The Blade of Safavid

A Historical Adventure
by Kent Merrell

The Blade of Safavid

An Epic Historical Adventure
by Kent Merrell

Meet the characters both historical and fictional on page 521.

If you dare to dive even deeper into their fascinating lives, sign-up now to receive regular "Historical or Fictional" biographical character videos. Enjoy these videos as well as Kent's blog posts and articles when you follow Kent at https://kentmerrellauthor.com/

Chapter One

Journal Entry: August 1, 1693 - London
Alexander Hincher - Ship's Surgeon

Flag Captain John Strong died on board. This is not good for me, we are still in port. I am the ship's surgeon. I feel a dread this may foreshadow what is to come. We are on the warship *Charles II*.

The ship owners paid the crew in full and promise payment every six months throughout our deployment. Captain Charles Gibson replaced Captain Strong. Rumor holds he is a notorious drunkard. Our first assignment is to sail from London to the northern Spanish harbor of Corunna.

    -Hinch

Liverpool, England 1748 -

Street lanterns dimly lit cobblestones glistening from the light drizzle. A man's stocky frame cloaked in black and silhouetted by light from the open doorway provided a perfect target. He stepped over the threshold, into the abandoned alley, and proceeded toward the wharf.

She followed only long enough to confirm his aim—the *Emerald of the Sea*—a recommissioned galley retrofitted into a merchant vessel soon to be sailing to the New World. If pattern held, he'd be on the *Emerald* the rest of the night. Satisfied, she crept away and entered the Nookery. More a hornets' nest than a library, of all the books available, only a few concerned anything but travel diaries or stories of the seas. Each volume was neatly organized on ancient wooden shelves. To its loyal patrons, the Nookery was simply their favorite tavern.

The proprietress, Mistress Lonnie, whose name proudly adorned the front door, was a collector of stories, a conspiracy lover, a purveyor of lore, and a psychic. According to neighboring shop owners, she was insane; gentle, harmless, and humorous, but insane. Enabled by the many patrons who enjoyed the folly of fanciful yarns about treasures, intrigues, schemes, myths, and legends, Lonnie spent her nights collecting and sharing these stories. The tales carried more charm in the dark, thus she slept by day, spun by night, and rewarded patrons with her own brew of ale.

Her tall slender frame was topped with long flowing braids that hung over her shoulders and contested her four decades. Lonnie appeared more a schoolgirl than the matron of a tavern.

A hush fell over the Nookery as Elizabeth stepped inside. Three nights now, she'd watched the patrons come and go. She looked for a pattern, formulating an approach, recognized the likely co-conspirators, and built the strategy to learn what she'd sought since she was a little girl.

Lonnie's warm, "Welcome, darlin,'" caught her off guard. "Here to share or despair?"

The chills from the surprising kindness felt like a spider inviting the fly in for dinner. *What does share or despair mean?* Elizabeth wondered, remaining close to the door so she could see who, if any, her answer would interest.

Pulling back the hood of her cloak, long blond hair tumbled over her shoulders. Striking blue eyes met Lonnie's warm brown ones, then slowly scanned the room lit by dual lanterns on each of the four walls.

Just loud enough for all dozen or so patrons to hear, she played her first hand. "Never mind, I'm sorry to bother you." She feigned a motion toward the door, as if to exit, then paused. "You wouldn't know about the Blade of Safavid?" Her eyes surveyed the room in hopes of finding a spark of interest.

All eyes turned to a puny little scruff of a man who, until Elizabeth spoke, hadn't moved. One eyebrow lifted and drug the rest of the wrinkled jowl with it, up from the ancient text holding him captive.

Silence. Silence broken only by his turning a page.

Old, piercing eyes transfixed her, hooking her like a tuna being reeled toward his table. At the slight motion of his eyes, she accepted his invitation to sit.

This is what you wanted; this could be who you've hunted these many years.

Hope replaced doubt.

His squint pierced her very soul. "The Blade of Safavid. You've heard of it?" he asked.

Is this a test? What answer gets him to share what he knows?

"In stories," she replied. The tiny upturn at the corner of his ancient mouth bid her to go on. "Stories my grandfather told of the blade, princesses, and pirates."

A voice from the other side of the room blurted, "Fella just left who's ya otta talk ta. Seems ta been huntin' that treasure 'is ole life."

An aged hand slowly lifted to silence the interruption while his eyes never left hers. He studied her for a long moment. "Tell me of your grandfather."

Elizabeth now understood the meaning of Lonnie's greeting: "Share or despair." She was expected to share if hoping to learn anything.

"My grandfather lived in a small fishing village on the coast of Iceland. He was an adventurer and a lifelong student. He met and married my grandmother when he was studying here in Liverpool. Before he settled down, he traveled the world. No one knows if the stories he told were true, nor did we care. He gathered us close, wrapped us in a large fur lined quilt, and enchanted us with magnificent stories. His deep warm voice filled our hearts with adventure and promise."

The memory was still vivid, even after so much heartache. So vivid, the aroma of her grandmother's lamb soup crept in from her memory to tickle her senses. Elizabeth paused and recalled the powerful sense of safety sitting on her grandfather's lap; a safety she hadn't felt in years. A safety she seldom felt since the day they attacked her home, savagely killing her mother. The murdering barbarians left her for dead and dragged her sister away screaming. That memory sent those of her grandfather fleeing like a bleating sheep from a hungry wolf.

The little man softly cleared his throat and brought her back to the present. "He told you stories about a blade?"

"A blade that held the key to a dynasty. . ." She paused, aware the room was silent. Like snuffing out a candle, her words extinguished all conversations. She reminded herself, *it's better they think you're a foolish girl on an innocent quest, rather than if they know you're on a manhunt.* Stay focused.

She continued, "I'm sorry. You probably think I'm another silly girl dreaming about the legend of some lost treasure kept alive by an old man trying to make his grandchildren happy. Please excuse me." She slipped her chair back to stand.

Surprisingly quick, his wrinkled hand caught hers.

"My dear, stories travel the world so they can live here. This is where tales are woven, spun, and knitted together into a giant yarn."

His long-awaited smile rewarded her ploy. Her shoulders relaxed, and she returned the smile. Only then did she notice two other men had joined the table. It worked.

Chapter Two

Journal Entry: August 10, 1693 - London
Alexander Hincher - Ship's Surgeon

A seasoned sailor by the name of Henry Avery is now first mate of this Spanish Expedition. In the spring of this year, Sir James Houblon, along with several London-based investors, assembled the Spanish Expedition Shipping Venture.

Our four warships: a pink, the *Seventh Son*, and the frigates; *Dove, James*, and the ship I serve on, the *Charles II*, commissioned by England's ally and our ship's namesake, Charles II of Spain are commissioned to prey on French vessels in the West Indies. Under a trading and salvage license from the Spanish we will sail to the Spanish West Indies, where our convoy will conduct trade, supply the Spanish with arms, and recover treasure from wrecked galleons, all of course while we plunder French possessions in the area.

The investors promise to pay us well, with the first month's pay in advance, which, as I mentioned, we received.

This is my first mission following the completion of my medical training at Cambridge University and receiving my license from the Royal College of Physicians. Though very young, I am hired as the ship's surgeon upon the privateering mission I described.

Tomorrow, we believe the four warships will sail down the River Thames in route to Spain's northern city of Corunna. This journey should take us two weeks.

- Hinch

Liverpool, England 1748

One small lantern lit the deck of the *Emerald*. No more were needed. The ship was abandoned for the night. Shipwrights, the craftsmen converting the once mighty man-of-war into a merchant ship, had finished for the day. Homes, taverns, and brothels sucked them into the night, leaving the ship quietly rocking in the tide. The entire port had long gone to sleep.

The waxing moon parted the clouds to reflect off the calm harbor. As the rain stopped, a lone figure quickened his pace. Tonight, he hastened past the *Emerald* and quietly hopped into a small boat, rowing out to the HMS *Kent*, a sixty-gun navy ship anchored offshore. The unwelcome moon silhouetted the *Kent* and his small boat. "Couldn't you hide just a few minutes?" he asked, looking up through the parted clouds. He reached his target just as the clouds heard his plea and hid the moon once more.

A ladder dropped, and he secured the boat and climbed onboard.

"A beautiful night, Mr. Jack. He's waiting for you below decks." Lucas, the ship's first mate, raised a hand to salute, but Jack quickly turned it into a vigorous handshake.

"Good to see you, Lucas." Jack released Lucas' nervous hand and took a quick glance across the water to confirm no one followed him. Small whiffs of low clouds hid patches of the town. Street lanterns and the occasional light burning inside taverns or homes dotted the hillside and added to the peaceful calm.

Jack bounded down the stairs, and without knocking, pushed open the door and stepped into the well-lit cabin.

The captain was standing, leaning over a large weathered oak table littered with maps, open books, and manuscripts. His raised eyebrow was all Jack needed.

"Not much new. I'm certain he knows more than he'll say. You're sure that old man is holding the last piece of your puzzle?" Jack asked.

Captain Joseph Remington's successful command of the HMS *Kent* had earned him great respect from fellow officers in the Royal Navy, and every man fortunate to sail under his command. Jack wasn't under his command. Jack wasn't under anyone's command.

Jack was among the few welcome in the captain's private cabin when the captain was not engaged in His Majesty's service. This night, the captain's frock coat lay draped over a night table and his vest hung open, several top buttons of his shirt missing. Jack admired how the man commanded such respect while in full uniform, yet appeared so common and was so personal once he removed the coat.

"He knows something or someone. I'm sure of it," Captain Remington said.

"I believe you're right; he's probably holding on to some sacred truths. He's old enough. He's drunk enough over the years, if he catches on fire, he'll burn for a week. But he still won't admit to knowing anything special," Jack said. "You're the captain of the mighty *Kent*. Why don't you charge in, lift him up by his filthy lapels, and command he tell you what you want to know?"

No response. Jack knew better. Captain Remington never compromised his position or used it personally...he thought.

The captain opened a small tattered journal that had been opened and read a thousand times. It nearly fell apart in his hands. "I've got two more assignments. Then I'll meet you in Antigua."

"Antigua?" Jack sputtered, "I'm not going to Antigua. You get me mixed up with your crew. You asked a favor. Chum up to the crazy old man in that cave they call a library and find out who he works for. I'll give it one more try tomorrow. Then I'm back to work."

"Work? Jack, you read books. People pay you to read books."

"It's called research, Captain." Jack's tone turned sour. Little did the captain know the extent of research Jack was capable of. Jack's love of the sea didn't include sailing on it. He'd studied and read and consulted. Antigua held no interest. Nothing across an ocean interested Jack. His interests were elsewhere. He checked his irritation and put it aside.

"Captain, that book you hold, would you like me to read it? I'll do you a favor and read it for free." The captain's smile pushed the irritation aside. Jack was the only one who noticed, anyway.

"Jack, this book is all that remains of one of the brightest men who ever sailed under my command."

Jack raised an eyebrow. The captain just accused him of being obsessed with books, but now clung to one like it was a life preserver in a storm.

"Looks more like a collection of notes."

"Precisely, the notes of an explorer. The notes of a..." The captain looked into Jack's eyes, and with the grin reminiscent of a father showing off a newborn son, "The notes of a researcher."

"Well, then it must be valuable. What was this bright exploring, researcher researching?" Again, Jack's tone lacked the respect due a Royal Navy captain.

The captain casually stepped around the table past Jack and closed the door, turned the key, and laid it on the table near the small oil lamp. "Please sit. It's time you knew." With one free hand and the help of his knee, the captain pushed a chair around to the corner of the table and leaned forward, locking eyes with Jack.

Chapter Three

Journal Entry: December 1693 - Corunna, Spain
Alexander Hincher - Ship's Surgeon

Two weeks became five months. Trouble after trouble delayed, detoured, and beset our ships. Anchored in the Spanish harbor, we await the Spanish letter of marque.

Worse still, after waiting another month, necessary legal documents still do not arrive from Madrid. Our ships must wait.

The sailors are in an unenviable position. With no money to send home to support their families and unable to find alternate sources of employment; they have become virtual prisoners in Corunna. We are in a foreign port, our sailors are eager for their next payment.

I have treated a variety of common onboard maladies. The malady of impatience is outside my medical training.

Before becoming our ship's first mate, Henry Avery served in the Royal Navy. Before that, he was a slave trader along the African coast.

> \- Hinch

Liverpool, England 1748

Elizabeth wondered how much she'd need to share before it was her turn to get answers to her questions. She placed her hand on top of the old man's, while assessing the table's two new companions and keeping her focus on the goal.

"Years ago, I was asked to care for a small class of children while the teacher was away," she began. "I found it easier to tell stories to the rowdy group than teach. When I told the story of a princess kidnapped by pirates and rescued by a daring rogue, a young boy complained he'd heard it before. I wondered how he had heard it before.

"When I saw my grandfather again, he was old but remembered the story. I asked about its origin. 'It's a true story, my dear,' he said. 'I heard it from the man who rescued the princess. I even handled the blade.' My grandfather grew tired. We agreed to talk more after he rested. He never woke."

"At's all 'e told ya?" It was the unbridled innocent voice on Elizabeth's right. The old man smiled. His lifted eyebrow repeated the innocent question.

"I never knew or cared if it was a true story. Now I'm consumed with the desire to know the rest of it." She glanced from face to face and settled on the wrinkled one, and his dark eyes sparkled.

"Dear," he started, "you may be the world's foremost authority on that story. If your grandfather heard it firsthand, he most assuredly heard more than the tidbits we glean from the sordid tales. Those are mostly filled with lies from the multitude of treasure hunters that pass through these parts."

Thank you, she thought. *Finally, you opened the door for my questions.* She didn't get to ask. He continued.

"That treasure hunts more'n fifty years ol', n tonight two blokes n a bird stumble in."

She turned to the voice and saw elbows on the table and hands cradling a long, thin face. *I may learn more from this plonker than the scholar.* "Two men?"

"One bin comin' every night. Goes right to tha mariner's books. Says e's studyin' trade routes."

"Could be." The old man let go of Elizabeth's hands and raised them, palms open.

"You think otherwise?" She turned back to the old man.

"He's smart, just not subtle. The books he scours don't match his conversations. He's snooping, wants to know more about people than routes."

What was this man's story? Did he have to share as she was? Inside, she began to fume. She'd watched him leave the tavern three times now.

"Says he's a student of the sea."

"A sailor?" she wondered.

"I say e's a brother of the sword," Plonker said.

"A soldier, then?" Elizabeth asked.

The old man ignored Plonker. "Possibly, but he's looking for someone. Not trade routes."

"Not a treasure?" she asked.

"Shared a banbury tale, too much rambling." It was the first time Lonnie spoke since her first 'welcome, darlin.' "'Twas chirping-merry, though. Tried to act like these arsworms 're old mates."

"How's his quest related to my grandfather's story?"

The banter ceased when the old man spoke, his tone serious. "We've seen and heard it all. Investigators, bounty hunters, treasure hunters, East India agents, but you're the first haberdasher of nouns and pronouns. They all end up here because sweet Lonnie there is daughter of old John Dann. But you knew that, that's why you're here."

Was this a challenge, a compliment, or an inquisition? I better choose my words carefully, Elizabeth thought. She bit her lip before answering. "That is why I'm here." *Am I that transparent?*

"My dear," he continued, "Mr. Johnson's biography is not as true as he claimed. Just another piece of pirate lore. Yet, like you, it leads everyone here thinking poor Lonnie can lead them to the treasure."

"Sir, do you believe a 'haberdasher of nouns and pronouns,'" she returned his challenging glare with confidence, "would be foolish enough to think after fifty years, if Mistress Lonnie knew where to find the treasure, she'd be serving a room full of dirty-beau's for fiddler's pay?"

Her turning of the slang tables brought raucous laughter. Plonker slapped her on the back with a hearty, "Aren't ye a grapeseed. Bring this bird a nipperkin!"

Am I part of the team now and chirping-merry?

Elizabeth's father knew his way around these kinds of men. When she was little, she'd traveled with him enough to recognize their general harmlessness. When they had too much to drink and turned into a swill-belly, she'd learned to get out of their way.

The old man didn't join the folly. "Sir Johnson's biography never mentioned the blade, nor did Midwinter's prostituted version of Johnson's account of Avery's attack."

What does this man know? "But you've heard my grandfather's story." She challenged his challenge.

"Once before."

This was a duel, who could pull information out of who. *This might be a long night,* Elizabeth thought.

Chapter Four

Journal Entry: January 1694 - Corunna, Spain
Alexander Hincher - Ship's Surgeon

Frustrations grow. Captain Gibson favors the drink more than calming the crew. Still no letter of marque from the Spanish giving us authority to plunder non-Spanish ships. Wages from *Charles II's* owners have not arrived. The men continue to feel like captives. My surgeon skills are under-utilized. I have repaired a broken hand and lacerated cheek following an onboard brawl.

- Hinch

Liverpool, England - 1748

Jack leaned back and crossed his legs, ready for a story. Maybe now he could make sense of the request to identify which piece an old man in an obscure book nook might be, in a grand puzzle he couldn't visualize. An old man who everyone only knew as ol' Denn.

The captain rested his elbows on the corner of the table, his attention set deep in his memory. "Many years ago, I was on the 50-gun *Biltmore* and just received my first command. A young bright sailor known by the nickname Cav sailed under my command. He took to navigation, shipwright, battle tactics, negotiation—everything required of a master sailor. He was as if born on the sea and salt water ran in his veins.

"Your love for books and—research," he winked at Jack, "reminds me a bit of him. Except he actually left the library."

Jack ignored the jab.

"A year later, following an extended journey to the New World, he became fascinated with the legends created by the stories told on the docks and in taverns. 'These stories couldn't possibly be true,' he once claimed. 'They were too daring, too fantastic, too unbelievable.' Yet, they continued to intrigue him. The stories of the courage, the creativity, the battles, and the escapes aroused something in the young sailor. Cav's skills at sea were unmatched. I feared he would seek a more adventurous assignment than mine. I didn't want to lose him. He was a lifelong student, aware and alert and constantly learning from everyone and everything. Studied like you, but he practiced what he learned."

Again, Jack ignored the jab. The captain's hands were busy, unconsciously thumbing through the notebook. He wasn't searching its pages. Jack knew that. It was as if he needed his hands to help tell the story. Jack smiled. This was the man who gave him a hard time about his disdain for adventure and got away with it.

A paper fell from the notebook. *Nice penmanship.* Jack picked it up and read the words, neatly written along the top. "Captain Henry Avery and his ship, the *Fancy.*" Jack's eyes moved from the paper to the captain.

"The pirate?" Jack asked.

The captain nodded. "The very one. Cav took an extended shore leave between assignments and visited the Old Bailey Courthouse in London. He studied the cases against various pirates who were caught and tried—and mostly hanged. While following a trail of testimony, Cav fixated on what he considered the most amazing pirate tale of them all. Avery, the pirate who plundered the greatest treasure… ever. Never caught, treasure never found. Captain Henry Avery and his ship, the *Fancy.* In time, I received command of the *Kent.* Cav came with me."

Jack felt like he was a child again, living the stories told to little boys before they go to bed, except without a nightshirt and blanket. The story of the pirate Henry Avery was an unfinished one, with endings as diverse as the tellers.

Captain Remington continued. "Avery's capture of that treasure ship set off a global manhunt—well, treasure hunt, like never before seen."

The names David Creagh, John Sparks, John Dann and several others were also neatly written on the sheet. Jack pointed to the one circled and underlined. "John Sparks? Who is he? What are these names?"

"Pirates, witnesses, sailors. But it was Sparks who fueled Cav's theory. In Sparks' testimony, he talked about a surgeon onboard the *Fancy.* He told about his kindness, his loyalty to the men, and his disdain for piracy. He talked about this surgeon refusing to take the plunder. A crew member they called Rudy apparently kidnapped two young Indian women off a ship called the *Gunsway* during the battle and hid them in the surgeon's cabin."

Two young Indian women? Now this story is getting interesting.

Jack turned over the sheet. As if whispering to himself, Jack mouthed the name HINCH. One word in all capital letters.

"Hinch. The surgeon," the captain echoed. "Cav believed he was the key to finding Avery and the treasure."

"Hinch," Jack repeated. "What about Sparks?"

"Sparks was one of the six members of Avery's crew eventually convicted and executed. During the trial held at the Old Bailey, Sparks pleaded not guilty. The jury found him guilty, anyway."

What about the two young Indian women? Jack wanted to know but didn't ask out loud. "What more do you know about this Hinch?"

"Cav searched everywhere. He even found original documents kept by those financing the voyage of the *Charles II*, the ship Avery mutinied and converted into the *Fancy*. Keep in mind, Cav was at sea with me most of the time. This research, as you call it, consumed him. He spent no time on land that he wasn't looking under some rock trying to find a new clue to the identity and whereabouts of that surgeon and his journal."

"A journal?" Jack's rapt attention spiked.

"Each of the crew members on trial shared versions of the attack, but Cav gave credence to Sparks' testimony the most. Sparks was the only man on trial to mention a journal."

"You think the old man in the Nookery can help you find the journal." Jack's smile broadened. "You're helping this Cav on his treasure hunt. You're part of this." Jack's sensible side wanted to scold this grown man, a serious Naval Captain, a seasoned veteran of the seas, for his childish foolishness. But curiosity won out.

"Where's Cav now? Why isn't he lurking around the Nookery interrogating an old fossil about an event fifty years old?"

"You're wrong Jack. I'm not on a treasure hunt, I'm on a manhunt. I'm not trying to help Cav, I'm trying to find Cav."

Chapter Five

Journal Entry: February 1694 - Corunna, Spain
Alexander Hincher - Ship's Surgeon

I've just returned to the ship. The captain sent me to assist a Dutch merchant ship where I provided needed medical attention to both crew and passengers. Having survived a pirate attack, many on board suffered from bruises, breaks, lacerations, and infections. They buried the dead at sea.

- Hinch

Liverpool, England - 1748

"You heard my grandfather's story once before?" Elizabeth asked. "When?"

From the first mention of the blade, the old man's mind was set to get this young woman into the hands of his benefactor and long-time associate. If he succeeded, he'd consider a debt paid. For decades, he'd regrettably been Nakhoda's eyes and ears. Yet, each time, the trail ran cold. Now it was as if providence had delivered a fresh new lead. And this time as a shapely young woman who heard the story as a girl from her grandfather. She heard it firsthand. What a prize… though unfortunate for her.

"Years ago…" The old man spoke slowly and deliberately, as if he were the grandfather speaking to his eager grandchildren. Every patron of the Nookery paid rapt attention. Plonker's eyes, wide as a child's, hung on every word. "… I served the East India Company as a buyer of spice and silks. Through a series of misunderstandings, officials held me for questioning."

He had grown apt at crafting wildly deceptive stories from slivers of truth. He smiled inwardly at his cleverness, *misunderstanding. If you call sleeping with the wife of the captain of the guard a misunderstanding.* He continued, "A commotion broke out and I was bid to join with a group of men who needed an Englishman as a guide and interpreter. On our journey, I made the acquaintance of the commander of the Shah's personal navy. As I aided his return home, he shared with me the stories of his daring attempts to rescue a princess and recover the Blade of Safavid from barbarous pirates."

The old man's eyes remained on Elizabeth. The room's quiet confirmed he owned the moment. Now was the time to set her on the path. "There is a man in the New World you must meet if you sincerely wish to complete your story."

I am sorry, my dear, but with this, I will consider my debt to him paid.

"This man will meet you in Antigua on the night of the fall equinox." Only a tinge of regret pricked his heart as his thoughts tried to justify his recommendation. *Whether he makes it or he doesn't, matters not to me. I have fulfilled my debt.*

"Who is he? How will I know him?" Elizabeth asked.

"He will seek you out." It surprised him that she didn't ask how to get to Antigua. He smiled within himself. *This woman is resourceful and brave. Hassan will have met his match. That is good too.*

"Please, tell me your name that I may thank you properly." She was now the one holding his hands firmly. Her confidence and lack of fear gave the old man pause. This was no innocent school teacher.

"My name is of no importance. No thanks is necessary." He released himself from her grasp.

She understood the meeting was over. He stood slowly; aged legs led him to a side doorway where he began putting on his cloak. Lonnie quickly came over and helped his frail hands secure it over his shoulders.

"Will we see you again tomorrow?" Lonnie asked.

A slight nod. "Rest well, Denn," she said as he shuffled out the door into the darkness. The rain had stopped and the moon played hide-and-seek in the clouds.

Plonker, with his stupefied blank look, represented the shock the entire room felt. They readied for a long engaging story only to be sorely disappointed. His abrupt departure also surprised Elizabeth.

Lonnie stepped to the table and cleared the cups.

"Darlin', ol' Denn is like that. You heard as much of that story as we ever have. Feel fortunate." Lonnie's tender voice was soothing, welcoming. She walked back toward the small rough-hewn table that served as the bar.

"Ol' Denn?" Elizabeth repeated.

"Dennison Hillis." Plonker said. "Bin sittin' in that seat fer twenty years. Knows more 'bout pirates 'n treasure 'an anyone. 'Cept maybe the feller he told ya ta meet in the New World."

Elizabeth stood up when the old man got up and realized she was still standing. She turned toward the door but paused and slowly turned back to Plonker.

"You said two blokes and a bird."

"One that's bin here just tonight, and the other comes once in a while. Mean lookin' nasty fella. Comes ta torment 'ol Denn, Won't talk about it though when we ask. I offered to take care of 'im once, but Denn said leave it."

"And the bloke from tonight. He's coming back?" she asked.

"Ol' Denn thinks so. Maybe you can meet 'im," said Plonker.

"Thank you." Elizabeth buttoned her cloak, pulled her hood back over her head and stepped out into the alley.

The moon won the tug of war with the clouds. Its light reflected off the wet cobblestones.

Elizabeth carefully worked her way through the labyrinth of alleys to the room she'd rented. It was small but comfortable. The lantern lit easily and revealed everything just as she left it. With one exception. A fresh bread loaf lay on the small dressing table.

Oh the kindness, she thought, appreciative of the elderly robust landlady. She was hungry and lifted the bread to tear a piece, beneath it lay a note.

"Someone followed you this evening when you left. Be careful." She turned the note over. There was nothing on the backside.

Elizabeth chose this small inn so she could easily monitor the harbor's activity. A small balcony accessible from the roof provided a view of the harbor. She'd rise early. Once she identified the second bloke, as Plonker called him, she'd confirm her stranger's next move and beat him to it. She added a third bloke or maybe a bird to her list of suspects. In the morning, she'd learn which it was.

Chapter Six

Journal Entry: March 1694 - Corunna, Spain
Alexander Hincher - Ship's Surgeon

Still no letter, nor wages. Neither Gibson nor Avery have answers. Fights breaking out and onboard illness because of stagnant lifestyles are not why I studied medicine. However, as the ship's surgeon, I am one of the few assets onboard useful for the captain. The captain barters, loans, and rents me out to meet medical needs on both ship and shore.

- Hinch

Onboard the HMS Kent, Liverpool Harbor - 1748

"Where is he?" Jack's legs no longer sat casually crossed. Elbows rested anxiously on his knees, holding his legs anchored to the floor. Open palms begged an answer.

"I lost him. He disappeared." The captain stood and retrieved a bottle from a drawer in his oversize armoire. He poured two glasses and handed one to Jack.

"When? How? Where?" Jack couldn't believe how casually the captain related this story. *You've lost a friend. Why are we not in a hurry? He could be in trouble.* Jack thought.

"In Newton Ferrers, nearly fifteen years ago."

"Fifteen years? So what's your hurry now?" Jack sat back; the immediacy of the search gone. "You think the old man knows where he is."

"I'm looking for three men." The captain set the bottle down after refilling his own glass.

Jack picked up the note. "Three men? You said they executed Sparks. So it's

Cav, Creagh, and Dann?"

"Dann died poor, thirty years ago, cheated out of a fortune. His daughter actually owns the Nookery. She knows nothing—an innocent plunged into a mystery. Creagh is who I want, and the man who kidnapped Creagh and Cav in Newton Ferrers."

"Kidnapped? Are you writing a novel? This story is getting good. Pirates, treasure, kidnapping." Jack held his glass out for a refill.

"Jack, Cav thought the same thing. More than once, he told me the stories were too fantastic to be true. But he followed the clues, anyway.

"When Cav visited the Old Bailey and studied the trial, he learned about one witness, the former second officer of the *Charles II*, David Creagh. Creagh was one of the few officers who refused to take part in the mutiny back in 1694. Cav convinced me that Creagh was in Newton Ferrers and I was foolish enough to indulge him. Me, Captain Remington of His Majesty's Royal Navy, sailed the HMS *Kent* right up the Yealm so a sailor could visit a drunk he suspected knew a surgeon years ago."

"That is fantastic." Jack chuckled. "Admit it. You wanted him to be right. You believed in the treasure hunt? You sailed this ship up the Yealm?"

The captain acknowledged Jack's tease with a tiny nod. "Cav went to the tavern where Creagh spent most of his evenings drinking. He never returned. The next morning we found two sailors murdered, a patron of the tavern stabbed to death, and no sign of Cav or Creagh."

Jack again hung on every word. "What happened?"

"Local constables were told Creagh sat talking with a sailor who must have been Cav. They never heard his name. They said another man, darker skin and powerful looking, with two mates came in and sat behind the sailor listening for a while. His mates sat at the bar. At a point in the conversation, the sailor jumped to his feet and fled from the tavern. The darker man commanded his companions to seize the sailor, and they dashed after him. The dark-skinned man—I assume middle eastern by how the men in the tavern described his accent, grabbed Creagh and pulled him from the tavern. When one of Creagh's mates tried to stop him, the man pulled a knife and cut him open."

"Where'd they go?" Jack didn't need the words; his rapt attention begged the question.

"We only guess they kidnapped or killed Creagh and Cav. That night, I saw a warship enter the river, but there was no sign of it in the morning. None of my men saw it."

"Who were the murdered sailors?"

"That's the mystery. Creagh's other mates claim the two dead sailors were the mates sent to capture Cav—if the sailor was Cav. According to the constable, those two dead sailors both end up dead at the hand of an expert."

"How was Cav with a blade?"

"As with everything he seemed to touch—expert. Long or short, he was quick and accurate. So if they took him, there was blood shed."

Jack stood, leaned on the back of the chair, pondered a moment and plunged in. "So Cav learns something important from Creagh, important enough to send him charging from the tavern. The eavesdropper hears enough of their conversation to recognize it's important enough to kill for; he wants Cav and Creagh. His mates are no match for Cav and three men and a ship disappear?"

"You're quick Jack," the captain said.

Both men sunk into silence.

After a moment, Jack asked, "You think the old man in the Nookery can help you find out what happened to Cav and Creagh?"

"Maybe not, but he knows something or someone."

"So Cav, picks up some global treasure hunt, cold some twenty-five years, he uses His Majesty's Navy to chase down clues all across the world for ten years, he gets close enough to get himself kidnapped or killed, and now a decade and a half later we're picking up a fifty-year-old treasure hunt?"

After the captain indulged Jack's summarization, he paused, giving Jack time to settle the question. "We're not looking for a ghost, Jack. I believe he's alive, or was two years ago."

"You lost him… twice?"

The captain nodded.

"Did your sailor sign with another captain? Ask the naval command and see where he's been." Seemed simple enough. *It's not that difficult,* Jack thought. He'd performed much more complex research for His Majesty's Royal Navy before. Jack found the assignments tedious, but curried a few favors in helping find a wayward sailor or two.

"He didn't sign with another ship. He disappeared. All evidence led to kidnap and murder. For thirteen years, I thought of Cav every time we returned to a port where he'd spent time with his research. Then two years ago, I found this." The captain pulled a beautiful knife from his waist belt and set it on the corner of the table before Jack.

Jack respectfully picked it up, as if an artist created it out of fragile glass. He'd never seen its equal. The highly polished blade reflected the light like a diamond. Jack swept his long, dark hair behind his ear when the blade revealed his reflection. He turned it over, examining the exquisite craftsmanship. He paused, lifting the note fallen from the small notebook. On the sheet's corner was a scrawled letter C that had no reason on the sheet of paper. However, on the knife's heel, a small stylish letter C perfectly engraved unmistakably matched the one on the paper.

"C for Cav?"

"C for Cav!"

"Or not." Jack frowned at the paper. "How does this old man help you find your sailor? How did you lose him?"

Chapter Seven

Journal Entry: April 1694 - Corunna, Spain
Alexander Hincher - Ship's Surgeon

What plagues the men aboard the *Charles II* are the stories and rumors concerning the adventures experienced by the crews on the many ships that come and go. The riches, the plunder, the success, the failure, the very reason these sailors sought the open sea is denied them. With wages, they could at least go ashore to take part in the vices known to sailors.

We buried our second onboard fatality. I am grateful it was not due to my failure of medical attention. A sailor contracted syphilis when he disobeyed orders, went ashore, and was accused of raping a whore. As an example, Captain Gibson had him hanged.

No letter, no wages. I have traded my services for medical supplies from other ships. I don't know why the ship owners are withholding wages. These men are desperate to provide money to their families and to enjoy even the most modest recreation ashore.

There is talk of mutiny. I do not take part, but I can't avoid the talk. Captain Gibson transitions from drunkenness to illness and is not providing leadership. First mate Henry Avery may even be behind the talk of mutiny. It strains my relationship because I continue to support Captain Gibson.

- Hinch

Liverpool, England - 1748

Frail hands lifted a key to unlock the door. Denn placed a hand against the frame to steady himself. Hinges creaked, the door pushed open. With his back to the door, a small fire silhouetted a man warming himself.

"You're entertaining a naval officer?" It was more a statement than a question from the intruder sitting at the fire.

Denn paused, stooped in the doorway. *Consequences, he reminded himself. Lifelong punishment for imagining he could dine with the devil and ever walk away. Had this, another of Hassan's spies, been spying on him? Of course he had.*

"An officer?" Denn removed and hung his cloak by the flickering fire. "More, another foolish boy who reads a book, thinking he can outsmart the countless fools who thought they could find a non-existent treasure."

"What does he want?" demanded the intruder as he stared into the fire, arms resting on knees and hands outstretched to steal every bit of heat.

"What they all want; a clue, a hint, an assurance their quest is not folly." The cramped home was no more than a single room with one tattered chair, a rumpled bed, a table containing a small basket of bread, and the fireplace that served as furnace and kitchen. A small iron pot hung from a swivel hook, but it was all enough. Denn spent his days on the docks and nights in one of several small taverns and often in the Nookery.

"If you will excuse me, I need to retire and you are not welcome here." Denn's calm request betrayed his anger and desire to throw the man into the fire and be done with his benefactor's obsession.

Knees popped as the man rose. Denn refused to cower to the man now standing a full head taller and thirty years his junior. Denn faced evil from men far worse than this creature and knew cowardice was the blood that runs through a bully's veins.

"Get out." Still calm, still firm.

The intruder broke the glare that had locked their eyes. "When the naval officer returns, find out who he is and what he knows."

Denn mumbled, "Fool, he's no naval officer."

"When he left you tonight, he rowed out to the *Kent*. Only an officer would do that alone." The man glared at Denn, enjoying his power. "And when you've learned who he is and what he wants, you don't need to tell me. You can tell Nakhoda himself."

Denn's blood turned cold. A chill no fire could warm. He said nothing.

"He's coming here to see you himself." The very words leaving the intruder's lips cast a dark omen on the room.

"When?" Denn finally muttered.

The intruder stepped past Denn, opened the door and stepped into the alley. He peered back into the small room and said, "Tomorrow, next day, next week. Does it matter?"

"You think he frightens me?" Denn stood firm, unruffled. It wasn't fear that gripped him, it was sheer hate. "It's you and your sort who should worry. You take his gold, pretend to search while you drink, whore, lie, and bully your way around. He's coming, just needing to talk to an old friend he can trust. Now get out."

Before taking his seat by the fire, Denn closed and bolted the door. "He's no naval officer," he mumbled to himself. *But what was he doing on the Kent? Tomorrow, we'll see who we're dealing with. Which port is the captain haunting now?*

If the parade of treasure hunters didn't weary him, the parade of hired thugs Hassan paid to snoop and scour the ports for clues did. Each one drifted through with a reason to harass the formerly staunch ally Hassan had. "Tomorrow that ends," he muttered. He shook his head imperceptibly. His mind resolved on a better plan. Disgust turned to peace.

He pulled an ancient logbook from an indistinct crack in the wall. In his own handwritten script, he read the notes made during his only visit to Hassan's private island in the New World. *This may be of help to the young would-be naval officer.* He created two copies of the notes, and tomorrow he'd find a way to share one with Elizabeth and one with the pretend naval officer. He finished by sketching a crude but accurate map. Retiring to the small goose down mattress, he laid his weary head on a woolen blanket that served as a pillow. Too tired to sleep, his mind reflected back to the night he met Hassan, the former commander of the Shah's navy, imprisoned for failing to secure the Blade of Safavid.

The night a prison break cheated the noose meant for Denn's neck.

Chapter Eight

We've still not been paid, so the men petitioned the captain for the pay owed them. If the men had been paid they would no longer be tied to the ship and could easily leave. So predictably, he denied the petition. The men's wives petitioned James Houblon as well and also failed. The sailors are desperate. They feel they've been sold into slavery to the Spanish.

The men threaten to strike and Houblon refuses to give in to their demands. Seeing how serious the situation is, Admiral O'Byrne wrote to England asking for the money owed to our men.

Unable to provide the wages, a change of leadership is inevitable, Admiral O'Byrne and our sailors argue. There is no way for him to maintain the trust he needs to keep the crews from this four ship expedition under control.

   - Hinch

Onboard the HMS Kent, Liverpool, England - 1748

"This is where you come in Jack." The captain sat, again opposite Jack's chair and lifted Cav's notebook. "Cav specifically mentions names and hometowns of each of Avery's men captured and tried for piracy. None of them provided information helpful to finding Avery's treasure. Though each became rich with the bounty taken from the treasure ship, most squandered their plunder with women, wine, and poor investments. Mostly, they were cheated out of their money. Creagh was a natural witness against the mutiny, but he would have no knowledge of what happened once the *Charles II* sailed and got converted into a pirate ship."

This reasoning made perfect sense to Jack. "Then why convince you it was important to take a navy ship to visit a tavern?"

"Exactly! Why did Cav and some killer want Creagh?"

"Because, as you said, Cav connected Creagh with the surgeon," Jack answered. This was getting interesting.

"That's the connection I want! Jack, we sail with the tide this morning. A glorious assignment of chasing pirates out of the Mediterranean is bound to keep me all summer."

"Pirates?" Jack asked. "Still?"

"Yes! Pirates! Find that connection. What does our old man in the Nookery have to do with Creagh? What does he have to do with our assassin from Newton Ferrers?"

Jack nodded. *Sure, I have nothing to do all summer but chase around a fifty-year-old treasure, which by now sits in the pockets of thieves, whores, and cheats.*

Standing, Jack asked a final question. "You said you lost Cav a second time. Why didn't you ask him when you saw him?"

The captain picked up his coat. Light peaked through a curtain. It was morning. "I never saw him again. I saw his work. I know he was alive two years ago. That's why I need you in Antigua when I finish my assignment sinking a rogue pirate ship that's returned to these waters. You're smart. Find the connection. When we meet, you'll have found the puzzle pieces we need. I know you, Jack. You can solve this mystery."

The Captain splashed some water on his face, combed his hair, buttoned his jacket, and called his first officer.

"We will meet in the fall, Jack. Clair's tavern, you won't miss it. Maybe you'll even be ready to settle down. Clair's a catch, especially for a man like you. The *Emerald* sails in August. I trust Captain Bentley will get you to Antigua. He knows how much I need you there."

He dismissed Jack and went above decks. Jack stood—alone in the empty cabin musing to himself. *How can he do that so effortlessly? I'm not his crew, I'm not enlisted. Like he said, I read books.* Sitting again, he picked up the notebook, opened to the page where Cav discussed the trials of Avery's men.

"Tonight the Nookery, tomorrow to London and the Old Bailey," he planned, whispering to himself.

Chapter Nine

Journal Entry: May 1694 - Corunna, Spain
Alexander Hincher - Ship's Surgeon

A mutiny is in the works. Going ship to ship, Henry Avery persuaded men to come on board with him, promising he would carry them where 'they should get money enough.'

Because of his experience and having been born in a lower social rank, he associated well with the men from the various ships. Avery fostered trust among many of the men and thus he is a natural choice to command the mutiny. The crew believes he will have their best interests at heart.

- Hinch

Liverpool, England - 1748

Elizabeth sat at the edge of the balcony, the early morning sun's rays pushing the low fog scurrying away like a mother shooing her children from the kitchen. She stood quickly, grabbed her scope. It was him, but he was disembarking from the wrong ship. She scanned the crew; the captain giving orders, hoisting sails, sailors jumping to work. *They're sailing with the tide—yes, naturally, but why was he onboard the British navy ship? Did I miss something?*

Quickly she moved her attention to the merchant ship *Emerald*. Shipwrights were beginning their day, just as she'd observed them do for days. Back to the small boat. He was alone. When he reached the dock, he hopped out and casually walked past the *Emerald*. Her eye caught another figure, seemingly on the same path. She surveyed them both through the glass until he disappeared into the early morning shadows. The second figure stopped, searching the growing crowd of workers. He lost him. *Did he know he was being followed?*

Elizabeth readied herself for the day and returned to the balcony. By midmorning, she'd not seen anything or anybody interesting enough to keep her attention. The two men she hoped to see hadn't returned. She left the inn through a small side door, taking the landlady's caution seriously. After a few turns and backtracks, she determined nobody followed her.

She arrived at the docks and casually made her way to the *Emerald*. Booking passage for a single woman might raise suspicion, so she decided to pretend her associates would do the same in time. She climbed onto the platform and went directly to the captain, catching the eye of many of the workers.

Concluding her arrangements with the captain, she saw him coming, the very man she'd hope to learn about. She wasn't ready for that right now. She thanked the captain and hurried off the ship.

Chapter Ten

Journal Entry: May 10, 1694 - Open sea nearing Cape Verde - Atlantic Ocean
Alexander Hincher - Ship's Surgeon

We are finally at sea. But not as intended.

With what I now write, this journal will either cause my death or prevent it. That all depends on into whose hands it falls.

On the 7th day of May 1694, the restless sailors mutinied. The *Charles II*, renamed the *Fancy*, is captained by Henry Avery, its former first mate of whom I have previously written.

Admiral O'Byrne chose to sleep ashore, which gave the men the opportunity they were looking for. At approximately 9:00 p.m., Avery and about twenty-five other men rushed aboard our ship and surprised the crew on board. Captain Gibson was bedridden, so the mutiny ended bloodlessly. A blessing.

I remained onboard with Captain Gibson and was in his cabin when men from the *James* pulled up in a longboat beside the ship and used the password "Is the drunken boatswain on board?" which was key to join the mutiny. Captain Humphreys of the *James* told Avery these men were deserting. Avery said he knew full well what was happening. When Captain Humphreys realized Avery was part of the mutiny he fired on the *Charles II*, alerting the Spanish Night Watch, and we were finally on the move. It forced Avery to make a run to the open sea. We vanished into the night.

After we sailed far enough to be safe, Avery brought all of us non-conspirators above and gave us a chance to go ashore. He even offered Captain Gibson command of the ship if he would join the cause. The captain declined, and I prepared to help him ashore in the longboat provided.

To my surprise and horror, I was the only man prevented from voluntarily leaving. As the ship's surgeon, they deemed my services too important. Once the longboat left, the men remaining onboard the *Charles II* unanimously elected Avery captain of the ship. We set sail.

Avery proves to have tremendous powers of persuasion. He convinced the men that since the original mission resembled piracy, only without the letter of marque to plunder French ships, if they were to plunder only ships that were not English, Spanish, and Dutch, they would be on the same mission.

With that reasoning, he convinced the men to sail to the Indian Ocean as unlicensed privateers. Stories held that only a year earlier a Captain Thomas Tew captured a tremendous prize in the Red Sea.

The crew settled the subject of payment, which of course was the cause of this mutiny. They decided each member would get one share of the treasure, and the captain would get two. I would not sign the articles, but they promised me payment, anyway.

We have now set a course for the Cape of Good Hope.

- Hinch

Deck of the Emerald of the Sea - Liverpool Harbor - 1748

"Pardon me." Jack stepped aboard the *Emerald* and hopped aside as a woman in a long blue cloak, her reddish blond hair falling out past the front of her hood passed, giving him only a quick glance.

He paused, spotted the captain, and walked toward him. Uncommon boldness and personal courage aptly defined Captain Brian Bentley. All six feet of him commanded respect when he entered a room or stood on deck. Thick dark hair complimented by gray at his temples framed his mature face. Uncommonly unwrinkled for a retired admiral with forty years at sea, Captain Bentley's countenance extolled peace and confidence.

"Who is that?" Jack asked Captain Bentley, watching the woman gracefully step from the platform to the dock.

"Elizabeth Farrow."

"What did she want?" Jack asked, still watching her walk along the dock.

"She booked passage to the New World. Intends to travel with me on the *Emerald's* maiden voyage."

"A maiden voyage with a maiden." Jack chuckled at himself. The captain didn't. "Who's she traveling with?" He continued to watch her. When she was finally out of sight, he turned to the captain. The captain's broad smile met Jack's.

"With you I believe. I now have two passengers. You at the pleading of Captain Remington and that maiden. She paid for her passage; you'll work for yours."

"I'm not joining you. Despite what you were told," Jack was adamant. "Who is she?"

"Jack, pay attention, Elizabeth Farrow. A young woman with responsibilities in the New World and she chose the *Emerald* to get her there. Must I remind you of your responsibilities?"

Dismissing the captain's jab, Jack took one more look over his shoulder toward the dock. "Traveling alone?" Jack didn't expect to see her, but hoped.

"She says a few acquaintances will join her. I hope you're not planning to lurk around Liverpool and harass me and my men all summer."

"No, I leave tomorrow for London. From there to Newton Ferrers, then back here so you may take my regards to Captain Remington." Jack turned back to the captain. "Do you know anything about the old man in the Nookery?"

Captain Bentley gave some directions to a shipwright mounting a jib. He then turned back to Jack. "Met him once is all. Well educated, served East India Company when he was young, left their employ and the rest is hearsay."

"Hearsay?" Jack repeated.

"It's the hearsay that holds Captain Remington's interest. He thinks something connects the old man to the Avery treasure. The old man comes and goes, associates with the less savory of men—and women, doesn't seem to have employment but is never in need of coin."

Jack followed Captain Bentley across the deck to where he gave instructions to another shipwright hanging a new door to the below decks.

"Be careful with the old man." Captain Bentley said, "He's not dangerous himself, but the company he keeps are not your type of men."

Jack smiled, uncertain if that was a compliment of his upbringing or an insult to his choice to study the seas rather than sail them. *If they only knew.* "Thank you, Captain, I'll keep my eyes open." Jack turned to leave then stopped. "May I lurk one more night aboard before I'm off to London?"

The captain gave a nod.

Evening didn't come soon enough. Jack walked the city with an eye out for another chance meeting with Miss Elizabeth Farrow. A casual inquiry at a few of the popular inns turned up nothing. Jack eventually entered the Nookery, acknowledged Lonnie's 'Welcome, darlin,' and returned to a shelf of books pertaining to astronomical navigation.

But where was the old man?

An hour passed, then two. Jack's impatience became noticeable to the other patrons. He sat, he stood, he paced, then as if a cloud parted revealing the sun's rays pouring through a storm, he recalled the old man had been apparently studying the same old book each night Jack had been in the Nookery. Instantly, he turned to the bank of shelves directly behind where the old man sat each night Jack visited the Nookery. Jack never ventured into that corner of the Nookery, fearing to disrupt the old man. He began scouring the shelves. Though he never saw the title of the book, its pitch-black cover was a sharp contrast to the various weathered brown leather books. It couldn't be hard to find.

Lonnie noticed his frustration and kindly asked, "Lost somethun, darlin'?"

All eyes were now on Jack.

"The old man, Denn as you called him, I was going to ask him something about the book he was studying. Is he coming in later?"

Lonnie slid up beside Jack, pretending to look at the various books he was pulling and replacing on the shelves. "Won't find it there, 'ats his book. Never shared it."

Jack turned, looking Lonnie in the eyes. Lonnie wasn't good at hiding feelings; Jack knew instantly there was worry behind those eyes. "Pardon me, I need to see him. Where else would he be? Home? Another tavern?"

"Lives up past the bakery," she said, "But ol' Denn won't be there. Said he's goin' away for a bit."

Jack bowed a thank you to Lonnie, turned and quickly stepped back outside.

Drizzle from the night before returned, erasing the inviting smell of fresh bread from a nearby bakery. The slight remaining odor gave Jack just enough pause to remember he hadn't eaten all day. He turned to give the bakery a second look when the shadows of two large men dragging a small body pulled him from all thoughts of food. The tiniest of resistance confirmed the person carried away by the two shadows didn't want to go along.

Jack circled the bakery to get a better look before charging in. At his abrupt appearance before the trio, one man released his prisoner, quickly pulled a knife, and lunged toward Jack. Without a second's pause, Jack took the man's lunge, turned the knife and rode the attacker to the ground, impaling the figure with his own knife.

He turned toward the other man still holding the prisoner. This man, as quickly as the first, drew a knife, but rather than lunge toward Jack, he drove the knife deep into the prisoner and then ran. Jack jumped to the crumpling body's aid. It was ol' Denn. Jack scooped him off the wet cobblestone to assess the wound. As he did, boots clamoring on the stones followed a scream.

With a weak hand, Denn pulled Jack close. "Don't let her go to Antigua. She must not go."

"Who?" Jack could hardly hear the faint whisper.

"Behind the lamp, what you're looking for is behind the lamp." Denn pulled a small piece of paper from his coat and slipped it into Jack's hand, closed his eyes, and went limp.

The sound of rushing footsteps grew louder. A small crowd rounded the bakery, led by a constable who was accompanied by the man who stabbed ol' Denn.

"There!" Shouts echoed off the buildings.

Jack laid the man down gently and disappeared into the night.

✝ ✝ ✝

Inside the bakery, the clatter of footsteps drew Elizabeth's attention away from a hot tea she was sharing with her portly landlady. Both women stepped to the window and pulled open the shutter just as a man cast in shadow pulled a knife from a man's chest and tucked a paper into his own pocket. Light from the newly opened window was just enough for Elizabeth to recognize the face when he lowered the man's head to the ground and turned to see the approaching crowd.

Moving to the door, she pulled the hood of her cloak up over her head and joined the crowd as it passed the bakery. Several of the men rushed forward

when they saw the assailant lower the man to the ground and rush off.

When they got to the still figure lying on the wet cobblestone, the drizzle turned up a notch. The soft rain elicited an umbrella held over the body and the constable bent to lift the man's head. Gasps filled the alley as they recognized the body. A second lifeless body was only a few feet away.

Chapter Eleven

Journal Entry: June 1694 - Cape Verde's Sotavento Islands
Alexander Hincher - Ship's Surgeon

We reached Cape Verde's Sotavento Islands. We sighted three English merchantmen from Barbados and the men tasted their first act of piracy. We robbed them of provisions and supplies. Of the three ship's crews, Avery persuaded nine of the men to join him on the *Fancy*, which now numbers ninety-four men.

- Hinch

Liverpool, England - 1748

Jack unfolded the tattered paper he received from ol' Denn. Its yellowed edges looked old, but the ink was new. It appeared to be a crudely hand-drawn map with three shapes he could only guess were some kind of landmarks. There was not enough information on the map to show what these landmarks represented. *Islands? Lakes? Continents? Mountains?* Or if it was a map at all. The size and distance were impossible to know nor where they were. Jack had studied countless maps in his passion to know a world he refused to explore, yet these markings did not look familiar. He folded and tucked the scrap into his vest pocket.

Whispering to himself, he pondered—behind the lamp. *What lamp? And she shouldn't go to the New World. Who? Lonnie? Did ol' Denn have a mistress? A sister? A daughter? How did he know what I was looking for? I don't even know what I'm looking for. I thought I was looking for you ol' man.* Jack's questions found no answer.

He squinted into the darkness, looking at nothing, yet hoping for answers. A cool wind splashed his face with rain, interrupting both his thoughts and protection beneath the shelter of a small archway connecting the livery to an inn. It overlooked the harbor, which now stood in complete darkness except for a single lamp shining aboard the *Emerald.*

I'm a fugitive. I only knew two people in the whole town. One sailed this morning, I can't endanger Captain Bentley, and the only other with whom I've shared one partial conversation is dead. Would Lonnie already know they think I killed ol' Denn? One way to find out. Grateful for the darkness, Jack slipped out from under the archway and carefully headed back to the Nookery.

The quiet of the alley added to the mystery of the night. Like every evening, most shops were closed with the occasional light coming from a second-story apartment. Rain fell, lit by a few street lights. The Nookery's door was wide open, yet the dim light shining from within barely climbed out over the threshold.

This is all wrong. Where are the patrons?

Bottles and mugs littered the tables, yet the once brightly lit tavern filled with lies and laughter of nights before had become a poorly lit den of foreboding. Jack cautiously stepped inside. Only one lantern remained lit. Each of the others was torn from the walls and lay shattered. A rustle of fabric drew Jack's attention. He turned to meet an enormous fist to his face sending him backwards. Crashing over a table, his head smashed against the hard floor. Everything went dark.

Voices woke him from unconsciousness. The last lamp torn from the wall was now burning on the tattered old table from which Lonnie served her legendary ale. His view from the floor and the shadow cast from the burning lamp revealed a small slit between two empty shelves.

Jack sat and discovered a body lying next to him. The soft light revealed the broken features of the former welcoming hostess of the Nookery. He quickly checked her for life. Lonnie was dead, and another man with a faint breath was next to her. Jack rushed over to his aid, but the man took his last breath.

Voices got louder and there was a rhythmic thud with the whisper of paper. Jack knew what it was. Every book was being thrown from their shelves. He climbed past the bodies to the tiny slit he'd seen from the floor. He grabbed the lone lamp and held it to the wall. There, behind the very spot where the lamp had hung, a thin leather-bound book blended so well with the wooden wall, it was invisible at eye level. With the help of his knife, he tried to fish it out.

"You!" The loud voice echoed through the tavern.

Jack pulled the thin book free and turned. At the sight of Jack's knife, a shot exploded—tearing through his left shoulder. Jack dropped to the floor and took with him the lamp, plunging the Nookery into total darkness.

Chaos filled the darkness. The blast of the pistol shot still ringing his ears, Jack crawled across the floor clinging to the prize he dug from the wall while trying to nurse a now bleeding shoulder. Members of the crowd who came with the shooter, who Jack only assumed was the constable he'd fled from just hours earlier, pushed into the Nookery just as Jack extinguished the light. They tripped over books, the broken table and bodies of Lonnie and one of her patrons. Jack got to his feet, nobody seeing nor aware he was not just another of the confused crowd.

"Careful, he has a knife!" Jack shouted to increase the chaos. He pushed and pulled at bodies in the darkness to help them stumble over each other. Fumbling for the way out, he squeezed out the door and fled once more into the darkness.

† † †

For the second time in two nights, he was unaware a lone woman standing in the shadows, watched him leave the Nookery. The hood of her cloak protected her from the increasing rain.

Chapter Twelve

Journal Entry: July 1694 - Guinea Coast
Alexander Hincher - Ship's Surgeon

They added slave trading. Along the Guinea coast, Avery tricked a local chieftain into boarding the *Fancy* under the false pretense of trade. Once onboard, Avery forcibly took the chieftain's wealth and his men's wealth, making them slaves.

Battles are minor and my service as a surgeon includes nothing more than a few stitches of an occasional cut and setting a broken bone or two.

- Hinch

Liverpool, England - 1748

"It makes me sick to my stomach. Three days and no sign of the killer. How can they let him get away? The whole town is panicked." Elizabeth's landlady set the fresh bread on the table at the window overlooking the harbor. Her non-stop grumbling faded as she made her way back down the stairs.

Elizabeth picked at her breakfast. *He's not a random killer. What was he after? Is he hiding on the Emerald? Does anyone else know his connection to Captain Bentley? Do I speak up? Is he working for Captain Bentley? He must not have gotten everything he wanted from ol' Denn or else he learned Lonnie had it. But what is it? Did he get it? Is it worth four lives? Maybe five? Is he dead lying in the wood? Does Captain Bentley even know his associate is the killer?* A thousand questions continued to pound through her head.

Captain Bentley appeared on deck. All morning, she'd been watching the shipwrights come and go, but this was the first time she'd seen the captain since the killings. She stood so quickly the bread tumbled to the floor when her leg struck the table.

Recklessly, she pushed out the door of the inn so quickly she knocked a tailor to the ground, spilling spools of thread across the cobblestone. As she anxiously stooped to help gather his trinkets, her eye caught the fleeting shadow of a man. A quick glance up was enough to recognize his step. *This man doesn't want to be seen. My landlady is right, I am being followed, and by the same man who followed the constable to ol' Denn's murder. Does he know I know Captain Bentley may be the only person who knows the killer's identity?*

She carefully stood, apologized, and accompanied the tailor to his shop. *There will be another chance to catch up with the captain. Until then, let's play a little cat 'n mouse. Time to be the cat.*

The shop door swung open as the tailor, arms still full, turned the shiny brass handle and leaned his body into it. With a casual glance, hoping to see she was still being followed, Elizabeth accompanied the tailor inside. A large ornately framed mirror hung on the back wall, giving the shop the appearance of being much larger than it was. It also gave Elizabeth a convenient view out the large front window where the tailor displayed two beautifully tailored fine men's suits.

She took in the finely constructed wooden shelves, light oaken tables, and the large window seats quickly. All perfectly stacked with fine cloth, spindles of thread, buttons and ribbons. The man was not just a tailor, he was a haberdasher, a seller of supplies for men's clothing. *How absolutely ironic. Me, a haberdasher of nouns and pronouns, accompanying a haberdasher to escape the mouse I now wish to catch.*

"Thank you." He took the spools of thread she helped him gather from the cobblestones.

She chuckled to herself. "A haberdasher!"

He lifted an eyebrow.

"The old man from the tavern called me a haberdasher of nouns and pronouns."

"You're a teacher?" Both eyebrows raised.

"More a student, these days." Elizabeth felt comfortable with this gentleman haberdasher.

He organized the spools of thread by color as he filled an open shelf. He was not a tall man, but surprisingly, his reach didn't appear unnatural as he placed a bolt of charcoal gray flannel on a top shelf.

"The Nookery?" he asked.

Of all the taverns, why would he guess the Nookery? Her wrinkled brow answered his question.

"What would a proper lady like yourself be doing in that tavern, and associating with the likes of ol' Denn?" His question was kind, more teasing than accusatory. There was something about this stranger, a tailor yes, very perceptive, yet seemingly harmless.

"I may not be the proper lady you think I am."

"Perhaps not. You were in a hurry. Yet, kind enough to put your task on hold to help a stranger gather his scattered notions and then accompany him on his way."

"The least I could do. I scattered those notions."

"Granted, yet you did not know where I might lead you. When does a woman follow a strange man to an unknown location?"

He emptied a small bag of rich brass buttons onto a tall leather topped cabinet and began dropping them by size into the small glass faced drawers. Elizabeth tried to balance her attention between his unique conversation and his precise attention to organizing his notions.

"Could you have been influenced to escort me when you realized you were being followed?"

His question caught her off guard as if he'd taken a pair of sharp scissors and stabbed her in the heart. His smile was innocent. His probing casual question was not.

"You must be someone of interest to ol' Denn's enemies," he said.

What does he know? What does he think? Who does he think I am?

"Milady, ol' Denn and I were friends enough for me to know of his troubles. He came to Liverpool needing to off-load some very fine silks from India. In fact, he was so eager to be free of the load, the profits he offered me were unconscionable. They made me very comfortable. He carried a burden of debt to someone. Someone evil. He knows secrets, well, knew secrets, precious to someone. He spent the last many years suffering the intimidation and pressure unfair to be carried by such an old man."

"You saw the man following me?"

A nod.

"You know him?"

"Seen him around. He comes and goes, mostly to torment ol' Denn. Part of a wretched team of thugs. Claims ol' Denn knows the clues to some treasure."

"Did he?"

"Come with me." He took Elizabeth by the hand and led her behind a long hanging curtain that provided modesty for gentlemen being fitted for suits. A small inconspicuous door led to a large storage room. The tailor lifted down a bolt of beautiful silk and respectfully unfolded it.

"Indian Silk. Fit for an empress," he said.

Elizabeth ran her fingers across it in reverence for its quality.

Slowly, her eyes moved from the silk around the storage room and finally locked onto the eyes of this new friend. But she saw none of the room. Powerful emotions blinded her. She was not looking into his eyes. Elizabeth was looking through this man that had just unlocked the fear, the pain, the hate and the contempt that had hardened her soul and compelled her on her quest.

Struggling within herself to maintain the composure expected of a lady, she fought the urge to turn this kind man into notions small enough to join the brass buttons she had just watched him organize.

"Please, tell me again where you got this silk." Her emotions were on hold, but the fuse still burned.

"As I mentioned, ol' Denn came to me several years ago with a cargo of the finest silks I'd ever seen. He was eager to be free of them. It all sold at top dollar, but this one bolt. It's the finest of it all."

As he spoke, Elizabeth's eyes never left his, while her hands never left the silk.

"I've yet to meet a woman worthy of its beauty or quality. Even if I did, I don't know if I would part with it, at any price."

"Didn't you want to buy more?" she asked, eyes still locked on his.

"Certainly. Denn said the source was lost, and he had no interest in finding it. From its profits, I made three trips to India searching for the mills that turned out this quality of silk. Each trip failed."

The storm inside her began to subside. Her breathing grew more even. She accepted and appreciated the honesty of this new acquaintance.

"You're troubled, milady. I've upset you, and for that I'm sorry. But I don't understand." His eyes did not shy away from hers. His confidence helped her heart continue to settle.

Elizabeth, now in control, broke her grip on the silk and his eyes. "This is my father's silk. Friends in India made it exclusively for him." She took several deep breaths. "Pirates took his ship, his cargo, his life, and my sister. Ol' Denn was my last link to find my sister. When that young man murdered him the other night, he took with him my hope. Now my only clue lies in a man following me."

She motioned with her head towards the shop's front door.

"Sir," she continued, "you said you've never met a woman worthy of this silk. I'm sorry, but you still haven't. Not with the hate in my heart and the blood that will soon be on my hands."

The tailor raised an eyebrow and looked her directly in the eye. Elizabeth met his with a wink, then she asked, "How would a proper lady dress if she were to be riding a horse for a few days?"

The tailor squinted back at her; unsure at first how to answer Elizabeth's question.

"A proper lady would not be riding a horse. She'd be in a fine carriage." The tailor stood a few inches shorter than Elizabeth, yet he stood unruffled, searching her eyes while looking for a motive behind her question.

Elizabeth wasn't sure she wanted to unravel her idea. "Suppose the lady needed to travel faster than a carriage and without the knowledge of others?"

"Would this be before or after the blood?"

This question brought smiles to both him and Elizabeth.

"As you can see, I've no interest in just evading. I may need to follow."

The tailor returned the silk to its shelf of honor; it having been offered to Elizabeth and her kindly refusing it. Perhaps at another time she told him, and he promised to keep it until her circumstances accommodated the gift. They returned to the front of the shop. The suit displayed in the front window gave them due reason to watch for someone outside. That someone, though clumsily, kept a discreet eye on the shop.

The tailor confirmed the man was a regular visitor to Liverpool and one of the few who tormented ol' Denn.

It surprised Elizabeth how quickly she felt comfortable talking with the tailor. He was open, confident, unruffled at her revelation, and appreciative of the quality of her father's silk. She needed help with the puzzle. When she described the man she watched pull the knife from ol' Denn's chest, the tailor concluded he was not one of the regular thugs. She shared the fact she'd seen the man who was following her with the constable chasing the murderer. Together, they concluded more than one party was interested in what ol' Denn knew.

"And I am one of those parties," she admitted.

When she shared how the killer had been on both the HMS *Kent* and the *Emerald*, her hopes fell. Captain Bentley, he told her, would have left for London by now and would not return for several weeks. Though not close friends, the tailor had consigned a large shipment of fabric on the Emerald, sailing in the fall with the captain.

Something held Elizabeth back from telling the tailor she too would be on the *Emerald* in the fall, and at ol' Denn's instruction.

After a few visits to and from behind the fitting drapes, Elizabeth thanked the tailor, and with a bundle under her arm, headed to an open market and back to her inn. The late afternoon sun broke through the clouds, showering the harbor with blinding golden sparkles.

That's odd, she thought as she pushed open the door to her room. She'd left so suddenly she knew she'd not straightened up her room nor locked the door behind her, but someone had been in here. Someone besides the landlady. The fallen bread remained on the floor, her bags were open and her books scattered. Her thoughts immediately went to her landlady. *Was she safe?*

Elizabeth straightened the room, placed the bundle in her bag, and casually made her way to the harbor. Inquiries made, she joined others in the short line waiting to board the *Brewster,* sailing immediately to Boston.

"You are not traveling alone, milady? Your husband will be sailing with you?" asked the captain of the *Brewster.*

"What kind of lady would I be?" Elizabeth said. "He will be in a hurry, I assure you. And please, see that he too sails with me in steerage."

Elizabeth carefully and deliberately joined the other passengers as they prepared for their journey to the New World. Mostly aboard were young men and families. She felt a bit out of place as a single woman, yet certainly the man after her wouldn't let her just sail off alone. For now, it was time to lose the mouse.

Standing nonchalantly near the rail to ensure her pursuer would accompany her, she waited, bag in hand. He took the bait. The mouse was bounding up the gangway. With her broad smile locked in place, she slipped down the steps into an empty cabin. She quickly unbundled and slipped into her new outfit, tucked her dress into her bag, and set it conspicuously outside a first-class cabin. With hair tucked into a handsome wool cap, she walked smartly back above decks and mingled with families as they excitedly waited for the tide.

As the captain ordered the gangplank removed, she quickly stole off the ship and joined those wishing their departing friends farewell. *I hope he enjoys the New World. I wonder how long he'll look for me? I'm going to miss that bag.*

The mooring ropes released, the ship set sail. Elizabeth let out a deep breath, pulled back from the crowd on the dock, and headed to the *Emerald*. One quick visit to learn what she could about Captain Bentley's visit to London, then to the livery to hire herself a horse. *Will they believe I'm the gentleman I'm impersonating?* She slowed her walk and tried to mimic the gait of a man. The new tall boots made it awkward. *How did men walk in these?*

Chapter Thirteen

Journal Entry: August 1694 - Bioko, Bight of Benin.
Alexander Hincher - Ship's Surgeon

We continued along the African coastline and stopped at Bioko in the Bight of Benin. The tide is out, and they careened the *Fancy*. As the *Fancy* is lying on its side, the shipwright and several men are making repairs to the hull. Along with it being razed, the men are removing part of the superstructure to make the ship faster.

I went ashore. A rare opportunity to gather what medical supplies I could gather.

We are back at sea and even I notice a difference in the agility and speed of the *Fancy*. While ashore, I met a village shaman who was placing a poultice on a woman's severely damaged leg. I watched as he chewed herbs to the consistency of paste. He then placed it on a plantain leaf and laid it on the torn flesh. It seemed to have an immediate effect. The woman relaxed with relief from the pain. He told me that if he changed the poultice each day, within a week she would heal completely. After learning about several other treatments he shared with me, I gathered supplies—mostly herbs and returned to the ship.

- Hinch

English Countryside, England - 1748 -

It had been years since she'd been on the back of a horse. Not since her grandfather insisted she was a lady now, and it was not becoming for the two of them to ride wildly through the countryside. Now outside of town, Elizabeth removed the hat and let her hair fall back over her shoulders, giving it to the wind as she gave her horse a slight kick.

With luck, she'd overtake Captain Bentley's coach to London by the time it reached Nottingham. With the condition of roads, she knew her horse could easily outdistance the coach by double.

She brought the horse to a comfortable trot. She didn't have to push too hard and didn't want to chance the need to stop too long to rest. Small farms came and went. The freedom was exhilarating. Each time she neared one of the small settlements, she'd return her flowing hair to its proper place under the hat. She still chuckled at how well the tailor had created the impression she was one of the gentry. He even accommodated for her ample female curves. Without a suspicion or close attention to detail, she was confident she could avoid being discovered. Not that she hadn't progressed in her journeys as a woman, but right now she needed the freedom to travel fast and without the restrictions or risks attached to a single woman alone on her own out in the country.

She approached a small stream winding its way through a small grove of poplars, their young leaves dancing in the cool morning breeze. A perfect place to stretch her legs and give her horse a well-deserved drink. She'd made good time. Though she was a day behind the captain's coach, she was certain she could catch him the next day.

Even on a horse with practically a perfect gait, she knew by day two her thighs would need serious attention, regardless of how well the tailor padded her trousers. It was important to keep her pace.

And then, she'd learn the identity of the killer who cheated her of the information she needed to get from ol' Denn, the man she hoped could help find her sister.

She slipped down off the horse, gave him a kind pat on his neck, "Thank you, old boy."

A loud crack disrupted the music made by the stream as it tumbled over the riverbed rocks. She turned so quickly she almost lost her footing.

Repulsion swept the surprise away like a gust of wind clears the dust. A vile stench of rotted meat escaped through yellowed teeth and hit her square in the face. If her horse hadn't halted her retreat, Elizabeth would have scrambled out of the reach of his pungent breath. As her head reactively jerked back into the neck of the horse, her eyes captured an instant picture of the loathsome man. Long greasy black hair fell past his dirt caked neck, landing on a worn shirt once maybe a brilliant orange, but now a sun-bleached rust-colored rag. When he reached his large hand toward her face, she instinctively ducked. Her knees bending to give her the only means of escape failed her. He was too quick. He grabbed her by the shoulder and held her upright. A scream certain to betray her true identity would do no good. She stifled it. Just as the word 'who?' tried to leave her lips, his deep graveled voice joined his offensive breath to silence her.

"I like your horse," he said, "and your boots."

As quick as lightning, a fist smashed her jaw and all went dark.

Chapter Fourteen

Journal Entry: October 1694 - Principe - Atlantic Ocean
Alexander Hincher - Ship's Surgeon

Our progress continued south along the African coast and my surgery work has comprised a pulled tooth and a few sick sailors, treated for stomach pain. We captured two Danish privateers near the island of Principe, where Avery's pirates stripped the ships of ivory and gold. We faced no battle requiring my services to clean up the damage.

However, there were seventeen defecting Danes who joined the *Fancy's* crew. I think they defected so they could receive medical attention, for three of them had venereal disease and one a badly broken and poorly healing forearm. I re-broke it and set it right, securing it between two planks with leather straps. With rum as the sedative, the pain was mostly tolerable.

On Principe, while the crew was restocking supplies, I secured more herbs. More importantly, I secured sugar and cocoa which I use to soothe the malady of bland on-board food.

- Hinch

Outside of Chester, England - 1748

"Is he dead?" The sweet girlish voice trembled as her father poked at the bloody body laying inside the barn door. The body didn't move.

"Get ma and get some fresh water. He's breathin' but probably not for long." The man laid down the rake, knelt and began peeling back the blood-soaked jacket. The blood was hardened, but the night's rain soaked the rest of the unconscious body's clothes.

✝ ✝ ✝

"Do I assume you're not this Dennison Hillis, who escaped from a Persian prison the night before they slated him for execution?"

Jack blinked back the clouds, holding a clear view of his surroundings at bay. He heard the words, but the voice was unfamiliar. A woman's voice. Young, but not a child. Eyes and head shuttered together trying to sweep away the confusion. She came into focus as he attempted to prop up on an elbow, only to collapse in pain.

A breath escaped, accompanied by a groan as he plopped back down.

"Where am I?" The words clung to a shallow breath.

"Chester. Well, near Chester actually."

Careful not to move his body this time, he rolled his head to see the source of the voice.

Sunlight creeped through flowered curtains to fall on long blond hair braided and falling over the woman's right shoulder. The freckles commonly found on young boys and girls had failed to disappear on this young woman. As if carefully placed by an artist, each freckle added to the next and seemed to dance across her smooth pink complexion.

A finely woven cream-colored bodice and blouse with a dark blue pattern contrasted against her light hair and skin, accented her figure. This was no farm girl. The surroundings were common for a farmhouse, and the clothes were also common. Anything near Chester either meant they were in the castle or on a farm. But the very visage of this woman caught Jack off guard. She was out of place.

"Well?" Her simple question brought his wandering eyes back into focus on her face.

"Well?" he repeated, trying to be a gentleman.

She held up the journal, a finger keeping the place she'd been reading.

"I assume, you're not this Dennison Hillis. If you were, I'd say you've aged well for being over sixty years old."

"Who are——"

A raised hand and extended finger cut off his question. "Let's determine who you are first." Emphasizing her marital status, she continued, "My husband and daughter find a soaked, unconscious man bleeding to death, lying in a pool of his own blood in our barn. I believe manners would justify learning his identity first."

This woman is definitely out of place, Jack thought. There was nothing to be gained from telling anything but the truth. Squinting his eyes against the light streaming over her shoulder, he tried to better focus on her determined stare.

"No, I'm not Dennison Hillis." *So that's ol' Denn's Christian name. She's reading his notebook?*

"Did you kill him?"

"Pardon?" His head involuntarily jerked back at the question. Pain shot across his shoulder. He winced, "No."

"Whose blood is on your knife?" She lifted the knife he'd pulled out of ol' Denn's chest, holding it with a lacy white kerchief.

"You believe he's dead?"

"Officers from Liverpool are searching for a murderer, probably bleeding, said to have killed four of Liverpool's citizens." Eyebrows raised, her head tilted slightly forward, pointing to his bandaged shoulder. "Got shot while escaping." His Majesty's Royal Judge couldn't have pronounced a defendant more guilty than this woman's gentle observation did.

"Why?" His question needed no more words. He mimicked the motion she made toward his bandaged shoulder; his attention fixed on her piercing green eyes. Again, he wondered how her freckles had survived the march into adulthood. As she shifted in the chair, the light changed and revealed a red tint in her long braids.

The tiny upturn in her smile confirmed the suspicion this was no ordinary woman. She was not only out of place here, but she had the advantage over Jack in every way.

She repeated Jack's question. "Why? This notebook. That's why you're not hanging from a tree across the Mersey."

"Forgive me, milady. You have me at a disadvantage. Mr. Dennison Hillis, who I'd met only recently, was violently murdered at the hand of two hoodlums. I arrived on the scene as they were attempting to secure what I assume was that notebook. When I intervened, they turned their attack on me. I killed one of them before the other, with that knife, pierced Mr. Hillis to the heart. As he lay dying, he whispered the location of that notebook and bade me to take it." Jack chose not to mention the map and wondered if this woman had found it. He carefully glanced around, spotting his vest and wondered if the map was still tucked in its pocket.

"The other two?" she asked.

"Were dead when I went looking for the notebook. The proprietress, Mistress Lonnie, and one of her patrons lay dead in her establishment when I arrived. The men responsible had ransacked the place looking for what I assume was that notebook. I interrupted their search and got knocked unconscious. When I awoke, I lay next to the two dead victims. From the floor, the lone lamp revealed the notebook's hiding place. As I retrieved it, the constable and friends charged in and began firing."

"Just as I supposed." Her smile was unconvincing, either in belief or doubt.

"Ah, he's awake." The voice yanked Jack's attention from the mysterious woman. Pain shot through him as he attempted to move his head and shoulders to watch the man enter the room.

"Lie still. Sorry about the hole in you. It took some digging to get that ball out. But if you don't hang, you will at least heal."

This man was more what Jack would expect in a farming village like Chester. From behind the six-foot frame clothed in a bright red shirt and black trousers, peered a mini version of the woman still sitting in the judgment seat. Strong, callused hands reached down scooping the little girl into his arms.

"Meet Margaret." She tucked her shy little face into the man's broad shoulder, then turned to peek out. "I see you've met my wife. Name's Victoria, named perfectly for the queen that she is and the victory I won. I'm John."

The sounds and smells of the small farm drifted through the now quiet room.

"Thank you. The prospect of healing outweighs the alternative." Jack carefully padded his bandaged shoulder. "My name is Jack. Yes, I am that fugitive. The four I'm accused of killing fell to an assassin's hand, not mine."

"They were after this, weren't they?" Victoria held up the notebook.

Jack nodded. "I believe so, though I've yet to see what's inside."

"Vic!" John's accommodating tone turned instantly serious. He was looking past his wife and into the yard. "Get Jack and Mags into the cellar. Now! They're here."

"Let's go, unless you're interested in hanging." Victoria quickly pulled the blankets off Jack. His relief to find himself wearing a very loose pair of John's trousers lasted only seconds. The pain shot through his body as Victoria helped him to his feet. Unstable from loss of blood, Jack appreciated Victoria's support. They climbed down into a dark, earthy, and dank cellar.

† † †

"Good day, sheriff." John rounded the barn as if he'd been caring for his livestock, acting surprised for the visit. "You and your men are out early."

"John." The sheriff nodded. "Four people in Liverpool were murdered, the killer's escaped."

"Who?" John demanded. "Who was murdered? You know my wife has family there."

"Wasn't them, John, relax."

John's heart relaxed, his feigned surprise and worry was working.

"Nobody knows why. A stranger who'd been seen coming and going stabbed an old man and his friend in the street, then tore up a quirky old tavern and killed the owner and one of her patrons. He took a ball in the chest and went down. He smashed the lamp and in the darkness he escaped."

"He escaped? You said they shot him."

"He's dangerous, John. You better keep your wife and daughter close. Don't let them out of your sight until he's caught. They say he knew his way with a knife. All four victims died with one stab to the heart."

As the sheriff and John spoke, several men with the sheriff, who John didn't recognize, led their horses around the garden and small coral. Normal enough for men hunting another man. John's heart pounded, realizing if they looked inside the barn they'd see the blood he'd yet to clean up. John had been more worried about stopping the bleeding than cleaning the barn.

"Sheriff! Look here!"

It was too late, they found it.

† † †

"Stay quiet, I must keep up appearances."

Victoria was up the wooden steps and out before Jack could respond. The cellar door closed, plunging the small earthen room into total blackness. Victoria went to the window and watched the sheriff dismount and enter the barn. A sense of foreboding enveloped her body.

The cellar door opened, Jack's clothes dropped to the floor, and the door slammed back down. He scooted over to take them. They felt dry and clean. His fingers explored, feeling for the map in the vest pocket. Nothing. He laid back down on the damp dirt floor as the pain slowly subsided.

Chapter Fifteen

Journal Entry: January 1695 - St. Augustine Bay, Madagascar.
Alexander Hincher - Ship's Surgeon

We finally rounded the Cape of Good Hope and are at St. Augustine's Bay, Madagascar, restocking supplies. The few ships we captured and looted gave the men enough action to keep them animated for the future riches Avery promised them, but it takes a persuasive captain to keep the spirits up when sailing months at a time.

- Hinch

Onboard the Chawbuck, Port of Birkenhead- 1748

"Captain, your old friend is dead," Krist said as he stepped into the captain's cabin.

Captain Ali Mutarid Hassan, known by his followers as Nakhoda, the god of the ship, lifted his weathered boots off the finely carved walnut table and turned to face Krist, his first mate and youngest son.

Krist stood tall, with only a hint of his father's Persian complexion. Standing side by side, few associated them as father and son. His blonde hair and startling blue eyes were evidence of his Icelandic mother's heritage. But in his twenty-five years, he'd grown to hate his father's obsession to find the sacred "Blade of Safavid" and seek revenge on those who kept him from it.

"The notebook?" The captain leaned forward, his leathered hands gripping the edge of the table as he pulled himself upright.

"They say the killer took it." Krist waited, watching his commanding father settle into thought. Captain Hassan sat in his cabin on the powerful

Chawbuck, now anchored in Birkenhead on the River Mersey.

Accustomed to his father's slower responses of late, Krist stood patiently, aware that his father, now at an old age, would ponder and consider his thoughts before continuing a conversation. It could take several minutes before he would return to the present. These sessions of deep thought demanded patience, a skill Krist had mastered through careful instruction and practice. Krist seldom asked what his father was thinking anymore. His father shared many of his conquests freely and his regrets rarely.

"Fools!" The captain slammed his fist on the table. Krist folded his arms, unmoved by the outburst. Despite his father's thoughtful appearance, once the pondering was over, his actions were immediate and final. "The messengers?"

"Above decks." Krist motioned with his head toward the stairs that led from the captain's cabin to the main deck.

The captain bounded past him and up the steps. The doors to the below decks slammed open as he charged through. Though they were only the messengers of this bad news, the captain's two spies stood visibly shaking.

A deep breath slowly exhaled readied Nakhoda for the report from his spies. His piercing and furiously dark eyes bore into their souls.

The taller of the two messengers respectively bowed his head, "Nakhoda, sir, Mr. Gasher and Mr. O'Donnel snatched Mr. Hillis to bring him here. A young naval officer intercepted, killing Mr. Gasher and Mr. Hillis. Stabbed both to the heart."

Krist slowly shook his head. Gasher and O'Donnel? Who trusted those two? Strong? Yes. Bold? Yes, but not cunning or clever. It was surprising they were not both dead.

"Where is O'Donnel?"

"The killer stole papers from Mr. Hillis' coat and fled. O'Donnel went to gather Mr. Hillis' collection of writings. The killer returned, then killed two more trying to take Mr. Hillis' writings. Mr. O'Donnel shot him, but the killer escaped."

"His writings?"

His father's voice lowered, a demand almost like a question. It impressed Krist.

The second spy, much shorter, had remained motionless and silent. Without lifting his head to look the captain in the eye, he said, "Mr. O'Donnel collected the books, writings and notes from both the tavern and Mr. Hillis' home. He only entrusted us with this." He handed a small leather satchel to the captain.

Captain Hassan pulled a half dozen poorly folded pages from the satchel. Opening the first, he recognized the handwritten note directed to him from his late friend.

> *"Mr. Hassan, my friend, your lifelong wait is over. I'm sending you a young woman in the fall. She'll be traveling to the New World and will meet you in Antigua. She is the first in our three-decade hunt with personal knowledge of the blade. My debt to you is now paid. I wish you well."*
>
> *Your friend - Mr. Dennison Hillis*

In a hurried note scrawled at the bottom, he read, *"A young naval officer may accompany her. Be careful with him. I believe he knows more than we know."*

"Where was this note?" the captain asked.

"Tucked inside Mr. Hillis' coat. The killer must have missed it."

A naval officer? Krist wondered.

Chapter Sixteen

Journal Entry: April 1695 - Johanna, Comoros Islands.
Alexander Hincher - Ship's Surgeon

The heat and boredom are the challenges the men face. We sit and wait here on the island of Johanna in the Comoros Islands. Avery refers to our time here as resting, but we are resting from what? On shore I try to learn from others about the medicines, the maladies, and the cures learned by the local native shamans. This practical education adds more to my skills than the books back in college.

- Hinch

English Countryside, England - 1748

Elizabeth blinked her eyes open. Her head pounded. Carefully, she opened and closed her mouth. Massaging her jaw, she confirmed it wasn't broken. She slowly sat up. The late afternoon sun witnessed several hours had passed. A glance confirmed the man had taken her horse and boots. Reaching up to feel what she expected to be a large knot on her head, a slight chuckle escaped her sore mouth. The hat had remained in place.

She stood and carefully walked around, hoping to find her boots. They were gone. *Maybe he just threw them away. As well as I'm hidden inside this men's outfit, my feet should have given me away. How did he not notice?* She freshened up as much as she could, composed herself, and stood on the grassy edge of the road. Nothing and nobody in sight in any direction. How soon would a carriage pass by, or would there just be more highwaymen?

If only she were the little girl of years ago, when she could run barefoot all day. Not anymore. *Do I wait? Do I walk? Where'd the brigand come from? Did he walk here?*

A search for tracks told little. Since the recent rains, only one horse had been here, hers, and there were no footprints but the few fresh ones. Her horse left through the small grove and across the fields.

Before long, the sun would set. Should she go back, forward, or follow the horse through the fields? Then she saw it. Why hadn't she seen it earlier?

A blinking light was resting right on the horizon, beckoning her. Elizabeth squinted, focusing her full attention; she rubbed her jaw, maybe her vision was still cloudy and her eyes imagining things. No, this was real.

At least her uncovered feet would be walking through fresh green spring grasses for a while. She left the shelter of the small wood and headed north. Could she reach the blinking light by dark? Did she want to?

Elizabeth crossed the small stream several times as it wound its way through the fields. Eventually it ran south and the beckoning light, changing now to a deep orange and beginning to rise above the horizon, was due north. She'd left the comfort of the soft grass hours ago; her feet were now cracked and bloody. The sun setting to her left matched in color the blinking light. A mill. She was being beckoned by the blades of a windmill reflecting off the setting sun.

A small farmhouse sat in the center of a cluster of small corrals, four or five, she thought. One small barn sat next to the windmill. Though the outside was peaceful and neat, this tiny settlement didn't feel right. Where was her urge to rush in and seek help? She approached cautiously. With sore bare feet, there was no other way to approach. A horse was tied to the rail next to the house. Her horse. Anger extinguished fear.

She was about to charge forward when the sound of pounding hooves drowned the clicking sound of the mill being driven by the soft breeze. It was too late to run. Elizabeth dropped to the ground and scooted behind a water trough. Riders on two strong and matching dark horses kicked up dust as they brought their mounts to a halt in front of the trough. They hopped down and bounded toward the farmhouse, not pausing. Pushing through the door, the two riders disappeared.

Elizabeth's heart slowed, and the lump in her throat slowly settled back down. She limped to her horse. As she brushed her hand along its mane, she whispered, "It's me, I'm here to rescue you."

Are all these horses stolen?

The overwhelming desire to settle a score overcame her urge to mount up and run. The darkness was setting in; she had little time. She couldn't just burst through the door and punch someone in the face. And there was the issue of her missing boots.

Elizabeth untied the horse and walked him around to the back of the barn, just in case she'd have to run. Though bloody and sore, she was grateful for the quiet of her bare feet as she approached the farmhouse. Voices from inside told her all was not well.

"Another horse?"

"My new favorite." She recognized that voice.

"The rider?"

"Pale and weakly."

Pale and weakly? Her urge to storm through the door and demonstrate pale and weakly was nearly more than she could bear.

"Where is he?" the deeper voice asked

"Dead. Fell off and hit his head."

"You fool."

"We're supposed to watch the old man, see what he does, and find out who he meets. Instead, we leave a trail of bodies. And this horse's owner is one more of them."

Elizabeth inched closer. Was the killer here? She couldn't run now. Were they talking about ol'Denn?

The door burst open. A tall, lanky man was followed by one much shorter and almost twice his width. Shouts of anger continued.

If they turn around, I'll join that trail of bodies.

She plastered herself against the wall of the house. Though in shadow, the two men could easily spot her. She was about to creep away when a third man stomped out, following the others. Though it was only a split second that she'd looked into his eyes before he'd knocked her out, she recognized the evil soul, the man who'd taken her horse and boots and claimed her dead.

Which way to run? Then she saw them. Her boots lay just inside the open door. Two quick steps she was inside the house with boots in hand. She turned to run, but once again stood face to face with her assailant.

"Shouldn't have come…" His words tapered off, turning from threat to question. He paused as he looked at her from top to bottom.

The hat didn't sit right, strands of long hair flowed from under it and past her ear to her shoulder. The open jacket exposed a trim waist leading to a fuller chest, and the feet, though dirty and caked with mud, were too fine. His grin turned her stomach.

Chills ran up Elizabeth's spine. She felt naked and the instinct to cover up, to tuck her hair back under the hat, to hide, to run. But to where? The man stood too broadly in the doorway, and she'd never get past him. She backed up slowly, one trembling foot at a time. When a table stopped her retreat, his grin grew wider and a slow growl climbed past his yellowed teeth.

Reaching down to catch her balance, Elizabeth's free hand rested on leather. Her quick glance took the chills running down her spine and sent them rushing back up to where they'd come from. Light from a small oil lamp illuminated the very ancient leather bound book that laid before ol' Denn the first night she'd entered the Nookery. Anger replaced her fear. The chills now running in the right direction fortified her backbone. Lightning fast, she grabbed the oil lamp and threw it square into the man's chest.

The shock of her quickness took his snarling grin and turned it to horror. The oil from the shattered lamp burst into flame, engulfing the man. He turned so quickly, his back now to Elizabeth, the house plummeted into darkness. She scooped up the book, and with boots held tight, dashed out past the screaming man. Two stunned faces turned to watch their partner fall and wallow in the dirt, followed by a shadow darting from the house and around the back of the barn.

Elizabeth shoved the book into an already crowded saddle bag and with a failed attempt to slip the boots over her muddy and swollen foot, tried to tuck them under her jacket. She sprung into the saddle, and as hard as her tender feet could, kicked the horse into action. It lurched forward just as a man rounded the barn.

The boots fell free and tumbled to the ground. There was no turning back. She charged into the darkness, a silhouette into the sliver of orange glow clinging to the horizon.

In the darkness, Elizabeth relied solely on her horse. They ran for what felt like hours. Regardless the distance, she'd be impossible to follow in the dark. That gave her peace. She didn't dare stop. Eventually, both she and the horse, too weary to continue, slowed to a walk and finally stopped. Elizabeth slid down and collapsed on the hard ground. Where was the moon when she needed it? So little of its light crept through the clouds, there was no way to know where she was.

Chapter Seventeen

I treat minor injuries of our own men, and at my insistence when the *Fancy* takes on extra crew members, I examine them for disease before they come onboard and infect our crew. We captured and looted a passing French pirate ship. Avery recruited forty of the crew to join him. As we are here in the Comoros Islands with nowhere to be, I insisted I quarantine these forty men on shore until I approve their joining our crew.

The last time we took on men from a pirate ship, we had an outbreak that was unnecessary.

- Hinch

English Countryside, England - 1748

"Is he alive?"

On bended knee, an older man held Elizabeth's wrist in one hand, her head with the other. He looked up at the woman in the wagon.

"He's alive. But I don't think he's a he."

The woman climbed down and joined him. She removed Elizabeth's hat and pulled the jacket free.

"Nope. Let's get her home."

The man gathered the hat and tied the waiting horse to the wagon. The sun broke over the horizon and began its new day. With a soft shake and tender, "Good morning," Elizabeth woke to the new day.

"Honey, let me help you into the wagon. Looks like you had a hard night." The woman took Elizabeth by the hand and helped her up.

Pain shot up Elizabeth's legs as she attempted to stand on her bare feet. "Who…"

"We'll get to that later. Let me help you up. Here, I need to take a look at those feet." The woman helped Elizabeth into the wagon, resting her alongside a large bag of feed. She took Elizabeth's bloody and swollen feet into her lap and began cleaning them off. Mud and blood soaked her apron as she gently poured water over one foot then the next.

"I didn't see no shoes," the older man muttered over his shoulder.

Elizabeth looked from the weathered man to the angel of a woman tending to her blistered and bloody feet. "Thank you. Who are you? Where are we going?"

"Home, dear," the woman said. "Port there is my father. Call me Ginger. And you?"

"Elizabeth," Elizabeth said quietly. She smiled, noticing for the first time the red twist in Ginger's tightly woven bun. It took a second look before she could recognize the difference in age. Her immediate impression that they were an elderly couple didn't fade quickly. His wrinkled hat sat atop long gray hair that curled as it found its way to the collar of a faded flannel shirt. Probably red when it was new, Elizabeth guessed. Yet, Ginger's sun-dried face carried the texture of leather. She had not aged gracefully.

The tenderness of the woman surprised her. Ginger dried each foot and gently worked a liniment of some sort into the battered skin. Muscles up and down her body released their tension, practically crippling her ability to focus on anything but the relief.

"Would I be impertinent asking how a young woman dressed like a man ends up barefoot on a secluded road with bruised and bloody feet? With a fine horse standing only feet away?" Ginger continued her magic as she asked.

Disappointed to leave her dreamland, Elizabeth leaned up on the bag of feed. "I was in a hurry to catch a carriage headed to London. It was essential no one followed or suspected me to be a woman traveling alone. I engaged a tailor, and well, I met upon a highwayman who took my horse and boots, leaving me for dead." She hadn't forgotten about the blow she'd taken to her jaw the day before. She worked her jaw in every direction and rubbed it tenderly.

"The feet," Elizabeth motioned to her newly saved feet, "result from walking the miles to find help. The help ended up being a farm which housed the very highwaymen who stole my boots and horse."

Whop. Whop. Whop. Whop. Whop.

The steady beat grew louder as the wagon approached the homestead. A natural sound, it hadn't drawn Elizabeth's attention.

"Whoa." Port pulled the horses to a stop and turned to face Elizabeth. "We're here."

"No, no, no, no, no, no, no." Elizabeth jerked up so quickly, Ginger nearly tumbled from the wagon.

She'd only seen the farmhouse in the late evening, but the rhythm of the windmill was unmistakable.

Whop. Whop. Whop. Whop. Whop.

She was back.

"What have you done? Why are we here?" Frantic, her head darted from the yard to the house, then the barn and corral, so familiar, but no sign of the men she'd fled the night before.

"You alright?" Port carefully stepped down off the wagon. There was no fear or threat in his gentle eyes as he looked at her.

"But I've been here. Last night, this… the windmill… over there." Her words stumbled over themselves as she tried to make sense of the certainty that this was the very place she'd escaped.

Port turned to Ginger. "Better get her inside and some food in her. Poor thing's a bit confused."

Together they helped Elizabeth from the wagon to the house. Elizabeth's eyes tried franticly to recreate the scenes from the night before and confirm this wasn't one continuous nightmare.

Whop. Whop. Whop. Whop. Whop.

She took one more glance at the mill as she limped through the doorway. Her feet were tender, but the care rendered by Ginger had genuinely helped.

Port returned to care for her horse. As it drank heartily, he opened the saddlebags and slid the old book free. Careful not to be seen, he slipped it behind the door of the barn.

Ginger quickly joined him as he began loosening the saddle. "The book, is it there?"

"Dunno. Give it a look."

"Damn." Ginger rifled through the saddlebags. A few foodstuffs, clothing neatly packed, no book. She pulled a pale green dress which had been carefully but tightly folded and shook it out. Almost by instinct, she held it against herself for fit.

"Gunna be a woman again?" Port asked. "Might take that to keep those animals from taking their anger and lusts out on her." He motioned to Elizabeth in the house.

"We gotta find that book. Must have fallen out." Ginger tossed the dress to Port, she took the horse's harness and tightened it back up. Dropping the saddlebags to the ground, she climbed up on Elizabeth's horse. "Get that dress on her. If I don't find that book, they'll need something to distract their anger."

She disappeared, the dust kicked up concealing her form as she charged around the barn and across the field, heading the same way Elizabeth escaped the night before.

Port righted the saddlebags, carefully returning their spilled contents, except for the dress. He retrieved the book from the barn, also picking up the boots he hid there earlier when he stumbled over them in the early morning darkness. He shuffled into the house.

"Who are you?" Elizabeth demanded.

She leaned against the table from which she'd snatched the lamp and thrown it at her captor less than twenty-four hours earlier. When Port stepped through the door, his tired eyes widened. Like a bearcat, Elizabeth wielded a large butcher knife she'd snatched off the now cold stove.

Port held up the boots in a gesture imitating a peace offer. "Don't know if these'll fit, but you better try." He took a cautious step forward and set them next to her, tossed the dress on a chair and plopped the book on the table. "Hope you've some stockings in there." He placed the saddlebag over the back of a chair. Elizabeth noticed his badly twisted leg as he shuffled to a trunk sitting in the corner of the room. With one eye on Port and the other rummaging through the saddlebag for stockings, she settled on the chair and carefully pulled the stockings over her tender feet. The first boot was painfully tight. She pulled the second one on.

Port stood as erect as his crippled leg would permit and turned, holding a pistol. Her eyes widened as the surprise was now hers. "Know how to use one of these?" He shuffled back over, taking the pistol by the barrel and handed it to Elizabeth. "Well?"

"You point this end at the person you're going to kill." Her confidence, mixed with confusion, created a twisted face that brought an enormous smile to Port's face.

"That's it, but not yet."

She lowered the pistol.

"Miss Elizabeth, you fell in with a nasty bunch. They'll be back and so will Ginger. If you're here, this will be a bad day for you. These men left a trail of dead bodies looking for that book, and that's just half the puzzle. Some bloke got some important notebook and disappeared."

Elizabeth visualized the scene where ol' Denn lay in his own blood as a stranger pulled a knife from his chest, took something from his hand and disappeared. She was more certain than ever Captain Bentley would be the key to the assassin's identity.

"Who are you?" she repeated. "Why are you doing this?"

"These fella's boss' worse than Satan hisself. Got spies and thugs in every port, looking for clues to a treasure lost some fifty years. Not money, he's got money, wants revenge. Nothin more worse'an 'at."

"Who is their boss?" Elizabeth lifted the book and opened the cover, eager to see why it was worth the lives of so many. She'd snatched it from the table last night in desperation and curiosity. Could these pages hold the answers to her quest? She'd seen this book before; it was the very book ol' Denn was reading when she first visited the Nookery. Her smile grew when she realized she'd even read another version of it. *The General History of Pyrates* by Captain Charles Johnson. She immediately saw it wasn't the book in particular, but ol' Denn's writings in the margins that made it worthy of so many murders.

Port interrupted her discovery. "Nakhoda is all they call him. An evil, murderous monster out ta'venge a wrong from a different time an' different world." He picked up the saddlebags and shuffled to the door. "Keep that pistol handy in case someone returns."

"Nakhoda," she repeated softly. *Persian?*

"What I heard is one of the pirates dun him wrong, took part of a treasure and escaped. Nakhoda still can't find him. Something about a princess, a knife, and breakin' out'a prison."

"The Avery treasure," Elizabeth mumbled to herself as she tried to read, walk, and watch Port.

Elizabeth followed him to the barn where he urged a saddle off its stand and dragged it to the corral. His shuffle looked as uncomfortable as Elizabeth's boots felt. They reached the corral and Port struggled to get the saddle up onto a tall white mare.

"Why are you doing this?"

"When you got away, they rousted Ginger an' me to go find you. They went too, ever' direction. When Nakhoda learns they lost the book, there'll be bad days."

Elizabeth's stare begged more.

"Murdered my wife and took my Ginger. Made her a slave. When I came searchin, they did this." He pointed to his mangled foot. Lifted his hat and exposed a scar that ran across the whole of his forehead. "Someday I'd get even, I promised, but if I ran, they promised to hurt my girl, so I stay. I'm a coward. So why do I help you, you ask? Hate. You get away, destroy that book, an' don't let them ever find you. At's my revenge."

Elizabeth knew that hate. It took years to turn hers into action—to revenge. Now she wanted to help.

With help from Port, Elizabeth settled into the saddle, pistol in hand.

"Now you head through that field as fast as this ol' mare'll go. Cross the river and run from the sun as fast as you can. This ol' girl can do it. Don't stop till it's too dark to take another step. Don't trust anyone. Find some trees and settle in. Don't take your boots off." He finally broke into a smile. "In the mornin', head towards London and don't stop till you get there and find the captain you're huntin', 'cause Nakhoda's men'll be hunting you. Their lives depend on bringing back that book."

Elizabeth listened to the instructions, leaning into every word, understanding why this old man would risk all to help.

"Now," he said.

"Now what?"

"Use that pistol. Can't let you just ride away. I'd have a bad day. How would I explain your escape, with me not putting up a fuss?" he said.

"Any requests?"

"I only have one good leg; I'd like to keep it." A tiny smile accompanied a wince.

Elizabeth raised the pistol. Port looked directly down the barrel. She pulled the trigger. A loud crack and Port flopped to the ground. Elizabeth turned the mare around, and following ol' Port's direction, charged away.

"Damn that woman." The ringing in his head was so loud he couldn't hear his own words. Port pulled his bloody hand away from where his ear was half the size it used to be.

Chapter Eighteen

Now northbound again with a crew of 150, the men are feeling like they own this ocean. Avery's only fear is the threat of the large and heavily gunned ships belonging to the East India Company.

In the next few months, Avery expects an Indian fleet to be making its annual pilgrimage to Mecca. We are sailing for Perim, to wait the pilgrimage's return trip.

- Hinch

Outside of Chester, England - 1748

Hours passed. To Jack, in the dark cellar, it seemed like days. After dozing off a few times, he got moving. Hunger overcame the expected pain. Each time he moved; the pain grew more faint. Never had he healed so quickly.

How long have I been down here? How long had John and Victoria nursed me?

He rotated his arm. Soon, even a full rotation was only mildly painful. He found his way to the steps and carefully pushed on the door. It did not budge. Another push, this time it cracked open just enough to reveal the sun was going down. He'd been in the cellar all day. He realized something very heavy sat on the door.

Am I a prisoner?

With a groan of pain, Jack pushed with his good shoulder to open the door enough to climb out into the small room between what he thought was a parlor and the kitchen.

Who are these people? Village peasants never have a home as nice as this.

The house appeared empty, but angry voices from the yard proved there was trouble.

On one good hand and knees, Jack crept through the ransacked house. Someone had thoroughly and disrespectfully searched for something.

Me? No, that notebook.

"We'll continue our search in the morning!" Jack heard a voice say. "Stay here with them in the barn where you can watch them."

Me and the notebook.

Knowing it was a futile thought that he might find it, the way the house had been searched, Jack crept back into the small parlor where he'd woken up earlier. The sun that had beautifully illuminated this room that morning was now casting a dim orange glow as if whispering a lullaby to the world. The chairs were turned over, and the temporary bed that had once been a comfortable couch was on its side. To listen through the window, Jack slid to the spot where Victoria's chair now laid on its side. His hand met a welcome piece of steel lying under a lacy white kerchief on the floor. Next to it lay a folded scrap of paper—he tucked the scrap into his pocket.

The door burst open and in charged a large man. The two recognized each other immediately. A venomous "you" escaped both men's mouths at the same time. The murderer and the accused paused, almost transfixed as they recognized the irony. A wicked grin formed on the man's face. The fading sunlight revealed darkened teeth as the grin turned to a threatening smile. Jack sat on the floor, shirtless with large bandages over his left shoulder and upper arm, and the very man who Jack watched plunge a knife into ol' Denn's chest stood above him, pistol in hand.

Jack returned the knife to its proper owner. Eyes opened wide, the evil grin turned to a gasp as the knife pierced the man's chest and heart. The pistol raised and fell, the man with it. He dropped to his knees and tumbled to the floor. Jack scooted over to the man and pulled the pistol from his hand. The back of the dead man's hand carried the same tattoo Jack hadn't paid attention to on the man he'd killed a few nights before.

What did Captain Remington plunge me into? What did the old man in the tavern know about the Avery treasure? I should have just walked up to him and asked. Research? This isn't research, this is madness.

Then his thoughts turned to John, Victoria, and little Mags. With the light from a small lamp, he returned to the cellar to get his clothes. As he tightened the belt of his trousers, he noticed a small crossbow with several small bolts behind the steps. He didn't wait to button his shirt. Reaching for the bow, he saw a sword, knives and two pistols. In the dark leather bag that hung next to the pistols, he imagined was powder and the balls to complete this tiny arsenal. He left the pistols, but with the crossbow, the dead man's pistol, and the bloody knife he retrieved from the now lifeless body, Jack slipped into the approaching darkness to see about his new friends.

† † †

Grumbling curses, though muffled, confirmed to Jack the men left behind to guard this little family were unhappy with the command. Jack was in no shape to make a grand or valiant entrance to rescue his friends. He expelled most of his energy getting his boots back on. How many men were there? He listened intently, hoping to make out and count voices. One, two? Nothing from Victoria or John. Were they safe? How about little Mags?

Jack soon realized this was not the local sheriff. He would know a family like this and he wouldn't be holding them hostage. *What happened to the sheriff?*

They want the notebook. And they don't know Victoria has it.

He smiled.

In the rising moonlight, four horses stood tethered, saddles resting on the rails of a small corral where inside stood several other horses Jack assumed belonged to John. Four men, one dead. Three men inside the barn? *Why the barn, not the house?*

One step at a time, he tiptoed around the barn. Another horse. Five men? In the darkness, he tripped and fell to his knees. Not just a horse. Its rider lay still in the darkness. He turned the body over to reveal the lifeless sheriff. The horse stood quietly and patiently for its rider. Leaning on the horse's leg for support, Jack stood. Again, he wondered what kind of men ol' Denn had been tangled up with. What was in the notebook and worth so many lives?

"Sorry, old girl." Jack lifted his good arm and leaned into the waiting horse to lend a little comfort to a beast who little understood what was happening.

The back of the barn was as tightly closed up as the front, but the sliver of light that seemed to crawl out between the cracks gave Jack a peek inside. One lamp sat between three men who sat drinking what had to be whisky. They'd had enough that their conversation was loud enough to have woken the sheriff if he was only sleeping.

He listened and confirmed their anger at being confined to the barn when a house was far better. These three, however, didn't let on they knew the value of the prize they were trying to find.

The crack in the door was too small. Jack couldn't tell where the family was being held. He needed a better look and scooted to another tiny stream of light escaping between two panels. There he spotted the family huddled together. Mags was sitting on Victoria's lap and John was leaning against a thick wooden post, an arm around Victoria.

I need these men out in the dark with me.

Jack scooted back to the sheriff's horse where he'd laid the crossbow, then crept back around to the horses.

Now, to get the horses to invite these men out to play. One by one, Jack removed the bridles, carefully and quietly. The third and largest of the four horses whipped Jack with his tail and turned to reject Jack's offer of freedom.

This is the one I need.

Jack backed off and went to the last horse. This one was black as black, its shiny back glistened in the moonlight. It also wasn't interested in Jack's attention, and though quiet, its skittishness was just what Jack had hoped for. An opinionated mare and an arrogant stallion. He scooted under the rail, and with the posts of the corral between him and the horses, he tied the bridles together. Neither horse reacted like they knew they were free of the corral.

With a slight encouragement, the two loose horses began walking away. Voices inside the barn, now mostly crude with vile threats, made for suitable cover for the horses' occasional whinny or neigh.

For the second time, Jack apologized to a horse. "Sorry about this." Then with the crossbow he shot the arrogant stallion right in the flank. It pounded forward, cracking the top rail of the corral, then lurched back, yanking the mare who joined in the fray. The two horses struggled, neither one able to let loose and run. It was like a dance with the devil. The commotion now too much to ignore inside the barn.

The barn door burst open, slamming into the mare, whose rear was in the way. A jumping kick slammed the door closed, knocking the first man out. The second pushed back through the door, charging out with pistol in hand. The stallion was now kicking wildly to free itself of the bolt hanging from its flank. A kick took the second man in the chest with both back legs, throwing him into the barn where he landed on the oil lamp scattering flame across the floor. The dry hay inside the barn practically exploded. With horses flailing outside and fire inside, the third guard had no idea what to do next. In his indecision, John helped him decide and knocked him flat with the shovel.

As quick as lightning, John pulled the lid from a large barrel and pushed it over, spilling water across the floor of the barn and extinguishing most of the flames. Victoria had a blanket in hand and was dragging it across the wet floor, beating out the flames that had climbed the walls. They quickly doused a few remaining spots with water pulled from the well. The first man came to his feet only to meet John's shovel. The second, badly burned, never moved again.

John got hold of the bridles and freed the now exhausted pair of horses. The stallion bounded off, bolt and all. The mare settled.

The fire out, the four stood speechless, staring at each other in the near darkness. The moon cast just enough light to see they shared a smile.

John broke the silence, tilting his head toward the house. "You got him first?"

"It was his knife, I just returned it," Jack said.

"So, you're not Dennison Hillis, and you're not his killer, who are you?" Victoria asked as innocently as if their friend the sheriff hadn't been murdered, their house ransacked, their family held hostage with life threatened, their barn set to flame, and a daring rescue taking the lives of three bandits hadn't just left them all standing in the cool of night.

"They call me Jack. On an errand for a man who will never appreciate what it took to tell him nobody knows where to find his old friend."

John handed Mags to Victoria. "We've a long journey ahead. Vic, help our friend here get his things. Pack enough for a few days. I'll take care of these three." He motioned toward the bodies scattered across the yard.

"A journey?" Jack asked.

"In the morning, their friends will come looking for you. They won't stop. None of us are safe until they have you. And this." John held up the notebook.

Jack let out a breath. The notebook wasn't taken or lost in the attack or rescue. Jack reached for it. As if not noticing, John tucked the notebook back into a pocket and turned toward the barn.

"You coming?" Victoria, with Mags in arms, turned and led Jack back into the house.

Chapter Nineteen

Journal Entry: September 1695 - Straits of Bab-el-Mandeb, Indian Ocean
 Alexander Hincher - Ship's Surgeon

The Islamic calendar determines the timing of the Hajj. It begins every year on the 8th day of the Dhu al-Hijjah lunar month. Avery feels confident he knows the approximate time the pilgrims will return home from this annual pilgrimage.

It is rumored this Indian fleet is the richest prize in Asia, perhaps the entire world. For the past year, this prize has been the *Fancy's* target and Avery's dream and vision. Any time spirits were low, discontent consumed the crew, or illness swept the ship, Avery jumped into action inspiring and influencing the men to trust in the future bounty.

As a captain leading 150 men to a very uncertain future, Avery's vision of unparalleled wealth, which he shared so confidently, was the only thing preventing a mutiny during the prolonged waits between the occasional capture or prolonged time on shore restocking supplies.

We reached the Straits of Bab-el-Mandeb this week and find we are not alone. Avery is joining with five other pirate captains. Many of our men were hesitant at the thought of sharing the bounty with other crews, but there are enough seasoned sailors who helped them understand that alone, the *Fancy* is no match for a convoy of ships, especially one certain to be accompanied with a gunship or two.

Joining our ranks to make a six-ship pirate flotilla are Captain Tew on his sloop-of-war *Amity* with a crew of about sixty men; Captain Joseph Faro on the *Portsmouth Adventure* with sixty men; Captain Richard Want on the *Dolphin* also with sixty men; Captain William Mayes on the *Pearl,* with thirty or forty men; and Captain Thomas Wake on the *Susanna,* with seventy men.

Each of these captains are carrying privateering commissions that implicated almost the entire eastern seaboard of North America. So they are all in the wrong ocean. Captain Tew is the most well respected, having captured some mighty bounty years earlier in these same waters.

Despite Tew's considerable experience, Avery got himself elected admiral of the new six-ship pirate flotilla. Avery is now in command of over 440 men as we lay in wait for the Indian fleet.

- Hinch.

Between Chester and Sheffield England - 1748

Mags, reigns in her tiny hands, took her turn driving the horses. She'd just woken up and insisted she sit next to John and have a turn. John wrapped the blanket around her and held her close. Having pulled through the night, the horses were too tired to run and the road was long and straight, surrounded by small hills and ravines, not very suitable for farms, so they had seen little life.

"Your friend Mr. Hillis tangled up with some bad folks." Victoria was thumbing through the notebook as soon as the dawning light permitted, the chill in the air notwithstanding. She added, "Jack, don't lose this notebook. The escapades of your recently expired friend Mr. Hillis and his associates are the makings of a great historical drama. Are you a writer?"

Jack blinked his eyes open. The sun rising behind her lit her hair with an iridescent glow, making it hard to focus. *Looks like I already lost the book, I've never even opened it.*

Victoria charged forward. "Mr. Hillis, your dead friend, did something that made the Persians upset enough to execute him. Didn't say what. He was in an Isfahan prison awaiting his execution when an Afghan army rebelled against the Safavid Shah Husayn and overthrew the Safavid Dynasty."

She paused, and gave Jack a nod as if he needed a moment to absorb the news. He did. "I'll try not to lose it," he answered, "And yes, I do write, but probably not a historical drama." *Yet, I may be living one.*

Jack wondered if her smile meant she realized he had already lost the notebook to her. She turned a page.

"During the rebellion by the Afghans, a prison break led by one of the Shah's former commanders freed Mr. Hillis and a group of really unsavory characters. They pillaged their way across India until they reached the port city of Sarat."

"All of that is in 'ol Denns notebook?" Jack lifted his hand as if to reach for the volume. Victoria paid no attention. The wagon continued forward as John, helping his sweet daughter think she was driving the horses, also tried to listen over the creaking wagon as Victoria shared the fantastic story.

"Looks like they became pirates, Jack." She paused, reading silently. Jack watched her eyes scanning the page. He decided to let her share the adventure. He leaned back, his elbow resting on the large soft bag. He guessed it was clothing Victoria hastened to pack and load on the wagon.

She turned another page. "Mu-ta-rid." She pronounced it slowly. "Mute-arid." She repeated, pronouncing a bit differently. "No it must be Mew-tear-id." She paused and looked at Jack.

"It's Persian," Jack said.

"This Persian, Captain Ali Mew-tear-id Hassan, is a former commander in the Shah's navy. Says his men call him Nakhoda."

Her eyes left the page long enough to beg the answer.

"God of the ship," Jack said.

"God of the ship?" she repeated. Her eyes remained fixed on Jack's.

"Though I don't write historical drama, I do read a bit."

She turned back to the book. "An interesting title, given he was in prison for letting pirates steal his ship when on some mission for Shah Husayn. He led a brutal prison break."

"Ol' Denn led a prison break?" Jack asked incredulously, shaking his head.

"No, the ship god led the break. Mr. Hillis joined the break to save his own neck and has never broken free. Been a pawn in the ship god's quest for revenge."

"Revenge?" John glanced back over his shoulder at Victoria. Instantly, he scooped little Mags off her seat and tossed her into Jack's lap. "Hold on!" he shouted.

John gave the horses a holler and a quick whip. They charged off the road across a small field, down into a ravine and over a hill out of sight from the road.

Victoria and Jack tossed and tumbled with Mags, who was squealing in delight.

"Vic, you and Mags stay here and stay quiet. Jack, come with me." John jumped off the wagon and led Jack back towards the road, clinging to the edge of the hill. Jack sensed the urgency and held his questions. Answers were coming soon enough. A dust cloud grew larger as it approached.

Jack saw seven or eight riders in a hurry. He heard John exhale as they pounded past the place where he led the wagon from the road.

"Recognize any of them?" He turned to Jack.

Jack shook his head no. "You think they're part of yesterday's bunch?"

"Don't know, but yesterday's bunch was pretty eager to find you and that notebook."

"And now they're anxious to find you and your family."

"Looks like it." John stood, heading back to the wagon.

"I'm sorry I got you into this," Jack said.

"Jack, do you even know what 'this' is?" John paused, turned back, and glared into the younger man's eyes. A slight shake of Jack's head was enough. "Let's go ask Vic. By now, she probably knows." A wink released the tension between the two.

Jack knew John was well aware of the danger. After all, he'd just disposed of four dead bodies. The bodies of those who, just the night before, threatened his family's lives. *Why was he so willing to help?* Jack wondered.

The two men cleared the small ridge. John burst into a full run down the hill. Jack's heart stopped. The wagon stood alone, its passengers missing.

John bounded up onto the seat, trying to get the best view possible. In the distance, a tiny head bobbed above the brush, followed by Victoria trying to keep up with her. His heart began to beat again.

"Had to go!" little Mags said as she skipped her way back to the wagon.

John's worry surrendered to relief, which just as quickly surrendered to anger. "What did I say?"

Victoria waved him off, "She had to go." She helped Mags back up to the wagon's bench, then climbed into the back with Jack. John's earlier relief was short-lived. Now certain the events of the night before hadn't gone as planned, John knew there was no time to lose in getting his family safely away from the violent horde.

They got back onto the road, John's eyes searching every direction.

"Jack, did your bit of reading include the fall of the Mughal and Safavid Empires?" Victoria returned to her casual investigatory inquisition approach.

"Was Mr. Hillis part of that too?" Jack asked.

"I'm not sure yet." Victoria's head was lowered over the book.

Her interest in the notebook amazed Jack. He stared, stunned at her tenacity to put the puzzle pieces together. *If I could only read it too. When is she actually quizzing me and when is she cross-examining me? Or is she just being rhetorical?*

Jack answered, "I know both empires rose and fell through fratricide. Inter marrying between families kept the two on somewhat amicable terms. When you imprison or kill the heirs to a throne, it becomes hard to keep an empire healthy." Jack paused his essay on the two once great empires and saw this was not at all what Victoria had been asking. Her look echoed that of a patient, but unmoved, parent waiting for the chatter of a child to end.

"If you're trying to place ol' Denn and Captain Hassan into the fall of two empires, it might help to know a time period. Any dates in that notebook?" Jack asked.

Victoria turned back pages to the first entry. "First date here is 1723."

"Nothing around 1695?" He asked, knowing the answer before even asking.

"Mr. Hillis seems to have started these notes when this god of the ship and seventy men pillaged and looted their way across India. Arriving in the port of Sarat, they captured the ship *Dover*, a twenty-gun frigate of the East India Company. They pirated around the horn and captured an eighty-gun Portuguese warship."

"Definitely a historical drama," Jack muttered. "How does a twenty-gun frigate capture an eighty-gun war ship? I mean no disrespect towards the Portuguese, but even they wouldn't give up that advantage."

John turned to Victoria, who kept reading as if she didn't hear the question. Jack looked up at John for support, who smiled like he was happy to share with Jack the joy and challenge of living with this woman. Mags had fallen asleep on his lap. The warm afternoon sun was welcome, following several weeks of clouds and rain.

Victoria's voice broke the rhythm of the horses, which had almost put Jack to sleep. "Some fifty years ago, pirates plundered the Indian Emperor's treasure ship. Those pirates kidnapped the emperor's granddaughter."

"Yes, I have read that much. We all know that story." Jack tried to remain calm.

"True, but it was your ship god who the shah sent to chase down the pirates."

"Why would the sultan send his naval commander to rescue the Mughal Emperor's granddaughter?" Jack asked.

"She was not only the Indian Emperor's granddaughter, the granddaughter was also the Persian Shah's sister, an heir to the Persian throne. With her there was a relic Mr. Hillis calls the sacred 'Blade of Safavid.'"

Jack sat straight up. His immediate reaction caught her off guard.

"You've read about this?" Victoria asked.

"This is not part of the history books. That blade is one of the relics that control the rights of rule in the Safavid Dynasty…" Jack's words tailed off. His thoughts led his focus somewhere off to the horizon. He was on the right track. It may have nothing to do with Cav, but somewhere along this journey, the paths had to converge. Again he reached for the notebook.

As if she was unconcerned, Victoria adjusted herself, and the book moved just out of his grasp.

John interrupted Jack's thoughts. "Vic, how did this Nakhoda captain capture an eighty-gun warship with a twenty-gun frigate?"

Jack mouthed a thank you to John.

Victoria gave her husband a smirk. "Patience, gentlemen. When the pirates sailed into the Port of Lisbon, your god of ships saw a ship he wanted. The *Dover* felt too tiny." She paused and looked John and then Jack in the eyes. "Do you want the details or just the short version?"

John said, "the short version," at the same time Jack said, "the details."

Victoria nodded. "When they sailed past the *Nossa Senhora da Conceicao*, an immense Portuguese warship, the pirates wasted no time in getting acquainted with its commanding officer, Count da Rio Grande. Over the course of the following week, Mr. Hillis and his ship god—"

"Nakhoda," Jack said. "Or Hassan, as you said his name was."

"Captain Hassan," Victoria consented, "learned the *Nossa Senhora* soon sailed for the Azores and Cape Verde off the coast of Africa. Pretending that to be the *Dover's* destination, and with Mr. Hillis as interpreter, Captain Hassan offered the count a considerable sum if the *Dover* could accompany the *Nossa Senhora* for protection. Mr. Hillis insisted the whole of their treasure be loaded on the *Nossa Senhora* for added safety."

"After two days out to sea, Captain Hassan sabotaged the *Dover* making it look crippled. Following a meeting between Mr. Hillis and the Count while onboard the *Nossa Senhora*, they determined the best course was to bring much of the crew aboard the *Nossa Senhora* and leave a small crew to sail to the nearby port of Funchal to repair the ship. The *Dover* would then sail on to Cape Verde and retrieve Captain Hassan, Mr. Hillis, and his crew after they made the *Dover* more seaworthy."

"The next morning, the Count became ill, as did many of his men. Mr. Hillis and several of *Dover's* crew pretended illness as well. Fearing a contagious outbreak, they confined these men below decks where the Count and several of his men died hours later. Fear spread throughout the ship, and as the *Nossa Senhora* had recently passed the Canary Islands, many of the Count's men fled the ship filling the long boats, leaving death behind."

"No longer outnumbered, Captain Hassan wasted no time slaughtering the few remaining Portuguese sailors. Mr. Hillis pronounced a mock blessing on the Count as they discarded his poisoned body over the port side of the ship. Captain Hassan returned quickly to the *Dover*, which was following at a safe distance. They retrieved the remaining crew and sunk the *Dover*.

"Making port in Casablanca, the crew wasted no time in converting the *Nossa Senhora* into a respectable looking heavily armed pirate ship with a Persian flair. The *Nossa Senhora* became the *Chawbuck*."

"The *Chawbuck*," Jack repeated. His head dropped back.

This drama is becoming historic, Jack thought.

Chapter Twenty

Journal Entry: September 1695 - Arabian Sea
Alexander Hincher - Ship's Surgeon

We now see the wisdom in the modifications made to the *Fancy* last year when we stopped to cut back the superstructure and remove a deck. We are clearly the fastest of these six ships. The *Dolphin* proved too slow. It fell behind. Avery commanded the crew to turn around, although all six ships are now in pursuit of the Indian convoy.

They spotted the convoy of twenty-five Mughal ships passing the straits en route to Surat. The convoy eluded the pirate fleet during the night.

It has now been two days in pursuit; we returned to the *Dolphin*, took its crew onboard the *Fancy* and put the *Dolphin* to flame. As we sail away, the flame and smoke make for an incredible sight.

Captain Tew in the *Amity* was the first ship to catch the convoy and took to battle the 600-ton Mughal ship *Feteh Muhammed*, which was the escort ship to the *Ganj-i-Sawai*. In the battle, they killed Captain Tew. We did not stop to offer my services to the wounded. We have now left both the captain-less *Amity* and the *Susanna* and hope to reunite with the *Pearl* and the *Portsmouth Adventure* and re-engage the convoy.

- Hinch

Sheffield, England - 1748

Tightening the reins, the wagon slowed to a gentle stop in front of an abandoned shop.

"The Checkmate?" Jack jumped off the wagon, glad to stretch his legs. The days and nights on a wagon may have been good for his healing shoulder, but was murder on his stiff legs. Several times he wished he could trade places with the horses. John joined him as he peered into the empty shop. The faded shingle hung as a memorial to a business long abandoned.

"This was where I met Vic. It's sacred ground to me. She was in here visiting her sister when I came in looking for a clock. Alex, the clockmaker, and who is now my brother-in-law, could build, repair, or create anything. The yarns he could tell! This shop became a gathering place."

"Your shoulder?" John pointed to the shop."Alex taught Victoria how to heal with natural poultices. Where he learned it nobody ever knew."

Jack raised and lowered his arm, rotated his shoulder and rubbed it just as he'd done a thousand times these last few days, amazed at how it had healed. Jack's raised eyebrows begged for more.

"Victoria learned to heal from Alex?" Jack asked.

"Alex never told us where he learned it. Fact is, never told us much of anything about his past. No family, no past, just showed up and became a fixture here in Sheffield."

"Where did he go?" Jack asked.

"The Americas, we think. Left a few years ago, never heard from him again. Vic thinks they're lost at sea. Otherwise, she says, she surely would have heard from them."

"You? What do you think?"

"Too much mystery. I think he's hiding somewhere."

"What did they say when they left?" Jack asked.

"Nothing. We came up to visit Vic's folks, and the shop was empty. Nobody knew anything. One morning the shop was empty. We thought the world of Alex. But what he did to Vic and her family by running off? I'll never forgive him." John turned and climbed back up onto the wagon. Jack hopped on the back. Minutes later they stopped again. This time in front of a substantial rock home surrounded by bright yellow and orange blossomed gardens protected by a waist high slate gray stone wall.

Mags lit off the wagon, carried by tiny pink bare feet, and bounded through the white iron gate. With no attempt to knock, the door flew open, and she disappeared inside.

"She's been here before." Jack smiled at John as he helped Victoria from the wagon.

"It's her home, as long as grandmother is here. Come in and meet Vic's family. You're safe here for now." John handed Jack one bag and hefted the other over his shoulder. Victoria was already through the door.

Jack stepped inside dropping the bag. A brick wall of a man covered in plaid flannel stopped him flat. "You're the one," Victoria's father said.

Towering half a foot taller and a hundred pounds heavier than Jack, the man squinted, eyes moving from top to bottom and back up to look deeply into Jack's eyes. "You don't look like a killer."

"Thank you," Jack whispered, trying to keep his breathing steady.

"No matter, you can't stay."

"Father!" Victoria stepped up to her father with an embarrassed rebuke.

"The wrong people are looking for him." Her father's stern pronouncement shocked the room. "You've left a trail of bodies. I trust because you're running with my daughter, she thinks you innocent. Maybe so. When authorities searched my daughter's home in Chester, their home was ransacked, the barn scorched with fire, four of their men were missing and their sheriff was dead. All that and the family gone," He turned from Jack to Victoria. "Naturally they knew you would return home."

Eyelids closed, Jack shook his head. "I am so sorry," he whispered.

"No, I'm sorry." Victoria's father hung his head.

"Don't be. You just spared your family a very uncomfortable death." With pistol raised, the voice stepped from behind a wall. Every inch of his greasy six-foot frame oozed hate. The smile coated each syllable uttered with disgust.

The room fell silent. Eyes bounced from Jack to the intruder and back, fearfully curious.

Victoria's eyes fixed on her ashamed father. "What did you do?"

The intruder ignored her. "You have something my master wants. You stole it when you killed his friend. It belongs to him and he wants it back. Give it to me now and we may spare your friends."

Jack's eyes, locked on the man, searching for answers. The tattoo on his wrist confirmed he was one of a legion of followers of an extremely powerful and evil master.

Jack asked, "You work for Nakhoda?"

The greasy smile grew wider. From the far corner of the room, John broke the silence. "Looks like checkmate, Jack."

As the man turned to see who was talking, Jack bolted from the room, bouncing off Victoria's mountain of a father, knocking him off balance and out of the way, as a pistol crack echoed through the house. With one leap, he was over the stone wall disappearing between houses, barns, and gardens.

Chapter Twenty~One

Journal Entry: September 1695 - Arabian Sea
Alexander Hincher - Ship's Surgeon

We are now in command of the *Fateh Muhammed.* It's unclear to me if the *Fateh Muhammed* was intimidated by the *Fancy's* forty-six guns or was just weakened by the earlier battle with Tew, but the crew put up little resistance.

Avery's pirates sacked the ship. I learned the ship belongs to Abdul Ghaffar, reportedly Surat's wealthiest merchant. Its crew told me, as I attended to their care, that Ghaffar was so powerful and wealthy he drove a trade equal to the English East India Company. They believe he will fit out in a year above twenty sails of ships between 300 and 800 tons.

Avery was eager to get me back on board the *Fancy* and my delay to help the wounded on the *Fateh Muhammed* angered him considerably. The entire crew knows I am a surgeon and not a pirate. They have respect for me and appreciate my attention to their well-being even though I find pirating barbarian. I choose not to let a man suffer or die needlessly, but I do not take part in the booty. I draw a wage as any ship's surgeon would. Avery and I are, however, in agreement that following this season in the Indian Ocean, they will drop me at a friendly port as an innocent from pirate atrocities.

Although the treasure from this capture is considerable, the shares for each crew member won't be enough to justify this year-long journey. Avery is eager to catch the *Ganj-i-Sawai.*

Once back onboard the *Fancy,* I attended to the crew as best as I can. Avery is insisting on all hands available to speed our overtaking this second Mughal ship. Most of the wounds are superficial because the resistance was so minor. In their anxiousness, our sailors are careless and two of the broken bones I have re-set and braced are from accidents where our own sailors tripped over themselves.

- Hinch

Sheffield, England - 1748

It hadn't taken Jack but a few minutes to search the back entrance of the Checkmate and find a bar to pry open the door. He remained away from the front windows he and John were looking in just minutes before.

Careful not to be seen, Jack explored the Checkmate's many closets, cupboards, drawers, and nooks. Most were empty, with only a trace of their original purpose. The Checkmate still maintained a feeling of hope, of vibrancy not actually present for years.

Darkness claimed the day. Jack felt comfortable extending his exploration into the front areas of the shop. When he bumped into a small cabinet, a squeak echoed through the empty hall. He pulled the cabinet away from the wall and a small bow fell free. He ran fingers along the squeaky strands. A violin bow? In the darkness, he swept his arm under the cabinet. It rewarded his hope. He pulled a small violin free from its hiding place.

A child sized violin. Somewhere, a small disappointed child was torn from her home without this precious treasure. Jack's thoughts paused, and he reconsidered his lament. Somewhere a small boy was triumphant in leaving behind this source of great aggravation, freed from tiresome lessons and practice. He smiled to himself. *Will I ever know?*

Hours passed. Jack sat still, pondering his options. He had none at the moment. Last time he ran in the darkness, he was bleeding and ended up endangering an innocent family.

Why did I ever accept the captain's plea to leave the university and chase a ghost? A ghost that will cost me my appointment at the university if I'm not back by fall.

He didn't know the village, the people, or where he might go. He couldn't leave without knowing the rest of the story inside that notebook. Yet he was certain John gave him directions.

A key clicked in the lock. The door squeaked as if it hadn't opened in years.

Which it likely hadn't. Jack froze.

"Jack, did you make it?" John whispered.

"John?" Jack leaned past a long counter, only to see a dim figure standing in the shadows. "Everyone ok?"

"Jack, they got the notebook. Vic's father resisted. They beat him up pretty bad. When they threatened Mags, Vic had no choice."

"I am so sorry." Jack put his head in his hands.

"They're still looking for you. Some pages were torn out, they claim you have them."

Instinctively Jack felt his vest pocket. Two days ago when he'd done the same the pocket was empty. To his relief, it was no longer empty. Looking heavenward he mouthed a 'thank you' comfortable John couldn't see his relief in the darkness. He still didn't know what the map meant, but a dying man who felt it was very important gave it to him.

"Your wife certainly knows everything that was in the notebook." Jack's tone rang with irony and jest. "So all is not lost if your family is safe."

"But you've got to get away. They're watching us too closely for you to have a friendly visit with Vic. They're convinced you killed their men." When John paused, Jack could guess what John was thinking. He was right. "They took one look at me… and… well, I don't look like a killer," John said.

"Your father-in-law said I don't either," Jack said.

"He changed his mind when you knocked him to the ground as you bounded from the house. He's a big man. For a scrawny kid like you to lay him flat hurt his pride."

"I imagine so. I'm scrawny? What about my pride?"

"We got to get you out of here tonight. Vic prepared some food. I've wrangled a horse you can take if you can crawl your way to that mill we passed as we entered the village this morning."

"Thank you. Again, I am so sorry…"

Both men came to a place they'd not planned. A goodbye.

"Where do I go?"

"Where were you going when you came to my farm?"

"To my grave… but you stopped me."

"Is that good or bad?"

"Don't know yet. But first, tell me about this shop. It's the first place I've ever been where emptiness and despair are drowned by hope and love. What happened here?"

"We don't know that yet. Vic's sister and her husband Alex were two of the most talented, loved, and cherished members of the community. They met at a ball where, by accident, Vic's sister and Alex got paired as partners for the Walzer, the scandalous dance where you hold your partner so closely your faces touch."

Jack wished he could read John's face as he shared this story. He wanted to know how that scandal was going over with John. Envy or disgust?

"Alex impressed her with his gentleness and grace despite his coarse facade. Granted, he was not an unhandsome man. Short dark hair and an olive complexion; we assumed somewhere in his northern European ancestry there had been a parlay with a race further south. He never shared his ancestry.

"Alex was at the dance at the request of the governor. He was relatively new to our village, but had made an impression with both merchants and gentry. Arrived in Liverpool on a merchant ship and traveled to Sheffield to set up a small shop catering to the repair of muskets, clocks, and fine musical instruments. The clavichord he sold to the governor was his own design and creation. Over the months, his unique set of skills put him in contact with every sort of the town's residents. His ability to converse with a slave, servant, or soldier, merchant, miller, or maiden, naïve, noble, or nobody, made Alex a friend to everyone. We all loved him.

"Even prettier than Vic, and as a daughter of a plantation owner, Vic's sister caught the attention of every eligible bachelor and a few less eligible sorts for miles around. But like Vic, she believed life should be lived, rewards earned, skills and talents developed. Those two sisters wanted to live, not be cared for. To them, anything less was a wasted life.

"Because of that, what most attracted her to Alex was not just that he was a friend to everyone, but he could do anything. His large hands could repair and adjust a delicate clock. They could create and tune a beautiful musical instrument. They could rebuild a broken pistol. And he could dance."

Even in the darkness, Jack's eyes widened as John described the man who, earlier that day, he swore never to forgive.

"Why didn't you marry him?" Jack couldn't resist.

John wasted a perfect scowl in the darkness.

"You asked what happened. This happened." John's tone changed noticeably. "One day the shop was empty. Everyone gone. Nothing. No word. No goodbye. Nothing."

Jack realized Victoria not only lost her sister, John lost a best friend, a mentor, a hero. And he couldn't come to reconcile it, he couldn't even grieve. John's tone was that of a scorned lover. Jack wondered if in the darkness a tear or two hadn't fallen.

John changed the subject. "Vic wanted me to tell you she thinks Mr. Hillis referred to you in the notebook. Said a young naval officer from the *Kent* was pursuing the Avery treasure, and was sailing with the *Emerald* in the fall. Didn't call you by name but described you. Are you an officer?"

Jack was stunned. How could ol' Denn know he'd been on the *Kent?* And what made him think he was an officer? *Why did he think I'd be sailing to the New World?* Only Captain Remington and Captain Bentley knew of those plans—their plans not his, plans that Jack had no intention of carrying out.

"No, I'm no officer, nor even a sailor. Must refer to someone else." Chills ran up his spine. "Did Victoria share anything else she remembered reading?"

"A young woman who knows about that sacred blade will meet Mr. Hillis' partner in the New World. Said he regretted sending her to that fate, but had to, to get free of an obligation."

"No name?"

"Didn't offer one," John said.

Ol' Denn must have changed his mind. His last words echoed through Jack's memory. "She shouldn't go to the New World." Now he knew 'she' referred to a young woman. *How young? Old enough to know about a sacred blade. The Blade of Safavid?*

Chapter Twenty~Two

Journal Entry: September 1695 - Arabian Sea
Alexander Hincher - Ship's Surgeon

The battle we sought for over a year is now upon us. After three days, the *Ganj-i-Sawai* is in sight, and the *Fancy*, the *Pearl,* and the *Portsmouth* are all now bearing down on the magnificent ship.

The *Susannah* could not keep up, so it looks like the six-ship pirate flotilla is down to three.

- Hinch

Weeks later, London, England - 1748

"Mr. Jack? Mr. Jack?" A timid knock sounded at the large walnut door carved with a depiction of the Owl of Athena who accompanied the goddess of wisdom and warfare from Greek mythology.

"Yes, Charles?" Jack's concentration remained fixed on the copy of the East India Company's reparations report made on the loss of the emperor's treasure ship.

"Your father is impatient to speak with you. He's in the library with gentlemen from the university."

Jack knew this was the news. His petition and presentation would have earned him the coveted position on the faculty and he would be a secure academian for the rest of his life—or else they turned him down. A rejection would make life with his father, his fiancé, and family unbearable.

He slipped the papers inside the desk and accompanied Charles down the stairs.

Broad smiles met Jack as he entered the library. Handshakes of congratulation felt more like a delivery of a verdict than a celebration of his acceptance to the board of regents and appointment to Cambridge University's prestigious faculty.

This appointment would fill the next several months with orientations, planning, and preparation for a glorious new era in Jack's life. The visitors left. Jack stood alone with his father.

"Jack."

"I know!" Jack's tone fell flat.

"You've been back two weeks and you've yet to visit Anne. That concerns your mother."

Concerned? What kind of word was that to express Mother's incredulous impatience?

His shoulder healed completely, the university regents had just granted the wish he and his family dreamed about, and he had a beautiful, wealthy woman waiting for him only a short ride away.

What else would I expect when my father's associates are the House of Lords.

"I'm on my way today. Father, can you help me secure a copy of the Proclamation for the Apprehension of Henry Avery?" He regretted his question the minute it left his lips.

"Is the captain still on that foolish treasure hunt? What are you doing for him now?"

"Father, please. The captain asked for one favor—which I granted. This request is mine, solely mine. Call it academic curiosity."

"Jack, that proclamation is over fifty years old. With a reward of £1000 sterling, if any person on the earth knew where Avery went, the world would know. Forget it. Anne needs you more than that ill-advised captain. Nonsense." Jack's father slowly shook his head.

You mean mother needs me to need Anne. He didn't say it.

Jack knew it was foolish, but he hungered for details. Details only available from two places—the Privy Council of Scotland's Proclamation for the Apprehension which offered the largest reward in history, or the East India Company's records of reparations paid to appease Mughal Emperor Aurangzeb's declaration of war against trade with England. He needed his father's influence to get him access to those records.

Jack ignored his father's dismissal. "Father, what do you know about the emperor's granddaughter's kidnapping?"

"What are you looking for?"

Jack decided it made no sense to parlay with his father. Captain Remington had failed seeking help from Jack's father, what made him think he could succeed?

"Enough of this," his father said. He picked up the official appointment notice and held it in front of Jack. "This is your future. Don't waste it."

A dead end. Jack knew it. Either his father knew something and wanted this puzzle to go away, or, in truth, there was no foundation in the Indian/Persian myth of a missing heir to the two dynasties. Was it possible neither the Persians nor the Indians admitted the blade was stolen? One more place to look and then off to see Anne.

† † †

An elderly gray-haired man plopped the large leather binder on the table. The sound echoed throughout the hall. Jack read the title page of the 1696 report issued by the High Court of Admiralty following the trial of Avery's crew.

Turning to leave the great hall, the man shook his head. "This report sits unexamined on my shelf for years, then in just two days, I bring it out twice."

"Twice?" Jack's sharp question stopped the older man. He turned back to face Jack.

"Yesterday, a lovely lady spent most the day reading and noting passages from that very volume."

"A lady? Young or old?"

"Compared to me, young. Lovely, well mannered, you know her?"

"Not yet. Did she tell you what she wanted?"

"Just to see the report. Excuse me, I'll leave you to it."

Jack watched him pull open the large mahogany door, and asked, "Excuse me, have you worked here long?"

"Well on forty years." The man paused for any other questions.

"You said this report sat for years?"

A nod.

"Do you remember who else you've shared it with?"

"There in the back. They make me keep track." The gray-haired man shuffled back to Jack and opened the report. There, tucked in the back, was a register containing names of the hundreds of treasure hunters, dreamers, students of law, and pirates. There it was. Jack saw the name Dennison Hillis.

Jack quickly scanned the register looking for another name.

Had Captain Remington ever read this report? What about his young sailor Cav?

"Thank you," Jack said. The man left, the door he closed echoed through the large hall.

The day passed quickly. Jack studied each testimony, the verdicts, the arguments, the charges. As a student, Jack read reports and cases until his eyes would fail him. Not this time. If anyone could dig a clue from his research, Jack could.

He made plenty of notes.

They arrested Mistress Lonnie's father, John Dann, Captain Avery's coxswain, on July 30, 1696 at the Bull Hotel. He had sewn £1,045 in gold sequins and ten English guineas into his waistcoat, which was discovered by his chambermaid, who subsequently reported the discovery to the town's mayor, collecting a reward by doing so.

In order to avoid the possibility of execution, Dann agreed to testify against other captured members of Avery's crew. *Selfish traitor.* As piracy was a capital crime, and the death penalty could be handed down only if there were eyewitnesses, the testimony of Dann was crucial. Of the twenty-four men captured, they convicted only six. Jack thought that interesting, how they dropped some charges of piracy and made charges of mutiny instead.

Jack paused and tried to recollect what Captain Remington said about David Creagh. He was second officer of the *Charles II* and one witness against the accused mutineers. Creagh testified that after refusing to take part in the mutiny, the mutineers allowed him and Captain Gibson to leave the ship.

In his testimony, he mentioned a young surgeon also attempted to leave the ship, but they forced him to remain on board. Jack noted that claim and created a timeline on a sheet of parchment. Details started to make sense and get interesting.

THE
TRYALS

OF

Joseph Dawson,
Edward Forseith,
William May,

}

William Bishop,
James Lewis, and
John Sparkes.

For several

Piracies and Robberies

By them committed,

IN THE

Company of *EVERY* the Grand Pirate,
near the Coasts of the *East-Indies*; and
several other Places on the Seas.

Giving an ACCOUNT of their *Villainous
Robberies* and *Barbarities*.

At the Admiralty Sessions, *begun at the* Old-
Baily *on the* 29th *of* October, 1696. *and ended on the* 6th. *of* November.

LONDON,

Printed for *John* Everingham, Bookseller, *at the* Star *in*
Ludgate-street, 1696.

Other testimonies and pleas of innocence varied among the accused pirates. However, it was the testimony of John Sparkes who was the only pirate to publicly express any regret. This was not for piracy, which was of "lesser concern"—instead, he was repentant for the "horrid barbarities he had committed, though only on the bodies of the heathen", implying that he had taken part in the violation of the women aboard the Mughal ships. His "Last Dying Words and Confession" declared that his eyes were "now open to his crimes" and he "justly suffered death for such inhumanity." Sparkes was also the only other man who mentioned a ship's surgeon.

Out of all the testimonies, only two people mention a ship's surgeon. One was a pirate they hung, and the other was an old drunk, kidnapped from a tavern in Newton Ferrers. Probably murdered.

As Jack put pieces of the puzzle together, his respect for the sailor Cav grew. Jack wished he could spend a few minutes with Cav's notebook Captain Remington had so thoroughly studied, but refused Jack to take.

The same subtle pieces of testimony that Cav noted, Jack also found important. According to Sparkes, the surgeon who was only referred to as Hinch, and another young sailor by the name of Rudy, kidnapped two young Indian women. After a great deal of negotiation and a flogging, they were allowed to keep the two women in exchange for their portion of the treasure.

These were expensive women, Jack thought.

When asked about these two Indian women, Sparkes admitted Hinch, Rudy, and the two women along with twenty slaves came up missing several days after the *Fancy* sailed from the island of Bourbon. Nothing more was known. The testimony notes included Sparkes' comment that he never saw Avery so angry and out of control than when he learned of the escape.

Almost as a footnote in Sparkes' testimony was the note that the surgeon kept a journal. *Why was that worthy of mentioning?*

Jack leaned back in the chair as his eyes wandered the room, noting nothing in particular. Questions, potential answers, and too many puzzle pieces danced through his head.

What am I even looking for? Nothing here, nothing in the proclamation, nothing in all these public documents has led the thousands of treasure hunters anywhere.

He leaned forward and turned to the back of the record and again scanned the names of the hundreds of individuals who'd done just what Jack was doing. Searching for a ghost treasure nobody had ever really seen.

Even Dennison Hillis, who searched through these records thirty years earlier, was searching.

But searching for what? The treasure? A crew member? Avery himself? Or something else?

I need another look at Denn's notebook. What did Victoria miss? Why was it so important that his partner Nakhoda...

Remembering ol' Denn's partner who would have been a Persian, Jack scanned the list name by name. Would he even have used his real name? There were names from every nation. A moment later, he found it. Right next to Dennison Hillis' was scrawled Ali Mutarid Hassan. The two were here together in 1725? Why? Jack kept scanning. The two were here together again fourteen years ago. *Whatever else they were after, they hadn't found it yet.* Jack concluded.

One more question. Jack returned to the testimony of Creagh. *Why did Cav need to meet with Creagh? Why did Captain Remington indulge him? What happened in Newton Ferrers?*

First, Anne.

Jack closed the report and scooted the heavy chair back. Its scraping feet echoed through the hall. Before closing the cover, he took one more look at the names in the back of the report.

"Elizabeth Farrow." He whispered the name.

Who is she and what does she want?

Jack set the report on the gray-haired man's table, thanked him, and turned to leave. On a bench laid the London Evening Post. On the far-left column, the decorative T started the first line:

"THE MURDERER OF FIVE CITIZENS OF LIVERPOOL REMAINS UNIDENTIFIED AND ON THE RUN."

His heart and breath stopped while his mind raced and eyes continued down the column.

> "Murdered in brutal attacks are Lonnie Dunn, proprietress of the Nookery, a local establishment, Emerson

Canton, dock worker and Nookery
patron, Greggson Tandy, sailor, Dennison
Hillis, long-time resident and theologian,
and Andrew Bills, sheriff of Chester…"

Chapter Twenty~Three

In the next few entries I will only briefly outline the disgusting victory of the capturing of what I now call the *Gunsway,* the name we English used to describe the Indian treasure ship *Ganj-i-Sawai.* The battle was decisive, brutal, and deadly. The victors were barbarians and the victims cowardly.

Muhammad Ibrahim captained the *Gunsway.* He should have been a fearsome opponent, mounting eighty guns and a musket-armed guard of four hundred, with six hundred other passengers. The *Fancy* with just over two hundred men took the *Gunsway* on alone. The crew of the *Pearl* seemed to be fearful to engage. They only took heart once Avery's crew were on the *Gunsway's* deck. The crew from the *Portsmouth* never engaged. I don't know why.

But the opening volley evened the odds. Avery's lucky broadside shot destroyed the *Gunsway's* mainmast. With the *Gunsway* now unable to escape, the *Fancy* drew alongside. A volley of Indian musket fire prevented the pirates from immediately clambering aboard, but then one of the powerful cannons onboard the *Gunsway* exploded. This blast instantly killed dozens of men and demoralized the Indian crew. On board any wooden ship, fires are death. Many of the crew ran below deck and fought to put out the spreading fires. That's when Avery's men took advantage of the confusion, quickly scaling the *Gunsway's* steep sides. The fight became a ferocious hand-to-hand battle that lasted two to three hours.

Some of our men told me they thought Captain Ibrahim ran below decks where he armed the slave girls and sent them up to fight the pirates. Since they outnumbered the pirates and out-gunned our ship,

I place the blame on the captain of the Indian ship rather than give credit to Captain Avery. Regardless, after several hours of stubborn but leaderless resistance, the ship surrendered. It was not an easy battle. It resulted in the death of hundreds of men from both sides. Lives lost for the sake of greed and lust. Many of the lives lost were in the defense of loved ones and duty. I mourn those losses and cast great blame at the feet of our Captain Avery. Many of the *Fancy's* pirates suffered violent deaths for the promise of riches.

I am mystified by the way a man's purpose and motivation can change so diametrically.

In the preceding year, they transformed from men seeking adventure and money to provide for their families waiting at home, into men seeking riches and bawdy satisfaction. Some of these men were noble at one point, some became my friends, some even promised to leave the ship with me to seek an honorable life. Now they are caught up in the basest of lust and greed.

Despite my most adamant protests, brutality, the violation of women, even torture became the fare for the next few days. There was no stopping them.

I was told some Indian women committed suicide to avoid violation. Only one member of the *Fancy's* crew displayed an ounce of dignity. A young sailor named Rudolph, Rudy to all of us, of whom I became quite fond. Orphaned at eight-years-old, Rudy learned about life the hard way. Talented in anything he gets passionate about, Rudy took to medicine and served my needs to have an assistant as often as the captain permitted.

Most of the day and night during this feast of the flesh, I spent my time repairing flesh, bone, and hearts, trying to help undo the damage, much of which is still taking place. I felt I was trying to dry the deck of a ship during a hurricane.

Nearing complete exhaustion serving the passengers and crew of the *Gunsway* for nearly three days and nights, they drug me off and returned me to my cabin on the *Fancy,* where I collapsed unconscious.

- Hinch

London, England - 1748

"Theologian?" Elizabeth set her cup down and took the paper in both hands, reading it aloud.

> "The murderer stabbed each victim to death with the expertise of a trained assassin. Local constables are uncertain of the motive and have been unable to link the victims in a way to identify a pattern. Officials believe Sheriff Bills stumbled upon the murderer as the assassin was planning to murder a family from Chester. The sheriff's body was found at the farm of the Chester family and evidence of blood indicates several other bodies suffered from the murderer's blade. The family has not been seen again."

Elizabeth reached for her cup and scanned the rest of the newspaper. *There's no description. Am I the only one who saw his face? Who else knows he stands around six feet tall with dark shoulder length hair? Did anyone else watch him rip papers from a dying man's hand and run? Or watch him freely come and go on the Emerald? Who knew he had spent days meeting with his victims?*

For two weeks, Elizabeth searched for Captain Bentley in and around London. By this point, she'd given up on finding him. She visited each of the places he was rumored to frequent, only to be a day or two behind. Concluding the captain had returned to Liverpool, she was determined to learn more about Mr. Dennison Hillis and his special associate she'd be meeting in the New World. She turned her interest from the paper to the old book, a book she'd studied for years. This time, however, it was ol' Denn's copy of the book, complete with his handwritten notes, which added a dimension only available from an eyewitness. She found small comments and underlined passages throughout, but the bulk of ol' Denn's attention was on the famed pirate Henry Avery and the *Fancy*.

The notes seemed to focus on the events following Avery's attack on the emperor's treasure ship. The book's author evidently gleaned most of his information from the same reports she'd read yesterday at the old Bailey. Some sources from India confirmed the author's facts, and yet others conflicted. There was, however, for Elizabeth, only one fact she wanted. What did ol' Denn know to help identify her family's murderers and sister's kidnappers?

Of the roughly three dozen famous pirates she'd studied in Captain Johnson's book, most had long since vanished, died, or been hung by the time those evil men destroyed her family. But with Captain Henry Avery, too many unanswered questions rose their tentacles during her search. Here again, a tentacle was reaching off the page and struggling to get a hold.

The word *estrella*—written and underlined, was in the margin alongside the paragraph describing the brutal attack of the emperor's treasure ship.

She continued reading from the book,

> "It is certain the Pyrates, which these people affirm were all English, did do very barbarously by the people of the Ganj-i-Sawai and Abdul Gofor's ship, to make them confess where their money was, and there happened to be a great Umbraws wife (as we hear) related to the king, returning from her pilgrimage to Mecca, in her old age. She they abused very much, and forced several other women, which caused one person of quality, his wife and nurse, to kill themselves to prevent the husbands seeing them (and their being) ravished."

> "These Pyrates had found "something more pleasing than jewels aboard," reported to be Mughal Emperor Aurangzeb's relative."

In her studies, Elizabeth had read this passage several times and gave it no attention until now. What did ol' Denn know? Or who? He said the Shah's general was hunting the princess and the blade. Why not the Indians?

She emptied her cup, folded her arms and stared at nothing.

That was over fifty years ago! They're all dead now. Forget them. How did ol' Denn get my father's silk? Did he kill my father? Did he know where my sister is?

The vision of the man taking something from the hand of ol' Denn and leaving him lifeless in the rain, pulled anger from its resting place. As it coursed through her veins, it turned to hate.

I want that murderer.

Elizabeth slammed the book closed. There next to it, the article in the paper reminded her it wasn't just Denn's life he took. An innocent sheriff and a family also fell victim to his savagery.

Her only hope was the captain. Yet, she'd exhausted every lead. Certain he'd have returned to Liverpool, she needed to make arrangements to return herself. Packing was easy, one dress, one fine masculine outfit, and an old book. She ran her fingers over its worn cover and regretted not having exposed the murderer when she had the chance.

"Estrella." The tentacle that placed that word into her mind set it firmly. *A word? A name?*

She left her things on the table, closing the door behind her. One more trip to the Old Bailey before leaving London. She needed another look at Sparkes' testimony.

The short walk brought her there quickly, and she entered.

"Hello, Mr. Underwood," she said.

"Here again?"

"May I review the report of the Avery trials once more?"

"Three times in three days," Mr. Underwood mumbled as he reached for the report. He hadn't returned it to its vault from the afternoon before.

"Three times?" Elizabeth repeated.

"A young man spent most of the day yesterday scouring through it."

Elizabeth immediately flipped it open to the back.

"Mr. Jack Remington," She uttered the name. Caution blended with hope, her heart pounding.

She closed the book. "Thank you, Mr. Underwood. I will be back later today, maybe tomorrow. Right now I must make an acquaintance." She slid the book back toward the gray-haired man and scurried from the Old Bailey. Once on the street, she looked both ways. Turning around, she stepped back into the Old Bailey.

"Mr. Underwood, might you direct me to a family with the name of Remington?" she asked.

"Lord Remington, of the House of Lords?" he asked.

Chapter Twenty~Four

It was nearly eighteen hours before I awoke. I learned they left the survivors aboard their emptied ship, which the pirates set free to continue on their voyage back to India. Evidently, the treasure satisfied the crew's greed for they pursued no other of the Indian fleet.

I returned to the deck disgusted and sick to my stomach at the sight of these barbarians. I saw we were at full sail, heading south as fast as we could. The crew now busied themselves counting and glorying in their treasure.

While the *Fateh Muhammed's* treasure of some £50,000 to £60,000 was enough to buy the *Fancy* fifty times over, it was the treasure of the *Gunsway* that entertained everyone's attention.

I noticed we were sailing alone and so assumed that while I was unconscious; they divided the treasure between the *Pearl* and the *Fancy*. I still don't know the truth of it, but the *Portsmouth* did not join in the battle, so Captain Faro's crew received none of the treasure. Captain Mayes and the crew of the *Pearl* parted company, having received a sum of coins purported to be the fair share. I am certain Avery used his profound negotiating skills to take advantage.

When all was calculated, the prize totaled somewhere around £600,000. Avery and his crew are easily the richest pirates in history.

Any words of rebuke or disdain would fall upon deaf ears, so I elected not to share my feelings. I sailed with the crew for two years; they know my feelings, my lack of approval, my utter disdain for piracy, but as a surgeon they know my dedication to their well-being. That dedication is now gone. I swore I would get off this ship at the next port.

And then it got complicated.

"Hinch!" Avery hollered as I approached the men standing around stacks of gold coins, jewels and silks. "Can we interest you in a mate's share? You've earned it."

"No, thank you. You know my feelings. I want none of your blood won treasure." Even as I finished my powerless refusal, the men sneered and laughed. One crew member even began collecting on a wager that once 'ol Hinch' saw how much his take would be, 'Hinch will change 'is mind."

"Then do I get the prize you have stashed in your cabin?" another asked, bursting into laughter. The laughter heightened as the men realized I was unaware of a prize stashed in my cabin. I didn't need to say "What prize?" my expression was enough to confirm my innocence.

"You can thank Rudy!" he hollered as I quickly hurried back to my cabin.

- Hinch.

London, England - 1748

"Jack, what do you know about this?" Jack's father held up the newspaper. He was sitting in a large leather chair just inside the library door, which, when open, gave full visibility of the home's entry.

Jack closed his eyes, bowed his head slightly while taking a deep breath, and turned to face his father.

"Father?" His tone intended to feign innocence.

"Five dead, murdered! A family missing, presumed murdered and the perpetrator loose. All while you were there."

"Excuse me? Where?" Jack worried his nerves would betray his guilt.

"Here," Jack's father turned the paper toward Jack to see for himself. "A stranger in Liverpool, knifes five people to death and disappears. All while you were there indulging the captain."

Indulging? Jack knew he'd never justify the time he spent with his father's estranged brother. Yet he needed to distance himself from the calamity of those several nights. The article said the family from Chester was missing. He hoped the writer just didn't know they were safe in Sheffield. *Were they safe?* He was grateful the writer didn't know the body count was really nine. Though he only killed five of them. "Does the story give dates?" Jack asked.

His father turned the paper back over and pulled the exact date. "16th of June."

"Captain Remington and the *Kent* sailed on the 16th. With his sailing, I had no reason to remain. I visited Sheffield as a favor to the captain and made my way casually home. I left just in time." Jack had collected his thoughts and was more at ease as he crafted a truthful denial of the charges he feared would eventually come his way.

His father turned back to the article.

"May I? When you are finished." Jack sat on a chair opposite his father. His interest in the article was real. Though he'd read it, he wanted to secure the details in his mind. He also knew his father would appreciate sharing an interest in such a rare and fantastic story.

A sharp knock on the door broke the silence. Both men turned to watch Charles open the door and invite a tall elegant well dressed woman into the house.

"Anne?" Jack said.

Chapter Twenty~Five

I appear to be a slave owner. I am not sure if curses are in order or blessings for my young friend Rudy.

I burst into my cabin and glanced around, thinking I might find a chest or bundle of pirate booty. But finding nothing out of the ordinary, I curiously stepped over to the small dressing room off the port side of my cabin and cautiously opened the door, afraid of what I might find.

Secured, both hands and feet, sat two Indian slaves, frightened and pale and both very female, looking at me with as much apprehension as a young woman could ever have. The surprise on my face must have been so genuine, and the look in my eye so lacking the look of lust found in the eyes of the other pirates, I visibly saw their tense and fearful muscles relax. I stood there for a while as my mind struggled to understand the complexity of the whole situation.

Where was Rudy? I was about to dash back out to seek my young benefactor, but I couldn't take my eyes off the beautiful eyes that stared back at me. I stepped forward and loosed the knots that held these young slaves bound. "Please remain right here," I told them as calmly as I could, "I will be back."

The crew broke into raucous laughter as I made my way back to where they were still dividing more of the spoils. "Where's Rudy?" was all I could muster in response to their various questions and jeers.

Avery stood and motioned me to follow. Locked in chains, my young friend Rudy tried to stand as we approached what the crew has turned into a brig.

Occasionally, when the behavior of a crew member or members is out of line, too far out of line, they used the brig to help a pirate sober up or to solidify a lesson he needed to learn. Punishments for crimes more serious than what time in the brig would satisfy, usually comprised flogging, being left behind or even hanging. In the two years we had been on board the Fancy, it was surprising how seldom we need the latter three.

Rudy in chains and having been flogged could only mean one thing. Rudy smuggled those slaves onboard and tried to hide them from the rest of the crew. Something impossible to hide when you are about to spend months together with a hundred lustful men. Women on board are forbidden.

As Avery turned to leave me with Rudy, he simply said, "You two have some catching up to do."

My first instincts were to become the pirate two years on board this pirate ship had failed to achieve and slit his throat for being so greedy, no foolish, no—I can't even think of a word to describe how stupid I thought Rudy's action was to try to smuggle two slaves on board and hide them in my cabin. I could do nothing but stand there and shake my head in disbelief.

Rudy's eyes didn't have the look of embarrassment or shame. He almost looked proud. A look that made me even more angry. Yet, I had loved this one young pirate, the only one that had showed any level of humanity, and I was not even a pirate. I knelt down and turned him around to look at his torn back. Without returning to my cabin for medicine, I cleaned the wounds the best I could with some water and the sleeve of my shirt.

"Why?" I asked as Rudy winced in pain while I cleaned out his wounds.

"Didn't you see them?" he asked. "Didn't you look into their eyes, see their faces, touch their hands?" Rudy asked these questions like a proud artist would point out his craftsmanship, not like a pirate lustfully bragging on a female conquest.

When Rudy spoke, I reflected back. Their eyes were beautiful, their features were perfect, their hands un-calloused. These women in my cabin were not slaves.

"Hold tight, I'll be back, this needs more than a cleaning," I told him, then chuckled to myself, as if he were going anywhere.

I ignored the jeers as I passed the crew and returned to my cabin to retrieve my medical bag. But I could not resist opening my dressing room door and taking a fresh look at my new cabin mates. Yes, these two were definitely not slaves. I motioned with my hand to stay put and closed the door carefully and returned to Rudy. After Rudy shared the entire story, I returned topside with bag in hand, and approached Avery, shaking my head in disbelief at what the young foolish Rudy had done.

"He broke the rules," Avery said, thinking I was ready to chastise him for the flogging and incarceration. "The only reason we were so easy on him was he offered to give up his share if he could use it to buy those slaves as a gift for you."

"Hope they're worth it!" Avery added as the men broke back into laughter.

Laughter stopped when I said, "Minutes ago you offered me a share of the treasure. With that share, which I now accept, I wish to buy Rudy. I apparently own two slaves, I want to own three." This time, I laughed along with the crew. "And, I need fresh clothes for the three of them." With that, I marched off triumphantly to my cabin where I dropped my bag and whispered to the heavens, "What do I do now?"

- Hinch

London, England - 1748

For the third time in as many weeks, Elizabeth watched as an ever-growing-familiar stranger stood between her and her mission. This time accompanied by an exquisite young lady. When the door opened and he escorted the lady to her coach, Elizabeth recognized his face immediately. With the grace of a murderer, so she thought, he slipped in beside her. With a single snap of a whip, the coach was off. Again, Elizabeth stood alone as her foe disappeared before her.

Does this lady know by morning she may be dead at the hands of Lord Remington's son?

Not again. Not this time. Dressed in her male counterpart riding clothes, Elizabeth adjusted the hat and mounted the tall white mare Port provided, pausing to think of old Port. Is his ear healing? I may have aimed too close to his cheek. At a comfortable distance, she followed the carriage along Downing Street toward Whitehall.

The coach stopped at Summerset House. Since being refurbished by Sir

Christopher Wren some sixty-five years earlier, Summerset House had fallen victim to a decline, as evidenced by its faded paint and poorly appointed gardens. After Queen Catherine left England in 1692, it became a grace and favor residence, owned by a monarch and leased at the discretion of the head of state.

Would I expect anything less? The son of a lord with a lady in favor with royalty. How poorly this will be for these parties, should I not get satisfaction.

Elizabeth, her horse, and the coach were the only things standing between the Summerset House and the slow-flowing River Thames. She rode past and secured the horse out of view. It was time to wait. This time he would not escape.

From her hiding spot she witnessed the driver and valet walk casually away from the waiting coach. They must believe this to be a long night, she thought. As soon as they were out of sight, Elizabeth quickly stole away into the coach. A quick search of the coach's interior gave no evidence that it was anything more than a coach. A lovely silk wrap sat on the seat, obviously overlooked as the lady disembarked.

What had she expected? Knives? A Pistol? Ropes? She shook her head in an effort to awaken her sensibilities. At that very instant, she heard footsteps approaching. The valet and coachman? From which door should she attempt to flee? The footsteps stopped, and the door flung open. A man bounded into the coach. Elizabeth froze, face to face with the killer.

As quickly as a rabbit can change course while being pursued by a hound, Elizabeth had a cocked pistol aimed at Jack's head.

"Please be seated," she said as calmly as her racing heart would allow. Her shock was equal to or greater than his.

Jack froze, half kneeling and half standing.

It was evident he hadn't returned to the coach to return home; he was simply retrieving the wrap for his lady. In the many weeks she'd practiced her male voice impressions, now face to face with the very killer she'd sought, she feared the practice failed her. *Does he believe I'm serious?* Her mind raced to re-focus on this, the conversation she knew she would eventually have. Had the uncertainty in her voice betrayed her advantage?

Jack remained motionless. "Please, sir, I beg of you," he said. "I've nothing of value. If you wish to keep the wrap you so favorably hold, it is my gift to you. You will not find any better." His voice was calm, un-stuttering, fearless.

He impressed Elizabeth. Even in the dim light, he was aware she was holding the wrap. Could he tell she was holding it like a woman? And the pistol like a man?

She dropped the wrap, collected her nerve and said with more confidence in the strong tenor voice she'd practiced, "I repeat, please be seated. I will not disappoint your lady friend by taking her wrap, as lovely as it is. What I wish is what you took from Mr. Dennison Hillis the night you plunged a knife into his heart. If you will provide me what you so viciously stole from him, I may let you live." Elizabeth's confidence grew as her voice maintained a low tenor tone.

Jack's eyes darted from the barrel of the pistol to his assailant, whose face was cast in shadow, and back to the pistol. "Who are you?"

"That matters not. As a witness to your murders in Liverpool, you must know I am not one to be trifled with."

"If in deed you are an eyewitness, you know I did not kill Mr. Hillis. Besides, you are too late. Mr. Hillis, his adversaries, and his accomplices have killed for the very thing you seek. They have retrieved them all. Mostly, I am nothing more than a victim, as was Mr. Hillis."

Jack's calm reply caught Elizabeth somewhat off guard. Here a man sat, pistol aimed at his face by a stranger and he pled innocence.

Of course he insists innocence. A killer like this won't confess.

"I watched you steal from the hands of a dying friend of mine and flee, twice leaving behind the dead bodies of innocent people. I am expected to believe you're innocent?"

Jack just glared. Elizabeth wondered what might be going through the mind of the killer. She knew if she let up even for one second, she could be his next victim.

"There is enough evidence that even the son of a lord will not escape the scrutiny and conviction of the several murders of weeks past. Please, sir, I implore you," she said.

As if the hound expected the quick dart of the rabbit under pursuit, Jack's hand was up on the pistol. As his fingers grasped the barrel, Elizabeth pulled

the trigger. There was a flash of gunpowder, a violent explosion, and Jack fell
motionless to the floor of the coach.

Chapter Twenty-Six

Journal Entry: November 18, 1695 - The French Island of Bourbon
Alexander Hincher - Ship's Surgeon

The *Fancy* will sail for the Bahamas tomorrow. Half way around the world. At least that is what we believe.

They've repaired the battle-damaged ship and as many provisions as a ship can carry are loaded on board. Besides the individual treasure, I calculate some 50 tons of ivory tusks, 100 barrels of gunpowder, chests of firearms and ammunition, which are still in the hold.

The shares each pirate received totaled about £1,000 per man, plus an additional share of gemstones. This is more money than a sailor will make in a lifetime. More than a sailor could dream about in a lifetime. But here on a small island, what do you do with that wealth? The sailors are not happy. There has been quite an argument about where to go next. There is no question now that Avery and his crew are marked men, and if I am with them, I too am in trouble.

The Danes and French crew members elected to remain here on the island of Bourbon. A mostly French island, Bourbon serves the slave trade, so ships coming and going are not uncommon. On the *Fancy*, the trans-world crew of only 130 is accompanied by 110 slaves. Tomorrow we will find out if Rudy, myself and our two young slave girls will also make that journey.

Avery recognizes that the wealth of foreign-minted gold and silver coins will be hard to spend without raising suspicion of its origin. Piracy in foreign waters has its challenges, a fact never discussed until the men are sitting here with nothing to spend their treasure on and realizing how hard it will be to spend back in civilization.

Avery purchased over 100 slaves. They will perform the worst of the labor on board the *Fancy* as they traverse the Atlantic, and slaves are the only universal currency that will not raise suspicion when the *Fancy* makes anchor in various ports.

They prefer the appearance of being merely unlicensed slavers to the appearance of being the richest pirates in the world who soon will draw the attention of every government. There is no way a treasure of this size taken from one of the world's greatest, wealthiest, and most powerful emperors will go un-redressed.

- Hinch

St. Bartholomew's Hospital, London, England - 1748

"This young man escaped death a second time. Notice this other scar, it's fresh. not more than a few months old."

"Who treated him?"

"It wasn't here. I don't recognize that work."

Jack heard the words, but as he struggled to recognize the voices, his mind drifted away. Hours passed. Again, consciousness struggled to return. This time, one voice was familiar.

"Lord Remington, he lost a considerable amount of blood. It required great skill to remove the ball which tore through a rib and lodged near his lung. He's lucky to be alive," the first voice said.

"He is also lucky Dr. Edmonds was available. We would never have attempted to dig out that ball," added a second voice.

"How soon can he assume his post at the university." This voice Jack recognized.

When can I assume my post? How about, "What happened? Will he recover? How is my son? Is he in much pain? We are concerned." Jack knew better. His father was all business. Good business, but business. *Maybe they covered all those questions while I was unconscious. Probably not.*

"Sir, this fresh wound, combined with his previous one, makes it difficult to say. We do, however, expect a rapid recovery. His body certainly knows how to heal."

"What previous wound?" his father demanded.

The doctor slid the sheet aside, revealing a large scar on his left shoulder.

Jack's mind fought with all its might to fend off the approaching cloud.

"This scar is recent. We did not treat it here. It was treated by an extraordinarily skilled practitioner. Together, we plan to investigate the methods used. It, along with these several other scars, tells us your academic son has spent some vigorous time outside the classroom." The doctor pulled the sheet back up.

"We all have some investigation..."

The cloud consumed the rest of the conversation. Jack's mind went dark.

† † †

Jack blinked his eyes open. He was alone. Once his eyes confirmed he was in a hospital, slow movement of his head gave him bearings enough to know he was in the care of the best London could offer. The room was spacious, with long white drapes covering the large floor-to-ceiling windows. He guessed it may be late morning or early afternoon. The brightness of the light pouring in changed intensity. Clouds were dancing with the sun.

He took a deep breath, as if to enjoy the fresh air. Piercing pain was enough to confirm what he thought he heard from the doctor about the ball lodging near his lungs.

Though he was alone in this large room, a rolling privacy partition blocked his view of its entryway.

Footsteps broke the numbing silence Jack hadn't noticed until it was gone. The partition rolled aside, and a nurse somewhere in her mid-twenties, he guessed, dressed in an all-white gown and hat took him by the hand.

"How are we this morning, Mr. Jack?" The kind voice was perfect to keep a dying patient calm and a healing patient hopeful.

Do they train nurses to speak like that?

As Jack turned his head to better focus on the nurse, his eyes caught hold of two women speaking to each other in the doorway. There stood a petite nurse, not over five feet tall dressed all in white, her pale skin nearly blending with the hospital gown. If it weren't for her dark eyes and red lips, she would have almost been a ghost. However, it was the other woman, tall, stately, with long hair flowing over a shoulder who caught his interest. She wore a pale green blouse accented with a woven vest tied up the front with a braided silken cord.

"Am I dreaming?"

"No, Mr. Jack, you seem to finally be awake."

Jack realized he'd voiced his thought. "Tell me please, who is that woman conversing with the other nurse?" Jack's urgent plea startled the nurse.

The nurse took a quick look over her shoulder. "You don't know her?"

"Me?" Jack turned back to the nurse.

"Why yes, you. She's visited you every day. You were robbed and shot in your fiancé's coach. Is she not your fiancé?"

Jack shook his head, hoping to clear it before taking a second look. He turned to look again; the woman was gone.

The second nurse moved alongside the bed.

"Mr. Remington didn't recognize his fiancé just now," the taller nurse said.

"Poor thing. The doctors warned the delirium might last awhile, with the amount of blood he lost."

"She's visited me every day?" Jack asked.

The nurse nodded as she ground and poured a powder into a small glass of liquid. She handed it to Jack. "This will help the pain, dear."

Within minutes, Jack was sleeping, deeply. Again.

† † †

Several days had passed, and Jack was grateful to be slowly healing. He enjoyed the company of the nurses, who were cheerful and always had a smile for him.

"Going to miss me?" a nurse flirted.

Jack took her hand, kissed it gently, and winked. "How can I? I don't even know your name?"

"You don't love your fiancé do you?" the nurse asked.

"Pardon?"

"A strange woman, lovely though she may be, diligently watches over you while you were in the most danger. You hunger to meet her."

Jack squinted his eyes to feign innocence.

"Jack, we're women too, not just nurses. You're as transparent as these dressing gowns."

Jack pulled the white sheet up to his chest.

"Then, your fiancé stops in and you can't be rid of her soon enough."

"Be gone with you. And no, I won't miss you at all." Jack said.

"It's Abbie. Good people call me Abbie." As Abbie walked away, she muttered, "Why do men always want the one they don't have?"

"That's not true!" Jack hollered.

If she only knew the gravity of the reason I must find that woman and keep her from traveling.

For the past week, Elizabeth watched as doctors, detectives, and family came and went. Posing as an interested girlfriend, the nurses gave her surprising access. As Jack was now awake and alert, she kept her distance. When Jack claimed he had not killed ol' Denn, his sincerity caught her off guard. The scene played through her mind over and over. He was right, she never actually saw him stab the old man. What she saw was him pulling the knife out of his chest and receiving a packet of papers.

Why did he have to grab for the pistol? Why was he so quick? Why did I pull the trigger? What was it he recovered from the Nookery and why did everyone want it?

After the first few days, the doctors and nurses relaxed as they realized he would not only survive but would likely survive well. She heard one doctor comment how remarkable his body was, so strong despite the loss of so much blood, and how fortunate it was a young man stopped the bleeding before rushing the coach to the hospital. They were still looking for that young man who might lead them to the shooter. In the excitement at the hospital, the young man who dropped him off disappeared,

Elizabeth found it interesting his alleged fiancé only came by once. During her single visit, both Elizabeth and the taller nurse sensed the lack of passion and tenderness. "How could she miss another woman attending to her fiancé?" the taller nurse asked. The two women both shrugged it off.

† † †

Alone in the quiet of the hospital room, Jack laid semi-propped up by two large feather pillows. He tenderly rubbed his new dressing and wondered how Vic, John, and little Mags were. With the first bullet wound completely healed as far as he was concerned, he marveled at how a country girl could weave such medical magic. He ran his hand along the scar. He knew a shattered rib would not heal painlessly. He'd suffered enough of those in the early years when his father permitted him to spend time with his uncle between school years. He would come back to London broken, bruised, and beat up.

Captain Remington loved Jack but hated to see him grow up weak, therefore he showed no remorse for the apparent mistreatment of his nephew. Nonetheless, Jack's father finally forbad his seasonal visits.

Young and headstrong and thinking himself invincible, he spent long days and nights learning from the talents of his uncle's best sailors. As he grew, other interests caught his attention, not the least of which were young ladies and the social recognition of his scholarly pursuits. He found the life of an academian was much more agreeable. He was learning the draw of power, prestige, and respect. With his father's position, there were no doors closed to him. Besides, he hated the sea. The romance of adventures at sea paled when compared to the discomfort, danger, and disregard for the pleasantries of his life at home.

Footsteps interrupted his pondering. "Mr. Jack, a package was delivered only moments ago."

Jack looked up, grateful it was the taller of his two caregivers. Though the care from the shorter nurse was gentle and thorough, Jack felt her paleness of complexion matched her personality.

The nurse plopped the package on Jack's lap.

"Did you see who delivered it?" he asked.

"Sorry, it wasn't your secret little friend."

"Has she been here?"

"Not since the detectives began showing interest."

The nurse dabbled with his dressing. Jack smiled at her attention. "Detectives?"

"Of course. The son of a lord returns from holiday where five people are viciously murdered, and then gets shot during a robbery?"

"A robbery?" Jack repeated.

The second nurse, her short arms full of clean dressings, dropped them on the foot of the bed.

"Oh, he's awake. I'll let them know." She turned and hurried out.

"Them?" Jack asked.

"The detectives and your father. They're anxious to know what happened. They've had someone lurking around for days. Your father says for protection. You must know something or someone, they say." The nurse conversed with Jack as if she were an innocent observer. Jack knew enough about innocent women to realize she was as curious as a woman could be. His smile at her curiosity helped mask his sweating palms and racing heart. *Would they try to connect his two injuries? Yes! Would they succeed?*

As the partition slid aside, in marched Jack's father accompanied by two men Jack didn't immediately recognize. The doctor was only one step behind, being trailed by Abbie, who didn't want to miss a single word.

The doctor attempted to intercept the men but was a few steps too slow.

"Jack, this is Inspector Clark," Jack's father began. "Your recent time in the Lake District, accompanied by an attack here in London, has garnered the attention of authorities. We're hoping to sort this all out."

Sort this all out? Jack's eyes darted from one man to the next, as if asking permission to speak.

I try to help my uncle, stop a kidnapping, they killed the victim, I kill a few bad people, get shot twice and lie here on what should have been my deathbed, and I need to sort this out?

Jack turned to his father. "How is Anne? I'm told she came to see me but my poor response frightened her away."

Way to change the focus, Jack. He wanted to wink at Abbie.

The inspector was the first to speak. His abruptness illustrated he had no interest in small talk. "Mr. Remington, we're trying to see if there is a link between the killings near the Mersey and the apparent attack you recently suffered. We understand you were in Liverpool when the killings took place."

Jack knew the days and hours better than anyone. How could these men place him at the scene of the killings? They couldn't, he knew that, unless someone saw and identified him. He had made no acquaintances with whom he shared his name. Only Captain Remington, his crew, or the men on the Emerald could identify him, and both captains were gone from Liverpool when the mess started. But then again, one young man had followed him to London and claimed to be a witness. A young man deadly serious about getting his hands on what ol' Denn gave Jack.

"Yes, I was. I was visiting my uncle; we both left the day before the unfortunate events we've read about in the paper." Jack motioned to the newspaper folded in his father's hand. "I struggle to see a connection, but may I assure you I hope there is not one. For all of our sakes."

"Please tell us what happened that night," the inspector asked, notebook in hand.

During one of his lucid moments after just arriving, Jack told authorities he surprised a thief when his fiancé asked him to return to the coach to retrieve her wrap. Startled, the thief shot him and the next thing he remembered was waking up in this hospital room. Jack repeated this same story for the inspector, with one embellishment—he concluded that when he awoke, he was under the care of this gracious doctor and his charming assistants. This time, a wink escaped his brow. Abbie's smile confirmed it arrived safely.

Jack felt convinced it involved his assailant promoting the connection between his two gunshot wounds. He hoped the scar so beautifully treated by Vic stayed out of this discussion.

"You said you never saw the shooter. Were any words exchanged? Was any motive alluded to? Any idea who brought you here?" The inspector rattled off questions, searching for any kind of lead to follow.

Jack watched his intensity, grateful he didn't pause between questions and expecting answers to each one. Instead, he shook off the need for direct answers with a slight shake of his head. Then he tried to become part of the investigation with his own questions.

"Doctor, do any of those attending to me when the coach arrived here know anything about my mysterious Good Samaritan? Did my coachman and valet have any response?" Jack knew these questions had been asked and unsatisfactorily answered time and time again.

Once again, there was no answer, and Jack leaned back against the pillows, his disappointment not feigned whatsoever.

† † †

Elizabeth knew Jack was going to be on his way home soon; Abbie confirmed that the night before. As she stood in the corridor and watched the inquisition through a reflection in the glass that separated her from the patient's room, she sensed a foreboding from the man accompanying the inspector. He had said nothing, not that she could hear the conversations, Abbie would fill her in later, but he fidgeted. His constant shifting from one foot to the other, hands in and out of pockets, his darting eyes were like a red flag to an anxious bull. Something was wrong, Elizabeth knew it. She'd felt this before—where?

At the farmhouse.

She wanted a clearer view. She had to get closer. How?

Just then, the interrogation ended. The inspector gave a slight bow to Jack, one to his father, and then swiftly walked toward the exit where Elizabeth stood wanting a closer look. She got it.

"That's him, I know it," the fidgeter said. "I don't care what the doctor or the lord says, I'm taking him to Nakhoda. He's the last person to speak with ol' Denn."

"You're lucky you didn't kill him in the Nookery. But who shot him this second time?" the inspector asked.

"A botched robbery, nothing more."

"I don't think so. Somebody knows he's hiding something."

"Tonight, he goes with us," said the fidgeter.

The conversation continued, but the two men were now out of earshot as they rounded a corridor and disappeared. Elizabeth desperately wanted to follow, but equally wanted to rush in and warn the doctor and Jack's father. She knew she couldn't do either.

"No, my dear friends, tonight Jack is going with me," she said.

Chapter Twenty~Seven

This may be the most blessed and terrifying day of my life. The tide was right, the winds were favorable, and the *Fancy* set sail. Hopefully, it will be hours, many hours, before Avery and his crew find my cabin empty.

Though the chances of Avery discovering my absence and returning to force us back onboard are slight, my anxiety to move on is great. Rumors of Indian warships seeking redress added to Avery's haste. When Avery realizes only ninety of his slaves are sailing with him, he will probably curse me rather than Rudy, who already got a cursing from me.

Rudy convinced me, however, that we would appear far more substantial traveling with a team of slaves rather than two young females who look more like members of a harem than slaves. I fear the next twelve hours may be the most dangerous of our journey— stranded here hiding in port waiting for the early morning tide when our passage will take us to Madagascar then north to the English run city of Bombay where we will return these two young slaves to their homes. Rudy traded a few of Avery's slaves for our passage.

- Hinch

St. Bartholomew's Hospital, London, England - 1748

Elizabeth's carriage slowed as it turned into the King Henry VIII gate of St. Bartholomew's Hospital. Compared to the night she charged through this gate to deliver a bleeding Jack to the hospital, this time sentries were there checking visitors. Dressed like a countess, she easily gained access. Someone of consequence must be here, she thought.

Her carriage stopped, and they helped her out just as they had on each of her previous visits. But it felt wrong. Something was amiss. She nodded a thank you to the footmen and hurried up the steps into the great hall, her dress rustling in the evening air. There were too many people. She tried to calm her racing heart. When she arrived at Jack's room, the race ended. Blood-soaked sheets and bloodied footprints seemed to glow in the lamplight of the empty room.

She raced back to the offices, hoping Abbie would have the answers she needed. Nobody was there. Elizabeth ran down the hall toward a commotion. Abbie was on a bed attended to by two doctors. Blood, rich and red, was spattered over her white uniform. She was alert, though. Her eyes caught Elizabeth's immediately.

"He's gone! They took him. We tried to stop them but they took him." Abbie said.

The doctor turned to see who Abbie was talking to. He was Jack's doctor, the same who attended him the night she brought Jack in. He recognized she was the regular visitor and answered her frantic eyes. "Miss Abbie will be fine. Just a few clean lacerations and if she will hold still we can have her back to work in no time."

Elizabeth came around the bed and took Abbie's free hand. Before the questions poured out of Elizabeth, the doctor turned to her and asked kindly, "Who are you? You've visited but never actually visited. Are you some kind of guardian?"

Abbie quickly piped in, "Miss Farrow here is simply an admirer. She won't admit it now, but if that fiancé makes one misstep, Miss Farrow wants to be Mrs. Remington." Abbie winked and Elizabeth got the message to let the question die there.

"Well," the doctor began, "Unless Lord Remington's men can catch up quickly and bring Mr. Jack back, neither of you will become Mrs. Remington. He's lost too much blood and without our care, blood loss or infections will finish him." The doctor turned back and pulled a sheet back over Abbie's bare shoulder. He stood, nodding to Elizabeth. "She's yours for a few hours, but she needs to rest."

The two doctors left the room and the questions poured out faster than Abbie had the strength or energy to answer.

From the fragmented questions and answers, the story took shape.

"This morning's inspector and his assistant were no more than bold highwaymen, impersonating a constable and inspector. They fooled even Lord Remington." Abbie talked as fast as she could between Elizabeth's onslaught of questions.

"They had Jack on his feet and claimed he was under arrest. Dr. Edmonds resisted and was the first one knocked to the ground. I was next, but this time a drawn knife left me bleeding. They dragged Jack past our bodies and out through the great hall."

Elizabeth interjected a question in between Abbie's race of words. "The blood in Jack's room?"

"His, mine, and from an ugly cut on Dr. Edmonds' scalp. They tended to him first." Abbie said. Elizabeth relaxed only slightly.

In response to Elizabeth's question about where they might be going, Abbie gently shook her head, looking like she was finally going into shock. She muttered, "Nakhoda. But I don't know where that is, maybe somewhere by Bristol."

Elizabeth asked one more question as Abbie closed her eyes. "Does Lord Remington know they kidnapped his son?"

"He has the Bow Street Runners out hunting. Elizabeth," Abbie's grip was getting lighter, "find him. If you don't, he will be dead." Abbie cracked her eyes and with them motioned toward a cupboard. "You'll need that." Abbie closed her eyes and took a deep breath and seemed to fully relax. Elizabeth touched her finger to her tongue and dipped it into the small mortar and pestle and back to her tongue. "Sleep well, sweet Abbie," Elizabeth whispered.

After one quick glance to ensure she was alone, Elizabeth emptied the contents of the cupboard into a pillowcase, the remaining powder from the mortar and pestle into a kerchief, and rushed out to the courtyard. Her coachman attentively swung the coach around and helped her in. "Back home please. Quickly," she urged.

"Bristol? Nakhoda? They'll be traveling through the Newgate past the prison. How appropriate," she said to herself.

Once in her flat, Elizabeth dawned her riding outfit, packed the supplies in the saddlebags on her big white mare, and headed west along the old Bath Road toward Bristol. With her pistol tightly secured to her side, she kept the moon over her left shoulder. She calculated Nakhoda's thugs would not be stopping for the night in any of the inns she passed. They had to deliver a wounded, bleeding prisoner to their boss Nakhoda before their prize either bled to death or died from infections. Did they stop the bleeding? From what she learned in the hospital, she calculated they had a two or three-hour head start. The old Bath Road was the only good road that would cross the country between Bristol and London. With a rest or exchange of horses, they'd be three days at best. She needed to catch them tonight. But then what? Who could she trust? Where could she take him?

Does he actually have anything worth shooting him for? I thought so. They think so. If he dies, did I kill him in vain? Can he help me find JoAnna? What am I doing?

She knew the Bow Street Runners would likely restrict their search to the city of London, even if they'd heard the destination might be Bristol. Then again, Abbie was under strong medication. She could have meant Briston, or even Boston.

Elizabeth was grateful for the moon, which gave her a somewhat clear view of the road and small villages she passed. The wonderful feeling of freedom she' felt just weeks before failed to break through the dread and concern she felt for Jack's life. This time, she knew she had enemies who would stop at nothing. Nor would she.

✝ ✝ ✝

It was nearing dawn; she wondered if she passed them or if maybe they were not headed to Bristol at all. A small settlement rose in the horizon. As she neared, a small light broke through the darkness, helping the buildings take shape. Her white mare welcomed the slower pace.

"Ol' girl let's keep it quiet." Elizabeth rubbed her hand along the horse's neck, hoping to keep the approach as quiet as possible. A coach and four lathered horses sat idly in a small courtyard. She stopped in the shadows and tied her horse, once again rubbing the neck and whispering appreciation to the mare.

She approached a young boy holding buckets from which the horses were eating feverishly.

"You're a good boy, thank you for caring for my horses." She put her hand on his shoulder. "So, my friends finally got here."

The boy looked up and could only see the slender silhouette topped with a clean-shaven face and a gentlemen's hat.

"If they're your friends, I hate you!" he said.

That sure changes my tact, she thought.

The boy's gaze dropped from Elizabeth to his task. The horses were reaching the bottom of the two buckets and though the buckets were much lighter as they emptied, the horses' eagerness to get every bite made it hard for him to hold on.

Elizabeth took one bucket. "Here let me help."

"Thanks," he muttered.

"I was trying to be polite when I called them my friends. My mother taught me to be kind." Elizabeth scrambled to position herself as a friend to the boy. "Were they mean to you?"

"They hit my pa."

"What happened?" Elizabeth wanted to be compassionate, to be a gentlewoman, but right now life required her courage, the courage she'd girded these many years. "Are they all inside?"

"One's with Pa gettin' fresh horses. Ma's in helpin' 'em clean up yer friend."

"One is injured?" she asked, hoping it was Jack, and he was still alive.

"He looked real bad when they came bangin' on the door."

"Just two mean riders and my sick friend?"

"Yeah. But yer friend ain't sick, he's bleedin' to death."

Elizabeth needed the fresh horses, a cleaned up and tended to Jack, and a few answers before she arranged for two dead kidnappers, all while keeping the family safe. And only one pistol. She touched it gently to give a boost to her courage.

"Can you help a stranger?" Elizabeth asked.

"Are you friends or just friendly?" The boy looked up into her eyes.

"The sick one is my friend. The two mean ones snatched him from a hospital after someone shot him. That's why he's bleeding. They hurt the doctor and a friendly nurse. I'm here to rescue him." She paused to give the boy time to decide if he trusted her.

"Ok," he finally said.

"Are you good at hooking up horses?" she asked. His bright teeth illustrated a proud smile. "What if the heel chain came loose from the trace?" she whispered.

The smile got bigger. "I'd get a whoopin'" he said. The smile didn't fade. She knew he understood her.

"Let's keep a big rock right here under this wheel. I promise you won't get the whoopin'. But will you help me make sure the heel chain gets undone when your pa and the mean man hook up the horses?"

Elizabeth slipped behind the coach as the boy's father and another man led two fresh horses up to replace the tired teams. Her new little friend was ready to get even with the men who hurt his family.

Morning threatened its arrival, and Elizabeth was torn between giving Jack all the care she hoped he was receiving and getting these two on their way in darkness. It wasn't a choice she was willing to force. She watched carefully as the new teams of horses were harnessed. Her new little friend led the tired horses back away. Light poured out into the yard as the door opened. Elizabeth recognized the fake inspector as he demanded his associate's help to bring Jack back out to the coach.

"You can't take him like this." A woman, Elizabeth assumed to be her new little friend's mother, took the man by the arm, pleading for Jack's life.

He flung her inside with one brush of his large arm. With all her heart, Elizabeth wanted to draw her pistol and leave the man dead right there.

Her husband bounded into the home. Seconds later, the inspector and the husband carried Jack from the house to the coach, the wife alongside and providing what little care she could.

With the coach door closed, both men jumped up in the seat and with reins in hand, a crack of a whip, and a loud 'hiya' the horses bounded away. The coach jolted, but stayed right where it was. The man with a firm grip on the reins flew off the seat head first, landing square on his face. The second man, stupefied, stood just long enough to look down at Elizabeth's pistol. A flash of gunpowder, a loud crack, and the man fell dead into the dirt. The man in the dirt turned just fast enough to catch a boot in the face. A boot loaded with such fury, if he ever woke, his face would never be the same.

Her new little friend arrived in time to see the first man lying dead in the dirt and a boot leaving the second man as still as the first.

Elizabeth turned to the woman. "I agree with you. He can't be taken like this." The young boy walked up to the man Elizabeth kicked and gave him a second boot. He turned to Elizabeth and smiled.

They carried Jack back inside and attended to his dressings. With the drug they gave him in the hospital, he remained unresponsive through the entire ordeal.

Light crept through the window. Dawn presented a new kind of day for this little family.

The boy and father stepped inside, having cleaned up the small courtyard to keep the neighbors from too much consternation over the previous hour's drama. At the sound of a gunshot, they were certain to ask questions.

"They're both dead," the father said, "your aim, both hand and foot…" He trailed off. His eyes fixed on Elizabeth, dressed like a man with the flowing blonde hair falling over her shoulders.

"Pa, this is Elizabeth. She needs help gittin' her friend back home," the kindly mother said.

Caught in the surprise of this woman who had just bested two highwaymen with no more concern for their survival than she would give a rattlesnake, he asked, "Where might home be?"

"Bristol." Elizabeth didn't know what else to say, but London wasn't it.

Chapter Twenty-Eight

In preparation to sail on an early morning tide, we boarded the
Falcon just before midnight and settled in a large bunk room Rudy
arranged for our small traveling group. The rest of our slaves (Avery's
former slaves) would travel in the slave hold below. Just before dawn,
Rudy woke me and the slave girls and quickly and quietly ushered us
off the ship. Piled silently into a long boat, we made our way from the
ship to an empty beach just outside the harbor. Rudy encouraged our
continued silence as we slipped past what in the darkness seemed to be
a fortress in the middle of the harbor.

Back on land, we scurried into the jungle and up a small hill just as
the crepuscular light of dawn revealed the silhouette of a 150 gun
Indian warship standing like a bastion in the center of the harbor's
entrance.

No ship would sail on the morning tide this morning. The *Fancy*
escaped its just rewards by one tide. Three thoughts battled for a place
in my racing mind. First, Avery was safe for now, the Indians sent the
wrong ship; that man-of-war will never catch the *Fancy*. It is too slow.
Second, I certainly couldn't safely return my slaves to their home in
India on that ship, it had the wrong intent and the wrong crew. And
third, the winning thought, "How in blazes did Rudy know to get us off
the *Falcon?*"

Now that I have a few minutes to record those thoughts of this
morning, I wonder why the question that consumes me now didn't

edge them all out then. "How do we get off this island and get these slaves back to India?"

- Hinch

The Old Bath Road, England - 1748

"How many times do I have to wake up to a new face, short on blood, long on pain, and wrapped in some sheet?" Jack groaned, wincing in pain as he asked, waking Elizabeth from a stressful, uncomfortable sleep.

She blinked her eyes open to see Jack wide awake, watching the countryside pass by over her shoulder.

"Hello," she said as she ran her fingers through her hair, certain it needed a proper comb. It did.

"Where are we?" he asked.

"Almost to Bristol. Maybe," Elizabeth answered, while still clearing her mind from her sleep's fog and trying to act in control.

"What day is it?" Jack asked.

"Friday."

"You sure?"

"I'm sure." Elizabeth had fallen asleep, but she was not sure how long she'd slept or even when she drifted off.

"Did you rescue me from Nakhoda's men?"

That question brought her up short. What did he know about Nakhoda or his men, or the kidnappers?

"Nakhoda?" She stammered out a question. He was ahead of her in this battle. She shouldn't have dozed off.

"Sure, Nakhoda, your friend in Bristol. Whoever gets this fool there first gets the reward. But did you have to kill your partners? Not that I care, mind you. There seem to be plenty of them to go around."

"I'll have you—" Elizabeth's indignation was stopped short.

"No, you won't have me anything." Jack cut her off and plunged in. "Miss Elizabeth Farrow, you are actually the ball in play here, not me. I don't know what you want. But I know there are very nasty people who want to get their hands on you. And if you insist on rushing into those hands, you'll do it alone, because I'm not going with you."

Elizabeth fumed. *How dare he talk to me that way? After what I've gone through to save his life, and he thinks I kidnapped him?*

"It's Saturday," Jack said.

"Saturday?"

"We stopped at the crossroads. I made a choice, Newton Ferrers. Some powder in your kerchief helped you sleep. You needed it."

"Newton Ferrers?" Elizabeth mumbled, confused.

"Miss Farrow, if you're traveling with me, you'll need to keep up. I've some work to do there."

Elizabeth held up the kerchief. Somehow, she'd forgotten it was full of the powder she took from Abbie's table. "Newton Ferrers?" she repeated.

"While we're getting to know each other. Where did you get this?" Jack held up ol' Denn's copy of the *History of Pyrates*.

Blood rushed from Elizabeth's face. Her hands quickly snatched the saddlebags lying at her feet. "You went through my things?" She regretted she wasn't sitting closer where she could slap his face.

"Your things?"

His smile infuriated her.

"Miss. Farrow," he held up the book, "this was sitting on your lap when I woke. Your *things* are perfectly safe. Besides a few *things* a gentleman wouldn't be going through." He stressed just enough to keep the blood from returning to her face, "Are there *things* in there a captive shouldn't see?"

Elizabeth was on the defensive, a position she hated. She also hated him for it.

"Mr. Remington, a captive you are not. My interest in you coincides with my interest in finding Captain Brinkley of the *Emerald*. My interest in that book coincides with my interest in . . ." her mind raced to pull together a workable story, ". . . learning the truths associated with lore, the legend, and the lies of piracy." She watched his eyes for any sign he might believe her.

The coach slowed to a stop in front of a small inn. The coach door opened and a smiling young boy greeted them. "Newton Ferrers, Mr. Remington." Right behind him stood a proud father.

Elizabeth looked from the boy to the father and back to Jack. *How much did they tell while I was asleep? He knows I killed two men? Does he suspect I shot him too?*

Jack smiled as he spoke. "Thank you. It was a great service to leave your home to bring Miss Farrow back to hers. As I promised, once you get us settled, the coach and the teams are yours."

"And the mare?" the boy asked.

Jack looked through the small back window. "I think we'll keep her."

The father helped Elizabeth from the coach, then with her help, Jack gingerly climbed down and shuffled to the inn. His strength was returning, but the shattered rib and wounded lung forced a careful gait. He had no bags. He was wearing baggy brown trousers and a checkered blue shirt given to him by the farmer. The only thing he owned was the vest he grabbed when they drug him from the hospital. It was wrinkled and bloody, but no one cared to deprive him of it. A new pair of boots would be his first investment, he told Elizabeth, though the pair he borrowed were a gift, the farmer told him.

Elizabeth kept a tight eye on the young boy who carried her saddlebags over his shoulders. With the reins in one hand, he proudly led the white mare to the hitching post.

Once settled, thank yous and goodbyes were said, and the farmer and his son were gone, proud new owners of a fine coach and four tired, but beautiful, horses resting back home.

"Newton Ferrers? You told them I'm from Newton Ferrers?" Elizabeth asked, her face tightened, frustrated she had lost control of their situation.

"Page fifty, Miss Farrow. Legend, lore, and lies? You're holding it in your hands."

Elizabeth relaxed her grip. Color returned to her knuckles. If it were alive, the book could breathe again.

† † †

Elizabeth and Jack sat together in the quaint dining hall. Likely the only patrons this inn had entertained in some time. The dirt floor was swept, tables and chairs were all carefully dusted, but the fire was cold and the service rusty.

An elderly woman entered from the kitchen with a basket of breads, cheeses, and a flask of wine. She poured a generous cup for each.

"You'll pardon me. Ma husband's passed. Few folk come by anymore, but you're welcome company."

Jack's heart warmed as the woman lifted the clean cloth keeping flies from the food. In any other given time, Jack would have generously patronized an inn like this one. For now, he regretted the feeling of obligation to Miss Farrow's generosity. He didn't feel like he even owned the shirt on his back.

"Thank you," Jack said, looking up into her gentle green eyes. She was not poor in appearance, he thought. Blue and pink flowers were scattered across an apron that protected a long peach colored skirt. In her prime, Jack thought, this woman was the catch of the town. "Please, what is your name?"

The woman warmed to both his thank you and his gentle entreaty for her name, uncommon kindness from strangers tired from travel. "Creagh, Violet Creagh."

Jack's eyes darted from the elderly woman to Elizabeth, hoping to see if that name meant anything to Elizabeth. How closely had she read the notes from the trial of Avery's men? Did she pick up on the fact that David Creagh was among the few who escaped the *Charles II* during the Avery mutiny? *Was this woman related to David Creagh?* Jack's heart beat wildly with the prospect that because he was shot by a thug looking for the very information he was charged by his uncle to find, he was now sitting in an inn owned by possibly the only person who could help him put that puzzle piece together.

The lights didn't appear to have come on in Elizabeth's expression.

What is she looking for? Why rescue me?

Jack returned his attention to his hostess. "Mrs. Creagh, as you can see, I'm not much good for anything right now. At the great benevolence of my dear friend here, Miss Farrow, my life is at yours and her disposal." When coming into the inn, Jack remembered seeing an ax leaning on the stand of the cutler's wheel. Mrs. Creagh had just struggled to cut a loaf of bread. "With that said, I do know my way around a cutler's wheel. It would be an honor for me to bring a blade or two up to the caliber of your fine baking." He tore a piece of bread from the mangled loaf.

Her gentle eyes threatened a tear. "As you wish. I would consider it a great favor."

As Jack dedicated his attention to satisfying his neglected appetite. Mrs. Creagh left the two alone.

† † †

Elizabeth was also hungry, but she couldn't quite pull her attention away from this man. Jack had not only taken two balls in the span of a month, but had also murdered her only hope of finding a link to the men responsible for her family's destruction and loss of her sister. Now, he so kindly respected a stranger? Yet her mind fought not to change.

Of course, he knows his way around a cutler's wheel. How else would he keep his murder weapons death-sharp? Still, the thought was losing its bite. It was true; she hadn't actually seen him kill ol' Denn. Yet, she knew ol' Denn hadn't expertly killed the stranger lying next to him. Too many uncertainties raced through her head. What about the family from Chester and the dead bodies found there?

† † †

Jack finished, pushed his chair back, drained the cup and looked Elizabeth directly in the eyes. "I met a man looking for that book. I didn't share that tidbit with the inspectors." Jack pointed to his bandages. "But the man who shot me was looking for that book. Too bad he didn't know you had it; he could have shot you instead."

Jack carefully stood with support from the large oaken table, and walked into the room where Mrs. Creagh was struggling as she cut fresh vegetables. Her smile welcomed him. He took the knife from her hand. "I'll start with this one." He picked up two others lying on a large maple cutting board. He ran his hand across its surface, admiring its craftsmanship. "May I?" he asked, holding the knives. A small nod of his head invited her to follow him out into the yard where he sat comfortably at the cutler's wheel.

He began it rolling with the push of a pedal. The wheel turned, but the conversation remained Jack's focus. "Mrs. Creagh——"

She interrupted him. "To all the young men holding my knives, I insist they call me Violet. And if you're as good at that wheel as you insinuate, it may be just Vi."

It felt good to smile so broadly. "Then Violet it is. For now." He held up the first knife.

The wheel continued to turn. "Violet, I was once told of a man who lived around here by the name of David Creagh. Might you know of him?" Jack ran the edge of the knife across the wheel. Sparks flew.

"Did he drink?" Violet asked with a wink.

"I believe I heard that. At least some ten to fifteen years ago he did."

Violet pushed the splitting log closer and sat.

"Mr. Creagh, your David, was my father-in-law. Spent a few years in Her Majesty's Royal Navy. Turned down an invitation to sail with mutineers, and when they were eventually captured and tried, his testimony resulted in their hangings. He was so shaken he took to the bottle. Never did fully recover."

"Violet, I have a feeling you've been asked about Mr. Creagh before."

Between volleys of showering sparks, Jack wiped the blade over his pant leg, followed by his thumb along the blade's edge.

"My response sounded that practiced?" she asked.

Jack smiled, took the blade in his fingers, and handed it handle-first to Violet. He picked up the next knife, which had seen some serious abuse, and began the sparks flying.

"But you didn't come here looking for me, did you?" She watched Jack pull the blade across the wheel with an expertise she hadn't seen in years.

"Total and complete coincidence," Jack said. "I'm an academic, not a treasure hunter. A friend of mine plunged me into a web of death and intrigue with a simple request to learn the background of an old man." He took the knife, poking at his bandaged chest, and with the back of the blade pulled the shirt aside to show the scar from the first shot. Her eyebrows told him she understood.

A small chunk of leather hung from the frame of the cutler's wheel. Jack wiped the knife across his knee and ran the blade along the edge of the leather, slicing off a sliver as if it were hardened lard. Again, he handed the knife to Violet. Wide eyed, she took the second knife.

"David isn't the old man?" she asked.

"David's a bonus. But too late. My friend is off chasing pirates and as soon as I help Miss Farrow find herself, I'm back to the university. In fact, my appointment there is waiting for my recovery and now my return."

"So Miss Farrow isn't your intended?"

Jack pulled the third blade across the wheel. Sparks flew further this time. He stopped mid blade, turned the knife over, ran it across his leg, spit and shined it. He raised his eyes to Violet and held the knife respectfully, rotating it in his fingers.

"Where did you get this knife?"

A small engraved C shined past the scratches and nicks The question was so earnest, Violet's shock denied her tongue utterance. Jack's piercing eyes finally cut through the surprise. He turned the blade so she could clearly see the C he so carefully displayed.

"A gift."

"A gift?" Jack repeated.

"David, drunk David, practically lived in the taverns in his later years. He made friends with a sailor who saved his life one night. They corresponded for a while. That knife was a gift from the sailor. David cherished it. When he passed, my husband gave it to me. It maintained its edge longer than any other. I suppose I wore it out, kinda like me."

"That friend, did you know him?"

"Is that who you're looking for?" she asked.

Jack was amazed how quickly Violet understood his thinking. Could he even hide his thinking? Should he?

"My friend is looking for the artisan who made this blade."

"I never met him. My husband did once, said he was a fine man. Your artisan and David shared some bond. Neither of us ever knew what it was."

"Did you ever learn where that correspondence originated?"

She shook her head. "David traveled to Sheffield from time to time."

Jack finished the blade, cleaned it, handed it respectfully to Violet and picked up the ax. Sparks flew, disrupting the parade of chicks crossing the yard.

"Would you like a little poultry in your stew?" Violet asked as she stood and joined the parade. "You can call me Vi."

Chapter Twenty~Nine

Journal Entry: November 25, 1695 - French Island of Bourbon
Alexander Hincher - Ship's Surgeon

After four days hiding in the forest overlooking the harbor, we are watching the *Bengali Sundari* leave. Rudy tells me several of the Danes and French crew members from the *Fancy* are on board. Their fate is certain. If they can't deliver Avery or my two slaves, the Indians will torture them to death.

Before Avery sailed, there was such an argument and misinformation about where to go next and by what route, the Danes and French crew members won't be of any help in finding the *Fancy*. A perfect ploy by Avery. He knew well enough to not leave behind a trail to follow.

I doubt Avery remembers my presence in his stateroom when he was studying the map of the Spanish main and his careful avoidance discussing the one small mark identifying an island he had drawn on the map. An island uncharted and on no other map. An island away from the currents, the trade winds, an island certain to be found only by accident or if you were Henry Avery, and only by calculated intent. The *Fancy* headed for that island; I am certain.

With that map carefully re-drawn in the back of this journal, if the need ever arises, someday, I will too.

- Hinch

Newton Ferrers, England - 1748

Violet rinsed the blood off her hands, placed the skinned chicken on the board, and let the newly sharpened knife do its work. It'd been a long time since she'd handled a knife this well-tuned. "You can call me Vi, the rest of my life," she muttered to herself.

Elizabeth watched the chicken give of itself as the joy filled Violet's face. "Looks like our friend out there didn't disappoint," Elizabeth said as she entered the kitchen.

"Nope." Violet looked up and smiled. "So, what brought you here?"

Me? Or us?

Elizabeth shook her head, raised her open hands, and shrugged. "Chance? Luck? Destiny? Curse?"

Violet continued with the chicken, giving a tiny glance upward to insist on a coherent thought. Elizabeth knew common courtesy required an actual answer.

"I'm searching and every avenue is closed." Elizabeth plopped down on a stool.

How long has it been since I had a grown-up conversation with a grown-up woman? Did Jack kill that chicken as easily as he killed those men?

Violet waited patiently.

This is a rare chance to talk with someone who, even if you don't know her, can't hurt you. Talk! You were more willing to talk to a wrinkled old man so you could manipulate information from him than you are a generous, kind, lonely woman. Elizabeth's heart ached from the inside out. *Where's Jack now? Killing a cow?*

Elizabeth finally fought her way clear of an emotional battle she'd always fought alone.

"I don't know how to answer such a simple question." Elizabeth confessed. Minutes passed. It felt to Elizabeth like hours. Then she raised her head, her eyes met Violet's. Tears threatened a revolt in both women's eyes.

How can she care? She hasn't even heard me yet.

"When I was young, evil men attacked our village. They abused and murdered my mother, then took my sister. I didn't stop them. I hid to protect myself. When my father returned, he swore to avenge my mother and find my sister. He left me with my grandparents and promised to bring my sister back. He never returned."

She wiped her eyes with the tail of Violet's apron. The chicken lay waiting for the knife's attention. Violet's eyes remained moist.

"For all these years, I've searched for clues. There are too many evil men. Every time I think I've found something, it's taken away. I found a sympathetic ear. The ear of a man who promised me resolution. The next night, he lay dead at the hand of an assassin. An assassin with the expertise of a knife."

She motioned with her head toward the yard where she hoped Jack wasn't practicing his knife craft for later.

The expression of disbelief on Violet's face was enough to back Elizabeth up.

"I actually thought he killed the old man."

"And now?" Violet asked, picking up the knife and finishing the bird.

"I don't think so. . . but I saw him with the dead man in his arms, the knife in his hands. What else can I believe?"

"What makes you now think he didn't?" Violet asked.

Elizabeth wiped her hand across her brow. "It doesn't feel like he's a wanton killer."

"So you chased him across England. Or is he chasing you?"

Elizabeth shook her head and put her head in her hands.

Violet wiped her hands dry and put her arms around Elizabeth's shoulders. "I think we're both safe for now. You need some rest, and so do I. I'll see what our blade expert is up to. Supper will be ready in a few hours."

† † †

When Violet found Jack, he was sitting next to the tall white mare in a small barn. With his stronger arm, he gently stroked her leg. He assumed Elizabeth used this mare to chase his coach. He was curious how this horse and her dress got along. Did she have some trousers in her bags? He regretted not 'going through her things.'

"She's beautiful." Violet said as she leaned against the rail that divided the mare from an equally beautiful black Flemish draught horse.

"Is indeed," Jack said.

"What are your intentions with her?" Violet asked.

Jack thought that an interesting question. He turned to look at Violet, hoping to hide his thoughts that he felt she demonstrated an unusual interest

in a couple of strangers.

"I have none, she doesn't belong to me," Jack said.

"I'm referring to Elizabeth."

With a quick change in thought, Jack repeated, "Well, she doesn't belong to me either."

There was silence for several minutes. Violet picked up a brush and handed it to Jack. "You might as well be doing some good."

This woman had a way, a snoopy way, but a kind way, of making you feel comfortable sharing. Jack couldn't help it.

"My intentions? Elizabeth got herself caught up with a man who got himself killed. Somehow, he convinced her there are people in the New World who will help her find answers she has spent her life searching for. Getting to the New World will get her killed, or worse, added to a harem. Although honestly I wouldn't envy the sultan who bought her." Jack smiled at his joke. Violet didn't.

"She thinks she's sailing with the Emerald from Liverpool. All I have to do is keep her away from there. Keep her busy for two more weeks and the Emerald will sail without her."

"Why is it your duty to protect her?" Violet asked.

Jack stood, leaning on the horse to brush her flank. "A dying man was laying in my arms and with his last breath had a change of heart. He begged me to prevent her from traveling to the New World."

"Did you kill him?"

Jack paused. He'd never met a woman so direct, so offensive, so meddlesome, yet, so without guile. Shrugging, he answered, "No." He paused again, "Yes. It was not my knife, but because of me, yes, he's dead."

With no words, Violet's silence entreated an explanation.

"Two men were escorting him somewhere he didn't seem to want to go. I intervened and seconds later, one lay dead… at my hand, the other stabbed the old man and ran with his satchel. I attended to the old man, who obliged me to keep Elizabeth from sailing. With a crowd of citizens approaching a stranger holding one of their own with a knife in hand, it seemed a good idea to flee."

"And here you are, looking for my father-in-law dead these fifteen years, and you, wanted by the law for murder, and all you want is to get back to the classroom," she summed up.

"Don't forget the old man's enemies. They think I have his satchel," Jack added, pointing to his broken and bandaged ribs.

"I'll bet a lot of good can be accomplished with a warm meal and a comfortable bed." Nodding, Violet headed back to the kitchen.

Jack grinned. *Who is this woman? Why didn't Captain Remington ask her to solve his puzzle? She gets to the point faster than anyone I've ever met. I wish I could spend time learning from a master like her.*

Chapter Thirty

Our troubles just intensified. I remained with my slaves these four days while Rudy, with his uncanny ability to be invisible, scouted the town, watched the Indians, and kept us fed. I breathed a sigh of relief as the warship sailed. I knew the *Falcon* would immediately follow—but without us. My relief was short-lived.

Pointing to the large warship leaving the harbor, my slave girl said, "That is my grandfather's ship, looking for the pirates who stole his treasure."

Pointing to the smaller frigate entering the harbor and passing the large warship, my little slave girl continued, "That's my father's ship, looking for me, but really he's looking for this."

She pulled out an incredible dagger, the Imperial dagger of Persia, 'The Blade of Safavid.' Possibly the most sacred, the most valuable, the most sought-after artifact of the Safavid Empire. No, this is no slave girl.

Incredulously, I stared into her beautiful dark brown eyes. "Do I want to meet your father?" I finally asked.

"You do not want to meet my father. And you will not. He is dead. It is my brother you do not want to meet."

In the three months we've been together, these were the first English words she ever uttered. And with those words, she proclaimed to me she was the rightful heir to not just one empire, but two. The granddaughter of Emperor Aurangzeb, and his wife the Persian Princess Dilras Banu Begum. As the daughter of Emperor Aurangzeb's firstborn daughter Zeb-un-Nissa, she is the rightful heir to the Mughal Empire.

Her father was Shah Suleiman I of Persia, shah of the entire Safavid empire. She is also rightful heir to the Persian Dynasty.

Rudy made quite a trade. He traded his share of a practically unspendable fortune for the most valuable slave girl in the world, the rightful heir to two of the world's greatest empires. And she has with her the one artifact that proves her identity and rights of rule, the dagger of Persia—'The Blade of Safavid'.

To a pirate, the dagger would be just another valuable relic, with its pearls, emeralds, and diamonds beautifully set in pure gold and silver. To the King of Persia, it means the throne.

Nobody here suspects we are not on the *Fancy*. When we slipped off the *Falcon*, our payment of slaves bought their silence. Rudy assures me they didn't know who we were, anyway. Nobody knows we're here.

- Hinch

Liverpool, England - 1748

Krist thumbed through the notebook. He decided to give it to his father later. His father's network of spies were made up of hoodlums, fools, and drunks, dependent on the dole paid for by his father's lucrative white female slave trade. Hassan knew both his son and his former friend, if you could call Hillis a friend, abhorred the trade, yet both failed to escape it.

Krist hated himself for it and hid behind his cowardice, branding it as loyalty to a father who raised him. Yet internally, he rejoiced in his father's setbacks and failures. Now he'd lost Hillis, his most consistent spy, through the failures of one of his bumbling lieutenants.

Snapping closed the notebook, Krist looked up. He knew the messenger who just entered knew nothing of its contents. Few of the men his father employed could read or write. This young man was no exception. Yet Krist offered the young man more respect than did his father, even though Krist pitied his ignorance.

"Mr. . . .?" Krist paused.

"Granger. Sir," the young man added.

"Mr. Granger, continue. Please." Krist leaned on the newly polished starboard railing of the *Chawbuck* and gestured for the young man to sit on a barrel.

"Sir, Mr. O'Donnel took me along with six of his other men to scour the nearby villages in search of the man who killed Mr. Gasher and Mr. Hillis. 'How far could he get?' Mr. O'Donnel said. 'I shot him square in the chest. He's lying bled to death somewhere.' When we got to Chester, Mr. O'Donnel collected the sheriff to help us in the hunt. I was snooping in a barn while Mr. O'Donnel and the sheriff was talking to the farmer and saw lots of blood. I know the difference from animal blood and man's blood, sir. This was man's blood."

Krist enjoyed the telling. This young Mr. Granger had a future. He nodded, encouraging the story to continue.

"When the sheriff decided to go git some local help, Mr. O'Donnel killed him. Said it weren't good. The farmer said he knew nothin. We took him'in the family, tied em up in the barn while we looked around. Mr. O'Donnel sent me with Mr. Baxter to bring help. We got back the next mornin and found Mr. O'Donnel and the three others dead behind the barn with the sheriff."

"And the farmer?" Krist asked.

"Gone. Mr. Baxter, he's a smart one. Knew the family was from Sheffield. We two and some others, headed out fast as possible. Arrived first and was waiting when they got there. That killer was with em. Got away. But we got that notebook. Mr. Baxter sent me to tell ya."

"And Mr. Baxter?" Krist asked.

"Was some trouble in Birchwood. Mr. O'Donnel said there was another book, one about pirates what had writin in it. Thought it was important. Left it in Birchwood for safe keeping. Your men there lost it."

"Did you see the book?"

"Yes, sir, but as I don't read, it made no difference to me. Was a big book. Mr. O'Donnel told the others to keep it till he got back from finding the killer."

"And?"

"Lost it. A bird took it."

Krist closed his eyes and took a deep breath, forcing his smile back inside. *How could there be a more humorous dramatic comedy? Or was it a tragedy?*

These are the best my father could hire?

"Thank you, Mr. Granger. When you see Mr. Baxter, please return here with him. My father would wish a detailed report."

Granger bowed, accepting the complement and command. Krist handed him a small handful of coins and wished him on his way. Krist was grateful he was the one who received the report. Mr. Granger didn't deserve the response he would have received from his father the captain.

Krist struggled to hide his smile as he considered this elusive officer who, even though seriously wounded, outsmarted Mr. O'Donnel, killing him and three of his crew after killing Hillis, Gasher, and how many others.

I like this officer. But who is he? How did he get Hillis to betray my father?

As he read, Krist questioned the wisdom in turning Hillis's notebook over to his father. Krist was born and grew up on the mighty 80-gun *Chawbuck*, a converted Portuguese warship. Unlike his father, he cherished any time he could spend on land. Even when anchored in the harbor of their hidden island in the New World, his father spent the majority of time onboard. Krist, in contrast, preferred the firm security of land beneath his feet. Today was an exception. Anxious for privacy, Krist retired to the one place he considered his own.

He tucked Denn's notebook inside his coat and began to climb. From the first time his father permitted him to climb the ropes to the top of the main mast as a little boy, the small platform had become his favorite part of the ship. Now a fully grown man, the platform didn't accommodate a prolonged visit. Many times he'd proposed expanding its size to accommodate a crew member who would be stationed as a lookout.

This view of the mighty deck still impressed him, yet the view across the Mersey to the harbor of Liverpool fascinated Krist.

Clouds adjourned their convention and its members began to disperse. Sharp rays of sunlight broke through small openings, highlighting random landmarks along the Mersey, showcasing Liverpool's bustling economy.

He sat, back against the mast, legs dangling, and read. Truly, this notebook would not favor his father if it ever fell into the hands of the magistrates. Krist heard many of these accounts from his father, yet reading them now from the viewpoint of another eye witness fueled the disdain for his father's brand of slavery. Krist read how Mr. Hillis and his father became associates; this was not new. How they'd captured and outfitted the *Chawbuck*. Mr. Hillis' account differed only slightly in who got credit for the innovations. A smile accompanied a chuckle.

The quest for revenge, however, was exclusively his father's. Krist read how Mr. Hillis felt imprisoned on the *Chawbuck* and loathed the taking of young white women from various coastal towns and selling them into the harems of Ottoman princes and sultans. The gentle rocking of the ship did nothing to his stomach compared to the thought of families being torn apart by his father's savagery. Yet he knew no other life.

Mr. Hillis shared his account of Krist's mother being kidnapped from the town of Ísafjörður on the coast of Iceland, and confirmed the tales of her surpassing beauty and grace. Krist had heard this story many times, yet hearing it from another's account brought him to tears. His heart ached for his mother and her family. A family he was never given the opportunity to meet. And a promise his father had never kept.

He smiled as he read that as captain of the ship, his father performed his own wedding. Tears erased the smile as he read how terrible his mother suffered as she gave birth on this very ship in tormented weather, dying only hours later.

He stood, breathing deeply. Arm wrapped around the mast, he continued reading. Mr. Hillis' notes elaborated more on the quest for revenge than the white slave trade, which made reading easier. Mr. Hillis and his father scoured the notes from the trials of Avery's men, and visited each of their home towns. They concluded, based on the testimony of a Mr. Sparkes, that a surgeon onboard the *Fancy* remained on the Island of Burbon when Avery and the Fancy disappeared, never to be seen again.

That is when the search took on a new direction. The ship's surgeon, along with twenty slaves and two young Indian women, had stolen Captain Ali Mutarid Hassan's Ship, the *Chappow*. Chills climbed Krist's spine as he read Mr. Hillis' account. From the pages, he could feel his father's rage, his passion, his hate; his father then knew where to direct his revenge.

† † †

Two men on horseback stopped at the dock. With decisive care, one climbed down and tenderly favoring saddle-worn joints, stepped down into a boat. The other quickly joined him. Hassan sat motionless as the sailor rowed him back to the *Chawbuck*. Krist half climbed and half slid down the ropes to meet his father on the deck. With the notebook tucked inside his vest, he welcomed his father back onboard.

"The *Kent* left Plymouth with the tide headed here. Gather the men, meet in Bristol in five days," Hassan commanded.

"You've not enough men to sail now," Krist said.

"I'll sail this ship alone if I have to. The *Kent* will never take it."

Krist knew the only true enemy his father feared was the Royal Navy, in particular the HMS *Kent*, which had chased him from one ocean to another. As his father issued sharp commands to the remaining men on board, Krist retrieved a small bag and returned to shore. Within minutes sails were hoisted, anchor raised, and the *Chawbuck* was moving.

Krist had little use for horses but he knew these had been rode hard. Still breathing hard, their lathered coats confirmed his father's anxiety to get the *Chawbuck* out to sea. Krist took the reins and walked the horses along the shore. He returned the horses to the livery and began gathering the crew. From tavern to tavern, he gave instructions for the crew to evacuate to Bristol. The door of the Nookery stood wide open and Krist stepped inside. The reports he'd heard had not done this quaint little tavern justice. From its fateful night many weeks before, it had not been touched. Broken lanterns littered the floor, tables were still turned over, and blood stains remained just as they had that night.

Who was the assassin? Too many unanswered questions. A navel officer?

He stepped in, returned a table and chair to their upright positions and sat next to the only window. Krist had been here only one time before as a child after his father agreed to let Mr. Hillis live out his life on land. For the past twenty years, ol' Denn had been the eyes and ears for Krist's father's spy network. Krist pulled the notebook from his vest, grateful he hadn't given it to his father in the haste. He continued where he left off.

He read how his father and Hillis sought out the medical schools in Great Britain, looking for a medical student graduating, or at least attending school in the early 1690s. After visiting seven additional schools, he found an Alexander Hincher graduating from Cambridge University in 1694, just months before the *Charles II* set sail for Spain. Alexander Hincher, became the surgeon he was chasing. Each of the spies had the name, but Hassan knew 'Hinch' would have abandoned that name immediately.

Krist read about several escapades, but none amounted to any serious clues. Truly, the trail ran cold and remained so—until now. On the last page of ol' Denn's notebook, he read:

> *"A young woman will meet Hassan in Antigua. She will be sailing on the Emerald. She may be the only person living with first-hand knowledge of the blade. Be careful, she may be accompanied by a skilled young man."*

Chapter Thirty~One

I once wrote that this journal could someday mean my execution or my exoneration. Execution seems the more likely. I am now the captain of a pirate ship. If I am successful, I will give it back to its rightful owner when I return my Persian princess to her home.

I am sailing with my first mate Lord Rudy, as he wants me to call him, eleven frail but improving-in-health slaves from the coast of Tanzania, (formerly the property of Henry Avery) and my two Imperial slaves. We sail on what they formerly knew as the *Chappow,* a quick and very agile frigate. They outfitted this frigate for speed not battle. She has a shallow draft and besides the mainsail they outfitted her with additional sails—both square and lateen-rigged. Rudy knows his ships.

My cargo have names. Once the princess revealed her fluency in speaking English, we learned the emperor named her after a famous and beautiful Persian queen—Astrella. Esther to us. Her companion, rightly named, is Leilyn, which we learned means beautiful woman with dark hair born at night. The Persians pack a lot into one name.

Since the *Chappow* legally belongs to the father of our prize crew member, Rudy felt no remorse in steeling it for his daughter. Its captain was a young and vicious sailor Rudy watched slit the throat of a slave who crossed him on the island. Rudy felt no remorse leaving the captain to fend for himself.

Esther's father, Shah Suleiman I passed away last year and her brother Shah Soltan Husayn took the throne. Esther thinks it's her brother who sent the *Chappow* in search of her and the 'Blade of Safavid'.

The Emperor Aurangzeb sent his ship to recover a treasure. That purpose paled compared to the Persian Shah's ship sent to recover the single most powerful threat to his throne. When Esther recounted the actual accent to a throne in the Safavid Dynasty or the Mughal Empire as anything but family friendly, it became clear our two companions' lives are in as much jeopardy as ours. The safest persons on board are our property, the slaves, who to some, are not considered people at all. This will be a dangerous journey.

- Hinch

Newton Ferrers, England - 1748

The next morning Elizabeth woke to the smell of ham sizzling. The aroma triggered every sense she had. Memories of her grandmother flooded in. Had Violet's inn imported the large feather beds from her grandparent's home, it could not have been more reminiscent. The morning air was cool as she dressed and ran a brush through her tangled hair.

Jack and Violet were deep in conversation when she entered the great hall, as Jack had named it. Violet turned and smiled as Elizabeth joined them.

"Morning, darling," Violet said, accompanied by an enormous smile. "Rest is healing. You look radiant."

"Radiant?" Elizabeth welcomed the compliment but hardly felt radiant. The hot bath the night before lifted her spirits and certainly aided in the deep restful sleep, but radiant?

"Mr. Remington has agreed to fuss around the inn and care for our many patrons today." She motioned around the empty hall in jest. "You and I, if you're willing, will ride down to Salcombe, a village made up mostly of smugglers and fishermen. I've a friend there you need to meet. I believe her story may add a new perspective to your upcoming journey."

My upcoming journey? Did I mention Denn's intent for me to meet his associate in Antigua? Or is she speaking rhetorically?

The fresh, innocent outlook for the day began to cloud over.

"Mrs. Creagh, I feel it would be an honor to spend the day with you and your friend."

"It's Violet to you, Elizabeth." Violet said.

Elizabeth nodded. She and Jack ate heartily. It was obvious to Elizabeth that Jack was regaining strength quickly. She saw the truthfulness of the doctor's statement that the man heals quickly. Since he was healing from her shooting, it was a relief.

Jack and Elizabeth finished breakfast and Jack went out to help Violet with the wagon. Violet had it nearly hooked up by the time he entered the barn. The wagon had a single bench and was pulled by the large Flemish draught horse. "You can trust me with the inn, Vi. Your patrons will want for nothing," Jack assured her. She and Elizabeth climbed up onto the bench and rode out of the yard. Violet thanked him with a smile.

The women shared small talk for the first few hours. As they neared the small coastal village, Violet began preparing Elizabeth for the visit she hoped would dissuade Elizabeth from traveling alone to the New World, and possibly help her understand she may never find her sister.

Violet pulled the carriage up to a small rock home that overlooked the harbor and the ruins of Fort Charles. Elizabeth found it interesting that at one point this small village was worthy of a fort. When she asked, Violet shared the brief history of the village and fort. She emphasized the fort had not only served the royalists during the civil war, but protected the residents from French and Spanish pirates.

A small iron gate hung between two pillars of the short stone wall that circled the rock home. Its garden was simple; a few late blooming flowers remained. At the sound of the carriage, a tall dark-haired woman opened the door. Recognizing Violet, she bounded to the gate and threw her arms around her friend.

These two must be more than friends, Elizabeth thought. *Sisters? Yes, like sisters,* she concluded. *When I find Joanna, the embrace will be like this, except with tears.*

The hug ended. Violet took Elizabeth by the hand and pulled her forward. "Elen, meet my friend Elizabeth. She's staying with me a few days, and I thought you might help. She's trying to find her sister."

Elen ushered them into the house. She paused, and whispered to Violet as they crossed the threshold, "Marauders?"

Violet nodded. "Any news concerning your brother?"

Elen shook her head.

"Any more news from Clare?"

"She's still waiting. Never met a girl with so much hope." Elen said.

"I miss that girl. Nobody can put on a meal like her," Violet said. "When she went to the New World, all of England lost. But especially me and my inn."

Violet turned to Elizabeth. "You would love Clare, she is your kind of woman—brave, smart, and independent."

Elen led Violet and Elizabeth into a small sitting room, lit by the afternoon sun. The light streamed past white lace drapes pulled to the side and tied with bright blue ribbon.

Elizabeth sat and turned to Violet and then to Elen, "I'm curious to learn about this Clare, especially if she is my kind of woman."

Mostly I'm curious to know what kind of woman you think I am. Is Clare willing to kill to rescue her sister? Is it Clare's hope that Violet is referring to?

The room was not large but served Elen's needs comfortably. The small kitchen area adjoining the sitting room was complete with a fireplace, wash basin, table with two chairs, and a tall table for food preparation. On one wall hung a large drape, behind which Elizabeth assumed was a pantry. The walls were painted a light pale blue which complimented the drapes. Opposite the front door they'd just entered was a second door, which no doubt led to the bedroom. It was tidy and comfortable. Elizabeth unconsciously accepted Elen as a fine lady, even if a bit out of place in a small out of the way village.

Elen poured each a cup of tea, sat in a chair next to Elizabeth, and to Violet's delight, began her story.

"This small fishing village was never a destination of any consequence. We're poor but content; always have been. I'm sure you saw the remnants of the fort. It was helpful when the royalists thought we were important. But the tendency of a village like ours to be attractive to pirates, isn't there."

Pirates don't pillage for fun. They want amusement and wealth. This Elizabeth knew.

Elen Continued, "To raiders, there's not much interest in a small, poor fishing village like ours. Yet, we've taught our daughters to hide and protect themselves with strangers. We've not always been successful. What enchants Violet here so much is how my brother foiled a kidnapping.

"A young Irish woman, this Clare you heard mentioned, was visiting from Ireland, Kinvarra, another coastal town, and she should have known better. She was returning home alone to her sister's when three marauders caught her. In one of the rare times they attacked our village, the marauders chose not to return empty-handed. Three of them had Clare in tow toward the harbor."

"You'll love this," Violet added.

"My brother, who had never been partial to women, any women, stumbled upon the three marauders. They made the mistake of arguing over who got her first. Lars, my brother, entered the negotiation.

"'Who gets her first?' he asked the marauders as he appeared to take part in her rather violent disrobing. But rather than join in the stripping off her clothes, he gently positioned himself between the sailors and Clare. They, somewhat drunk, assured him he would be last if there was any left.

"He surprised them by assuring them he didn't want any. Not with a sick, infectious, dangerous tramp. He said it as just an innocent question. He wanted to know which of them would be the first to suffer with the rashes, the bloody vomiting, wrenching, painful death caused by her yellow fever. And if their captain would wonder how they contracted it.

"The men stopped grabbing at her clothes and paused. When one man accused him of lying just to have her himself, he tore the back of her dress wide open, exposing her bare back to the sailors. He showed them a large red streak running down her back and told them it was just the beginning. He told them with this kind of woman, it would lead to yellow fever, smallpox, and scabies. He told them this woman only stalked the village at night when others were safe at home.

"When he told them to have their way with her, she slapped him so hard, he said it made his face numb. Lars turned around and left. He just walked away, leaving Clare holding on tightly to her ripped dress, trying to remain somewhat covered.

"Clare said the three sailors just stood there not knowing what to do next. She stood staring as Lars walked into the shadows from where he had come. She was clinging to the remnants of what had once been a somewhat modest dress, now bare on the back and only barely covering the front. Like the raiders, she didn't know what to do either.

"The two raiders looked to the apparent leader who they referred to as Scotty. He finally motioned for his companions to leave. He looked at Clare up and down.

He looked at his hands, and questioned if she infected them. 'I need rum,' he said, 'for my hands and my head.'

"Standing alone now, half naked, Clare said she was in shock. As the sailors rounded a building and were out of site, Lars approached with a cloak and gently wrapped it around her. When she released the grip on her dress to pull the cloak tight, the remnants of her dress hit the ground.

"When he asked her if she had some place to go, she pointed out she had no clothes to go anywhere. He offered to bring her here."

Violet interjected. "We believe how Clare tells the story more than Lars. When he offered to take her home, she told us she said to him, 'You're not afraid of my yellow fever, my smallpox, my scabies or any of the other infections fatal diseases a woman like me might carry? You made me out to be a common dirty whore.'"

"Lars' response tells you a lot about my brother. He said to her, 'If they believed you were a whore, they would have finished what they started. I made you out to be a sick, infectious, dangerous tramp. That's all.'"

"That's all?" Clare said.

"I would have loved to watch this interchange," Elen said. "He claimed victory, saying to her, 'It worked, didn't it? You've kept your virtue, your assailants left, and unless you are coming with me, you will stand there naked, because that cloak is coming with me.'

"He brought her here. I got her dressed and over the next number of months they saw each other frequently and made big plans for a new life in the New World."

"So what was the rash?" Elizabeth asked.

Elen explained, "Lars has, well, Lars is… he's a genius. There's not much he can't learn. This all happened during his toxicology phase. With a friend up in Sheffield, he created some ointment that irritates the skin immediately. Mostly it was harmless, except that it acts fast and makes you miserable. And with a little help from another lotion he made up, it goes away just as quickly."

Violet added a detail. "When he tore her dress, he spread the cream on her back."

"When I challenged him on using Clare as a genie pig, he claimed he had to make it real. He offered to use his antidote to clear it up. I stopped him right there. I put the antidote cream on her back," Elen said.

Elizabeth's mind struggled to find relevance in this story. Was Violet trying to get Elizabeth to become attracted to Jack? If she knew Jack was healing from a gunshot wound she inflicted, would she then share this charming story about how two lovers fell in love after the woman shot the man? No. Her mind finally decided. The story is about raiders, marauders, the very pirates who killed her mother and took her sister.

"Clare and Lars, where are they now?" Elizabeth asked.

"This part of the story is less fulfilling," Elen said. "Lars went from toxicology to chemistry, to metallurgy and then horology. His varied interests each exposed his uncanny ability to learn quickly. His keen understanding of people and subtle wit made him a friend to all, which made it easy to get others to teach him each of his new passions.

"Lars learned about a clock maker from Doncaster. His new fascination with keeping time began when he met a ship's captain who had purchased a pocket watch in Sheffield. He traveled there to learn from a clock maker turned metallurgist by the name of Huntsman. He became involved with Huntsman's brother and the brother's friend in a scheme to establish a cutlery manufacturing business in the New World.

"After just a few days in Sheffield, Lars met and worked with another clock maker by the name of Mudge, and as Lars learned how the movements of watches worked, he saw a flaw in the lever mechanism. Within a few days, he had designed a new lever which Mudge felt would be a grand breakthrough in watch making. Mudge rewarded Lars with a small commission and a handful of beautiful signature watches they designed and built together."

Elen pulled open a drawer and lifted out a beautiful pocket watch and handed it to Elizabeth. Elizabeth's inhaled breath illustrated her approval.

"Huntsman and his friend invited Lars to join them and travel to the New World. He accepted the invitation and was certain Clare would accept his proposal of marriage and start their new life in the New World. Clare was up for the new life with Lars in the New World. She however, couldn't join him immediately and they agreed to meet in St. Johns, Antigua in the fall."

"Two years ago," added Violet.

Elen continued, "When Clare's ship arrived in St. Johns, the news that Lars' ship never arrived devastated her. 'Lost at sea,' they said. To her credit and stubbornness, Clare couldn't bring herself to believe Lars was lost, and would not someday meet her there. She stayed put, took a job as a cook in a small tavern near the port, and determined to prepare for Lars' eventual arrival."

Elen pulled and unfolded a letter from the open drawer.

"Dear Elen, no word from Lars yet, but soon. The tavern is now mine. Oh, how I wish I had your fresh vegetables. Yet, I don't know if these scurvy sailors here would appreciate them, anyway."

Elen put down the letter. "Still hopeful. Soon is an elusive word, Elizabeth. Gives hope, but not to me. I lost my brother to the sea."

I'm not afraid of the sea, Elizabeth thought. There's no use in Violet bringing me here to convince me not to sail. Elizabeth began to feel this journey to Salcombe to meet Elen was a setup to discourage her. She resented that.

"But it's not about the sea, Elizabeth." Elen interrupted Elizabeth's downward spiraling thoughts. "You're looking for your sister. I assume she didn't have a bumbling savior like my brother who kept her from humiliation and lifelong servitude."

Maybe there's more here, Elizabeth admitted to herself, nodding at Elen's words.

"Making slaves of foreign conquered peoples is an age-old abomination used for domination, subjection, and control. You need to know it takes a different type of man to rip a girl of his own kind from her home and sell her as property. It's an evil unimaginable."

This was not new to Elizabeth. She knew what kind of villainy had destroyed her family. She saw the evil in their very beings. Her hate needed no additional fuel. She continued to struggle to understand Violet's purpose of bringing her to meet Elen. It was at this point Elen connected the pieces.

"Elizabeth, the men that took your sister are animals. They've lost claim on humanity. They're unworthy of forgiveness. There's no reconciling their actions with mercy. Are you ready to confront that fact if you eventually find the monsters that took your sister?"

Elen paused, waiting for Elizabeth to absorb those thoughts. She continued, "Are you ready to be the judge, the jury, and the executioner? You cannot walk away. It will be you or them."

Another pause.

"You will yield to their power. You will become their victim with a similar fate as your sister, or you will yield to hate that will drive you to destroy them."

Another pause.

Elizabeth felt the truth wash over her. *Could she kill these men? Yes, and she must.*

"Someone must stop them!" Elizabeth said.

"Yes." Elen said softly, "Are you ready to be the one who does?"

"Justice must be satisfied! Civilization demands it," Elizabeth said quietly.

"And those that mete out justice live with that responsibility. It's hell, Elizabeth."

Where is this woman coming from? What does she know about watching your family destroyed and then letting it go?

Elen watched as Elizabeth struggled. "I've lived with that responsibility. I have blood on my hands."

Violet bowed her head, bracing for the story.

"The decisions I made were right. However, I'm not sure I was the right one to make them. Let me tell you who you're likely looking for."

Elizabeth sat silently, watching Elen with rapt attention.

"It's like a dragon snatched your sister, burned up your home, and left you singed. You've spent your life looking for the dragon that likely traded her for gold. You think if you can find the dragon, you can coerce it to tell you which monster traded the gold for your sister. If you succeed, you'll then need to rescue her from that monster. The dragon will not give up the gold; you must destroy it. The monster will not give up your sister, you'll need to steal her back, and likely over the dead body of the monster."

Elen gave Elizabeth a moment to ponder her words, then continued. "Elizabeth, I've never met a dragon, but I've cut the claws off a monster. Elizabeth, even some of our own people have become monsters. Like my Clare and your sister, humans are prizes to be sold to monsters throughout the Ottoman empire and Barbary Coast, the dragon tears apart and sells black families to the monsters right here in England. For the pretty young girls, their fate is horror.

"A local landowner bought one such black family. He sold the father to coal miners up north. Harriet, the mother, and Chloe, the young daughter, who was no more than thirteen or fourteen years old, worked the gardens and provided domestic help."

"Mrs. Calhoon, the owner's missus, was kind enough to let Chloe keep a small garden from which she gained some independence, in hope to someday purchase her family's freedom. With Harriet's help, Chloe grew the best of vegetables."

"Mr. Calhoon and his oldest boy Simon were like the devil, two monsters when it came to treating their slaves. One day I was up to their plantation, little Chloe was bruised up badly. When I asked about her, I was told to keep to my own business. I couldn't do that. Young Simon abused that young girl. Abused her bad."

"I went to the magistrate and made such a fuss they had to threaten me to let it be, after all, little Chloe was not my property and the Calhoon's had every right to treat their property as they want."

"I already hated the dragon, but watching the monsters lit a flame unquenchable in me. I tried to bring a doctor but was refused. I fumed about my helplessness for months."

"Toward the end of season, I was up to the plantation to get some of Chloe's squash. When I asked for Chloe, Harriet broke down and cried. My indignation forced it out of her. Simon took Chloe to 'teach her how other black children work the fields.' he said."

"My heart cried in anger. I insisted to know where, but Harriet forbad my interference for fear of what the Calhoon's might do. But the motion in her eyes betrayed her.

"I ran through the pasture and across the small meadow into the nearby woods. A muffled scream guided my path. When I came upon Mr. Simon abusing that young innocent girl, there was no going back. I elected myself judge, jury, and executioner."

"That young arrogant evil monster wasn't even embarrassed to be caught. He sneered at me telling me to leave them be. He should have left her alone and he should not have left his scythe in the field. I took it in both hands and with all my strength, I de-fanged a monster. Lying there in pieces, he wouldn't hurt anyone ever again. I lifted Chloe up and held her crying in my arms for the longest time. We both knew, no matter what we claimed, the truth would not protect us."

Elizabeth sat silent. Could she destroy the monster that held her sister?

Elen continued. "We buried Simon. I cleaned the scythe and left it in the nearby field. I took Chloe with me and hid her away. Even Harriet didn't know the fate of her little girl. I lied that I was unable to find Simon, and the matter played out that Simon took Chloe away and both were lost."

"Did they ever learn the truth?" Elizabeth asked. "Harriet had to know. You couldn't leave her to grieve!"

Elen looked firmly into Elizabeth's eyes. "Elizabeth, once I bloodied my hands, I could never return life to the way it was. Nor would I. The dragons and the monsters will never quit. My job as judge, jury and executioner demanded more from me."

She let Elizabeth ponder.

"Weeks passed. Harriet became so distraught, and Mrs. Calhoon, fearing what her son may have done to Harriet's little girl, agreed to sell Harriet to me to rid herself of the daily reminder."

"Shortly after I purchased Harriet, my dear brother visited and introduced Harriet and me to his new manservant and the manservant's young daughter, who he purchased from up north."

The song of a nightingale interrupted the silence of the small room. Elen stood and replenished the tea.

Elizabeth watched Elen closely, struggling to understand why Elen ever thought what she did could be wrong. Simon deserved to die. And so did the dragon who destroyed her family and the monster that had her sister.

Elen set her cup down, folded her hands on her lap and waited.

Minutes passed, then as a kindly grandmother would, talking to an innocent granddaughter, she took Elizabeth's hands in hers. "Elizabeth, what I did saved a little family. It also destroyed another family. Until I meet God Himself, I fear I won't ever have the peace to know if what I did was right. If you ever find your sister, and I will pray that you do, I hope you will find peace in the decisions you will be forced to make."

Chapter Thirty~Two

Elevating Esther and Leilyn from the stable of slaves to precious cargo
leaves Lord Rudy and me with a crew of eleven slaves. I am fortunate,
again, to have a first mate with extraordinary skills of acquisition. He
chose the twenty of Avery's slaves that seemed to have the most potential
to enhance our journey. And that is without his knowledge of what our
journey would entail. Truthfully, I did not understand what it would
entail until I met, personally, our cargo. We will take them home.

Since we are technically in Esther's family's ship, we let her rename
it. Appropriately we are now sailing north easterly on the *Caspara*, by
definition, 'she who is the keep of treasure.' The *Caspara* has no slave
hold, and it doesn't need one. These men chose freely to sail with us. We
offered them freedom. They could accompany us or they could stay on
Bourbon. If they stayed on Bourbon, they would be caught and sold to
the next slave ship. Of the twenty slaves Rudy helped escape the Fancy,
he traded five to the Falcon in exchange for our passage. When two left
the protection of the jungle, someone captured them and two others
refused to join us on our journey. Their fate is certain.

It's Black Moses, my new boatswain, who made negotiation with our
slaves possible. Moses is a tribal chief from Rwanda, taken captive
by deceptive traders and sold to a Dutch slaver. He and two other
slaves escaped in the commotion of a pirate raid. They killed his
two companions in the attempt. Trying to return to Rwanda, slavers
captured him again in Tanzania and returned him to the slave markets.
Being a large and powerful man, he was purchased and condemned

to a galley ship. Again, he escaped, overpowering and killing five of the crew members during a storm. In the attempt, he was picked up by another ship he hoped would be friendly. They were not. Moses was aboard the Falcon on his way to the slave markets in Madagascar when Rudy recruited him to our cause, as Lord Rudy tells it.

When Rudy heard him threaten a guard's life, in English, Rudy sold the story that ol' Moses wasn't heading for the slave markets but was heading to the gallows for killing five different masters and twenty guards in the past six months. With a few pieces of eight on the side, the guard forgot to secure Moses' chains. Rudy, along with fifteen of Avery's twenty slaves, including Moses, slipped off the *Falcon* just minutes before the warship showed up.

I promised Moses his freedom anytime he wants it, but begged his help for the next few weeks as a translator for my crew. He flatly stated he would stay, and if I betray him, he will tear my head off with his bare hands. I believe him.

- Hinch

Newton Ferrers, England - 1748

"She's gone, Jack," Violet said as he entered the kitchen. "She left this."

Violet pushed a small bag toward Jack. It jingled in his hand as he lifted it and pulled out a note.

"Violet, I thank you for yesterday. I know what I must do. Here is enough to cover our stay and to get Jack smartly attired before you get him back home to the university." — Elizabeth

Jack feigned offense. "Smartly attired?"

Violet laughed with him. "You know where she's going?"

"The New World. Into the belly of the beast," Jack said, folding the note and tucking it back into the small bag.

"And we'll get you smartly attired and back home?" Violet asked.

"I think you know better." Jack said. "If I can get Captain Bentley to sail without her, my job is done. My ribs will not let me overtake her on horse. Can you get me to a ship in Plymouth?"

"I can do better. We'll get you there smartly attired." Her whole countenance made it evident Violet enjoyed being thrown into the intrigue of these past few days. A welcome diversion from the loneliness.

Bristol, England - 1748

Elizabeth pushed the door aside. This was the third tavern she visited that evening. Each tavern progressively became more filled with debaucheries. What did she expect? The closer she got to the harbor, the easier for the sailors to find what they had missed out at sea. Ale, rum, perfume, and body odor blended to give the senses the duty to either escape all together or sort out the one to cling to. The large hall was pungent.

This tavern was more crowded. A young woman approached her when she entered. A test, Elizabeth thought.

Will this woman believe I'm the man I hope my clothes project?

So far in her journey, the tailor's artistry never failed. All she had to do was keep her hat on tight, her vest buttoned, and not say too much.

Her confidence improved with each encounter. Besides, she'd now shot three men, but only one fatally; outsmarted the son of a lord, escaped capture twice, and now stood in one of Bristol's popular taverns, propositioned by a pretty young girl who could not tell she was a woman.

Just don't get in a brawl. A clap from one of these men and you will go tumbling as you did the first time you got careless.

She patted the pistol strapped to her side. Carefully scanning the many patrons, she wondered, which ones were here waiting for their two dead kidnappers and Jack?

"Aside, wretch." The booming voice proceeded the jolt by a fraction of a second. Elizabeth stumbled. If not for the young woman she'd have hit the ground. She got her balance, let go of the girl, and watched three men bully their way into the heart of the tavern.

"We're gone with the tide. Drink up swine, and get onboard, lest you wallow your miserable lives here in hell."

The man spewed several other demeaning commands before turning to leave. Elizabeth's eyes caught his. There was no light, no color, just evil. Chills filled her spine. The hate surfaced immediately, replacing the initial fear. She had seen those eyes before. She stood motionless, shocked, caught completely off guard.

He marched past her, back out into the growing darkness. How long had she stood there frozen?

"Hell? This is heaven," A sailor said, raising his cup and pouring its contents down his throat.

"Hell?" another added. "Sailing under Scotty is hell!"

"Maybe I'll stay here and sail with," the sailor paused looked at the buxom girl on his lap, "Wat's yer name wench?" Elizabeth didn't hear her reply. "With Lizzy," he shouted.

Scotty! She thawed immediately. Scotty? Her mind flashed back to her conversation with Elen. Scotty was the name of the raider accosting Clare.

"Your hands are so soft." The gentle voice brought Elizabeth back to the present. She hadn't noticed the young woman was holding her hand.

"Oh, you poor thing, get out of here, run as far as you can!" Elizabeth said. She pulled her hand free and charged from the tavern. Which ship was sailing with the tide? She followed several other sailors as they left the tavern.

"The belly of the beast?" she whispered as she stood at the edge of the harbor and watched sailors pile into small boats and row out to a large ship silhouetted by the sliver of light winking good night to the shore.

Elizabeth stopped one sailor struggling to keep his cap on, and asked, "What ship is that, and who's the captain?"

"Fool. The *Chawbuck*. There's no captain. Just Nakhoda!" The man joined the sailors in the last boat headed to the ship.

✝ ✝ ✝

Onboard the Chawbuck - 1748

Onboard the *Chawbuck*, Krist watched the last of the crew scurry up the ladder. On shore stood a lone figure silhouetted by the light of the tavern.

"Who did we leave behind?" he asked.

"Don't know him. Not one of ours," Scotty said.

The figure turned and walked back toward the tavern.

"Just as well," Krist said. "He walks like a woman."

The two stood watching as the figure disappeared.

"Anything from our two friends from London?" Krist asked.

"Nothing. Coach and all disappeared," Scotty said.

Chapter Thirty~Three

Journal Entry: December 1695 - Indian Ocean
Alexander Hincher - Ship's Captain

If the winds continue favorably, we will reach the coast of India within three weeks, possibly sooner. This is the fastest ship I've ever sailed with.

Lord Rudy and Moses are quite the pair. More like jousting partners than master and slave. Continually teasing and teaching each other and training the slave crew. My crew required more medical care than I previously thought. Though they looked stout, malnutrition and other maladies had weakened them. The *Caspara* is remarkably well equipped for a ship's surgeon. If the *Fancy* were this well-equipped, I could have made the lives of the crew less miserable.

With the proper food and medical care our crew has taken to the sea with vigor, with Rudy and Moses' training; the crew has purpose. Because of the way slave owners treat slaves and consider them as property, I feared a slave would not take to freedom, and initiative, and self-discipline. They prove my thinking completely wrong. My slaves, now freemen, act like men. They respond to instruction, to training, and they accept correction. They also think and solve problems once they felt the freedom to do so.

- Hinch

Liverpool, England - 1748

Jack regretted not returning to Sheffield or even Chester to learn how Violet's father-in-law, David Creagh, and his relationship with associates in Sheffield might somehow connect him to John and Victoria. His analytical mind scrambled to connect the pieces. The winning thought though, was: *The Bringhurst will be sailing and I've got to get a report for Captain Bentley to give to Captain Remington, and keep Elizabeth off the Emerald.*

It felt good to be dressed smartly once again. He strutted across the deck. It impressed Jack how quickly the tailor fitted him out. Violet certainly knew her way around. During the two days he waited in Plymouth for the ship to Liverpool, she arranged for his outfit, passage to Liverpool, and then back to London. If weather permitted, he could be back to the university, whole and smartly attired.

The boots needed some time to mold to his feet, but the trousers and shirt complemented his old vest smartly. The barber trimmed up his hair and beard. Jack laughed at himself for how good it felt. He wondered if this was what Elizabeth envisioned her investment would produce.

Tomorrow afternoon he would be in Liverpool. His plan to thwart Elizabeth's embarking was taking shape. He didn't know how well she knew the town. The one day he had hoped to see her again earlier in the summer, she eluded him so he knew he couldn't chance just bumping into her. With the handful of Nakhoda's men and the local constabulary still on the lookout for ol' Denn's killer, he regretted Violet didn't have her tailor turn him into someone else.

He knew it was up to him to keep her off the ship. At gunpoint? Abduction? Distraction? Persuasion? Seduction? Jack settled on self-preservation—the truth. If he couldn't simply tell all and let reason and her sense of self-preservation keep her off the *Emerald,* then what else could he do? But he had to find her first.

Relief washed over him as the sloop entered the harbor, and the *Emerald* came into view. His tense shoulders relaxed and breathing became easier as they did. In the many weeks since he was in Liverpool, there was no knowing if plans had changed and the ship had sailed early. By his best calculations, he had only one day to find Elizabeth, deliver the report to Captain Bentley for his uncle, and be on the *Cunningham*, a merchant ship returning to London. He could do this, he repeatedly told himself.

Harsh, un-deliberate movements reminded him his ribs were still healing, but he'd made short breaths a habit so he moved and worked mostly pain free. His first stop, the *Emerald*, was only a hundred feet away when he saw the local constable walk down the gangplank. If he recognized that face, Jack knew the constable would recognize him, even if it was in poor light when they last saw each other. Jack ducked into a small shop and watched as the constable walked up and down the docks. How many others around here would know his face?

Is he still looking for me?

"May I?" Jack said to the shopkeeper as he pulled a cloak over his shoulder as if trying it for size. He stepped out of the shop for a better view and saw the constable watching other passengers leave the very sloop he'd left. The constable was one passenger too late.

Jack returned the cloak and hurried into the alley, away from the dock. He would start his search for a tall white mare. There it stood in the third livery he visited. It arrived the night before, he was told.

So she beat me here by a day.

When he asked about the woman who brought it in, the smithy yelled from the forge, "Warnt no woman, t'was a man, kinda weakly looking, but she'd bin rode hard this one."

"How old?" Jack asked.

"Six, maybe seven," the smithy swiped grime from his hands.

"The man, not the horse," Jack said.

The smithy smiled and winked at Jack. "Twenty? Thirty? Forty? Don't matter, really. We let him a nice Cleveland Bay weeks ago, and he returned this." He pointed to the mare. "Good trade for us."

He? She had a man rent her a horse? Of course, she would have accomplices. Maybe her financier? But who is working for whom? Jack decided he should be grateful Elizabeth has no more need of him.

I'll let him worry about her.

Jack's decision to abandon Elizabeth lasted only moments. Curiosity, rather than honor, turned the decision. Besides the Cunningham didn't sail until Thursday.

"You say the same man rented and returned?" A nod was all he got; the smithy returned to the forge. The young man tending to the horses shrugged.

With each alley, each inn, each shop, Liverpool felt tense. It was weeks since the killings.

Is this feeling just me?

Twice he neared the docks. Both times he spotted the constable. There was no way to get to the *Emerald* and get his report to Captain Bentley's hands. It must be done tonight, he concluded.

He worked his way back to the Nookery. He expected it to be boarded up possibly with rough-hewn timbers over the windows and door to keep out— keep out who? He wondered. But instead, it stood wide open.

Looking all directions, he was back inside. The limited light from the door and single window revealed enough to see nothing had been done other than the removal of Mistress Lonnie and her patron. The few books remaining on the shelves would be interesting if he were traveling to the South Pacific; a subject that once fascinated Jack since it seemed to be the last frontier for ocean-going explorers. He bent to pick through a handful of books lying next to the turned over chair once reserved for ol' Denn.

Jack recognized the titles on a couple of them, standard fare for students studying maritime history. Jack turned Denn's chair upright and sat down with the one book unlike any he would expect to find in the Nookery. "The Safavid Dynasty."

He opened it to a highly marked section, "The rightful heirs to the Safavid throne," he read aloud. The light was too dim. He moved over to the only other chair set upright, which was next to the only window. He sat for only a moment. His curiosity didn't justify the risk being caught at the scene where weeks before they nearly killed him while he was searching for Denn's notebook.

He tucked the book under his arm and stepped back into the alley.

Chapter Thirty-Four

My anxiety for our safety lessens as we approach the Indian shores, but I have seen what men on a pirate ship can and will do. Three days ago, we spotted what appeared to be the Pearl in pursuit. It quickly disappeared, either because of our speed or they saw the flag under which we sail.

The food has surpassed any eaten in the past few years. A well-stocked galley and a very skillful Leilyn has proven to turn this journey into more a pleasure cruise than an escape. The only real obstacle Leilyn faces are the distractions caused by Rudy. More than once Moses has threatened Rudy to leave Leilyn alone so she could prepare our meals. I reminded Rudy I own her and he needs to leave her alone.

On a comfortable ship in a favorable wind, a sailor's life often becomes boring. On this journey, it has been anything but. Esther has proven to be an incredible hostess. Her care and attention to each of those on board is most remarkable. We tease Rudy for not having brought the women's wardrobe along, but we don't complain how these two Persian women can make a pair of men's britches and shirt look so good. Their beauty is not lost on any of us men, but Lord Rudy doesn't even try to hide it. Yet, his admiration for beauty is more childlike than lustful.

Raised as an heir to both an Indian and Persian throne, Esther is very accomplished. She speaks fluent English with a most delicate accent, French with that same flair, Arabic, which I don't understand at all, and Persian, which I am trying to learn myself out of my fascination for Esther's culture.

- Hinch

Liverpool, England - 1748

"Oh, Jack… Jack, Jack, Jack. What are you doing back in Liverpool? And what, may I ask, is that tucked under your arm?" Elizabeth whispered as she watched him step from the Nookery. "And in plain daylight?"

Her desire to explore the Nookery needed to wait. This time, she would not assume his destination. She followed as discretely as possible. His movements were much more guarded this time and he constantly looked around.

He knows he's a suspect and people are looking for him.

Elizabeth followed him down toward the docks. He made a quick check and darted back into the alley, nearly catching her. She already saw the constable and his men watching those coming and going. Did they know he would be back in Liverpool? Was it Jack they were looking for?

She followed until she saw Jack enter a small inn—her inn.

Is he looking for me?

After many minutes, he didn't exit. Circling the building, she entered through the back entrance which she used with the landlady's permission the last time she stayed here.

The landlady welcomed her with open arms. "I wish I had known you were coming, Miss Farrow. A gentleman just rented your old room for the night. Will you be here in Liverpool long? He said he is leaving tomorrow. Tonight you may stay with me."

"Not to worry. I appreciate your generosity. I've made arrangements with a friend. I just wanted to stop in and say hello," Elizabeth said. "But you could do me a favor."

"Anything." The landlady was still holding both of Elizabeth's hands.

"When I was here before, you so kindly warned me I was being followed. The man upstairs is the man following me," Elizabeth said cautiously.

The landlady's eyes widened with fear.

"He's harmless," Elizabeth reassured her. "But a nuisance. He is a cousin of mine who is insistent on my returning home to marry his brother."

Every muscle tightened on the woman's face. She squinted her eyes while gritted teeth showed between cringing lips. Elizabeth could not ask for a more disgusted look on the landlady's face.

"So, I would just as soon not let him know I am back. But I would love to visit with you again sometime at the bakery." Elizabeth said. "I will come by again before I leave."

† † †

"I'm sure she will." Jack muttered to himself standing in the dark stairway. "It's my turn now." He shuffled up to the balcony, hoping to see what direction Elizabeth might be headed. He watched her cross the narrow cobblestone street and enter the inn that, for all intents and purposes, could be this inn's twin.

On his way to the room, two young women passed him in the narrow dark hallway. Their intent with another resident of the inn was unmistakable. The idea was irresistible. Jack quickly returned to the hallway to find the two waiting at their client's door.

"Ladies," Jack said, "will you please do me the favor of helping a stranger learn the secrets of the harbor?"

Apparently eager to help a potential future client, the two ladies followed Jack to the balcony of his room. Hoping Elizabeth was already in position to spy, he took advantage of their eagerness. He asked about the ships, the shops, the sailors, and the constable, who was still surveying the many passengers and crews along the docks. They pointed and giggled and talked and flirted. If only he could see Elizabeth's reactions now. After a few minutes, he put his arms around both ladies and escorted them back into the room. He closed the door with a quick glance and a hope to see if he might catch Elizabeth watching. He ushered the two ladies back into the hallway, and on their way, thanked them for their help and chuckled as he hoped Elizabeth saw it all.

† † †

Elizabeth slammed her window shut. She had seen enough. *Those two harlots will keep Jack busy the rest of the day.* The disgust she felt for him right then surprised her. The disgust turned to disappointment, then to anger.

She had become appreciative of the riding outfit the tailor so masterfully created for her. It was time to refresh it and secure a new dress before sailing to the New World.

The tailor's giant smile needed no words as Elizabeth entered the haberdashery.

The tables turned; Jack opened a small window giving him a clear view of the room across the road where he'd seen Elizabeth's shadow watching him. After a few minutes watching, he saw she took the bait. She left the inn and hurried up the cobblestone street. Using the back entrance he learned could be very helpful, he followed her.

She wound her way through the shops and markets, and without the slightest concern, he watched her enter a haberdashery. Large windows covered the front of it, making it easy to see all going on inside. It also made it easy for them to see him. Jack ducked behind a cart loaded with barrels being loaded from a mill.

The haberdasher greeted Elizabeth in so friendly a manner, Jack realized they knew each other well.

Her accomplice? Her employer? Or does he work for her? Certainly her financier, Jack concluded.

Shifting from side to side to stay hidden as young men loaded barrels onto the cart, Jack watched as the tailor took Elizabeth by the hand and led her to the back of the shop. The two disappeared. *A lover?*

The cart now loaded, drove away leaving Jack standing in full view. With the tailor and Elizabeth in some back bordello, his eye re-focused on the beautiful suit displayed in the window. As he approached to admire it, two voices, one he recognized from many weeks earlier cried out, "Stay right there!" The constable, not twenty feet away, reached to pull a pistol.

Jack darted so quickly to run, he stumbled in pain. He'd been so careful the past many days to protect his shattered rib, he had almost forgotten it. Recovering from the shock of the pain, he turned a corner, and at the fullest run he could endure, wound from alley to alley. Oh, how he wished he knew this town. His only hope, with the constable away from the docks, was to get to the *Emerald*. Could he do it without it becoming a trap?

The sound of footsteps on cobblestone behind him helped him forget the ribs until heavy breathing added to the pain. Jack neared the docks and felt he had no choice. Plunging into the harbor, he dove as deeply as he could. Searing pain made it nearly impossible to hold his breath. He had to find something to hide under or behind. The shadow of a small craft above him heading away from the dock would be his only hope. Jack surfaced next to the hull of a skiff being rowed out to a large ship anchored away from the dock. Fortunately, the oarsmen were too busy to notice they'd picked up a human barnacle.

Jack couldn't see past the skiff to the dock and didn't know if the constable was close enough to see him dive into the harbor or if he was still searching the town. Yet, he regretted the officials now knew he was back in Liverpool.

The skiff reached its destination. Its oarsmen tied up and began unloading supplies on a large ship. Forcing will against pain, Jack took a deep breath and dove. He surfaced on the opposite side of the ship. With a deep breath, he could float without too much effort. It was taking the deep breath that hurt. After a moment, he made it around the ship to the anchor chain. With an arm wrapped around it, he let his body settle.

Who was the man with the constable? He'd seen him before as well. As Jack's body relaxed, it also cooled. He knew he'd need to get out and get dry before too long. He could certainly swim, but he knew they would catch him if he didn't wait until dark. His mind raced to put the pieces together.

He got it. The pieces fell into place.

The man with the constable! One of Nakhoda's men. They knew ol' Denn instructed a young woman to get to the New World to meet ol' Denn's partner. It was now evident they figured she would sail on the Emerald which sails tomorrow. They also thought ol' Denn betrayed that partner, so when I came along and foiled the abduction, I'm in league with ol' Denn's betrayal. Nakhoda's men know I didn't kill ol' Denn. Is the constable one of them or just being used?

Jack tried to climb the chain. The strain on his ribs was too much. Though it had only been a few hours, his body felt like it had absorbed the entire ocean. He wondered if he'd sink the minute he let go. Finally, the sun called it a day and set. Before total darkness set in, Jack swam around the ship to see what might be happening on shore. Too much activity.

He spotted the *Emerald*. One light shown on deck and there was another he hoped was the captain's cabin. The sleeping quarters where Jack had spent a few nights during his fateful visit to Liverpool had a porthole large enough for a man. He also knew a change of clothes he'd left behind awaited him. If he could get close enough to see if it was open, he might scale the side to safety.

His wet clothes added so much weight he shed the shirt, trousers and boots. He was grateful his vest remained in the inn. Did Elizabeth realize he hadn't been in the room all afternoon? Did she think he and his female companions were making their visit an over night experience? He was too tired to smile, but his lips couldn't resist.

Hand over hand, and with help from bare feet, Jack inched his way up the side of the ship. The cold water was a mixed blessing. The numbness it caused stifled much of the pain but made it hard to tell if his toes were holding on to anything secure. His numb and bare feet finally met the floor of the empty sleeping quarters in his former cabin.

Quietly, he inched his way to the door and looked toward the captain's cabin. Was he alone? Jack wondered. Do I barge in mostly naked? No. In the darkness, he rummaged until he found the bag housing his clothes.

Blessed be Captain Bentley for not throwing them out. Is he still expecting me to sail with him tomorrow? How many times did I assure him I wasn't? I could just hide out right here.

That wasn't an option. Dry and dressed, Jack quietly went to Captain Bentley's cabin, and with a soft knock, pushed the door ajar and peeked inside. No sign of life.

Captain William Bentley's cabin was spotlessly clean, yet cluttered with a life's collection of artifacts gathered from what seemed like every port on the globe. Finely carved ivory from Africa, beautifully woven silks from India, Chinese blankets, golden Inca statues, weapons of every kind, indigenous clothing from countless tribes and peoples, and his favorite, a bone whaling knife with the scrimshaw walrus tusk hand carved by the chief of an Inuit tribe. The stories his sailors told about how the captain acquired these treasures were treasures of their own. The room was like a monument to a mariner's life adventurously lived.

Jack spent many hours in this room during the summers he was with his uncle. Captain Bentley and Captain Remington were as close as two men could be, short of being twins.

"Jack?" The familiar voice both startled and calmed in that one word.

He turned and faced his dear friend. Captain Bentley's smile was a mix of pleasure and curiosity, but the raised brows asked the questions.

"I see you found your bag." He motioned to Jack's outfit.

"Thank you."

"It's you they're looking for isn't it?" the captain asked.

"By name?" Jack asked.

The captain shook his head. "Just by description. You killed ol' Denn?"

"Captain, no. It's a long painful story. But the short version is, ol' Denn was tied up with some Persian captain they call Nakhoda. He offered to deliver Miss Elizabeth Farrow to them to pay some debt. He changed his mind and got himself killed. She still thinks she must sail with you tomorrow, but it will get her killed or worse. I'm here to keep her off your ship."

"Don't know if we can do that, but that is a story I'd like to hear," Captain Bentley said.

"As you can see, my options are limited. I've got to get off the *Emerald,* get the full report I've prepared for Captain Remington back to you, keep her away from this ship so you can sail, then get myself back to London where father and the university expect me to begin the fall session of classes."

"All while they patrol the docks and markets?" The captain added, "The only thing you can possibly do now is stay right here. I'll find and send someone."

"Tonight?" Jack asked.

"Where is she staying? I'll go," Captain Bentley said.

"Levendar's Inn, the balcony room, right building. If she knows I'm behind it, she'll refuse to stay." Then, Jack added, while the captain buttoned up his coat, "There's a book in a satchel along with my vest you'll find in my balcony room of the left building. Would you be so kind?"

The captain left Jack standing barefoot in his museum of a cabin. Jack slipped up to the main deck and watched as Captain Bentley passed lamp after lamp on the dock. Jack realized they added these since he enjoyed the darkness of the docks several weeks ago. A man stepped out from behind a post and joined the captain, confirming the patrol would be out all night.

He tried to visualize which lights might be his and Elizabeth's on the small rise. Would she be there, or maybe still with her haberdasher?

An hour passed, then two. Lights across the hillside went dark, one by one as time wore on. The captain should be back by now. Jack saw no other movement on the docks. How many other patrol members were out watching?

Should I chance it, leaving the ship to check on the captain?

He rushed back to the cabin, this time with a small lamp. He rummaged, looking for something to put on his bare feet. Nothing.

Can I borrow something from Captain Bentley? No.

He heard the hurried footsteps on deck. Fearful the patrol might be with the captain he hesitated to rush above decks.

"Jack!"

That was all he needed to hear. He rushed up the steps.

"Your problems just got bigger." The captain was panting. "Miss Farrow was not in the room you told me. The constable's man insisted he accompany me to the inn. The landlady let us in, only to find a member of the patrol lying dead in his own blood, the room terribly disturbed."

Jack could hardly believe a word of it. "The landlady knew nothing except she saw a slender man with a satchel over his shoulder rush down the stairs and out into the darkness."

"No sign of Miss Farrow?" Jack asked with a panic in his voice.

"A dress hung on the post and other clothes were scattered on the floor. From the landlady's description, it was Miss Farrow's things. The landlady said the woman's cousin was hunting for her and suspected he took Miss Farrow and killed the man when he tried to protect her."

"Her cousin?" Jack said.

"She said the cousin was staying in the identical room in the left building. We rushed over and found it empty except for this book…" the captain held it up, "this satchel, and this vest."

Jack couldn't believe his ears or his eyes, and something smelled fishy about this entire story. He took the items from the captain. "I can't thank you enough captain."

If only I had some boots.

"You didn't tell me Miss Farrow was your cousin. And I'm having a hard time seeing how you killed one of the constable's men in her room, swam to the opposite side of the *Emerald*, and climbed through the porthole after kidnapping your cousin."

"Yes, I'm the cousin. All part of the long story that gets longer." Jack resigned himself and plopped down on a crate yet to be loaded into the cargo hold.

"I know that man, the assassin. Believe it or not, he's a tailor, a haberdasher. He's in league with her for some nefarious yet innocent looking scheme. Maybe she's being used, a pawn, or maybe she's even the mastermind and yet a superb actress." Jack said, head down in his hands.

"You think so?" the captain asked.

"I don't know." Jack looked up, eyes searching a dark sky for answers.

"When the landlady described the cousin, she described you. She was less certain about the man she saw dart from Miss Farrow's building. As far as officials care, it's you. Put one more notch in your belt."

"Notch in my belt? Knot in my noose!" Jack said, standing. "I need to go to the haberdashery. Are there any boots on this ship?"

Both the captain and Jack knew men were watching every ship. There was no way to get off and on without being seen. Unless you're willing to take your clothes off.

Jack shared his plan with the captain, who reluctantly agreed. He left the satchel, complete with the report of what he'd learned from Denn's notebook, along with the book about the Safavid Dynasty he took from the Nookery.

"With what I saw at the inn, are you certain Miss Farrow isn't safer here with me? You are," the captain said.

"With you, yes. It's when you get her there, then no. Thank you, captain. I hope to see you upon your return if you are ever back in London. This may be my last visit to Liverpool."

With necessities in a small watertight bag, Jack went the way he came.

Out of view of any patrol, Jack climbed out of the water well away from the docks, pulled on tight black trousers and shirt, tucked his hair into an uncomfortable black cap too tight for his head and black slippers Jack was certain had been fit for a child. He crossed several fields and passed farm houses before circling back toward the town. In total darkness and from this direction, no one would be looking. He crept up to the haberdashery. Placing his hand to his brow and the glass, he tried to see if there was any life inside. Nothing. Wouldn't she come here for hiding? Or was she actually kidnapped?

Jack stepped across the small road to see if he could see any movement in the apartment above the shop. One small light flickered behind a pulled curtain. He snuck back past the Nookery and tried to follow the vague directions to ol' Denn's house Lonnie had shared with him those many weeks ago.

Wandering in the darkness provided no hope. Keeping close to the shadows cast from the various street lamps, he made his way back to the tailor's shop, his only hope to find Elizabeth again. The inn was under too much attention; he was certain she'd not return there.

Sunlight broke over the horizon, bringing with it a new set of dangers. The light from the tailor's apartment remained on the rest of the night. Jack waited and hoped. The truth, he kept telling himself. She will listen to the truth. A lamp flickered on inside the haberdashery. Through the glass he saw her.

Elizabeth followed the tailor out from where Jack saw the tailor lead her the day before. The rich dark green split overdress was laced at the top and contrasted sharply with the white blouse and underskirt. Jack saw she was dressed to travel. The tailor helped her into a long black hooded cloak. She captivated him.

The sound of an approaching cart broke his concentration. He realized he was standing in the middle of the road. He stepped back out of sight. Morning broke, the streets were alive again. How could he get to her? Dressed like a corpse, all in black, how could he solicit her attention without drawing attention from everyone else, especially the patrol?

A small carriage pulled up to the haberdashery. Its valet opened the door and loaded a trunk on the small platform in its rear. He then helped Elizabeth in. She wished the tailor goodbye, and the carriage was off. With no other options, Jack leapt into the seat beside her.

"Please, please, it's me and I mean you no harm," Jack said pulling off the cap, and letting his matted hair fall to his shoulders.

Stunned, Elizabeth called back the scream she so nearly let loose. "Jack? What are you doing here?"

"Miss Farrow, don't go. You can't go to the New World!" Jack wanted to yell it, but held back. He wanted to ask a hundred questions, to find out about this mysterious woman who rescued him, who paid to make sure he was smartly attired, who provided a way for him to return home, who now was heading to her death or worse—servitude.

Her eyes continued scanning him from top to bottom. It was obvious to Jack she was struggling to make sense of this strange visitor.

"Miss Farrow, several weeks ago, I was here in Liverpool. On assignment from a dear relative, I became acquainted with an old man whom this relative thought had information to help him find an old friend. An innocent request. The old man was connected with some very bad people who were taking him to meet someone he did not want to meet."

Jack paused, looked deeply into her eyes, took a deep breath and continued, seeing he had her full attention. He saw they were approaching the dock. He had to speed it up.

"Miss Farrow, I interrupted them. In the scuffle, I killed one of the men but the other stabbed this old man to the heart and fled before I could stop him. As this old man lay dying in my arms, he gave me some papers and begged me to keep 'her' from traveling to the New World."

The carriage reached the dock and stopped directly in front of the *Emerald*. When the valet stepped down, Jack saw the constable approaching the carriage. Jack dove under the seat. The valet removed her trunk and set it on the ground.

Elizabeth quickly stepped out and met the constable before he could reach the carriage.

"Good morning, constable. Would you be so kind as to help me with my trunk?" She led him to the back of the carriage where it rested.

Nodding, the constable picked up the trunk and began carrying it up the gangplank.

"I've left my gloves; I'll be right with you." She hurried back to the carriage.

"I've practically given my life and now risk my career to protect you from sailing," Jack whispered. "The old man begged me and the 'her' he referred to is you! He knew you are in danger."

Elizabeth froze. Hearing the footsteps approaching, she turned and took the constable by the arm. "Thank you so very much. To find chivalry is refreshing."

The carriage rolled away. The constable offered his arm and escorted Elizabeth onboard the *Emerald*.

Chapter Thirty~Five

Journal Entry: December 1695 - Tanzania, Eastern Africa
Alexander Hincher - Ship's Surgeon

Though perfectly clear for her, I still struggled to piece together Esther's family tree. An Indian princess is her mother and a Persian prince is her father. One grandfather is the Mughal Emperor who married a Persian princess who is the direct descendent of the first Safavid Shah. Her other grandfather was Shah Abbas II, Shah of all Persia.

Even as I write this, I confuse myself. Regardless, Esther is an heir to two empires, and one of them wants her out of the way. What the other empire wants is unclear. That is what we will find out in a few short days.

We are sitting offshore in a small inlet, planning how to get our passengers home. This is not a simple feat. Esther has been insistent, ever since we left Bourbon, that we not return her home. Because I know best and am so damned stubborn, I never listened to what she was saying. Being my captive, she was fearful of me knowing the truth. I finally understood.

- Hinch

Liverpool, England - 1748

When the carriage arrived back at a livery, Jack slipped out from under the seat. Checking for anyone watching, he hopped to the ground. On the carriage floor sat a small pouch tied with a pink ribbon. It jingled in his hand when he picked it up. "Oh, sweet Miss Farrow," he said.

He darted from the yard into cover behind a barn. He opened the pouch. There was plenty to get him smartly attired and back to London. He sat down, a tired failure. He broke an oath given to a dying man. What he learned from ol' Denn's notebook convinced him Miss Farrow was certain to become another member of an Ottoman harem, if she lived that long. What drove her to risk her life?

No, it isn't a risk, it's suicide.

Slowly, he shook his head back and forth. Nothing could change what had happened. She was Captain Bentley's problem now. Maybe he would kick her off the ship. But no, not even delusion could deliver any hope of that. His thoughts wouldn't settle.

Jack got up, considering where he could safely get smartly attired.

Should I try a ship back to London or go overland?

Returning the black cap to cover his hair, he made his way through the alleys and back doors to the only tailor he knew; Miss Farrow's partner. Maybe that suit in the window would fit.

A bell rang as Jack entered the haberdashery. He hoped the patrol would keep their eyes on the harbor while he got himself smartly attired.

"Welcome, may I guess you're in need of something special?" the tailor asked, looking Jack up and down.

"A dear friend of mine recommended you. He said you may be the only tailor in England who can do something respectable with this." Jack motioned from shoe to cap with one long wave.

A big grin accompanied a confident nod. "Where should we start?"

Jack lifted his foot, untied a very uncomfortable shoe, and dropped it to the ground. "Here."

The sun reached its daily apex. Jack stepped from the haberdashery confident Violet, Miss Farrow, and Anne would be impressed. Throughout his fitting, he gently probed for information that might leak the relationship the tailor had with Miss Farrow. Nothing surfaced. He stayed far away from revealing any knowledge of the killings or his knowledge of ol' Denn so as not to raise any suspicion. After all, Jack knew he fit the description of the killer perfectly.

With hat and cloak in place, a walking cane and exquisitely fitting boots, he looked like the son of a lord, like a professor of maritime studies from a highly respected university in London, like a member of the gentry—like

Jack Remington.

With a smartly wrapped package under his arm, he walked directly toward the docks. Locating the constable, Jack walked confidently up to him and took him by the hand.

"My good man," Jack said, "Will you please guide me to Captain William Bentley. I've a package and a message for him to take to my partners in the New World."

The constable offered a slight bow and walked Jack over to the gangplank of the *Emerald*. Jack recognized the constable was struggling to decide if he might be the man they hunted. Jack met and kept his eyes on the constable with confidence and borderline arrogance. Though inside, nerves wreaked havoc, Jack calmly added one more element to the ruse. He asked, "May I call on you later tonight to pay respects from Lord Hawthorne in London? Lord Hawthorne asked me to be sure to send his regards." Jack didn't know if the constable knew a Lord Hawthorne or not, or even if there were such a lord, but the constable certainly should think if Lord Hawthorne was paying respects, it could be an important meeting.

Jack bowed and marched up onto the deck of the *Emerald*. The constable stood still, mouth open, staring as Jack casually crossed the deck and disappeared from view.

Within the hour, the *Emerald* hoisted sails, raised the anchor and began a journey to the New World.

Chapter Thirty-Six

I am not convinced we are doing the smart thing returning Esther to her home. I now have what I think might be the entire story. Esther and Leilyn have been together as long as they can remember. They are like sisters, yet Leilyn has no royal blood. She is the daughter of a servant who Esther's mother took in when a man raped and murdered her mother. The Kotwal, their local magistrate, caught and executed the perpetrator. Her mother's death left Leilyn alone, and as her father was unknown, she became Esther's companion.

Esther's mother is the firstborn of Emperor Aurangzeb (the very emperor whose treasure ship we sacked). Aurangzeb married the Safavid Princess Dilras Banu Begum. Many men courted their daughter, Esther's mother, Zeb-un-Nissa though she never married.

According to Esther, she is an uncommonly talented poetess, well educated and extremely independent. Her father trusted and relied on her for her talent and wisdom. Yet her independence frustrated him. When she became pregnant with Esther, they concluded the father was none other than one of her suiters, the Shah of Iran.

When he, Shah Sileiman I, claimed fathering Esther, an awkward relationship between India and Persia continued. I can only imagine. Just as we know Emperor Aurangzeb to execute rivals to his throne, even family; it holds that the Shah secured the Persian throne the same way. These leaders kill even fathers, sons and brothers to eliminate rivals to their thrones.

Emperor Aurangzeb, we learn, imprisoned Esther's mother fourteen years ago for her unwillingness to adhere to his strict religious tenants. Not to mention his daughter's infidelity. Esther studied with the finest tutors and was free to visit the palaces and other lands. At the request of her mother, Esther and Leilyn were permitted to travel on the emperor's own treasure ship on the Hajj.

Shah Suleiman I (upon whose ship we are sailing) died last year and his son Shah Soltan Husayn has taken the throne—Esther's alleged step-brother. When Esther and Leilyn left Dehli where her mother is imprisoned in the Salimgarh Fort, she entrusted Esther with the sacred Blade of Safavid. Shah Soltan Husayn is after that dagger, and according to Esther, he will rid himself of any competition for the throne. He will have her executed.

Certain that her brother is not personally searching for her, we don't know what other ships, other bounty hunters, other fortune seekers are hunting for Esther and the dagger. Thus, we are rethinking our plans. We are certain no one knows Esther is not still on the *Fancy* headed to the New World. We do know that the former captain of the *Chappow*, is angry that we took his ship and will most likely feel the displeasure of Soltan Husayn when the Shah learns of its disappearance.

Therefore, it is unlikely the route between us and Dehli will swarm with spies.

- Hinch

Departing the Port of Liverpool, England – 1748

With wind to fill the sails, the *Emerald* left Liverpool and land behind. Within minutes, land was only a speck behind them.

Jack breathed easier and freer as the constable and his men became mere dots and Liverpool disappeared on the horizon. They pointed and gestured in vain. He wished he could hear their conversation as they waited in vain for him to get off the ship, nor was he ever going to pay his respect for Lord Hawthorne. Maybe now they'd stop searching and might soon forget. Maybe the trail of dead bodies would no longer condemn him. Time for Jack to turn his attention to other affairs.

From the corner of his eye, Jack watched Miss Farrow step up onto the main deck and spot Jack comfortably leaning on the rail chatting with the captain.

"Mr. Remington?" she said, waltzing up to him and the captain. "What a surprise to have you with us on this journey." Elizabeth's eyes scanned up and down, examining his outfit.

"I met a fine tailor. Thanks to a cousin, he helped me get so smartly attired," he said.

"A cousin?" she asked.

For the next several weeks, the winds were fair, the sea calm, and the *Emerald of the Sea* lived up to its name. Once a well-armed frigate in Her Majesty's navy, both the ship and Captain Bentley retired from the navy and now served as merchant marine. Jack busied himself with the crew, putting into practice what he'd learned from his uncle's sailors during the many summers spent with him. It felt good not to run for his life. It felt good to work; it felt good to avoid Elizabeth.

He admired the work the shipwrights did in converting the *Emerald*. When he had time at the helm on the quarterdeck, completely re-built with the finest elm, his view across the decks to the forecastle overwhelmed him. The *Emerald* shined. The gun decks now served for cargo and as cabins for the few passengers and crew quarters. Jack took advantage of a cabin below the former gun decks for quiet and privacy.

Many a night by candlelight he spent studying the Safavid Dynasty.

It was during this study he found the missing link that bothered him from the first time Captain Remington invited his help and Victoria read to him from Denn's notebook. He sat back, head relaxed on a pillow, eyes following the flickering shadows from the candlelight. He'd found a missing puzzle piece. It became clear why they sent a Persian general to rescue an Indian treasure captured by pirates. The Mughal Emperor's own granddaughter was part of the treasure taken. Why a Persian Sultan cared finally came into perfect focus. The princess was believed to be his sister, an heir possibly competing for the throne.

"Nakhoda is that general," Jack whispered to himself. "But how does Elizabeth fit into this puzzle?"

Chapter Thirty~Seven

Journal Entry: December 1695 - Tanzania, Eastern Africa
Alexander Hincher - Ship's Captain

Lord Rudy, the ultimate adventurer, and his new best friend Black Moses are proposing an overland trek to Delhi to rescue Ester's mother, Zeb-un-Nissa, from the prison, kill her father, Emperor Aurangzeb, and place Esther on her rightful throne. Then, kill the Shah and place Esther on the throne to rule the Safavid Dynasty. I think he and Moses have been smoking too much jungle weed.

I proposed we seek an audience with the one person and possibly the only person we know who loves and cares for Esther's welfare. We will attempt an audience with Zeb-un-Nissa. We will make landfall near Sarat, the most dangerous part of our journey, and then trek to the Salimgarh Fort to meet Esther's mother.

- Hinch

At Sea, Atlantic Ocean - 1748

The blast shattered the cabin wall, showering the room with broken shards. Not an elegant stateroom to begin with, Jack chose it for the privacy it afforded being a lower deck. It was now rubble. The only piece of the cabin's furnishings still intact was the solid mahogany table hurled like a child's toy across the room. Landing on its side, the sturdy table pinned Jack against the far wall, shielding him from the other flying pieces, which would have certainly caused a painful death.

It took a few minutes for Jack to recover from the shock of the explosion. He shook as his mind fought to get its bearings. His eyes and throat burned as the air filled with the smoke of burned gunpowder.

Are we listing to starboard? Or am I just dizzy?

Regaining his bearings, he realized the ship must have taken hits along the waterline. Jack knew it would be but moments until water came rushing in.

Too heavy to return the table upright, Jack struggled to his feet and pushed the table upside down onto its top.

"Who's firing on us?" he mumbled as he staggered across the room. He got angrier as he neared the gaping hole, struggling to see out through the smoke.

"Pirates, filthy pirates!"

The broadside of a large warship stared back at him. From the unique curvature of the ship's hull, he concluded the ship was Portuguese built. An added motif on the gun deck doors gave the ship a unique flavor. Middle Eastern? No, Persian.

"Miss Farrow is getting just what she wanted," he mumbled.

Jack wanted to help above decks, but he would not make any difference in the battle, and he certainly didn't want to be here below decks when the pirates came searching for passenger and crew hiding below. The cabin was a total loss. Water rushed in.

The temporary deafness caused by the blast gave way to the sound of pounding boots, clanking swords, and the occasional crack of a pistol. Jack realized the battle was raging above decks. As the increasing water lifted the table, Jack saw his way out. Now somewhat floating, he pushed the table away from the door, opened it, and finding the way clear, dashed up the steps and into the captain's cabin.

Jack quickly stepped past the artifacts, slipped open a secret drawer in the captain's desk and secured the one item hidden there for safety. He pulled a map from the satchel, then folded and tucked it into his pocket, hurrying to Elizabeth's cabin.

"Elizabeth!" he yelled, darting from cabin to cabin. Leaving the last one, he saw her starting up the stairs to the main deck, a pistol in hand. Surprised by the pistol, he paused for a second, and then in one powerful swoop, grabbed her around the waist and pulled her down the stairs to his room. Her shock was in his favor. Though healed from his pistol shots, had she struggled much, he'd not be able to get her into his shattered room.

"If you stay, you die! If you don't die, you join a harem. If that's what you want, use that pistol right now on me. But I'm escaping, and so are you!" Jack's forceful command was enough. Elizabeth lowered the pistol.

Jack motioned to the now floating table and gave her his hand. She climbed on, hands wrapped around the table legs.

He pushed the table out the large hole and joined her.

Looking up between these two massive ships, Jack wondered how things could go so wrong. What should have been a routine trade journey for the *Emerald* from Liverpool to St. John's, Antigua in the West Indies, turned into a sea battle between a warship and a woefully under-gunned merchant ship. The *Emerald of the Sea* was once a powerful force in Her Majesty's Royal Navy. With piracy nearly non-existent in these waters, it was decommissioned and they converted it into a merchant ship which was now poorly armed.

The large, rounded sides of both ships prevented Jack from seeing what was happening above decks, but he watched Captain Bentley escorted across a plank onto the pirates' ship. Jack felt like a coward abandoning the ship and the captain, but had no other choice. He felt duty bound to protect Elizabeth and the map now folded in his pocket.

† † †

The noise of the raging battle above them drowned the noise of the large table as it bumped and banged between the two ship's hulls. All it took was one sailor to look down and all would be lost. Standing, Jack kept the makeshift craft close to the pirate ship as he worked his way toward the opposite side. He hoped through the smoke and the commotion, he and Elizabeth would appear as debris if they were seen.

A body splashed into the murky water. Captain Bentley, face down, sank so quickly Jack couldn't reach him. He leaned his head against the ship's hull as his stomach convulsed; anger, sorrow, and guilt fought their own battle within him. No one prepared this crew for battle. Jack knew he could not have prevented the murder of his family's friend.

The makeshift craft approached the rudder. Directly above them hung a long boat. If only he could get to it somehow.

Impossible.

Jack held tightly to the rudder and knew for now nobody could see them, but once the battle ended and the ship set sail, there was no way to stay out of sight. He didn't really know where they were or if there was any chance of finding land. Oh, how he wished he'd paid more attention to their progress today. The captain indulged Jack's wishes to study the many maps found onboard. He had cluttered the walls of his cabin with them.

"You impetuous fool." he groaned to himself.

There were no choices that made sense. Finally, he looked to Elizabeth, not for guidance or even comfort, but more to see if she were still there. Her look was nothing but disdain. He read her thoughts exactly; he saw she knew there was no hope.

Chapter Thirty~Eight

Journal Entry: February 1696 - Kenya, Eastern Africa
Alexander Hincher - Tribal Shaman

With translation help from Moses, each of our slaves chose to travel with us on our journey. I promised freedom anytime they want, but with the best living conditions they've ever had, their choice is easy.

We stay clear of the ports and islands where this ship or the princess might be recognized. North of the Zanzibar islands we put in to a small river inlet on the coast of Kenya to careen the ship before resuming our trek northward. As the tide allowed us to beach the frigate, Rudy took charge, and along with Moses and our slaves careened the ship.

Eager to explore local plant life and find the same herbs I found when I sailed with the Fancy, Esther and I ventured inland. Pleased to locate the same herb from which I had learned to make the healing poultice, we gathered arms full.

I heard a muffled scream. Two tall Africans captured Esther. Faces painted with white accents and one holding a club and the other a long, pointed spear, it was clear we had stumbled upon two warriors. Maasi was my guess.

- Hinch

Onboard The Chawbuck - Atlantic Ocean - 1748

The murdered Captain Bentley thrown overboard, Captain Ali Mutarid Hassan, captain of the 80-gun *Chawbuck*, a Persian man-of-war was now also captain of the damaged frigate, *Emerald of the Sea*, secured only ten feet away by a series of ropes the pirates used to pull the ships side by side.

"Clean this up," he demanded. "Bring the passengers and crew on board."

Captain Hassan was strong and surprisingly agile for a man well advanced in age. His shoulder length hair and dark complexion, combined with the scars and wrinkles of a man who'd spent his life on the sea, commanded immediate fear and respect from soldier and civilian alike.

He crossed the platform between the two ships and inspected the crew and prisoners as they crossed to the *Chawbuck*. The damage inflicted upon the *Emerald* was fatal. It would never sail again. The sea flowed into the ragged opening in its starboard side.

Angered he hadn't spotted the young naval officer who eluded and killed a dozen of his men, along with the young woman Mr. Hillis promised to send him, Hassan inspected the ship. He started belowdecks knowing he didn't have long before it would fill with water. He stomped from cabin to cabin and room to room, many already succumbing to the rising water. When he reached the cabin with the large breaching hole, the water was already knee deep. He waded in through the cold and dirty water.

The remaining maps on the wall confirmed this was the cabin where the elusive young man had been, and likely with the young woman. He cursed at the irony.

Looking out the enormous gaping hole and destroyed furniture, he knew this blast destroyed his chances to find the one person linking the treasure to its probable resting place. The young officer's dead body was likely making its way to the bottom of the turbulent sea, taking with it hope of finding the retribution he'd been hunting for all these years.

Disregarding the cool but murky water that filled his boots, he gathered the remaining maps from the walls and bounded back above decks. The *Emerald* listed starboard and it wouldn't be but a few more minutes before the sea would take another victim. With passengers and crew onboard the *Chawbuck,* they pulled the platform. The enormous gaping hole would assure the complete loss of the *Emerald of the Sea*. One of Captain Hassan's few remaining sources of hope.

The pirate ship cut its tether to the *Emerald*. A wave sent from the sinking *Emerald* washed over the two floating below, pulling Jack's grasp free from the rudder and setting them adrift.

Chapter Thirty~Nine

Journal Entry: February 1696 - Kenya, Eastern Africa
Alexander Hincher - Tribal Shaman

Speaking, what I understood was Swahili, they took us both into the heavy forest to a small village. The village was in a large clearing away from the forested river's edge. We were separated and confined to small huts built from sticks and mud. Who I assumed was a tribal leader questioned me several times. I spoke no Swahili and he no English.

My worries for Esther made my worries for the ship and crew pale. After all, Moses and Rudy could care well enough for the ship. There's no better team than those two.

I sat alone in the small hut, on a somewhat hard bed large enough for two people. The ceiling was too short for a man to stand properly, so I assumed it was not inhabited during the day. The two warriors and the several women I saw when being brought to this place were all taller than me.

It was dark inside, but the shadows outside moved through the day, telling me it was late afternoon. The warriors finally removed me from my confinement.

As my eyes adjusted to the late afternoon light, I saw Esther and I were not the only captives. There stood Rudy and Moses talking with the tribal chief as if they were best friends.

This was a tribe with whom Moses could communicate. It appeared they made a bargain. They brought me over to the chief where I learned I was the bargain. There was no sign of Esther, or anyone else from the ship.

This tribe was a Bantu tribe, and like other Bantu tribes were not traditionally a warring tribe. They were driven from their homes by marauding warriors looking for slaves to sell in Zanzibar. A major slave port in this eastern coast of Africa, we intentionally avoided it.

Though Moses negotiated the bargain, when I heard what it was, it was vintage Rudy.

When enemy warriors attacked the village, they found it deserted except for the very ill wife and daughter of the chief. The wife was too ill to run, and the daughter refused to leave her side. In anger, the warriors stabbed the girl and left her and her ill mother to die. The mother was too sick to bring a good price, and they feared she infected the young girl. We assume the enemy warriors believed the tribe abandoned the village because of this illness.

The villagers just returned before they brought us to the village. The young girl is in terrible shape and the mother deathly ill.

Rudy, through Moses, assured the chief I was a great white healer and could heal both the mother and the daughter.

- Hinch

The Island, West Indies - 1748

Jack brushed hair back from his face as the early dawn silhouetted a forest-covered mountain rising dramatically from the ocean shore. Blinking awake, Jack remembered he was not lying alone on the shore. The hair he brushed from his face was not his own. A sweet fragrance enlivened his senses. Perfume?

This surprise was not unpleasant, but it was considerably awkward. His new companion was quietly sleeping in his arms, and for more than one reason, he hesitated to wake her. He recognized the scent and the beautiful fingernails on the hand resting on his chest.

The last time someone laid in my arms he was bleeding to death. I hope this ends better.

A quiet lapping reminded him they were near the water. The warm moist air, blended with her perfume, filled his lungs as her quiet breathing against him filled his imagination.

They had spoken seriously only briefly during the journey, and when they did, it was about the fratricide associated with the rise to power in both the Mughal and Safavid Dynasties. Jack never divulged his possessing the book taken from the Nookery and the many hand-written notes concerning the relationship between the Mughal Emperor Arrangzab and his Persian wife, Dilrus, and how that complication was at the core of Nakhoda's apparent quest.

Jack admitted to himself he still knew nothing about Elizabeth. Of the several other passengers, she was certainly among the most pleasant to look at, but her interest in his plans left him unsettled. For that reason, he questioned her motives. Why would a young woman risk traveling unchaperoned to the New World? Something about her was amiss. He understood why ol' Denn sent her, but why did she want to go?

Regretfully untangling their embrace, Jack arose. He carefully rested her head on a wrap she had likely used as a blanket earlier in the night. Her tangled reddish blond hair fell across his hand like silk and he brushed the few grains of sand from her perfectly smooth cheek.

Elizabeth lay there motionless. All he could do was stare—a luxury he enjoyed once before when he watched her sleep in the coach as they rode to Newton Ferrers. The peace in her face reflected a purity he liked, a purity missing when she was awake. It impressed him how her dress, though somewhat rumpled, remained relatively clean. Its tone of blue complemented her hair and her complexion. Onboard the *Emerald*, he hadn't paid attention to her shoes so her fine boots were a surprise. He bent to gently wake her but when his fingers rested on the soft fabric of her gown, he let go.

Coward, ever the coward, and this woman was in your arms of her own free will.

He shrugged off his regret for leaving her embrace and turned, walking along the shore. A rugged, majestic mountain rose straight out of the ocean, sealing access to what lay beyond. Its twin at the opposite edge of this shoreline flanked the small patch of sand. Inland access required a rugged climb into a dense jungle. Jack explored the jungle's dense edge. He found no path.

Could I be the first human to explore this island?

With his back to the forest, Jack folded his arms and stared out at the same sea that swallowed the *Emerald* and spit him and Elizabeth out on this small secluded beach.

This is all wrong. This is definitely wrong.

His mind dashed back to his youth and when he spent time with his uncle; when he'd spend hours watching the tides, the surf, the winds, and the waves upon both calm and turbulent seas.

There's so little surf.

By the time Jack covered the length of the beach and returned to his sleeping companion, the sun peaked over the tree line, waking Elizabeth.

Chapter Forty

Journal Entry: February 1696 - Kenya, Eastern Africa
Alexander Hincher - Tribal Healer

They took me to a small tributary at the river where the shamans attempted to heal a woman by bleeding her. They'd placed the woman on a stone in a small river. She sat naked with her back to the shore. Various shamans shot small darts into her back. Each dart drew drops of blood. Occasionally a dart drew more.

I tried to convince the shamans there was a better way. We climbed over the stones in the river and took the sick woman back to shore. I taught the shamans to find a vein, and I bled her. I don't believe in bleeding as a cure, so I took very little blood. Just enough to leave the shamans with enough respect from other members of the tribe. It impressed them how efficiently I bled the woman.

I then showed them how to mix an herbal cocktail from local plants and fed it to her. Within hours she looked better. She responded to the herbal medicine so well; I concluded the potency of these local herbs to be more pure than those secured in villages on the western coast of Africa.

They then allowed me to attend to the young daughter. She was badly hurt and lost a lot of blood. The blade of the spear cut through her hip and badly damaged the joint and the flesh. The shamans gave her up for death and were eager for her to die while under my care rather than their own.

I gathered herbs and chewed them to the consistency of paste. I cleaned the wound. The shamans had packed it with some herbs which stopped the bleeding but infected the tissue. I carefully applied

the paste into the open gash which bled when I cleaned it. The
young girl's pain immediately lessened. She relaxed. The torn flesh
now covered with my poultice seemed to welcome the relief and the
bleeding stopped.

The sun was setting, and the tenseness of the situation lessened.
They brought Rudy, Moses, and me food, but they still guarded us as
prisoners. I never inquired what the bargain called for if I failed. It
couldn't be good. We knew nothing of Esther. During the night Rudy
was Rudy and located the hut where they kept Esther and Leilyn. To
my shame, I never even thought about Leilyn. They were safe but kept
as hostages.

We were kept this way for nearly ten days. Each day the guard became
less oppressive as the young girl and her mother recovered. The young
girl sat up and tried to walk after the eighth day. The mother recovered
well enough to prepare and apply her daughter's poultice each day.

On day five, Esther and Leilyn joined us. Because we were not married,
it was insisted we sleep apart. Ironically, they offered us other female
companionship. Throughout the ten days in captivity, Esther and Leilyn
developed relationships with some of these tribal women. Apparently,
there was enough Arab influence in the language of the tribes along
the coastal region and several words carried a similar meaning, so they
could communicate—if even rudimentarily.

They gave us leave to return to our ship.

The woman I healed was the first and favored wife of the tribal chief.
Moses told me that though I had saved her life, I had also saved the
lives of the shamans. I should have not been surprised that shamans
from different tribes would have different skills in healing. What I
learned from shamans in western Africa were new to these shamans.
The chief told them if she died they died. They were eager to reward me.
Recognizing the importance to let them do so, we asked them to gather
a large quantity of these local herbs, which they did.

As we set to return to the mouth of the small river where the ship was
now ready to sail, the chief met us. In his gratitude, he gave me three
gifts. The eldest daughters of each of his three wives for me to marry.
Moses told me there was no way to refuse. "It would be an insult that
would bring grave consequences to our party," he said.

These Maasai women are genuinely beautiful. It appears I am
assembling a harem.

- Hinch

The Island, West Indies - 1748

Jack stood above Elizabeth, holding a small bundle of bananas. She wiped sleep from her eyes.

"Breakfast?" He pulled a ripe banana from the bunch and handed it to her.

"Thank you, um, didn't we…" Elizabeth stuttered…

"Yes, we did, or should I say you did. When we crawled up onto this beach, and found sleep, you were over there."

"Sorry, but there was only one way to stay warm. Thank you for breakfast." She swallowed a bite of banana.

"Do you still think me a coward?" Jack asked.

"You cowered in your cabin and stopped me from protecting the captain," she said.

Jack had no desire to re-ignite the fury he'd suffered the many hours they drifted before finding this beach.

"You can't think us helpless females, Mr. Remington."

"It's Jack. We are alone here."

"Mr. Jack, as the battle raged above decks, we joined the fray. When I went below to secure a weapon, one, I might say, I'm proficient with; you prevented me from returning to—"

"To the fray?" Jack interrupted. "To a fate worse than death. Might I say!"

She bit her tongue. She, too, was unwilling to rehash either battle from the day and night before. Elizabeth took his offered hand as she got to her feet.

"You know what they do to women taken captive." Jack couldn't resist.

This was the first time he ever gave serious thought to what other passengers did during the attack. They did not man the ship for battle. The guns had been transferred to other navy ships when it was decommissioned. Yet, privateering and piracy were near extinct in these waters. It should not have needed guns. What went wrong?

Elizabeth brushed sand from her dress. "Captain Bentley surrendered the ship to those barbarians, and they were about to march him away. That's when I came down for the pistol. They would not have taken me without a fight."

"But they would have taken you," Jack said.

"Like you did?"

How could he answer that? Her penetrating light blue eyes seemed to search for a way to examine his thoughts and motives.

The tiniest of movement drew his attention to the hem of her dress. Her eyes followed his, where a small crab clung on for its very life. With no alarm, she reached down, freed it, and gently sent it on its way.

Well, she's not as silly as others.

She changed her focus. "What now?"

"I imagine he'll scurry off and tell family and friends about the nice lady on the beach. They'll come, knock on your dress, we'll invite them into our open air dining hall, sit around my table, and have crab soup for supper."

That drew a smile. A lovely smile. He liked that smile; it complimented and softened her expression that clung to the hope of a serious answer to her question.

"I don't know what's next. But I know we are free, and we're alive." He lifted the bananas, "and there's plenty of food to keep us that way for a while. I am grateful for that."

"By free, you mean lost on a strange island?"

"If it is an island."

What answer is she expecting? The captain insisted to everyone on board that I was the pilot. Did she hear the captain deny to Nakhoda we had a pilot? A coward and an incompetent pilot? I'm losing ground here.

"You don't know? Wouldn't it be on one of your precious maps? The maps you studied for the entire journey?" she asked. Her mocking tone demonstrated her continued irritation with him.

She's testing me. What does she know? Do I try for another smile? Has honesty ever worked for me?

"We drifted through the blazing sun and in the dark for two nights. And last night, did you notice the lack of even the slightest breeze? Look at the surf."

She turned. "There isn't much."

"Right. How we washed up here has baffled me all morning. We're not lost. This island is lost."

Despite the warmth of the rising sun, he noticed goose bumps surface on her bare arms. She shook the sand from the wrap and pulled it tight.

"No, Miss Farrow, I don't think this island is on one of my maps. I apologize for not bringing one with me on our journey."

His curt and snippy reply caught both of them by surprise.

"I…"

As she replied, Jack raised a finger. "Don't. I'm sorry, you did not deserve that."

For Jack this was uncharted territory, not the island, the apparent adversarial relationship with Elizabeth. Her evasive responses to his inquiries about her interest in ol' Denn's knowledge of the Avery treasure, and her motivations for rescuing him from two of Nakhoda's men, served as a powerful deterrent to further attempts in learning the truth.

His apparent rescue of her from who Jack assumed was Nakhoda himself, only fueled her hostility. She made it more than clear, it was a cowardly kidnapping, not a rescue. Regret and pride took alternating jabs at Jack's thoughts. *Why does she want to march into her own destruction?*

During his most civil interactions with her, he'd only learned she lived with grandparents she dearly loved when her family was unexpectedly lost. A couple times she let feelings of her father slip out in ways leading Jack to believe she felt he was among the greatest of men and Jack would never live up to her image of true manhood.

His pursuit of academics added nothing but disdain to her image of him. "A likely token given the son of a Lord," she said during one of their conversations.

"First thing, we better find water," he said.

They spent the rest of the day poking in and out of the dense jungle only deep enough to prevent themselves from getting immediately lost. Eventually they found a small spring providing them relief from the thirst and heat of the late afternoon. Too cautious to spend a night in the jungle, they returned to the beach and quietly watched the setting sun paint a masterpiece with the distant clouds.

Chapter Forty~One

Journal Entry - February 1696 - Mahi River, Gulf of Khambjat, Arabian Sea
Alexander Hincher - Ship's Captain

After considerable discussion, we will not sail into Sarat on this ship. With none of its customary crew or its captain, it will create a stir when someone recognizes it. We are therefore sailing past Sarat and will attempt to sail up the Mahi River as far as it will take us. From there, we will go by land to Delhi.

- Hinch

Onboard the Chawbuck - At Sea - West Indies - 1748

Captain Hassan hadn't said another word. His anger prevented all rational thought. He stood nearly motionless for two days. His rigid grip on the helm and hostile glare kept the unsettled crew at a distance as they sailed back to the harbor of his own island. Only twice did he leave his post and only briefly. When he questioned the passengers taken captive, he learned but little about the pilot, his alleged naval officer, yet the female captives confirmed the loss of one of their own. From their description, the name didn't register, but he knew it was her. Another unfortunate loss. Spies had alerted him of a competitor seeking the treasure he believed belonged to him and him alone! That competitor sailed to the West Indies on a former man-of-war converted into a merchant ship. Easy, oh so easy.

When told his young naval captain escaped his men and the constable in Liverpool, he put the *Chawbuck* to full sail.

When he sighted the *Emerald*, it sailed at full mast in clear water. The new competitor and his officer were being handed to him. No ship could outrun the

Chawbuck. He personally oversaw its modifications. Modifications he learned in the Great Shah's personal navy. The *Chawbuck* came across the *Emerald* two full days before they had even hoped to find it. Winds were favorable, and they followed for most of the day before approaching. Their approach was friendly. They were flying the Persian flag.

Why did they refuse to pull up? There was no way the *Emerald* could outrun or out-gun the *Chawbuck*. That foolish captain had to know that, so why did he try to fight?

How could my gunner miscalculate a warning shot? Across the bow, not through the mainmast. That fool captain fired back at me. He gave me no choice but to end the battle with a direct broadside attack. Fool!

One passenger. One passenger is all I wanted. That miscalculation by the gunner set off a chain of events that killed the one person on earth with the last piece of a puzzle I've spent a lifetime seeking. Slitting the poor man's throat didn't help.

All hope was gone.

Unless…

Chapter Forty~Two

We sailed past villages, countless temples and several small ports, and sadly encountered the remnants of villages destroyed by marauding highlanders. Is there a place where a people can be safe to enjoy life without fear? The seas are not safe and coastal villages are subject to the ravages of countless pillaging peoples. Now, even several hundred miles up river, we find marauders equal in their treatment of humanity as the pirates we despise.

In Africa, we found tribes capturing another tribe and selling their captives as slaves. I hope to find civilization one day before I die. Civilization I define where one man treats another man as an equal, with equal rights, privileges, and opportunity. Where one man cares for another because it's right, because it's his nature.

- Hinch

The Island, West Indies. 1748 -

The next morning, the two laid quietly.

"We're not alone," Elizabeth said, breaking the calm silence. "I know you smelled it. I'm pretty sure you're a man, and if I learned anything from my father, men don't miss a step if that step leads to a good meal. Hopefully, as a man, you're looking for a challenge."

Was that a compliment?

"I smelled it," Jack said, "I'll climb back to the summit and see if there's a hint of the direction it came from. You should stay here."

"Just because I accused you of being a man, you don't have to prove it, protecting the helpless girl. And what, you go, get eaten by cannibals and I die alone here on the beach? Why don't I go? That way if I get eaten, you're free of the responsibility to protect the girl and you can live happily ever after, alone on a beach?"

Jack opened his mouth, but nothing came out.

"We're going together," continued Elizabeth, "for two reasons. First, you're not going alone, and second, neither am I."

Do I sense fear? That's a first.

Finally Jack said, "Well those are certainly two good reasons."

He stared at this very resolute woman. That is not at all what he thought. He never thought she was weak or that he needed to protect her. Stop her, yes. But to protect her? Maybe. He actually didn't know what he was thinking, but it wasn't that.

Sometimes, a guy just needs to think nothing at all. And if he says something smart or dumb, it means nothing at all. This woman is so, so, complicated.

For the next few hours they struggled to get through the thick vegetation and make the climb. It was not so steep as it was constant. At the point of exhaustion, they came across another small spring, and relief for their thirst. They sat on a fallen tree as the peace in the jungle was only broken by the sound of an occasional bird. Suddenly, they turned to each other. Jack tilted his head up, leaning into an invisible flavor in the air. The scent of cooking food crept through the trees.

Is that pork? No, it's sweet like pork, but not quite. Elizabeth was right; I am a man.

Exhaustion fled. As quietly as possible, the two climbed their way around the crest of the hill. The growth was too dense to see much, but they detected smoke working its way through the trees. The sound of faint voices also crept through the trees, noise of a family, children, a mother giving instructions. Relief washed over Elizabeth's face, confirming to Jack she too knew these weren't savages, nor pirates. She stepped ahead of Jack, and knelt to see between the branches of a thick fern and a mossy fallen log.

"Do we just wander in?" Elizabeth whispered.

Jack didn't answer. After waiting what seemed like a long time, she turned to find Jack, arms raised, his rugged face drained of color. A large man several inches larger than Jack, maybe in his forties with solid powerful shoulders and piercing brown eyes, was holding a very sharp machete, just inches from Jack's chest. He motioned with his head for her to stand next to Jack. She froze in place, paralyzed by shock.

He motioned another time. She didn't move. Jack broke the silence, "I think he wants you to come over here by me."

"Thank you," the man said, and Elizabeth climbed to her feet and joined Jack.

"And no, you don't just wander in, at least not and keep your head," the man said.

"Forgive us, we don't know the customs here, we were shipwrecked day before yesterday and…" The blade lifted to Jack's throat. His mouth closed and his eyes widened.

"Where's your ship? Where did it wreck? You're on the wrong side of this island for a ship to wreck. Trades will pull you away from this side of the island, and besides, there's no shoal or reef to wreck a ship, and no weather to cause it. Try again."

The deep, powerful voice reverberated through the trees transfixing the couple.

Elizabeth cautiously asked, "Have many visitors wandered in and lost their head?"

The man let out a resounding, menacing laugh. "Who are you two and what do you want? No, we don't get visitors, we get pirates, Visigoths, and Vikings. Why do you think I'm out here patrolling these jungles? Which are you?"

"We aren't any of those," Elizabeth said.

Doing his best impression of courage, Jack said, "We're visitors, and if we're the first visitors you've ever had, then we're even. We don't know how you want us to pay a visit and you don't know how to receive visitors. Hello, I'm Jack and this is Elizabeth. It's a pleasure to meet you?" Jack's courage faded. He cautiously reached out his hand, but the machete stood firm, inches from his throat.

Eyeing Elizabeth up and down, the man turned to Jack and asked, "She your wife?"

Jack stuttered out a weak reply, "Uh, uh, no."

"Good," said the man, "I need a good wife and this here Elizabeth will work just fine. From the looks of her, she's young, strong, just the kind of jungle woman I need. Come on, woman, if you're not his, you're mine. Law of the jungle. And you can call me Glen."

The man lowered his machete, and Jack took his first full breath since the blade was initially raised. And with that first breath, he found the courage to object.

"Wait, I mean she's not my wife, yet. The wedding's next month, we were sailing to meet her parents when pirates took our ship. We escaped and floated to this island."

The machete went right back up to Jack's chest.

"Prove it," Glen said.

Using one finger Jack, gently lowered the blade away from his chest. He reached out and with both hands took Elizabeth's hand and held it up, showing a beautiful diamond ring on her finger. Elizabeth's eyes widened again. She was as shocked as Glen was. Glen saw it in her face.

"That proves nothing." Glen huffed.

Elizabeth pulled Jack into her arms and kissed him deeply. When she finally gave him a chance to breathe, he stood limp, more shocked by her embrace and kiss than she was with the appearance of the ring on her finger.

Glen pounded him on the back, nearly knocking him to the ground. He burst into laughter. "Well done! Rosemary wouldn't like me bringing a wife back, anyway."

Jack regained his balance and some of his composure. "Who's Rosemary?"

Glen's laughter returned. "Why, Rosemary is my wife, the mother of my four children. Come and meet her. If you two actually arrived two days ago, you've probably had little to eat besides a banana or two. Rosemary's a splendid cook. You'll love her. And my children will love having some new friends." Glen's tone then got serious. "If you're telling the truth, we need to have a little talk about pirates."

The Island

The Settlement
Rag's Fjord
Glen's Cove
Rosemary's Harbor
Lost Ship's Graveyard
Washed Up Beach

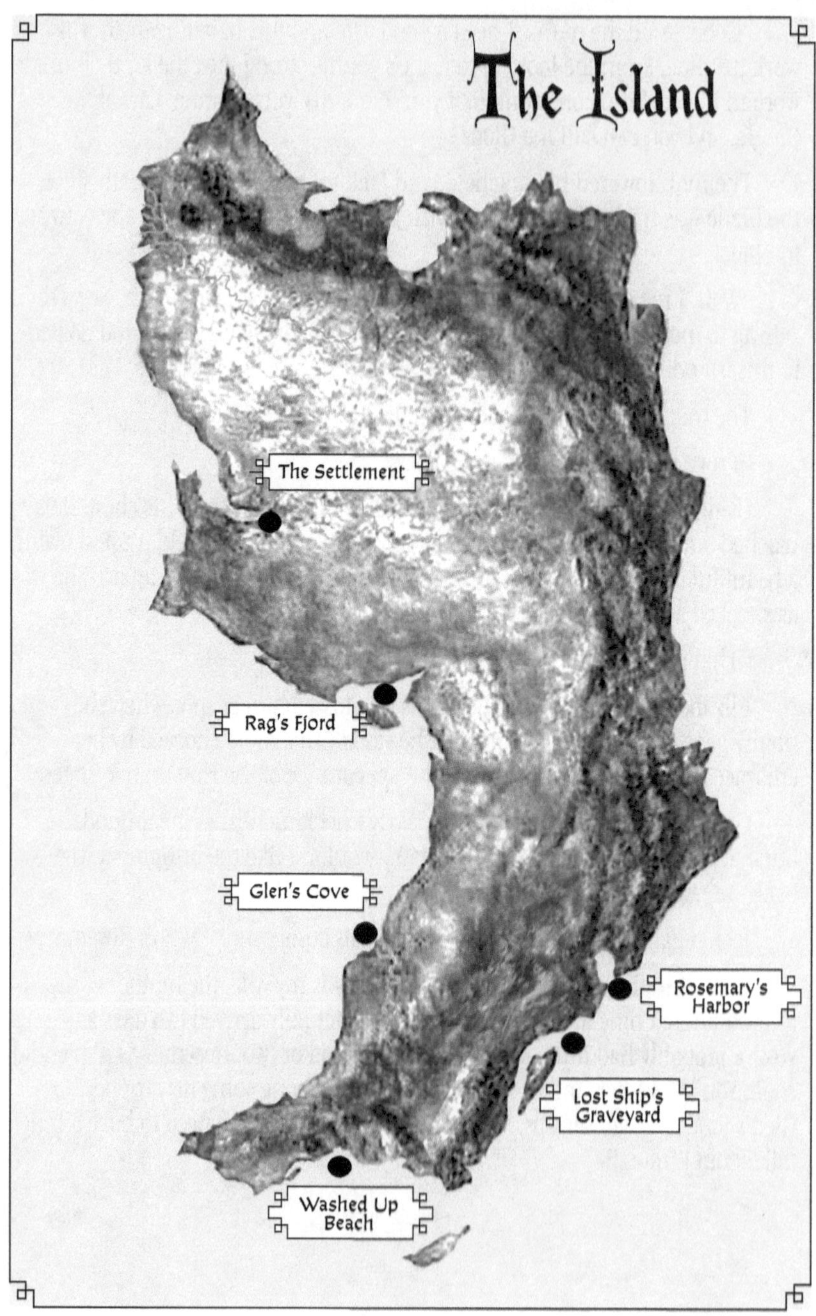

Chapter Forty~Three

Journal Entry: March 1696 - Mahi River, Rajasthan, India
Alexander Hincher - Punt Passenger

We sailed up the Mahi River as far as our ship will allow and made port. We encountered few ships the size of ours, mostly small boats.

If we knew the duration of our trip to Delhi, we could arrange for the care of the *Caspara*. We don't, however, know how long we may be. We expect our journey will take us several weeks over land to reach Delhi. We don't know what our fate shall be.

This is home country for Esther. Her mother was born nearby and her grandfather the emperor rules this land, so we are very careful. Until we learn from her mother who is a friend or foe, we hesitate to contact anyone who might know the royal family.

Lord Rudy has been out in the villages surveying our best route to Delhi. With coaching from Leilyn, they made acquaintance with several prominent citizens. I must admit, I am concerned about the arrangements Rudy might make.

As we remained mostly onboard these many days, we noticed the fine spices grown in the area. Spices have become a major crop for the landowners here. Local farmers grow, harvest, and then transport these spices down the Mahi River in small boats called punts. Once they reach the port, other ships transport them to the ports of Surat and Bombay.

- Hinch.

The Island - West Indies - 1748

This turn around in fortune was as much a shock to Jack and Elizabeth as the kiss and the ring, but they fell in line behind Glen. The machete in Glen's hands proved lethal to brush, branch, and vine as it cleared the path down the hill and into Glen's forest homestead.

Not to be overheard by Glen, Elizabeth whispered to Jack, almost mouthing the words without a sound, holding up her ring wearing hand.

"Where did this come from?" Elizabeth paused, "does she know you took it?"

Jack, quite pleased with his surprise, whispered back, "I try to keep one with me in case a helpless girl needs rescuing from a Visigoth, Viking, or pirate. But while we're at it," Jack holding up his arms in a mock embrace and pursing his lips, "what was that all about? Not that I mind."

Elizabeth responded, "I always try to keep one of those with me in case a young hopeless lad needs rescuing from a very sharp machete in the hands of a Visigoth, Viking, or pirate."

The two followed Glen for a couple hundred yards into an secluded cove accented by a small stream which flowed lazily toward a small lagoon a short distance away.

Two figures rounded the edge of a small building. They exploded into a mad dash toward Glen. Dark brown ponytails bounced as the young girl tried valiantly to keep up with the young boy bounding toward him, giving him barely enough time to sheath his machete.

Glen scooped the two up, their flailing arms loose to the wind as he spun them around. A third girl, older than the two in Glen's arms, made her way around the edge of the building. Her beautiful smile instantly changed to a frown when Jack stepped from behind Glen. It softened slightly when Elizabeth appeared behind Jack.

When Glen, with two giggling children in his arms, reached the teenage girl, she turned and stayed close to him as he quickly approached the small homestead. She could hardly keep her eyes off the two strangers as she walked beside him. The two little ones hardly took notice of the strangers.

The first building was the small house built out of a collection of logs, branches, mud and an occasional piece of well sawn lumber. The pieces of lumber were obviously collected as salvage from a well-crafted ship of some sort, due to the fine and intricate patterns carved into them. Jack appreciated its innovative craftsmanship.

This is no temporary jungle hut.

Next to the house was an ingeniously designed stone fireplace upon which sat a large pot boiling, emitting the sweetest aroma Jack thought he'd ever smelled, an aroma that had found its way through the trees and had entreated Jack and Elizabeth to find its source.

The crowd rounded the corner. An exceptionally beautiful woman stepped out of the small building. Immediate upturned eyebrows didn't lessen the beautiful smile, they just revealed stunning deep brown eyes. In her late thirties or early forties, her soft olive complexion could pass for late teens. Long black hair hung comfortably against a pale blue dress that to Jack, looked out of place for a woman living in a jungle. She stepped toward Glen and traded a gentle kiss on his cheek for the young girl, who now in her arms displayed identical color and complexion. If not for the thirty-plus years difference in ages, they could have been twins.

How did the Visigoth win the hand of a lady of this beauty and grace? Probably at the point of a machete.

"Well, what have we here? Or should I say, who have we here?" she asked. "Do I get to meet your new friends?"

"Meet Elizabeth and Jack, soon to be married and recently lost on our beloved island."

When Glen called it an island, a terrible thought shot through Jack's mind.

Does lost refer to both us and the island?

Glen continued, "Meet my Rosemary. The finest wife, mother and cook on the entire island." Proudly he continued, "Jeremy and Jenny, my twins, and Lydia, who, as you can tell, is the prettiest young woman on the island."

Lydia, all five feet of her, remained half shielded behind Rosemary. The three girls, Rosemary, Jenny, and Lydia were enough to stop a man's heart. Clearly, all three were related, yet Lydia carried more of Glen's strong nose and firm cheekbones. Still, as pretty a young girl as Jack had ever known, she didn't appear to be as weak or fearful as her current timidity portrayed.

But there is something about Rosemary that looks familiar.

Elizabeth stepped forward to meet Rosemary, "I can see why Glen is so proud of his family. It is our pleasure to meet you. He mentioned you had four children?"

Rosemary answered Elizabeth's query, "Lizzie, our youngest is sleeping. She is the only true native of this island and she pretty much sleeps, eats, and, well, does what babies do.''

Jeremy and Jenny weren't shy or afraid at all. They took Elizabeth's hands and offered to take her exploring.

Rosemary gave orders, sending the two little ones and Glen off on an errand and invited Jack and Elizabeth to follow Lydia to wash up.

"I'll have some food ready in no time," she said.

Jack thought Glen was not exaggerating when he proclaimed her the prettiest young woman on the island. Lydia was a lovely junior version of her mother. Jack hadn't yet met any other young women on the island, in fact, until a few minutes ago he did not know if anyone actually lived on the island, but he was willing to agree with Glen.

Walking side by side and not hiding behind a parent, Lydia was not yet nearly as tall as Elizabeth, but more slender, as he would expect a young teenager to be. Her dark brown hair reached halfway down her back and was braided in a unique twist Jack hadn't seen before. Her brilliant blue eyes were a surprise as her parents both had dark ones.

As Lydia led Elizabeth and Jack across the small clearing to what looked like an actual bath house, also crudely made but substantial, she stayed close to Elizabeth. Jack noticed that too.

Lydia gave instructions and hurried back across the clearing to the house.

"Wow," Jack exclaimed, turning to take in the view of the cove, "What is this?"

"Well, Jack," Elizabeth began, "I think it's where you wash up, take care of other duties..."

Jack turned around shaking his head at her answer, "You know that's not what I mean. You have this man out patrolling the jungle for... who knows what, or who, he has a family with a wife who seems to..." his hands moving to encompass the scope of the cove, he trailed off not knowing even how to finish his question.

Elizabeth gave Jack a few moments to formulate the end of his question, encouraging it with her gentle motion to lend her ear to his next words. Finally, she finished it for him.

"You mean how does a man have a family, a beautiful family, a happy-looking family, a well-fed family, out here in the middle of nowhere, tucked in some secluded cove?"

"Precisely," Jack finally muttered.

They finished washing up and returned to the house. As they arrived, Glen and the little ones were getting back from a short hike up the hill bringing with them an arm full of coconuts. Glen quickly cut the tops off, providing fresh coconut water for the guests.

That machete is certainly sharp!

They sat around a large table similar to the one Jack commandeered. The table, elements of the small house and even the steel top of the oven were not local. Their English origin gave Jack hope of a nearby port. They enjoyed a feast of sea turtle, fruit, and a vegetable dish which neither Jack nor Elizabeth had ever tasted.

"That's pepinello," said Jeremy, "It's good for you."

Every bite was delicious. Rosemary steered the conversation away from any details, insisting these two needed to concentrate on eating first. As the meal ended, proper questions gently began. First, Jack described the attack on the Emerald. He kept his eye on Elizabeth, curious if his modified version of their escape met her approval and backed up their claim of engagement. Guile was not Jack's talent, nor was fiction.

Why isn't Elizabeth helping me out here? She's enjoying my misery.

He told how the aroma of Rosemary's cooking the day before had prompted their exploration. Though interesting, the story didn't come to life until Glen rescued it from Jack.

"For years, we've suspected if there was an attack on this side of the island, it would be on that beach; the only logical landing spot. As I was patrolling, two suspicious figures, as quietly as a herd of elephants, crept from the beach and pounded their way through the thick jungle toward our home."

Wide eyed, Jeremy asked, "How could you see through the jungle?"

Rosemary gently placed her hand on his arm. Stories like this could get very long if every question got asked and answered.

Glen answered anyway. "I was at Dead Man's pass, which as you know, overlooks the beach, and I noticed someone had landed. They were probably going to move here because they left a table. But I didn't see the people. Then I saw movements among the tips of the trees. They were headed our way. What kind of dangerous people are these who attack an island and leave a table on the beach? I wondered. Then I knew. The table was a signal, a sign, that they found the island where treasure was buried by pirates. There were probably a hundred pirates waiting offshore in a giant ship for the signal it was safe to attack. I had to find out. Like a jungle cat, I followed the movements in the brush."

"You said you saw the trees move," Jenny corrected.

"Yes, and also the brush. These two pirate spies weren't very careful. They probably grew up in the city."

"They probably don't know how to play hide-n-go-seek!" It was Jeremy this time.

"Probably not. But they were getting closer and closer. I wanted to come to warn you and to put out the fire so they wouldn't find our home. But I knew your mother would be unhappy if she couldn't finish the supper. So, I stopped them myself. I crept in closer and closer. Like a snake in the grass I slithered and crawled through the ferns and the palms."

"We don't have snakes, papa," Jenny clarified.

"That's why they didn't see me. They weren't expecting something to slither through the brush. Then I saw them. A strong pretty girl leading a frightened man toward our home."

She wasn't leading; she was just . . .

Glen winked at Jack as if he could read his thoughts. Jack relaxed. He was as curious as the rest to hear how this story ends. Glen held everyone's attention but when he mentioned the pretty girl, all eyes shot toward Elizabeth. At the frightened man comment all eyes pushed back to Jack. Added to those eyes were big happy smiles.

"Then it was my chance. I silently slipped in between them and took the man by surprise with my blade." Glen plopped the machete on the table for drama. "He knew I was serious and would cut him gill to spleen if he moved. When the woman finally turned and saw their devilish plan was foiled, she surrendered to my demands to stand next to her man. Speechless, both of them. I had them; there was no escape. Then the most remarkable thing happened." Glen's intentional pause gave Jenny the cue.

"What happened?"

"Elizabeth here, took ol Jack in her arms and gave him the biggest, longest, most passionate kiss I'd ever seen. She was saying goodbye, 'cause she knew I was going to slice him up."

"Yuk." It was Jeremy.

This time it was Lydia, "Shush."

Jeremy ignored her.

"Glen." Rosemary didn't need to say more. Her look and tone said everything.

"Ok, so let me back up. When Jack thought all was lost, he begged me not to kill him and take Elizabeth as a slave. He said they were getting married, even showed me her ring so I might believe him."

Elizabeth's hand was on the table, and when Glen mentioned the ring, Jack noticed she had been caressing it. All eyes turned to the ring, which she proudly displayed. An extra heartbeat surprised Jack. Her hand was as beautiful as the ring. It looked at home.

"Then what?" Jeremy brought everyone's attention back to Glen.

The baby woke and alerted everyone it was now her turn to eat

"Well, I figured Lydia needed a new friend and if I killed Jack, you wouldn't have someone new to cheat at kickball. So, I brought 'em home."

Jack's many questions remained unanswered. He'd lost his chance.

Well, it doesn't look like anybody's going anywhere. Time for questions later.

Rosemary turned to the children, "While I take care of Lizzie, you two take Jack and Elizabeth down and show them the lagoon."

Glen got up and readied to go with the kids. Rosemary snagged his shirt, "You, come with me."

Jenny took Elizabeth's hand and Jeremy grabbed Jack's arm and bounded toward the lagoon with visitors in tow. Lydia watched them scurry off, turned, and cleared the table.

Chapter Forty~Four

Journal Entry: March 1696 - Mahi River, Rajasthan, India
Alexander Hincher - Entrepreueur

My fortunes do not cease to increase as long as I have Lord Rudy by my side. We are now partners in an Indian spice empire. Rudy calls it an empire; I think it more of a small plantation. We invested in the Sahakari spice plantation. Our partners are a co-op of three farming families.

Avery's former slaves will stay on here and work the plantation, but not as slaves; as free men. I offered freedom to these men as we traveled the African coast, but knowing they had little hope of keeping their freedom or ever returning home safely, they elected to continue with us. As free men, they work as part owners of the plantation. They each receive a plot of land and will receive training in the art of spice cultivation. As contributors to the co-op they will all profit from the venture.

Using the *Caspara* to transport the spices, they will bypass the middlemen in Khambhat and deliver product directly to Bombay. Rudy convinced our partners the increased profits will easily justify our ownership in the new 'enterprise.'

We offered Moses a large plot of land and the captaincy of the *Caspara* while Rudy, Esther, Leilyn, my harem and I travel to Dehli. He declined. He convinced me our needs were best served if he traveled with us to Dehli. His consideration for the safety and comfort of my small harem is touching. Rudy, of course, teases him about his attention of our three Maasai princesses. I don't blame him. I wonder what it looks like to those we encounter—a Scot, an Englishman, a large and powerful black slave and five beautiful women of African and Indian descent.

Using a small punt owned by the co-op and no longer needed to make the journey down the Mahi, we are traveling up river another hundred miles, where we will take our journey overland north to Delhi. If not for our ancestry, we would look like any other group traveling up river.

From time to time, Esther or Leilyn shares their knowledge of a village or a temple we pass. As I wrote earlier, this is their homeland.

- Hinch

Onboard the Chawbuck - Hassan's Private Island - 1748

"Captain, the HMS *Kent* anchors in port at St. Johns," Krist said as he stepped into the captain's cabin.

"Do you know why it's here?" The captain leaned forward, his leathered hands gripped the edge of the table and pulled himself upright.

Chasing you.

"Your spies say it's escorting the *Emerald* back to England." Krist stood watching his commanding father settle into thought.

Captain Hassan sat in his cabin on the powerful *Chawbuck,* now anchored in the harbor on his own private island. There were hundreds of these islands scattered throughout the West Indies. Many years ago, a small band of interlopers, having pirated a small slave ship, discovered and populated this island. They found it prime for a small plantation. They settled, put the slaves to work and built a small isolated community.

Years later, Captain Hassan and his crew on the *Chawbuck* stumbled upon the island and made it home. Its deep protected harbor was ideal to anchor and hide the large warship. He killed the interlopers, took the slaves, and turned the island into a safe harbor to manage a very profitable white slave trade. Many an Ottoman and Persian harem relied on Captain Hassan's trade. The profits provided the funding during the last many years of his life's quest.

Krist stood patiently, leaning against the door frame, boots crossed at the ankle. He imagined his father was repeating the questions he'd vocalized so many times before. "How had he failed? Where was the blade? What happened to the princess? Where was the treasure of the *Gunsway?* How had he been so careless as to lose his ship? Where was this ship's surgeon he hated so much?"

As if never pausing for even a second, the captain looked up directly at

Krist. "The HMS *Kent*, a fine ship, captained by a fine officer. We will see that it never returns home. They could not yet know we destroyed the *Emerald*."

"There was no talk of its loss. Only questions of its being late." Krist replied.

"Good," the thoughtful captain said. "Is the *Sally* ready to sail?"

"Yes, father."

"Tomorrow I want you to go. I wish to remain here on the island."

"Yes, father," Krist replied as he stepped from the cabin.

Krist sailed with his father his entire life, never knowing a home on land. Even with the manor house on the island, his father spent most of his time here in the confines of the *Chawbuck*. When in port, Krist much preferred to stay on land. He didn't know a mother.

Krist's grandparents offered to keep and raise Krist, but his father insisted he keep the boy. Krist loved his father, but loathed his work. Nothing in this work brought satisfaction to Krist. Island exploration was the closest thing to peace he found. Hassan was convinced Avery hid the treasure somewhere in these islands, most of which were on no known map. The main islands were located along the currents and trade routes, but there were countless others away from the main trade winds.

Most of these islands were the small remnants of ancient volcanos and nothing but piles of rocks. Others were empty but for beach and sand. Still others could feature a deep harbor, beautiful sandy beaches, and lush forests. Hassan taught his son well how to navigate these waters; winds, currents, tides, or not.

Several years ago, the captain and his son were stranded without wind, current, or tide. For three weeks they sat in the heat, no land in sight in any direction. Unprepared for this delay in their travel, they nearly starved to death. Two crew members went mad. Hassan slit their throats and tossed them overboard.

Since that experience, island exploration relied on the *Sally*. They gave her the nickname after the famous Persian battle of Salamas, where the Persians crushed the Greeks. *Sally* was a galley ship similar to the ancient Persian and Greek trireme warships.

Powered by sail and oars, the *Sally* was Hassan's insurance against ever finding himself stranded in the doldrums again. He believed Avery's treasure was on one of these hidden islands and practically impossible to find if you were sailing with the trade winds alone.

Powered by eighteen slaves and square sails, the *Sally* was reliable. Mostly, wind in the sails saved the slaves from the arduous labor of powering the *Sally*. From time to time the *Sally* would need to use those ores to explore during a calm sea.

Years ago, in the Gulf of Sidra, Hassan traded a cargo of young Irish girls for the *Sally*. It was returning from a trade mission in the eastern Mediterranean when Hassan met it off the coast of Libya. The *Sally* came fully stocked with galley slaves and a few crew members familiar with its nuances. When Hassan attempted to include several of the female passengers from the *Sally* as slaves with the young Irish captives, three of the *Sally's* male passengers objected. He shot them and dropped their bodies into the sea.

Hassan and Krist sailed the *Sally* to the New World, chaperoned by the *Chawbuck*. Krist was a natural at the helm.

Tomorrow he would sail.

This journey will again likely prove to be interesting, but unproductive exploring, Krist thought. In similar journeys, the area had provided visits to some exquisite islands upon which Kirst felt he was the first man ever to set foot.

Chapter Forty-Five

We are on foot traveling north. After leaving the farmlands near the river, we walked days at a time encountering no other life. This feels like a sacred land, untouched by a human. The countryside comprises wide open grasslands, patches of small thickets of scrub and what appear to be large forests. It's warm and dry, but the signs of animal life keep us from venturing deeply into those forests. We haven't needed to yet.

Raised in the untamed lands of Africa, Moses knows the dangers of wildlife. He assures us we will encounter more wildlife as we travel further north. Our two natives tell the stories of the wild Bengal tigers they heard so much about as they grew up. I assumed, as a princess, Esther grew up a very sheltered child. She has proven this assumption erroneous. She and Moses have arguments over the animal droppings we encounter along the way.

Regardless of their disagreements, they both feel the habitat conducive to be the home of India's big cats.

- Hinch

Deck of the Chawbuck in Harbor - Hassan's Island - 1748

Krist set sail early the next morning, heading due south toward the same calm waters where they experienced the doldrums years before. At full sail and making around eight knots, it would only be a few more hours before the *Sally* would need the oarsmen.

† † †

Hassan stood on the deck of the *Chawbuck*, one hand resting on the deck's swivel gun the other brought rum infused coffee to his lips. Otherwise motionless, he watched as the *Sally* left the harbor. The early morning, light streamed through the partly clouded sky and radiated off the sails, a sight he never tired of watching.

As Krist was cautious, thorough, and more than competent at the helm, Hassan didn't worry about the safety of his ship or his son. Hopefully, on this voyage he'd find the lost island.

As soon as the *Sally* vanished over the horizon and was out of sight, Hassan returned to his cabin. He compelled his aging body to keep moving. With crew ashore, he didn't have to pretend he wasn't in constant pain. Each step demanded resolve.

On this quest, he would never give in. Hassan sat in his cabin, recalling this entire journey. He reached for a journal he and Hillis snatched from the archives of the Royal Medical Society.

In their search for the identity of the pirate surgeon, Hassan overheard Creagh tell the young sailor in Newton Ferrers about a chief. He and his partner Dennison Hillis spent months working their way into the Royal Medical Society where they hoped to find a chief of the Royal Medical staff who may have had a son serving on a ship. They found in the records that an Alexander Cavinaugh served as chief of the medical staff from 1690 to 1704. In 1705 he died of a lung infection. Dr. Cavinaugh had only one son. Named after him and his mother, who died giving birth. Alexander Hincher Cavinaugh went to sea following his completion of medical school. He disappeared, never heard of again. When Dr. Cavinaugh died, all his possessions went to charity as per his will.

Among the effects in the Royal Medical Academy Archives, they found this journal. Thanking the clerk for his kindness for sharing it, a bag of gold coins helped the clerk ignore its disappearance.

Both Hillis and Hassan scoured the journal looking for anything that might give them an idea of the 'new home' Dr. Cavanaugh had referred to in a note written to his son that his son never received. The note was tucked into the back of the journal and read:

"To my dear son, your happiness brings me great joy.
Your journey has been a glorious adventure and your

adherence to the principles of truth brings me great hope. Your beautiful Persian princess will make you a wonderful wife. Your mother would have loved her, as I now do. As you have told me, you and she will never be safe. This I understand, but I hope to see you again before my days on earth end. May God protect you as you journey to a new home far from the reaches of your enemies."

Your loving father.

A P.S. at the bottom of the note simply stated. *"Thank you for the lovely verse, I cherish it as a token from an angel."*

The poem was printed on a beautiful parchment, folded carefully, and tucked in the back of the journal.

By the Poetess Diwan-i-Makhfi.

You with the dark curly hair and the breathtaking eyes,

your inquiring glance that leaves me undone.

Eyes that pierce and then withdraw like a blood-stained sword,

eyes with dagger lashes!

Zealots, you are mistaken—this is heaven.

Never mind those making promises of the afterlife:

join us now, righteous friends, in this intoxication.

Never mind the path to the Kaabah: sanctity resides in the heart.

Squander your life, suffer! God is right here.

Oh excruciating face! Continual light!

This is where I am thrilled, here, right here.

There is no book anywhere on the matter.

Only as soon as I see you do I understand.

If you wish to offer your beauty to God, give Zeb-un-Nissa

a taste. Awaiting the tiniest morsel, she is right here.

"Zeb-un-Nissa, poor Zeb-un-Nissa," he uttered to himself, "an actual heir to two great world empires, imprisoned by her own father. And her daughter the only surviving heir, hunted, only to be killed… by me."

Hassan smiled and shook his head slowly, considering the irony. Zeb-un-Nissa's mother was a direct descendent of the first Persian shah, Shah Ismail I, and her father was the Mugal Emperor Aurangzeb. Hassan had never met the princess, her father imprisoned her several years before Hassan joined the Persian navy under Shah Suleiman I.

When Shah Suleiman I died, they crowned his son, Shah Sultan Husayn. That's when Hassan became commander of the entire Persian navy. Husayn's crown wasn't threatened by Zeb-un-Nissa, she was still in prison. It was Zeb-un-Nissa's only daughter who was a threat, Husayn's stepsister, the Persian Princess Astella. A legitimate heir to the Persian Safavid Dynasty.

Zeb-un-Nissa was religious and known for her passion for helping the faithful make their pilgrimage to Mecca. It was at her insistence the Princess Astella traveled in the security of her grandfather's fleet to Mecca for the Hajj.

Hassan rested his boots on the table, leaned back and laughed at the thought of a few pirates being able to attack the massive Indian fleet and the powerful *Gunsway* and its captain so easily giving up. What cowards these Indians were. A Persian ship would never have given up.

Why Zeb-un-Nissa smuggled the Blade of Safavid and sent it with her daughter was still a mystery to Hassan. His only guess was to protect her daughter's legitimacy as an heir to the Persian throne. Hassan always thought that foolish. She of all people knew and even witnessed the fratricide associated with the accent to a throne. The princess would never live to rule, regardless of whatever 'blade' she possessed. Zeb-un-Nissa knew that. She watched her father assassinate his own father and brother. *Foolish! So very foolish!* He scoffed.

Now these many years later, the princess has claim to nothing. The Safavid Dynasty collapsed and the 'blade' has only symbolic relevance. To Hassan, that symbolic relevance related to his revenge for losing his ship, and the failure of his mission to recover the 'blade' and rescue the precious princess.

He lowered his legs off the table, stood slowly, shuffling over to a finely carved walnut table holding the platter of fruit, breads, and drink. He slowly refilled his cup.

Chapter Forty~Six

Journal Entry: March 1696 - Rajasthan, India
Alexander Hincher - Potential Prey

We passed several herds of deer over the past several days, but this morning we found the first signs of their predators. The fresh remains of two dead deer. The tracks surrounding the kills show we have more than one very large predator.

Moses, the warrior, takes the stance of a protector. Rudy teases him but is grateful for the appearance of security. It was late in the afternoon when we realized we, too, were being tracked. We spotted movement in the tall grasses growing parallel to the woods.

To our relief, we encountered a small herd of deer. When we spooked the creatures, they bounded away from us toward the woods. We saw no more signs of our follower.

By evening, we reached an abandoned farm. A single farmhouse made of tree branches and a small corral. No recent sign of any inhabitants, however. We consider ourselves blessed and secured it as our night's lodging. Moses blessed what he called a boma and calls it a gift from the gods. I have many times wondered what his feelings were about 'the gods.' He has not opened the door for me to ask.

The sounds of the wild were 'enlivening' as Rudy described it.

- Hinch

The Island - Glen's Cove - West Indies - 1748

"You went up to get coconuts and came back with a couple strays. What a morning. And you mistook them for pirates?" Rosemary asked struggling to hold back a laugh.

"The story I told was true."

"Stomping like elephants? When was the last time you told the truth? I mean the unvarnished truth?" she asked. "Can you even remember that far back?" she teased.

"I watched them for a while and saw they were looking for us. They can hear and smell. I just couldn't walk up and say, "Hello, I'm Glen, how do you do?" We'd like to have you for supper." He gave her a wink. "How often do we get strangers wandering around our island?"

"Funny how two love birds escape a pirate attack without being seen and drift to our island on a chunk of wood. One kiss in the jungle and you believe they're engaged?" She raised her eyebrows to accentuate the question. "I've seen no other signs of endearment between them. Are they just shy?" Rosemary asked.

"Oh, they are not engaged, that's for sure. That ring was not there when I unnerved Jack with my blade. Ol' Jack did some smooth slight-of-hand getting that ring on her finger. Surprised her as much as it did me when he slipped it on her hand. And that lifesaving kiss? She's a quick thinker; that was their first kiss. The shock of it returned the color to his face faster than my blade removed it. I don't blame him. Every time a pretty young woman grabs me and kisses me, I'm in shock."

Rosemary's eyes did not need the words to ask this question. "Oh? And exactly how often does that happen?"

"Well, I just know they're not engaged. In fact, I think they're trying to figure out what to do with each other and what to do to get back home."

"I have the same question. How do they get back home?" Rosemary said.

She continued feeding the baby, but her gaze never left his face. She knew the unspoken truce was about to be broken. If Jack didn't force the acceleration of their efforts to get off this island, she would. Their failure to escape the paradise of this lost island was the only wall standing between them.

"Well?" She didn't let go.

"Just believe me, please... You know what Walt and I are doing. It won't be long. We'll soon be off this island, weather or not."

Her feigned smile said he was excused, for now. Rosemary knew there was nothing he'd rather do than leave this discussion for another day... or year. She respected his ability to stick it out without permitting the discussion to evolve into a fight. She stood, handed the baby to Glen, and shooed him out.

He took the opportunity to leave the discussion for another day. With baby in arms, he left.

Eventually, without help from the weather, I'll have to do something bold. Maybe these two visitors can help me do something bold. Glen concluded.

† † †

Elizabeth turned to the soft sound of approaching steps. Her immediate smile softened Lydia's wrinkled brow and tight, youthful face. The cautious approach surprised Elizabeth. She'd expected a young teenager to be more carefree. Maybe she was unhappy being left to clean up?

At Elizabeth's urging, she joined her on the large, smooth rock divinely designed and placed for an audience to enjoy the games. For a few quiet minutes, they sat and watched Jack playing with the twins on water's edge.

"This is amazing," Elizabeth broke the silence. "How long have you lived here?"

"Too long." Lydia's curt response surprised Elizabeth. "Yes, it is nice. It's safe, we have everything. Everything but..." Lydia's tone of voice was sweet, not harsh or complaining, yet her simple comment explained everything. However, it sounded more like she was quoting someone else.

"The twins have each other. Mother has father, and they are wonderful, but I have no one."

She must really hunger for friends. I'm a complete stranger and she's so open. Was I that open? Though different in many ways, Elizabeth felt a unique connection to Lydia's struggle.

That statement triggered a question Elizabeth hadn't yet asked, which surprised her. Were there other families on the island? If so, how many and who and how did they all get here? The surprise of Glen, the family, the remarkable home, fireplace, and bathhouse literally wiped out the bigger questions. Their first question: "How do we get back home?" was brushed off with a "You don't; this is a lost island."

Elizabeth wondered how Jack accepted that answer. She figured since he just had a brush with a machete and probably the first passionate kiss in his life, he was still in shock.

Dropping all reserve to ask adult questions only of adults, yet to be tender, Elizabeth asked Lydia. "Are there others on this island?"

"No young people. Our families get together and the adults talk about survival, the storm, what we can do for protection if the wrong people come to the island, and sometimes they talk about being rescued. When they talk, mostly me and the twins play games and have fun. But I don't have friends."

Elizabeth's mind was reeling like crazy. A thousand questions that had slipped her mind were all back and a thousand more joined them. But the number one question winning the battle to be asked first was: *"How can I help this sweet young girl, who seems to hurt so much?"*

So, out it came. "Lydia, if you didn't live on this island, what would you want to do with your life?"

"Music!" Elizabeth hardly finished the question when Lydia answered as if she'd waited her entire life for someone to ask.

"Music?" Elizabeth repeated, tipping her head with eyebrows raised.

"Music! I love music. I want to sing. I want to dance. I want to be part of everything music. I want to play the violin and the flute and the piano." Lydia said this with so much passion, it caught Elizabeth off guard.

"How long have you been on this island?" Elizabeth asked again.

Her question wasn't meant to find out the number of years as much as a desire to get a bearing on how much Lydia was exposed to music in her life before the island. So many questions needed answers, but Elizabeth felt sensitive about Lydia's tender feelings.

"I was nine when we left our home. I hated to leave my friends, but the twins were babies so they didn't care, and Mother just wanted to support Father's dream to start fresh in the New World. They told me I would make new friends and I could take music lessons in our new home."

"What happened?" This was the big question and Elizabeth just couldn't wait any longer.

"They call it 'the storm'. I don't remember much except I was afraid. Mother held me and the twins below while the ship was thrown everywhere. Mother and Father don't talk about it and when the adults of the island get together, they send us off to play. We ended up here, and that's all I know." Lydia concluded her statement with a tone of despair.

Elizabeth sensed Lydia wanted to continue talking, but she withdrew slightly as Glen approached, holding little Lizzie. It was quite a contrast, powerful Glen holding that tiny little baby girl. For being such a Visigoth slayer, he was so tender with his little girl.

"May I?" Elizabeth stood and reached out to take little Lizzie from Glen. It was so clear Glen loved his little family, but Elizabeth couldn't but wonder if he understood how his sweet Lydia was hurting so much. As Elizabeth was now showering attention on the baby, Lydia got up and followed Glen to the water's edge where the twins were having fun besting Jack at skipping stones across the lagoon.

With Lydia's seat empty, Rosemary sat down beside Elizabeth. "Beautiful isn't she?"

"Precious," responded Elizabeth.

"I watched how you and Lydia were getting along. You are an answer to a prayer. Well, lots of prayers. She loves us, she loves her little brother and sisters, but this island is no place for her. There is no future here," Rosemary said, placing her hand on Elizabeth's arm as if they'd been friends a lifetime.

It surprised Elizabeth how forthright Rosemary was. In so few hours, both Lydia and now Rosemary were extremely open with a stranger. Just as with Violet, conversing with another woman began awkwardly, but quickly soothed her. Elizabeth recognized Lydia and Rosemary were social creatures and the comfort and safety of this beautiful secluded forest cove couldn't meet their needs.

They're prisoners here. Am I now one too? Her stomach tightened to the thought this might be the end of her quest.

"Do you ever plan to leave this place? Not just here," her head and shoulder motioning the small homestead, "but the island? I haven't explored the island and certainly don't know what else is here. Until last night, we didn't know if we were alone on it or not. I have so many questions, forgive me," Elizabeth said apologetically.

To Elizabeth's relief, Rosemary seemed eager to talk. "We were on our way to Antigua, where a new home—new life awaited us. We joined families who'd combined their life savings and chartered the *Bringhurst,* a large and very fine ship. The captain and crew were quite competent, but rowdy. When the storm became violent, Glen encouraged them to put in at Port Henry, which he insisted would be a safe harbor until the storm subsided. But they laughed and mocked his cowardice and told him to go below with the women. Once you know my Glen, one thing you will never accuse him of is cowardice."

Rosemary continued. "The storm caught us head on. We were certain we would drown. Only one other of the men, Walt, stayed topside with Glen, which is how we know what little we know about what happened up there. A giant wave slammed against the port side of the ship and washed all but a few of the crew overboard. Unfortunately, the few most vile of the crew is who survived. The wave severely injured the captain when the storm slammed him against the rail nearly washing him overboard. Glen took the helm, and together with Walt and the reluctant remaining crew, eventually brought the ship about and kept the ship somewhat upright until finally he caught sight of this island. Despite the wind and storm, the ship made a safe landing. Well, we all call it a landing, Glen calls it a wreck."

Elizabeth sat holding little Lizzie, transfixed, while Rosemary recounted the story. When Rosemary paused, she stared off in the distance. Elizabeth came back to the present and recognized how she had been gently rocking little Lizzie and holding her a little too tightly to protect her from the storm Rosemary was describing. She relaxed a bit, almost apologizing to poor Lizzie. Elizabeth saw Rosemary wasn't watching the kids, Jack, and Glen play. She was reliving some scene in her mind.

Patiently, but anxiously, Elizabeth waited for Rosemary. Finally, she continued.

"Something happened during that storm, something terrible. It broke my Glen. It's unspoken, so I don't know what it was. But we lost part of him that day." Rosemary trailed off.

Of the hundreds of questions Elizabeth wanted answers to, it was the new one that found utterance.

"Which part did you lose? I mean, I've known him for only a few hours, and I met him at the tip of a machete, but I don't think I know many men as complete as Glen," She waved her hand motioning to how he was delighting the children.

Smiling and agreeing with her assessment of Glen's playful part of fatherhood and his care for the family, Rosemary shocked Elizabeth with a question of her own.

"What about Jack? Short of being a father yet, isn't he a complete man? You're marrying him after all." Rosemary's smile added emphasis making Elizabeth's heart skip.

Elizabeth could only stammer out an, "Uh, well, um."

As if the stammering was in relation to her comment that Jack was yet to be a father, Rosemary teasingly added an addendum to the question. "You don't have children yet, do you?"

Elizabeth smiled, then chuckled, realizing Rosemary was teasing. "Tell me about Jack. You must love him very much to risk so much to be with him."

This was not at all what Elizabeth wanted to talk about. The volume of questions she wanted answers to revolved around getting off this island, killing a monster, and rescuing her sister. But it was Jack who brought the conversation to an end.

Glen had made a ball from what looked like fabric sewn around a collection of the fluffy ground cover growing prolifically along the base of some larger trees. One of the twins kicked it up toward the two women and Jack came running up the beach to retrieve it.

Elizabeth tossed Rosemary's line of questions to him. "Jack, Rosemary was asking if you're a father yet."

There couldn't have been a more random question and Jack couldn't have been caught more off guard. Elizabeth was proud of herself at the dismay she'd created on his face.

"What have you two been talking about up here?" he asked.

He looked at Elizabeth holding the baby, then back to Rosemary. His total look of bewilderment caused the two women to burst into laughter. That frightened Lizzie, and she began to cry. Elizabeth stood up, handing the baby to Jack. He dropped the ball to take the baby. She picked up the ball and ran with it down to join the kids and Glen.

Elizabeth regretted the end of her conversation with Rosemary, but the line of questions had taken an uncomfortable turn for the worse. Escape was the only choice. She dropped the ball and kicked it awkwardly toward Jenny. It was time to play.

† † †

Lizzie immediately stopped crying and stared up at Jack, who stared back in amazement. Jack held her tenderly. Rosemary stood to take Lizzie from the surprised Jack, but sat back down and smiled.

Jack joined her on the rock as Rosemary said, "You've got quite a girl there, Jack."

Jack was looking at Lizzie when he said, "She is something."

Rosemary smiled and said, "I was talking about Elizabeth."

Jack could only mutter, "Oh, you have no idea."

Rosemary then asked, "Do you?"

This question pulled Jack's attention away from Lizzie and back to Rosemary who was staring directly at him. "Do I?"

Rosemary repeated the question a little more completely. "Do you know what kind of girl you have there? Elizabeth, I mean?"

Jack shifted his seat, repositioning Lizzie in his arms while trying to stir up some confidence in his answer. "Of course, I do. Someday I am going to marry her, after all."

"After all what?" Rosemary asked. "When are you going to marry her? After you get off the island?" Her pause was unnerving. "After you find a minister?" Another pause. "After you've known her for more than a few days?"

Jack froze, stared back at Rosemary and felt she was staring into his soul. If she only knew what he'd done was to protect her. He let that be. "How did you know?"

"Glen told me. Inside that big playful husk is a giant of a perceptive, observant, brilliant, and very..."

Jack inserted, "Romantic?"

"No." Rosemary continued, "Protective and fearsome warrior."

Jack turned to face her. "About that," Jack questioned. "Here we are in what most any decent man would consider absolute paradise. A beautiful wife," he gave a slight bow of the head, "happy and loving children, plenty of fresh food, your own personal spring. You're protected in this," Jack gestured with his free arm, referring to the expanse of the beautiful secluded cove "this glen. Do you call it a glen? That would make it Glen's glen." Jack chuckled to himself and then continued. "There is nothing missing. Yet, it's just a feeling, but there's something wrong. Something amiss. And when I began the question, Glen quickly reminded me of his machete and asked if he needed to get it out again. I let it drop. You don't have a machete close by?"

In a pained smile, Rosemary turned to look back at the lagoon. Jack followed her eyes and head to see where Elizabeth had joined in what looked like a very one-sided game of kickball. She and Lydia were no match for the cheating tactics of a father and the two young twins who had no conception of rules.

"No, I leave all the machete action to my warrior. Jack, we're not alone on this island and our neighbors are not all friendly. We can't stay in this 'paradise', but there is no way off either. Something happened to Glen when we wrecked on this island. He's always been protective, but until he feels confident he can guarantee our safe escape, we are all held hostage here. Welcome to paradise."

Chapter Forty-Seven

Journal Entry: March 1696 - Rajasthan, India
Alexander Hincher - Potential Prey

We elected to travel a more north-westerly direction to avoid the forests. We don't feel prepared to challenge a Bengal tiger or two. According to Leilyn, the tigers are not normally a predator of humans until they feel threatened, but Rudy says Moses looks too threatening to take a chance.

By mid-day we encountered a small village built alongside a small spring. Surrounding the village were fields freshly cultivated. Unlike the earlier small 'boma' this looked to be an active village. There was no one working the fields, however. We could see people in the village. As we approached, we saw them very agitated.

Strangers visiting didn't appear to be too uncommon, for they gave us very little attention. As we passed the fields and entered the village proper, we witnessed great concern, weeping, and commotion at one of the small stone and mud houses.

Leilyn and Esther hurried to the scene. They are native to these lands where the rest of us were obviously foreigners.

They quickly learned the cause. Tigers attacked several of the village's children. The report was a tiger killed one child and badly wounded others before someone heard their cry and men from the village chased the tiger off. They also told us one child was still missing.

They put me to work immediately. Esther offered my surgical skills, and I began patching up the viciously torn flesh. I became immediately grateful for our boma the other night. The power and damage from these large cats is shocking. One boy not only has his flesh torn away, but the impact of the attack broke his leg.

Using medications I carried in my pack, I soothed the pain and sewed the flesh back together. This will not be a beautiful scar if he lives, but if he does live, he will have stories to tell. Fortunately, his artery was not severed or he would be dead already.

The other two children are not so bad, but they too will have scars. I wonder what kind of stories they will tell when they gather together and pull off a shirt or raise a pant to show what a tiger can do.

I am certain these young boys are like any boy in any culture where the story will grow each time they tell it.

I was not aware what else was taking place while Esther, Leilyn, and I worked on these three boys. But Rudy and Moses went with several men from the village in search of the tiger.

To our total dismay, our three Maasai princesses followed along and then went in search of the lost child. They returned with a very frightened but safe young girl. The joy was unmeasurable. The princesses followed the tracks from the point of the attack and found this little one hiding high in a tree. It took some coaxing to get her to come down.

It was late in the evening when the men returned. We were sitting together near a small fire when they delivered a large tiger to the village as a trophy.

The success of the day in saving three lives, rescuing a threatened little girl, and killing the large tiger would have been such a triumph if the grief over losing a dear little boy did not overshadow it.

- Hinch

The Island - Glen's Cove - West Indies - 1748

The game ended abruptly when little Jeremy got too excited and kicked the ball into the lagoon and went chasing after it. Jeremy was an accomplished swimmer, even at such a young age. The ball was not. It took on too much water and once back on shore, all it could do was sit and leak.

This was not the ball's first adventure into the lagoon. Glen picked it up and set it on a rock where it could dry out in the hot afternoon sun. He winked at Elizabeth, recognizing her look of relief.

"The island's heat's a bit uncomfortable compared to that on the ship." He knew well that onboard a ship the constant breeze kept things comfortable. Here there was none. Elizabeth nodded in agreement.

"Well children, looks like it's time to get to work." Glen motioned to Elizabeth and then to Jack where he sat with Rosemary, "We've got to get these two a place to sleep tonight—two places to sleep tonight," he added, winking at Elizabeth. "We don't want them curling up together on the beach again. That would just be too improper, especially at my home."

"Elizabeth can have my bed. I can sleep on the ground." Lydia immediately offered. With a nod of Glen's head, that deal was done. Jeremy followed suit and offered his bed to Jack.

With a chuckle Glen replied, "Jeremy, that is thoughtful but Jack will not fit in your bed."

"Then he can sleep in your bed," Jeremy generously offered.

"Where will I sleep?" Glen questioned.

"On the ground," Jeremy proudly said.

"And Mom, where will she sleep?

"With Jack."

"Let's get to work, Jack is getting his own bed—outside." Glen wasn't about to explain all of this to his little twins. Elizabeth and Lydia smiled at each other.

"Thank you, Lydia, that's kind, but I will be most happy to sleep on the ground and I don't want to put you out." Elizabeth took Lydia by the arm as they walked back toward Jack and Rosemary.

The group reached the large rock where Rosemary and Jack were quietly sitting enjoying Lizzie.

"Well," Glen said to Jack, "Looks like you made a new friend. You seem to move fast with the girls."

"Glen!" Rosemary's stern but simple rebuke merited a slight raise of an eyebrow.

"What? It's just that Lizzie doesn't take to strangers very often." Glen said, trying to defuse his poke at Jack.

"Lizzie doesn't take to strangers? Jack and Elizabeth are the first two strangers she has ever seen. And they are not nearly as strange as you make them out to be." Rosemary got to her feet and reached for Lizzie.

"Well, if they are not so strange, Jeremy volunteered my bed and suggested Jack sleep with you tonight."

Rosemary turned quickly back to Glen and sat back down, "And what did you say?"

"I'm still thinking about it."

Elizabeth smiled at the shock on Jack's face. Lydia's grin lit up her face.

Glen scooped up Lizzie from Jack. Marching back to the house, he dictated the sleeping arrangements.

"Elizabeth will be in with Lydia. Lizzie, Jeremy, and Jenny will be in their own beds, I will be in my own bed with my own wife, and Jack will sleep—outside!"

"Well, there you have it—Glen, lord of the glen has spoken, and I get the biggest room of all. All to myself." Jack's voice was proud and bold, with only the slightest tinge of relief as he stood. They all headed to the house.

† † †

When they reached the house, Glen grabbed Jack, "There's a secret to sleeping well on this island, especially if you're alone, outside. Let me show you that secret."

As the two of them climbed the hill behind the house, Jack began the conversation. "Glen, today is one of the most interesting days of my life. You and Rosemary and your family are remarkable, but you know, Elizabeth and I . . . how do we get back home?"

"What took you so long?" Glen expected this request. It surprised him it took Jack so long to ask. "I know you didn't accept my first answer to that question."

"Pardon me?"

"Jack, your face has been asking that question all day. Why did it take your lips so long to utter the words?"

"Well—I, or we . . . " Jack started.

Glen unsheathed the machete, which disrupted Jack's answer. He cut a vine and pulled it free from the branches it clung to.

"We all want to get home, Jack. None of us want to stay here. But we can't leave."

Glen watched as Jack struggled to find his words. He knew what was going on in Jack's head. It had gone on in his own. He smiled, putting the machete away, though, the machete had inspired Jack to propose to Elizabeth. Could it inspire a fresh solution? Is Jack what Glen needed these years?

"It may appear harsh and final, but Jack, there's no way off this island. Not now anyway."

Jack squinted his eyes and slightly raised his hands, ready to ask.

"Jack, our ship was already off course when the storm hit. It was not a storm; it was a hurricane. The captain ignored the signs. We argued. He and the crew were fools. We should have all drowned. It carried us completely out of traditional trade routes. Only God knows this island exists. Only through His providence did we get dropped here.

"There are no strong currents, no reliable winds of consequence, no tides favorable to getting off this island. Your arrival and where you landed backs up my calculation of where we might be. I've sat for days watching the wind, the tides, and current on that beach. There are only two beaches on the entire island. One thing troubles me though. If you were only days from Antigua when pirates attacked the *Emerald,* you sailing to this island—well, sail is figurative—you drifted as you said almost two days. Any craft under sail will miss this island. It troubles me why the *Emerald* was this far south."

"I need to rethink our position," Glen mumbled to himself as his blade sliced through a growth of brush.

"How do you know all this?" Jack finally found words.

"Observation. And I've had a little experience with navigation," Glen responded.

"You say there's no chance at all to get off this island? Have you ever tried?" Jack's tone became more firm.

Glen looked directly into Jack's eyes. Jack didn't flinch.

I like his spirit. Well, now that I'm not holding a blade to his throat. He's on a lost island with an attractive woman, what's his hurry? What's in Antigua that can't wait?

In that flash of a second as they stared at each other, Glen recognized every thought, question, and concern that had troubled him these past few years was now crowding Jack's mind. Glen's defiance softened.

"Tried and died. Most of the crew perished during the storm. The captain died from injuries. We buried him. The few remaining crew, convinced they could go for help, piled into the long boats. A month later, one boat drifted to your beach with two dead, bleached, and bird pecked bodies onboard."

"What happened? What went wrong?"

"They left the island, Jack. That's where they went wrong. Now let's get a bed made for you. If you're going to find a way off this island, you'll need a good night's rest," Glen said. "There are plenty of questions running through your mind. I know. They ran through mine a few thousand times as well. They still do, almost every day. The questions are excited to have a fresh mind to exhaust."

Glen cut armfuls of soft ground cover free and loaded them on Jack.

"Once you've spent some time with our neighbors in the settlement, you might have some ideas we've not thought of. You'll like the people over there. They'll like you."

"Settlement?" Jack asked, arms full of what felt like soft velvet rope.

"Jack, I'm glad you're here." Glen said. "We needed you."

✝ ✝ ✝

The next morning the family gathered at what they considered the dining room - which was at a table similar to the one on which he and Elizabeth escaped. He assumed it was taken from the wrecked ship. Cleverly fashioned from small tree limbs and lashed together with something Jack had not seen before. The chairs were creatively fashioned so each member of the family sat comfortably at the table, regardless of their size. Jack leaned over to see even the twins' chairs with longer legs brought the children up to the level of the table.

What would he think of next, a chair for the baby?

Rosemary prepared a delightful breakfast of fruit and fish. The aroma of the fish as she cooked it was a reward by itself. Jack regretted his urgency to leave the cove. He smiled when he remembered his comment about Glen's glen. The morning pleasantries evolved into the good-byes. Glen fashioned a small bag and filled it with fruit and dried fish and a flask full of water.

Glen gave the couple a detailed description of the island and gave them instructions on what and who to look for as they trekked across the island to the harbor where they would find the remnants of the wrecked ship. Lydia volunteered to accompany them, but Glen denied her that adventure.

As they prepared to leave, Jack pulled Glen aside and whispered, "Your family is not alone here in the cove. We had a visitor last night."

Glen whispered back, "I wondered where he was."

"You know him?" Jack asked.

"We're stranded on an island, Jack, and have been for two years. We traveled from the old country together. I know everyone. You will too. Be careful. Take care of Elizabeth."

As he said that, Glen gave Jack a look that frightened him. He also offered Jack the machete.

Glen slapped Jack on the back, almost knocking him over as he said goodbye. Finished giving hugs, Jack and Elizabeth headed up the hill in the opposite direction from which they had entered the small homestead the morning before.

Chapter Forty~Eight

Journal Entry: March 1696 - Rajasthan, India
Alexander Hincher - Potential Prey

They gave us a comfortable bed for which we were grateful, but when we arose, I found Esther in the home of the grieving parents, comforting and soothing their loss. I went to what they turned into an infirmary to see to my patients. To my surprise, two Indian men I did not meet the night before were attending them.

I approached to introduce myself and learn what they were doing, but we didn't understand each other. I needed Esther or Leilyn. I stepped out to look for one of them. I saw Leilyn leaving a small building that served as the kitchen; she brought a broth that smelled marvelous; gave me a smile and entered the small infirmary. I followed her back in. She too was surprised to see these two men caring for the patients. She had words with them, words I didn't understand. She left the broth on a small table and stormed out.

She returned immediately with the village leader talking and gesturing passionately. When they entered, I followed them back in. Again they had words I didn't understand and the two men glared at me, glared at Leilyn, then said something very foul. Still I didn't understand, and they stomped out, practically yelling something as they stormed through the village in the direction I assumed we would be going.

I am embarrassed that my thoughts were 'I hope we never meet them again.' My thoughts should have been for my patients. Once I got hold of myself, I slipped over to them and helped Leilyn feed them some breakfast. At one point, Leilyn held up a spoon to my lips for me to taste her broth. It was wonderful!

A few moments later Aadarsh, the villages guru, entered the infirmary
and whispered to Leilyn. I'd watched her countenance transition
from happy when she left the kitchen, to passionately angry as she
confronted the two men in the infirmary, to joyful and playful as we fed
my three little patients, to fearful as she spoke with the village's guru.
She is a woman of passion.

When they finished, Aadarsh bowed and left. In stepped a young woman
named Kairah, who quickly took the bowl of broth from me and ushered
me out of the room without a word.

As Leilyn and I walked toward the small building where I spent the
night, she explained that we had to leave immediately. Aadarsh sent
others to get Rudy, Moses, our three Maasai princesses, and Esther.
They handed a large bundle of food to Moses, assuming he was our
slave and should carry out the servant's duty. He and I exchanged
glances, and we both smiled. Though Moses looked the part of a
warrior, he could be good natured.

Aadarsh himself led us out of the village heading directly into the forests
where we and my patients encountered the tigers. We couldn't help but
wonder what we were up against. Little was said. Leilyn felt confident
following him, so we put our trust in this man we barely knew.

We encountered several signs of tigers before we turned and worked
our way out of the woods. We saw another settlement on the horizon; it
appeared to be moving as if the buildings had legs. The closer we got,
we recognized that indeed they did.

Elephants, large, no giant elephants. The closer we got, the larger they
appeared. A large, jovial man greeted Aadarsh. We learned he was the
mahout, the keeper of the elephants. There appeared to be hundreds of
these magnificent beasts. There was no way to count them, as we could
hardly see past the first few in front of us.

After a few words with the mahout, Aadarsh explained several things to
Leilyn and Esther, and left the same way we came. Speaking as quickly
as I could, I thanked him as he walked away. He didn't understand me,
but I hoped he understood how grateful I felt. 'Maybe this was one of
those men I would want to live in my civilization. With no reward, no
motivation, no apparent purpose, he served a small band of strangers.
I thought. 'Maybe he was just paying us back for saving the child.' No
matter, my gratitude was sincere.

Our new host, the mahout, turned to us and welcomed us to his
elephant caravan. He said his name was Sangha, he smiled when he
said 'it means handsome.'

- Hinch

On the trail - The Island - West Indies - 1748

"How did you sleep?" asked Elizabeth once they were clear of the family.

"Alone." *Well, not really alone. She doesn't need to know that.*

Elizabeth smiled as she teased, "Disappointed not to cuddle up
with Rosemary?"

Jack walked ahead of her and tripped on a vine, nearly falling when he
turned to challenge her tease. Her wide grin invited a retort.

"And get impaled with Glen's machete? No thanks."

"Where did this come from?" She gently spun the ring on her finger.

Jack side-stepped the question. "So why doesn't he at least try to get off the
island? Glen is not lost; he knows where he is. If he had a map, I bet he could
pin-point within a few miles exactly where we are."

"So you wonder why he doesn't use that knowledge?" Elizabeth asked and
then answered herself, "I think because he lost his nerve."

"He doesn't dare?" questioned Jack.

"Jack, Rosemary told you Glen saved the ship. When Glen told you there
was no way off the island, he gave you enough viable reasons as to why we
can't. Enough that you're convinced he knows exactly where we are. Did you see
the home he built? And that oven? I think nothing is out of his reach. The only
thing can be nerves."

"Glen saves everyone, obviously knows this ocean, builds a life for his
family and is nervous? I'm not arguing but, please. Believe me, that machete
was in the hand of a very confident man," Jack said.

"Ok, you know men. In fact, I believe you think you are one. So tell me,
when does a man stop dreaming of more?"

Jack stopped cold.

Elizabeth continued. "There's only a few reasons men give up and settle.

There is a reason Glen isn't willing to try to get off this island. I don't know what caused it, but he lost his nerve. According to Rosemary, six crew members survived. They took the long boats, where did they go? We know at least two are dead. Only the man they call Walt witnessed what happened during the storm. His report, according to Rosemary, makes Glen out to be a hero. I doubt Glen is obsessed with a fear of disappointing people. He can't possibly doubt his own ability. There's something else." Elizabeth conjectured.

"You think if he wanted to, they could get off this island?" Jack motioned for Elizabeth to take the lead up the trail.

"They'd be off this island," she said. "You didn't answer my question."

"What question?"

"When do men stop dreaming?"

Jack shook his head, trying to see if by shaking it he might follow her train of thought. It didn't work.

Actually, that's a good question. Is she asking about Glen—or me?

"Well?" Elizabeth sprang over a fallen, rotted tree, waking Jack from his mind's puzzles.

The frond of a tall fern slapped his face. Jack hadn't considered the trail they'd be following or noticed the foliage nipping at their legs. *Is this the right trail?*

Elizabeth gave the slightest of glances over her shoulder, but never broke stride.

Stepping over the log, Jack answered. "For me, the biggest roadblock is success. Something a little risky happens, even a little dangerous, a little scary, and you get through it safely and land someplace comfortable, you hesitate to push your luck. You consider yourself victorious and settle. Even if it wasn't your dream. Even a mediocre comfort is better than taking the risk of losing that little success. You wonder if it was worth it, anyway."

Slowing, Elizabeth faced Jack. "You say Glen's afraid to push his luck. I say he lost his nerve. We're saying the same thing."

"That's not what I said."

"What did you say?"

"I said... oh, never mind."

"There's no never mind here. You said success is a roadblock to reaching a dream. Whose dream?"

Jack mustered his courage. This casual conversation was becoming a full on exploratory, an exercise he once cherished at the academy. An exercise in which his logic and reason once gloried.

"Elizabeth, success can be a roadblock to reaching a goal. You know what a roadblock is, don't you? Back home, did they ever close a road? Make you take a detour?"

I'll take that scowl as a yes.

"Failure is also a roadblock. So is distraction, ignorance, lack of resources, weakness, laziness, addiction, anything can get in the way."

Jack surprised himself. *You still got it.*

She turned and continued up the path, seeming to shrug off his eloquence. "So, why are they still on this island? Glen's lazy?" She missed his sigh and mock surrender and didn't wait for an answer. "What's your dream, Jack? And what's the roadblock?"

My dream is to end this conversation, and the roadblock is a woman with too many questions.

He reached into his pocket. Content ol' Denn's map was safely there, he stepped over a small stream. "Fame, fortune, glory. Same as any man. This island is just a minor detour."

Elizabeth didn't even flinch.

Did she hear me?

Chapter Forty~Nine

Journal Entry: March 1696 - Rajasthan, India
Alexander Hincher - Apprentice Mahout

Sangha became an instant friend. He is as friendly and jovial as Aadarsh was serious and quiet. Aardash took his role as village guru seriously. And it appears Sangha takes his role as elephant keeper just as serious and is having a wonderfully fun time doing so.

He ushered us past the elephants and provided a delicious lunch under a large canopy put up to protect the other mahouts and riders from the scorching sun. The elephants are being prepared for a journey which we will apparently join.

As we enjoyed the shade of the canopy, Leilyn shared with us why we were so quickly ushered out of the village. At Aadarsh's instruction we didn't speak all morning; it was as quiet of a journey through the forest as possible.

The two men we encountered at the infirmary were Marathas, a powerful opposition group to the Mughal empire. The angry man claimed to be Valen, the Maharaj Kumar, son of the Maharaj, the Maratha king.

Leilyn smiled as she explained how even petty leaders take upon themselves titles, even un-deserved titles to look important and to exercise power over others.

I didn't understand the danger until Leilyn told us that Valen claimed we were sent from Aurangzeb to spy on the Marathas. It wouldn't be long until they would send a force to track us down and take us captive. Aadarsh escorted us from the village himself so none of the other villagers would be in danger by knowing where we went.

Esther knew well how her grandfather treated his enemies. The Marathas would be merciless in their effort to find us and especially if they recognized we were traveling with his granddaughter. She expressed her concern for the villagers. Though they were of the Vaisyas caste, they would not get any respect from the Marathas.

My little patients looked good this morning, and that was my only consolation. If we hadn't come by, the tiger would still be loose and the young boys would be dead. That is the only reason Aadarsh risked helping us escape Valen's vindictiveness. I wonder what set him off in the first place. Was it Leilyn or was it me?'

We spent the day traveling directly through tiger country. High on the elephants, they never threatened us with danger though we watched tigers and they watched us throughout the day. As we dined tonight, Sangha assured us that tigers are not typically nocturnal hunters therefore we are safe. I happen to know better. I appreciate his effort to help us feel safe.

I notice, however, there are several guards with muzzel-loaded flintlock muskets surrounding the camp. I guess that is just in case nobody told the tigers they are not nocturnal hunters.

- Hinch

Ship Graveyard Overlook - The Island - West Indies - 1748

Glen stood on the edge of a small clearing, overlooking a small rocky cove which had become the resting place for several lost ships. Glen estimated the caravel to be from the late 1500s, the carrack about a hundred fifty years it's junior and the barque to be the youngest of the several wrecked vessels, maybe only forty or fifty years old. None of them contained any treasure. Each looked damaged by sea battles. He wondered how the other ship, a small schooner came so far south, being it looked to be of English origin.

These abandoned ships were now joined by their newest friend, a beautiful well outfitted galleon that too was badly damaged, abandoned and left to drift, the *Emerald of the Sea*. This small rocky bay had become a gathering place for the casualties of the eastern sea. Over the past two years, parts of these ships were salvaged to help the island residents become more at home. None of the ships were deemed salvageable enough to ever leave the island.

Glen figured they abandoned these ships and left them to sink, but before they lost all buoyancy, wind or current or providence brought them to this resting place. Glen knew any ship under wind power and command of a captain would miss this island by over sixty miles. That gave Glen comfort. *But how did the Emerald arrive so quickly? As I said to Jack, I need to rethink our island's position.*

One day soon, he'd have to hike down to the bay and explore Jack and Elizabeth's ship.

As Glen turned to return to his cove, he stood face to face with Hunter. Hunter was the vilest of men. As far as Glen knew, he was the only person on the island who knew Satan personally. If Glen didn't hope that one day the gods would permit him to send Hunter back to hell, he would have unsheathed his machete and been free of the filthy swine right then. He had to wait for God's timing. It was Hunter's deception and taunting that caused the captain to sail into the storm, which eventually brought them to this island. Glen would be free of his past had Hunter not discovered him and Walt back in Sheffield and then decided to followed them to Liverpool.

Hunter was the only reason the island paradise wasn't an island paradise. He seemed to ooze around the island like a parasite. He never seemed to take part in the actual work of life here. His woman, Joanna, was virtually a slave. As much as the others, particularly the women on the island, tried to befriend her and support her, she remained apart. It was painful for the others to watch her provide for this vermin.

Lydia asked several times why Hunter couldn't get jungle fever and just die. The others had all thought that too, but it took the voice of an innocent to vocalize it.

Glen didn't know how much Hunter knew about his past, but he knew it was too much and that Hunter was dangerous. He didn't want to admit there was anything to know, so Glen avoided any reference to any other reason Hunter would follow them to Liverpool than make the decision to travel to the New World.

"What now?" demanded Glen.

"You've got friends," scowled Hunter. "How did they get here? And what do they want?"

"What they want," Glen answered, "is what we all want, and that is to get off this island."

"Yes, they do, everyone does." Hunter said, "Everyone but you."

Glen used to hate himself for permitting his disgust for Hunter to ignite a flame of hate within himself. Though he'd learned to breathe deep and calm himself with these unwelcome encounters, his knuckles turned white as he reached for his machete by habit then remembered he sent it with Jack.

"And how did they get to this island?" Hunter asked again.

"They floated. Go down to the beach and look for yourself. You'll find their vessel safely stored there, a very buoyant table."

Glen had shown everyone the ship's graveyard as he called it, and they had thoroughly examined each stranded ship, but he was not anxious for Hunter to see that it collected an additional casualty, especially before he checked it out himself. *Perhaps, it may offer some new options,* he hoped.

He offered to accompany Hunter to the beach, "Here, I'll go with you. Maybe together we can sail away," Glen said, not at all trying to hide his displeasure.

Chapter Fifty

The elephant caravan has been in the service of both the Hindu
Maratha and the Muslim Mughals. Sangha is not a political man.
He is Kshatriya by birth, which means he should be part of the Hindu
caste serving as warriors. He laughs at what he should be and the
stations determined by birth. Because so much of life here in India
is determined and controlled by birth, he has to be careful with his
opinions.

We learned the people in Aadarsh's village are Vaisyas, destined to
be herders and farmers. Some may become artisans, but the boys we
saved were of the Dalits caste or untouchable caste and shouldn't have
received the care we provided.

Had they been the Shundra, which are simple laborers, it would have been
permissible. 'These children should have been working,' Valen said. The
fact they were not where they should have been when the tiger attacked
was karma. They should have been left to die. Our interference disrupted
their circle of life.

"They should punish the village," he demanded. Sangha laughed as he
shared all of this with us as we sat and talked tonight.

"Valen, and his kind," he said, "think they have the wisdom of
Brahmins, the power of the Kshatriyas, the value of the Vaisyas, while
the rest of us bow to their superiority. In reality," he continued, "his
kind are no more than elephant dung the Shudras and Dalits have to
clean up."

"What kind of God would create men to be rulers over other men?" he asked. "Believing in that kind of God makes no sense."

I wondered if it was a genuine question seeking an answer or if it was just a way to share an opinion. I hesitated just long enough to know. He answered it himself.

"You have the God of Israel they call Jehovah. The Christian God they call the Christ. In Islam they have Allah. We Hindus have several among us which are Brahma, Shiva, and Vishnu. Your friends, the Maasai, have Enkai. Then there's Buddha. My friends, the list goes on. How many gods are there? But more important than how many gods, the question is, 'what makes it worth being a god?'"

I struggled to understand that question, let alone answer it. Before I could even try, he added to my dilemma by asking, "Do any of these gods know who you are?" He continued. "What do they want you to do, or even better, what do they want you to become?"

He saw I was not keeping up with the questions, so he smiled as he asked one more. "If God knows you, and He helps you become what He wants you to become, what is His reward?"

Sangha stopped and emptied his third or fourth chalice of wine. I wasn't accurately keeping track, but this man could drink. Were these questions coming from a drunk?

This was an interesting way to think about gods. I became curious as to how a Hindu merchant could come up with these considerations. He apparently has been around and has had discussions like this with every kind of man.

What did he know about these gods? I wanted to choose my words carefully because I didn't want to challenge our host and I didn't know how he might respond. I quickly learned he welcomed open discussion.

I was ready to ask which of these gods he followed when he set down his chalice and continued his questions.

"Think about it. If you were a God," he asked, "why would you create an earth? Why would you create man? What would you be trying to accomplish?"

I never thought God had some kind of motivation, he was just... God. Was this Sangha really a Brahmin rather than a Kshatriya? I wondered. No, he was just a man who wanted to think God knew him. That he was someone with an intimate relationship with God, a child of a God, with unlimited potential. And he wondered what God's purposes were.

I studied medicine; I study humankind. I am passionate about preserving life. I have respected peoples of all extractions and have seen the best and worst in man. I hate to admit, I never ever thought God might have a personal purpose as a God. Did God actually have a plan? What did He want?

I know many priests, some rabbis, some imams, and I've recently met a guru, but not one of them got me to thinking as this mahout has. It took and elephant keeper to help me think about God as something or someone who might actually know who we are, and care. Someone who has something He wants to accomplish.

'What's God's job?' That's the question I want an answer to. Tomorrow, I hope to spend time with my new Guru Sangha, the mahout.

I have not had this kind of intellectual discourse for a long time. Actually never.

- Hinch

On the Trail - The Island - West Indies - 1748

"What makes you say Glen knows exactly where we are? The hurricane blew the ship off course. He was lucky to find a piece of ground to wreck. According to Rosemary, Walt told everyone when the captain went down and most the crew were swept overboard, Glen saved everyone. You think he chose where to wreck the ship?" Elizabeth asked.

Trying to answer carefully and accurately, Jack replied. "I'm not saying he wrecked on purpose or that he chose this island to wreck by accident. When he told me there was no way off, he said the tides, the trade winds, and the currents all placed this island in a position where it would be too difficult to find by accident or on purpose and practically impossible to leave. To even make that statement he would have to know more about tides, winds, and currents than a family man from Sheffield, England would know. Glen is a mariner. What kind I don't know, but there's more to him than he lets on."

Jack continued, "How old do you think Glen and Rosemary are?"

"What? What does that have to do with anything?" Elizabeth asked.

"Glen thought we could reach the ship by nightfall."

Elizabeth grew up in a home with one sister. A sister who as each day passed got further away. She'd never learned to understand men. What Glen's and Rosemary's ages have to do reaching the others by nightfall mystified her.

Chapter Fifty~One

Journal Entry: March 1696 - Rajasthan, India
Alexander Hincher - Student of Theology

The ride high atop Sangha's elephants is surprisingly smooth. The gentle rolling motion is relaxing and comfortable. If we hadn't rested well last night, the rhythmic motion would lull one to sleep.

Rudy did his best today to extinguish my enthusiasm. We traveled together all morning. Esther and Leilyn were together on their own elephant and Moses and my harem were together on one of the lead elephants. Moses took quickly to being an elephant mahout. His elephant, Gihanga, as he calls him, responds to his direction with little encouragement.

When I shared my newfound discovery-of-thought with Rudy, I asked, "Why does God do what He does?"

With almost no thought he said, "Love."

I spent hours, thoughtful, deep pondering hours, considering this question. I was not about to accept a trite, superficial answer like that.

"Love?" I replied, not as a question but as a challenge.

"Yea, God is love. Says so in your Bible," he said. "We love Him because He first loved us. Love."-

Rudy didn't understand the meaning of my question at all. I want to know what God wants. What does He expect to get out of being the God of a world full of every kind of human possible? Good, bad, bond, free, male, female, strong, weak; what's His reward?

Why had I expected to have the same kind of intellectually stimulating conversation with Rudy as I did with an elephant keeper?

I recognize in the past two years, cutthroats, murderers, rapists and the like surrounded me. I was fortunate to learn from wise shamans, laiboni's, and sanusi. I met people of grand character even if they were low in station. But nothing kindled the flame of my thoughts like this has. Rudy almost doused the flame.

- Hinch

On the Trail - The Island - 1748

Jack and Elizabeth reached a rise in the trail clear from the thick forest.

To the far left, the coastline meandered in and out, meeting a lazy ocean. Jack thought how Glen was right about the location of the island; no waves of consequence. As a young child, Jack lived in a coastal town and it was his common practice to sit on the hills above the shore and watch the breakers crash into the rocky shore. Here there were none.

The heat that had become almost intolerable earlier in the afternoon was giving way. Jack noticed the slight breezes were almost vertical in nature and so mild they couldn't be considered wind. Nonetheless, the breeze was welcome.

In the same way that Jack scrutinized the coastline, Elizabeth did the same to the large, rugged cliffs on their right. The ragged, craggy cliffs rose majestically above the jungle forest and seemed to span the entire length of the island. Elizabeth pointed to the far right.

"We've come quite a distance, if that ridge dropping out of sight is the one that dropped into the ocean at our beach," Jack said.

"What's on the other side of this cliff wall?" she asked.

"Glen didn't say. I don't know if he knows. I can't see if there's a way over it," Jack answered.

"You're a coastal boy, right? Other than when you sit in a comfortable classroom, I mean. Well, I'm a mountain girl. There's not a mountain that can't be climbed. It's a matter of planning and preparation and perseverance."

"Perseverance?"

A mountain girl? I know so little about her.

"Yes, perseverance. It's actually a noun and a character trait, meaning determination, persistence, tenacity. Look, school boy, even you should know what it means."

Is this the true Elizabeth? Maybe I'd be better off with the constable. Get her alone in the jungle, she turns into a cat.

"I know what the word means, believe it or not. I'm just saying that wall of sheer rock looks like it needs more than perseverance. It needs a generous scoop of insanity," Jack said.

At a fork in the trail, they naturally followed it to the left where they'd seen the coastline. Soon they were plunged into dense jungle. The trail, which they assumed would be easily followed, disappeared from time to time. After several hours, they reached a small clearing, they realized they wouldn't make the settlement by nightfall. Neither of them was willing to continue in the pending darkness.

Jack employed his great skills recently learned from Glen and made a comfortable ground cover and the two settled for the night.

Did Glen know I was going to need this?

Since neither Jack nor Elizabeth wanted to take credit for, nor blame the other for getting lost, the conflict Jack half expected never materialized. They settled in and drifted off to sleep.

Chapter Fifty~Two

Journal Entry: April 1696 - Rajasthan, India
Alexander Hincher - Unwelcome theologist

Esther and I shared an elephant these last few days. I wearied her with my questions and theories of possible answers. She is very kind and wise. Many times she set my unique thoughts straight.

Esther directed my attention toward the followers of each of these gods. With a simple question, she turned my focus.

"What do the followers of each of these gods think their reward is if they follow their God?"

This morning we discussed what her people believe is their purpose for life on the earth. "What do they seek?" I asked. "What is the reward they expect if they follow the path their particular God has communicated?"

That question brought up several more, such as "How did their God communicate what is expected? Is there a written scripture? Is it an oral tradition? Is it a revelation to some special living person like a prophet? Or, is it just the thoughts of each individual?"

Esther didn't provide many answers. She did, however, help direct the questions I hope will lead to the right answer. The question I still want answered is "What is God's reward? What is in it for Him?"

I pretended I wanted to learn to handle an elephant, so I traded. Esther rode with my three Maasai princesses and I with Moses. I rode with Moses, so Moses and I could talk about what God wants.

The former tribal chief was understanding about my questions. He knew exactly what I wanted to know. He thought me foolish for wanting to know, but he understood how the knowledge of someone's motives would help them be motivated. He thought me crazy to want to motivate God.

He shared this legend told to him by his village elders.

The great king had four sons. He raised them to become the rulers of the four kingdoms. To prove their worthiness before receiving dominion over these kingdoms, he insisted they talk with the Snow Leopard who lived atop the great mountain, and learn from him how to love the people they would rule.

He took his sons to the four corners of the land and gave them instructions how to find the great mountain. He told them it was not a race, there were kingdoms enough and each would receive his dominion no matter when they finally learned the secrets of the great Snow Leopard.

With great anticipation, each of his four sons began their quest.

Kibo, the eldest, was smart, cunning, and very capable. He had great confidence in his ability to reach the mountain and meet the Snow Leopard. He started very strongly and made substantial progress. Along the way, he became acquainted with many wonderful people. He learned about many wonderful cultures. He ate many wonderful foods. He was excited to become the king over these peoples.

Mawenzi was the second oldest. He, too, was very capable. He was wise and very faithful. He loved his father and wanted to please him. Mawenzi also met great people. He became acquainted with new cultures, had new experiences, and was excited to become the king over these peoples.

Shira, the third son, was like his older brothers in that he was very capable and also enjoyed all the new experiences and new people. He was anxious to reach the mountain and meet the Snow Leopard so he could return and rule these people.

The youngest of the sons, Auphrika, was not as big, strong, or wise as his brothers, but he loved his father and trusted in his promises. As he met these new people, he came to learn they were ordinary people; some of them were kind and good and others were selfish and unkind. He enjoyed the new experiences just as his brothers did and he realized that as he learned from these many peoples, he loved them.

The people recognized Kibo, Mawenzi, Shira, and Auphrika as the heirs to the great king and they treated them with great reverence.

After many months traveling, the journeys became much more difficult as they got closer to the mountain. Fewer people were willing to help; the food and the excitement waned. Each of the sons faced challenges that tested their courage, their strength, and their dedication to the cause.

Each of the sons eventually reached villages at the base of the mountain where they found relief from the difficulties of their journey. Again, they found the wonderful food, the wonderful people, and the pleasures afforded heirs of a king.

Kibo shared stories of how he faced the challenges during his journey. He told how he outsmarted robbers and killed poisonous snakes. The people loved him. When he prepared to climb the mountain to meet the great Snow Leopard, the people laughed at him. This made Kibo angry, and he asked why they laughed. They laughed because nobody could meet the Snow Leopard, nobody ever had. Some said the Snow Leopard was dead. Others said the Snow Leopard lived on another mountain, and still others said the Snow Leopard never really lived; he was just a story told to children.

Kibo knew he could climb the mountain, and he wanted to be king over all the land, but he believed the people of the village and he never climbed the mountain.

The people welcomed Mawenzi like a king when he reached his village at the base of the mountain. The people loved him. They honored him and gave him the grandest home on the hill. It was a palace. The people showered him with praise. Mawenzi loved these people. When it was time for him to climb the mountain to meet the great Snow Leopard, the people were shocked at his selfishness and foolishness. This made Mawenzi angry. He asked why they treated him so.

They told him how hard it was to climb the mountain, and how long it would take. He would have to leave the comfort of his palace on the hill and travel many, many days. They reminded him how wonderful it was here in the mountain village, how much they loved him, and that he had everything he ever wanted right now.

Mawenzi remembered how unhappy he was during the difficult parts of his journey and how happy he was right now. He didn't want to be that unhappy again. He concluded climbing the mountain to meet the great Snow Leopard was not worth it. He never climbed the mountain.

It surprised Shira he ever made it to the mountain village. He met many people who were kind to him and helped him. He was sure he wanted to be their ruler. He wanted to live with them and to be happy. When the journey became difficult, he found fewer people willing to help. Many times, he doubted he could even make it to the mountain village. He knew without help from very generous people he wouldn't. He had a hard time. Shira's mountain village people welcomed him and honored him. It felt good and safe.

When it was time to ascend the mountain and meet the great Snow Leopard, the people gathered around and wished him well. They were sad and worried. They cried for him. This made Shira angry, and he asked why they reacted so. The people told him about the hardships he would face. They warned him that only a powerful man could climb the mountain. Some even told him they believed he could not do it. They were sad for him.

Shira believed them. Even though he wanted to meet the great Snow Leopard, and he wanted to be the ruler over these wonderful people, he didn't trust he could do it. He never climbed the mountain.

Auphrika was the very last of the four brothers to reach his mountain village. It took him a long time. He stopped along the way to help one village build homes. He stopped along the way to help find lost children. He tarried in one village to help repair a broken water dam. When he finally arrived, the people welcomed him as warmly as others had welcomed his brothers in their mountain villages.

When it came time for Auphrika to climb the mountain, some people laughed, some people thought him foolish and greedy, others cried for him. This made Auphrika sad. He asked each why they responded so. They told him there was no great Snow Leopard. They said becoming the king of the land was not worth the work it would take to climb the mountain, and still others said he could not do it. They said no man could climb such a hard mountain.

Auphrika thanked each of them for their concerns and he left the village and climbed the mountain.

He loved the people of the land, and he wanted to be their ruler. He wanted to make life better for them. He believed his father. He believed the great Snow Leopard would meet him and help him become a great ruler. He believed he could climb this mountain, for he had done many hard things in his life, and this mountain would be as any other hard thing. He climbed one step at a time and did not give up.

When Auphrika reached the top of the mountain, he saw the great Snow Leopard had prepared a fine dinner for him, and greeted him. Auphrika looked around and saw three empty seats at the table. "Where are my brothers?" he asked the Snow Leopard. "They are much stronger and faster than I am. They should be here waiting for me."

The great Snow Leopard winked away a tear and gently said, "Kibo does not believe I am real. He did not climb the mountain. Mawenzi does not believe the reward is worth the effort to climb the mountain, so he did not. Shira does not believe he can make it to the top of the mountain, so he did not climb."

Sadly, Auphrika bowed his head and wept for his brothers.

"Come with me," said the great Snow Leopard.

He took Auphrika to the pinnacle of the mountain and said, "Look around you. As far as you can see, this is a glorious land with great people. They need a ruler to lead them, to teach them, to love them. I give it all to you. I will call it Auphrika."

Moses ended the story and turned to look me directly in the eyes. "Our gods expect us to climb the mountain and he will meet us there. If we do, God will give us a kingdom. Each of us must find our mountain and climb it."

So many new questions begged answers, but this man fascinated me so I let him continue.

"As Mwami of my people, I am king. My people consider my appointment divine. I am of Renge lineage of the Singa clan. I even held the Kalinga, our sacred drum. To them I am part god."

"Look at me. I am king and have been sold as slave four times. If my kingship is divine, where is my God? I cannot protect my people. Many are dead, they sold others. Families are destroyed. What kind of Mwami am I?"

"My God created the Hutu, the Watutsi, and the Twa. Each has a mountain to climb and God will reward each. My God did not create them subservient but to serve."

"To serve whom?" I couldn't help but ask.

"Each other. Not as slaves, but with love. Like your Jesus taught. When I was a boy, I could not understand why Kibo, Shira and Mawenzi could come so close and not climb the mountain. I have learned to base my life on trust. Trust in myself, trust that my God will reward my life, and trust that my reward will justify the life I live."

A procession of cavalry soldiers on beautiful Marwari horses cut our conversation short when they galloped past us and approached Sangha who was leading our elephant caravan. Moses encouraged Gihanga forward so he could hear the conversation. It was very animated. Whatever the soldiers wanted was in contrast with what Sanga wanted.

As they argued, several soldiers turned and slowly examined the occupants riding in each of the howdahs. The Marwari are not a tall horse so it took some stretching for the soldiers to see into the howdahs mounted on the back of the elephants, especially the taller elephants. They took a particular interest in the howdah containing my harem, Leilyn, and Esther.

That bothered Moses. He lost interest in the conversation between Sangha and whom we assumed was the captain of the cavalry. I could see Moses was about ready to turn Gihanga around. One soldier quickly returned to the argument between Sangha and the captain. He said something we could not hear, turned with his handful of soldiers, and returned the way they came, galloping away.

Sangha said something to the captain. It was unintelligible to us, but certainly a string of words not meant for tender ears. The cavalry galloped off ahead of our caravan. Two of the trailing soldiers remained behind and became our escorts.

If you can decipher a man's disposition by the way he drives an elephant, it was clear Sangha was very upset. I thought if he could have, he would have his elephant stomp the two soldiers to dust.

After a while, our curiosity and concern got the best of us. Moses urged Gihanga up alongside Sangha. He glanced over. His face confirmed my conclusion he was not happy. After a few minutes, the escort soldiers were far enough away and Sangha practically whispered, "Tonight we part company. You will be in the care of God. He no longer trusts you in my care." He then surprised me and gave me a wink accompanied by a wicked grin.

- Hinch

Clare's Tavern - St. John's, Antigua - 1748

"That story gets better each time you tell it!" Clare proclaimed as she plopped the drinks loudly on the table in front of Amos and his three new acquaintances.

"Oh shut it, Clare," Amos replied, dismissing her even though she was already leaving the foursome to tend to the others demanding her attention in the tavern.

It was supper time, and the tavern was full of both regulars and newcomers. Being so close to the port, sailors, merchants, traders, and wanderers joined with the locals to make Clare's tavern the most popular tavern in the West Indies. Though alcohol flowed, the real draw was Clare's cooking. The lack of wenches for hire validated the fact that patrons came for the food. There was not a better meal anywhere. It was practically impossible for anyone to prepare a better meal and serve the hundred visitors Clare hosted on a Saturday night. Other nights she featured various stews, chowders and soups along with remarkable assortments of breads, but on Saturday the fare included a pork or beef entrée and when those became scarce, Clare could take wild turkeys or a collection of fish and make a feast for a king.

Other taverns or inns featured dishes more commonly influenced by the African and Indian peoples brought to these islands as slaves or indentured servants. But Clare's definite western European touch provided a unique and distinct allure.

The one thing Clare missed the most from her homeland were the plentiful variety of vegetables. Here on the island there was plenty of fruit and wonderful spices, yet Clare missed the potato. Potatoes had only become popular in her native Ireland a few decades earlier, even though potatoes found their way to other European cities by the returning Spanish conquistadors over a hundred years ago.

Oh, what she could do with a potato. And her efforts to get the local plantation owners to grow potatoes proved ineffective because of the blight that was so common with root vegetables. She found some success with a sweet potato, but still a regular Irish potato could not be matched.

The years Clare spent in the islands was not so bad. She seemed to blossom where ever she landed. And this time, life landed her on the island where she was to meet her betrothed, a Norwegian sailor by the name of Lars.

She waited patiently. Occasionally, rumors surfaced regarding the ship upon which Lars sailed. Some rumors held it was lost at sea. A few swore the ship wrecked on some distant shore. Others said pirates captured and scuttled it, taking the passengers as slaves to be sold on the Barbary Coast. They sold black slaves locally, but white slaves were taken and sold in the coastal cities of northern Africa.

Clare clung to the hope that someday Lars would find his way to her. Not that she was desperate; she was a tall, strong shapely woman and her somewhat light complexion and reddish blonde hair made her an irresistible target for lust, longing, and lewd advances from the many men that visited the tavern. From time to time, a decent man made his way to her tavern and showed interest, but Clare was attracted to and remained loyal to Lars, even these several years.

As night wore on and guests finished their meals, their drinks, their stories, lies, and laughter, the guests paid their tabs and wandered out into the night. The tavern was empty, except for Amos and his three new friends.

"Amos, it's time to go home, climb under some rock, or catch a ship. I'm ready to close up," Clare said as she cleaned and washed up the tables.

"One more round and we're gone," Amos begged.

Amos never left his bill unpaid, but Clare never figured out where he got his money. He didn't have a steady job, and he seemed to always associate with the most unique of strangers. These three were no exception. They were not typical European sailors. Darker skin and eyes led Clare to assume they were from the coast of North Africa.

The Golden Age of Piracy in these waters came to a close nearly twenty years ago, but the occasional visitor from the southern Mediterranean validated the rumors that piracy was still very much alive in other parts of the world. Clare thought these three could easily be part of the Barbary Coast pirates, who from time to time wandered through these islands.

Though the slave trade was one of the largest import businesses bringing ships across the Atlantic, they believed an occasional cargo of white slaves found its way back to the human flesh markets in North Africa.

Clare couldn't help but wonder whenever these types of sailors arrived in port if their purpose was anything but sinister.

As Clare brought a fresh tray of rum to the table, she heard the discussion was not about human trafficking, but to her relief, it was about Amos' pet topic. The Henry Avery treasure. The only thing she heard from the visitors as she left the table were the words "Blade of Safavid," which meant nothing to her.

Chapter Fifty~Three

The soldiers made their own small fire apart from the rest of the caravan, letting us speak freely with Sangha. Sangha shared little while others could hear. He told us the emperor sent the soldiers to provide reinforcements to the siege on Jinji Fort. The captain who had so vehemently argued with him earlier today was also commanded to retrieve the Mughal Emperor's own son. The young prince betrayed the Mughal soldiers there at Jinji Fort.

Sangha told us the Maratha army and the Mughal forces have been at war for nearly ten years.

"The Jinji Fort has not fallen in that time, and anyone who thinks adding my elephants to the force will help them now is a fool. I refuse to take my elephants into a hopeless battle," he said.

When I asked Sangha for details of his plans, he only said the plan will start with him helping us escape before the reinforcements to our escort soldiers arrive in the next day or two.

Esther remained silent but I could tell she was very upset. Finally, and very carefully, she filled in the blanks.

"That captain," she said, "is Emperor Aurangzeb's trusted vizier. If grandfather sent him, it is a very serious matter, and Mr. Sangha, you are in terrible danger if you resist."

Sangha then surprised all of us with his revelation.

"Princess, I am not the one in danger. The vizier's men recognized you. He sent several soldiers back to bring an escort to return you to your grandfather. They said 'To escort our passengers on their way'. That can only mean they plan to escort you back to your grandfather."

Anywhere else in the world an armed escort returning a granddaughter, kidnapped by pirates to her grandfather, would be a welcome blessing.

Esther adamantly dispelled that misconception. It did not surprise her that her uncle the prince could be sympathetic to the Maratha. She told us he was the illegitimate son of her grandfather's Hindu concubine. Making an alliance with the Maratha was a betrayal that would cost his head. Esther's family tree continues to fascinate me.

Her uncle was not Esther's concern; the concern was being returned to her grandfather and used as a pawn to punish her mother. Although her Persian family had a more threatening purpose for finding her, Esther is not willing to see her grandfather until she visits her mother.

There will be no time to finish our discussion about the motivations of a god and his purposes for those over whom he is a god. We will probably never meet Sangha again. The camp is all asleep, the fires out, and the elephants' breathing are the only noises of the night.

† † †

Shortly after midnight, Sangha slipped into our tent and by the light of a waxing moon quietly woke Rudy, Moses, and me, leading us to Esther's tent where we woke them. His instructions were clear and short.

Travel back the way we came. Move quickly, so we reach the village of Tonk before sunrise. Seek Maneet in the livery, his family will care for us.

As Sangha stepped out of the tent, Esther humbly asked, "Why such kindness? My grandfather is not kind to the Hindu".

"I love your mother and loved your father. Your grandfather is conflicted. Power and control are very hard to balance with love and family."

Then he looked at me and even in the darkness, his deep brown eyes penetrated into my soul as he said, "When God succeeds, His glory increases."

We quietly slipped out of camp and practically ran the six leagues to reach Tonk before sunrise. Sangha provided water sacks and some

breads and cheeses, but we traveled as lightly as we could on foot.

Moses complemented Sangha's wisdom in having us travel the way we came earlier that day, rather than cut through the wilderness. I thought it was to keep us safe from animals, but Moses pointed out the cavalry would wipe out our tracks as they approached the caravan. With no tracks leaving the caravan, there would be no way to track us.

I can hardly imagine how Sangha will explain our disappearance. He is clever and will probably leave it in God's hands. He is like that. I have never met a man of such great faith. Faith in a God who he believes knows and is interested in him.

We reached the outskirts of Tonk well before sunrise. All was quiet and dark. Exhausted, we now faced the challenge of finding a livery owned by a man named Maneet. I never considered what kind of network of friends or enemies we would encounter as we traversed this country to Delhi. I laugh at my innocence. Of course it wouldn't be simple. Nothing important ever is.

Esther is the heir to two dueling thrones in an empire that comprises competing ethnic, religious, and political identities, where the lines between friend and enemy even cut through families. Esther's uncle has betrayed her grandfather and will probably lose his head. Her mother is in prison for several offenses, even though she, we are told, is Esther's grandfather's favorite daughter and heir to his throne.

- Hinch

Mountain Pass - The Island - 1748

Glen didn't trust Hunter for one minute. His very presence on the island threatened Glen's family and he knew it wasn't an idle threat. But what kept him from removing that threat right that minute angered Glen.

Every time Glen ventured into the mountain, he worried about the safety of his family, but knew Hunter had equal confidence that if he ever harmed Glen's family, there would be no place on this island or on any other island he would be safe from Glen's wrath.

For now, Glen wanted assurance that Hunter hadn't found the mountain pass and gained access to the other side of the island. Glen had actually found the pass soon after they all arrived on the island and he was returning from there when days before, he spotted Jack and Elizabeth on the beach.

Once he knew Hunter was safely heading the other way, Glen hurried up the steep slope to see if there was any evidence Hunter had found the access through the cliffs. All he found was the careful camouflage he put up himself. The pass was secure.

Glen carefully made his way back to the leeward side of the island, cautious not to leave tracks. He climbed down to the *Emerald*, taking a moment to examine the damage. If Jack and Elizabeth were right, and slavers captured the *Emerald*, it would likely be pirates from the Barbary Coast; he hoped not Persian.

He worked his way the long way back toward the cove, he gathered as many berries, papayas, and passion fruits as he could carry.

When they heard Glen singing as he approached, the twins, as always, ran to welcome their father home.

† † †

Rosemary had no interest in the honors of people. Though not religious, she had a very fine reverence for a God she knew, knew her. How could she ever consider life on this planet as an accident, a mere existence without a purpose? She felt it her duty to become the finest person she could, and to help others do the same.

Because of that, what most attracted her to Glen was not just that he was a friend to everyone, but he seemed able to do anything. His large hands could repair and adjust a delicate clock. They could create and tune a beautiful musical instrument. They could re-build a broken pistol. And he could dance. He was ever developing and learning.

That Glen couldn't get them off this island was a mystery to Rosemary. The time would soon come where Rosemary would need answers, proper answers. He insisted the plan he and Walt were working on would safely get them off the island, but if she understood correctly, it too depended on help from the weather. Until then, she loved the peace, the security, the love of her children, the relative comfort of the cove, and the love of her Glen.

Still, the fact was they now had visitors on the island who were not eager to stay. Her children were growing up and would need more than a loving, protective father and mother to provide for them. Rosemary knew change was coming. She also knew change brought uncertainty. Hardship, challenges, pain, and stress would likely accompany that uncertainty, but hopefully rewards as well. For Rosemary, hope rather than fear accompanied this expected change.

That hope is what most attracted Glen to Rosemary. Yes, she was extremely beautiful. He loved the way her long black hair freely caressed her shoulders as they spun on the dance floor. How her eyes sparkled and her smile could melt a heart were certainly a bonus. But it was her absolute confidence, her positive and undaunted hope of the future, that drove Glen to give up everything to have her. And he did.

Her confidence extended past herself and gave confidence to everyone she met. But Glen was the biggest recipient of her confidence.

"Lydia, would you like to accompany me to the plateau?" Glen's voice boomed across the clearing.

Lydia's eyes lit up, she hurried and joined the twins helping him unload his arms full of fruit.

Glen wrapped his arm around her, "Tomorrow, we'll make sure our new friends made it safely."

Chapter Fifty~Four

Sangha's god followed us to Tonk. We entered the small village in the light of a moon ready to set. One small lamp lit a window in what looked to be a barn. We carefully approached and peered inside to find a man saddling a Marwari just like those ridden by the cavalry. He turned our direction as if he heard us and Esther caught her breath. It was the man who had recognized her on the howdah.

As quietly as possible, we skirted away from the building into the shadows. A few moments later, the large door opened. The soldier rode out and headed back toward the caravan. We stood frozen as he rode past.

As if time stood still, we watched him disappear. Moses broke the silence. He whispered for us to follow him back into the building. As we turned and looked into the open door from where the soldier had exited, Rudy stood with his arm on a man's shoulder. The light behind them silhouetted the two men. We hesitantly stepped into the building.

Until I die, I will never know how Rudy can make friends so instantly. It was Maneet, and we were standing in his livery. He closed the door and ushered us past six other Marwari's which he was saddling up in preparation for the other soldiers.

He opened a small door on the floor of a back room. "Please forgive me, but I have other guests you will not want to meet. When I am free of them, I will come to you. Rest quietly. You are safe for now. I will be back."

We climbed down into total darkness and sat quietly on what felt like large blankets laid out on bales of hay. It wasn't long until I could hear the sounds of deep breathing. Our little group was sleeping. I apparently joined them, for I awoke when the ceiling opened and light entered the small hideout. "Hello, my friends. Please forgive my lack of hospitality but we have work to do."

We climbed up and out of what we learned was a hideout Maneet built for his family in times of trouble. He led us into a comfortable room where his wife had prepared a nice supper. It was light outside, and I guessed it to be midday. The warm meal was welcome. I was about to ask questions when Maneet silenced me with a raised finger.

Looking at Esther and Leilyn, he said. "I assume you are the emperor's granddaughter. Right now, an entire army is looking for you. The soldiers who recognized you in Sangha's caravan met with Ali Khan's reinforcements headed to Jinji."

"Late last night, they stopped here to rest the horses before reaching Sangha's caravan this morning. They talk too much. As they talked and drank last night, my wife listened. These few have sympathies for the Maratha's and decided you would bring a handsome reward from Ramal at Jinji Fort. Last night we sent our son Tanek to warn Sangha to wait for the whole cavalry before letting you go."

"We would have passed him," I said.

"No, he took the forest trail," Maneet said.

Just then Tanek entered the room, out of breath but wearing a giant toothy smile.

"Sangha sends his thanks and thought you might need this." Tanek said as he handed a beautiful tiger skin bag to Esther.

She opened it and blushed in embarrassment to see it held an ornately carved and jeweled box housing the sacred 'Blade.'

"You left so quickly last night you left it hidden in your tent." His smile never wavered.

Tanek can't be over ten or twelve years old, but his confidence is that of an older, mature young man. Then he said, "You are as beautiful as he said you were. I wish I could tell my friends I was in the princess's service."

He sat down at our table and just stared. I didn't blame him. I've been doing the same for months.

- Hinch

The Settlement - The Island - 1748

Louisa entered the small settlement carrying a basket full of cherimoya fruit. The fruit was plentiful in this area of the island. It was Louisa's custom to gather a small basket each afternoon. She used its sweet juices to flavor the Guinea fowl she prepared for dinner. Though Guinea fowl was not native to this island, one family brought several with them onboard the ship. They multiplied well and took to the climate here on the plateau.

Except for Glen and Rosemary, the families on the ship elected to settle on the plateau rather than venture deeper into the island. Though it was still tropical jungle, its undergrowth was not so overwhelming. Water was plentiful and nearby groves of fruit were abundant.

"Is Rags back?" Louisa asked as she stepped over the small footbridge that seemed to serve as the entry into the small settlement. It would be considered a village if it had more than four curious homes.

All together, there were only the five families scattered across the plateau. They resigned themselves there was no way off the island and so they settled in and made a life for themselves. Though they explored, the mountain range that acted as a sentry, the range divided and protected the other side of the island. They had only circled the island once on a make-shift raft. All they found was sheer rock rising ominously out of the sea. Only Walt seemed to have any knowledge of tides and currents apart from Glen, who absolutely refused to discuss how he successfully took the helm during the storm and how he knew the island's location forbade a successful escape.

So, resigned to a life rather devoid of stress and pressure, or hope and ambition, the residents of this secluded island lived from day to day.

"He's still off hunting," replied Walt.

Walt sat with his bare feet in the small stream that worked its way across the plateau and down toward the ocean where it gently disappeared into what seemed to be an eternally calm sea. Walt was cleaning the few fish caught in the nets Rags had fashioned.

Rags seemed to be a man of all trades but a master of none. He was a thinker, always with an idea, he would pursue it until it appeared to have a glimmer of hope of succeeding, but then would have his attention captured by something else. Louisa and Walt loved Rags. They looked at him as a son; yes a grown-up son, only Walt's junior by a few years, but his childlike curiosity and enthusiasm made it easy to love him like a happy little boy.

The net Walt used to keep the settlement in fresh fish began as an automatic harvester. It was to be attached to a team of posts secured into the lagoon's bottom. They would secure floating casks to the seaward side and when the tides flooded, bringing fish, the net would rise letting the fish come in. As the tide ebbed, the net would lower with fish trapped beneath it. At low tide, they would simply walk down the beach and collect the fish.

Walt wanted so badly to explain how it wouldn't work since the tides on this island were so small, but he didn't have the heart. But before they even tried it, Rags had a better idea and left the automatic harvester untested. Walt and the others didn't mind because the net served well in the hands of an experienced fisher, Walt.

The settlement's residents ate well, thanks to Rag's net and Walt's expertise. Not to mention Ben's farm and Glen's ability to catch the large sea turtles.

"Is he still after the boar?" asked Louisa.

"I hope he is successful this time." Walt hollered so Louisa could hear as she was now nearly out of earshot.

Louisa was not one to sit still or to sit and wait for an answer. She and Walt had been married for nearly as long as Glen and Rosemary. Glen and Walt became friends almost immediately after Glen arrived in Sheffield.

Some said Walt and Glen became fast friends when Glen learned of Walt's expertise with steel making.

Chapter Fifty~Five

Journal Entry: April 1696 - Banas River, Rajasthan, India
Alexander Hincher - Apparent Wealthy Englishman

It's now been a week traveling in a punt down the Banas River. We stay out of sight as much as possible. We are in a country where our little group looks a bit out of the ordinary, and no doubt the rumors of the Mughal Emperor's granddaughter traveling across the country are circulating. We will soon be the target of every sort of bounty hunter.

What makes the danger more acute is that we are back in Esther's home country, where people know her and will easily recognize her. Enemies of the emperor will be plentiful. We hope it is still too early for her Persian father's people to be looking for us.

Tanek convinced his father it would be wise for him to serve as our guide. Who would suspect a young boy sailing down a river to be transporting such a valuable cargo? Young boys grow up early in the country.

He and Rudy are two of a kind. The British developed enough relationships throughout the Mughal Empire that people are accustomed to dealing with them. At times, Rudy professes to be teaching his young apprentice, and at others Tanek professes to be hired to escort a wealthy Englishman down river. It is Esther who we try to keep out of sight.

Esther and Leilyn have long since shed the trousers and shirts for their customary Indian dress and they converted my harem from the colorful African tribal dress to that of Indian farm women. It made little difference to their natural beauty, but it helps them blend in, somewhat. Moses remained quite attentive to the needs and care of these five women.

The Banas merged into the Chambal and Tanek says we will meet with the Yamani in a few days. He tells us stories about how he and his father once sailed all the way to Delhi together. We've had no sign of danger these last few weeks. This morning when Tanek relieved Moses at the pole he recognized the concerned look. They have become good friends. Though Rudy and I take our turns at the pole guiding and propelling the punt down river, mostly we travel with the speed of the river flow. Most fishing punts are shallow, but ours has higher walls making it possible to keep its passengers hidden.

Moses kept his eyes on what looked like three or four men keeping pace with the punt. We all agreed we had company. They kept with us for most of the day. It wasn't until we rounded a bend we lost sight of them for a few hours.

The Chambal River eventually reaches the Yamuna, which then flows up to Delhi, which I assumed was our intended course. Young Tanek laughed when he realized I thought we could go all the way to Delhi in this punt. "The Yamuna flows too fast the wrong way. I am not strong enough to push this punt up stream."

- Hinch

Clare's Tavern - St. John's, Antigua - 1748

"How many times do we have to do this?" Lucas asked.

"At least one more," Captain Remington answered.

"You chose this commission based on a rumor that is now two years old. And the trail we followed was cold back then. The treasure is spent or lost. The hunt is over." Lucas tried to sound convincing.

"Possibly the treasure hunt is over, but the man hunt is not."

This same discussion, or argument depending on the point of view, was playing itself out for what seemed to be the thousandth time. The only change was the venue. This time Captain Remington was leading his first mate Lucas into a popular tavern they had visited countless times over the past two years.

"When Jack joins us, the few missing puzzle pieces will come together," Remington said.

"And if your Mr. Jack didn't sail with the *Emerald?*" Lucas said, "He clearly told you he wouldn't."

Lucas had great respect for his captain, and the captain's obsession to find his friend was a lucrative one for Lucas. The guilt of serving two captains was long since washed away by his dual income.

"I know Jack. He'll get his hands on some tidbit of information and dog it down until his excitement to tell me all about it will hurry him here," Captain Remington said.

"I hope you're right," Lucas said.

For both our sakes.

Lucas caught the eye of a beggar sitting on a rotted mat next to a small bowl containing a couple of coins. The rags covering his sun browned body complimented his visage of poverty.

"Excuse me for one moment," Lucas said to the captain. He pulled some coins from his pocket, and stepping over to the beggar knelt at his side, listening carefully while dropping the coins.

"The *Emerald* is lost, scuttled. Yer capin's friend and the girl drowned dur'n thatack. Nakhoda's beside hisself. Stay clear lest you want 'is full wrath. Promised to sink the Kent when he sees it, Ya know 'e can," the beggar whispered.

Lucas stood and caught up with Captain Remington. The beggar slithered back into the hole he came from. So, the captain was right, Jack did sail. Lucas thought. And Nakhoda lost him in the attack. Lucas smiled. Poetic justice. Lucas hated Nakhoda like most of his men did, but his assignment to follow Remington and keep the *Kent* one step behind the *Chawbuck* proved to be challenging and lucrative. It might be time to retire.

Since the disappearance of Nakhoda's most vicious spy, Hunter, Lucas, though never in personal contact with his boss, rose to become the most vital in keeping the Royal Navy at bay and keeping Nakhoda aware of Captain Remington's progress. Which wasn't much, until now.

As he caught up with Captain Remington and entered the tavern, he decided to collect the reward he'd certainly receive for the intelligence he'd provided concerning Jack and the woman traveling on the Emerald. Once proved correct, he'd retire and get lost in the colonies.

Just as they'd done each time they were near Antigua, they visited the tavern to speak with a young woman who was also anxious for a ship to come in—a ship two years late.

Chapter Fifty~Six

Journal Entry: April 1696 - Rajasthan, India
Alexander Hincher - Venturer

It's nice to be on foot again. We traded the punt for a cart pulled by a mule that looks like it has already earned its place in heaven. Rudy insists it is a good bargain. I am grateful we don't have to carry the food and water on our backs. We are now heading due north towards Delhi. Tanek is still pleased to be in the princess's service as he pays her particular homage.

In reflecting on the conversations with Sangha those many weeks ago, I look at people and their motivations differently. Though we talked about the motivations of the gods, I apply the legend Moses shared with me repeatedly in my head.

- Hinch

Onboard the Sally - Open Sea - West Indies - 1748

As predicted, the *Sally* slowed, the sails hung limp; the wind stopped. Krist signaled to the coxswain, and the oarsmen began their work. Krist was eager to find land. On some trips, they could see from one island to another. Other trips, they could spend days with no sight of land at all. He hoped this was not one of those times.

The *Sally* was following the same winds the *Chawbuck* did countless time before. Now, diverting from that course, the *Sally* began her descent towards the windless doldrums.

It wasn't but just a few hours when what looked like a small rock came into view. Depending on its actual size, Krist estimated it would take them several hours to cross the distance, which he estimated to be some ten leagues away. As they approached the land mass, it looked like it extended straight out of the calm ocean.

Krist lost his enthusiasm for his find. The sheer volcanic rock breaching the water left little hope it could be inhabited. There was no evidence of a beach or inlet. Krist estimated the island to be maybe ten miles wide and maybe two hundred yards high at its tallest point.

The oarsmen slowed, and the *Sally* came to a coasting stop in the calm waveless water. They elected not to drop the longboats and explore.

Krist turned to his coxswain and motioned to have the oarsmen bring the *Sally* around the island. It was no different on the other side. This was just a volcanic stump. It kept everyone's attention as they circled it. It wasn't until Krist gave directions to complete the circle that he noticed what seemed to be this island's twin about another fifteen leagues off to the port side of the *Sally*.

The sun was retreating from a star-filled sky. The *Sally* dropped anchor and readied for a peaceful night. They would advance to the twin island tomorrow.

Chapter Fifty~Seven

Esther is now our guide. This is her homeland. We are resting in the home of one of her mother's childhood tutors, Bibi Hafiza Mariam. When Aurangzeb jailed Zeb-un-Nissa, it forced many of her friends to become practically invisible. Bibi was chief among her friends. Esther and Bibi embraced and tears flowed down their cheeks like rivers.

She gave us places to rest, but the home is tiny and I am concerned a worn out mule pulling a tattered old cart accompanied by eight strangers will attract the wrong attention. We arrived after dark and it concerned me to see what might happen in the morning. Still, those concerns didn't keep me from falling into a deep sleep.

When I awoke in the morning, I was alone with Bibi. Her peaceful countenance practically erased my concerns as I ate.

"Thank you," was all she said.

After what seemed a very long time, she answered my questions without me even asking.

"They've all gone ahead. You are safe here in Agra. They will meet you at the Bageche Temple. For now, come with me. She wants to show you something special. You can leave your things here."

She allowed me the few minutes to conclude this journal entry.

- Hinch

Jungle - The Island - 1748

Rags finished tying off the end of the trip line to a small sapling holding on for dear life once it took the bulk of the pressure from the hog trap he was making. Just as he let go and stepped back to admire the newly set trap, the sapling gave way and the much larger tree whipped back up into its full and upright position. This second sapling, having also lost its tug of war with the much larger tree, flew up and over the tree it was expected to hold in abeyance, flying nearly a hundred feet.

Rags stood, hands on his hips and exhaled as the small tree took to the air.

Rags was like a big kid. He was actually an adult, who was never one to run out of ideas about how to get off this island. Most of his inventions, though few were ever put to the test, enhanced the quality of life on the island. His automatic fish harvester, though failed in its automation, made fishing easier for Walt. His paddle wheels would depend on the right storm, and his lighthouse finally became a playground for Glen's children. It was his enthusiasm and love for ideas that endeared Rags to the residents.

Rags was one of the few bachelors on the island. Originally, he was on his way to meet and marry his one true love when the storm interrupted his journey.

He was confident his fiancé would be faithful. He claimed she would be full of hope, and was as anxiously preparing for their reunion as he was in trying to procure a way off of the island.

Climbing back up the tree, Rags grabbed hold of the rope and swung out away from the trunk. As he did so, the leverage and weight of his body again bent the tree over, softly landing him on the ground about fifteen feet away from where its trunk met the rich forest soil. At nearly two hundred pounds, Rags was stout enough and strong enough to manage the tension of the tree's resiliency. The tree played tug of war with him.

Now, to secure the rope with a trip mechanism to trigger the trap.

Rags hadn't thought the small saplings would give up so easily. In search of a new victim, he secured the rope to a branch on a fallen mahogany tree. Just as he did so and let go to admire his work, the larger tree stood straight up again and yanked the branch off its trunk, hurling it up and over the canopy.

"Humph." He muttered, "All I need is a castle under siege. I've got a catapult."

Chapter Fifty~Eight

With my journal returned to me, I continue the story. Bibi led me from her small house through the streets toward the river. As we walked, she spoke in very hushed tones, not to be overheard but certain I would hear every word. She told me that if I was fortunate enough to meet Esther's mother, I will have met one of the most wondrous women in the world.

Bibi served the princess as a tutor. They rewarded her when the princess, at the age of seven, memorized the Quran. Bibi told me great stories about the princess and her keen intellect, her talent with languages, with verse and how loved she has been by her father. He had been so proud of her and he counseled with her because of her wisdom.

I learned about Esther's grandmother, Dilras Banu Begum. She and Aurangzeb married right here in Agra, and apparently conceived Zeb-un-Nissa here as well. Agra is, therefore, a special place for the family. It was easy to see Bibi loved Esther's grandmother. She talked about her with great respect. She described her as beautiful, vivacious, charming, and fair colored. She also said she was a proud and self-willed woman and her husband stood in some awe of her. Bibi even quoted Aurangzeb as having said she was a woman of extreme imperiousness and he would love her until the end of her life and would never wound her feelings.

Esther's grandmother, Dilras, was a princess of the Safavid Dynasty of Persia, a direct descendent of the first Safavid Shah. Bibi reminded me that Zeb-un-Nissa, and thus Esther, are as well.

Though Aurangzeb has other wives, none could replace Dilras.

Everyone mourned her death at the young age of thirty-five.

Bibi was at Zeb-un-Nissa's side initially as a tutor, but their relationship become closer when Zeb-un-Nissa's mother passed away. She was only nineteen when her mother died and was twenty-one when her father took the throne. Bibi did not go into the details of Aurangzeb's ascension to the throne. She didn't need to; Esther already gave me those details.

Esther has not shared with me anything about her father, so I took this occasion to ask.

Bibi laughed when I asked. Then she related tale after sordid tale, told by the people of Zeb-un-Nissa's trysts, affairs, and follies with her various suitors. Some of them made me laugh.

Then she got deadly serious. "The princess had only one love in her life. Many came to call and she would interview them. Her mother arranged for a meeting with a Persian prince."

He was kind. Not militant, nor arrogant. He appreciated her poetry, and they fell in love. When Esther was conceived, Zeb-un-Nissa was put away, and the true Persian prince disappeared. Aurangzeb reported the child belonged to Shah Suleiman I, who claimed it true. But Zeb-un-Nissa refused to marry the shah and eventually she was imprisoned for it.

Esther has been a reminder of the contention between Aurangzeb and Zeb-un-Nissa. Curious people circulate stories that the imprisonment is because of Zeb-un-Nissa's political differences, religious differences, her love of poetry. The stories are as numerous as the people telling them.

"Is Esther's real father still alive?" I asked.

"You are one of only a handful that knows the truth. Even Esther does not know," Bibi confessed.

As we talked, I became so interested in the conversation I paid no attention to where we were going until we stood before the most magnificent building I have ever seen. Bibi led me to a mausoleum, the Taj Mahal.

The brilliance of the white marble, the architecture, the total spirit of reverence of the grounds captivated me.

"She's inside waiting for you," Bibi said. She turned and walked away.

The feeling of the place was indescribable. It moved me to tears. Emotion welled up inside me. Though it was just a building, a monument of cold hard marble, the beauty of it, combined with the peace I felt, planted in my heart a hope there is still goodness in the world.

I quietly removed my shoes and stepped inside. Esther was kneeling all alone next to one of the two tombs. She slowly looked up at me and with a tear in her eye she smiled, inviting me to join her.

As I knelt, she whispered. "I want you to meet my great-grandmother Mumtaz Mahal."

For a long time, we knelt in reverence. There was not a sound. Slowly she stood, and taking my hand, helped me up and we turned and stood before the second tomb.

"I'd like you to meet my great-grandfather, Emperor Shah Jahan. He built all of this so the world would know of his love for her."

Again, we stood silent. The reverence she showed was palpable. My hand remained in hers.

A screaming young woman broke the silence; it was as if I was being pulled back from a beautiful dream.

"Princess, take off your clothes and give them to me!"

The beautiful dream then became a nightmare. This young woman, who appeared to be about the same age and build as Esther, was also removing her clothes and she handed them to Esther. As the two young women quickly exchanged clothing, we heard shouting men approach the sacred building.

The young woman, now dressed in Esther's clothing, clung to me as if she were my lover. Esther disappeared so quickly I didn't see where she went.

"There," a man shouted, "take them!" All went dark when something hit the back of my head.

- Hinch

Canyon's Edge - The Island - 1748

Jack blinked his eyes open. Looking around, he noticed Elizabeth's jungle bed empty. He got to his feet, brushed away some wrinkles and saw Elizabeth standing, arms folded with her back to him. *What is she thinking this morning?*

He was about to ask when a large mahogany branch crashed through the trees and landed just behind them. Quickly they collected themselves and were on their way.

"What was that?" Elizabeth asked, turning one more time to verify nothing was immediately following them.

Jack didn't turn around, he kept moving, machete at the ready. They were forced to retrace their tracks a few times but after a few hours, they eventually came to a complete stop. The trail ended abruptly.

† † †

"I don't think we're on the right trail," Hunter heard the woman say as she overlooked the massive gorge standing between them and where she suggested they would reach the other families stranded on this island. The morning sunlight highlighted the couple against the distant jungle.

The canyon wasn't that wide, maybe only a few hundred feet, but it was deep. The sheer drop-off made it impossible to climb down and up again. They would have to go around. That's when he would get to know them, he thought.

Hunter feared these two were spies sent to the island. What he needed to know was who they were working for. They made immediate friends with Glen; the perfect spies, young, innocent, and feigning to be in love. An easy trick to gain favor with residents on this island. He had to get to know them in the right way, to know what they knew, and who they were working for. Hassan or a competitor? More than one person wanted what Glen had, and whoever that person was must think it was on the island. Yet, Hunter spent years searching and found nothing.

Did Hassan think Hunter failed, so he sent others to find the treasure? Hassan never shared what Glen had or its true value. But Hunter concluded it must be a treasure so vast, so valuable as to dedicate a life to finding it.

If these two worked for Hassan, Hunter must appear to be in control of the island, but if they worked for a competitor, he must thwart their plan.

Enough thinking. It's time to meet these visitors before they make

Just as Hunter was about to step out of the cover of the jungle, a squealing hog bounded from the brush, headed directly at the woman. In her shock, she nearly did Hunter a favor by plunging into the chasm. It would be easier to handle one spy rather than two. Her companion was close enough to grab her and keep her from stumbling off the edge.

The hog stopped as if yanked off its feet only a few feet from reaching the couple standing there in shock. The hog got back up and changed direction. That's when Hunter saw a rope tied around the hog's front leg. On the other end of the rope was a large branch tumbling and crashing behind it. The branch caught on a large rock, bringing the hog down right in front of the couple. The man quickly jumped on the rope and wrapped it securely around the large rock. As he did, a second man came crashing out of the jungle breathing heavily and seized the rope.

"Rags, you fool!" Hunter cursed under his breath as he stepped back into the jungle's protection.

Hunter watched as Rags and the new visitor stood face to face, looking like neither man knew what to say.

Chapter Fifty~Nine

Journal Entry: May 1696 - Uttar Pradesh, India
Alexander Hincher - Hostage

I now continue the story. When I awoke, I found myself draped over the back of a horse, tied both hands and feet. By the pain in my chest and stomach, I knew we had been traveling for some time. I tried to turn to see who had me prisoner and could only see enough to tell that my new pretend lover was on the horse next to me. She, however, was not tied up as I was.

After what seemed to be another hour, our procession stopped. They loosed the ropes that held me on the horse and I tumbled to the dusty ground. I felt like my ribs were broken and someone had turned my insides, inside out. Then I realized the crack on my head provided equal agony. I laid there motionless, enduring the pain.

Finally, a pair of large dusty boots appeared and kicked me over onto my back. As I looked up, the brightness of the sun behind him only let me see the silhouette of a man I am sure I wouldn't have recognized if I could see his face. As I squinted to protect my eyes from the glare, he bellowed something I didn't understand.

"He wants to know where your friends went," a voice said, translating for me.

All I could do was groan. I was in so much agony. The dusty boot struck again and added to the pain.

"You better answer," was all I heard before everything went dark again.

When I awoke for the third time today, the pain remained, but my effort to grasp the situation was much greater. I didn't want another meeting with that boot. My eyes focused much faster this time because I willed them to do so. They had me tied up and lying on the floor inside an unfamiliar room. My companion, still dressed in Esther's clothing, was also tied up, but was sitting on a chair. She didn't look hurt, which was a relief.

I heard arguing in an adjacent room but couldn't make out what they were saying. The door burst open and this time I saw the face of the owner of the boots. I had seen that face twice before. Once when he was on horseback eyeing Esther and Leilyn sitting atop Sangha's elephant. The second time when he left Maneet's livery heading toward Sangha's caravan.

I understood the angry conversation this time. They were arguing over my companion's identity. I will never forget the disgust in the senior officer when he shouted 'This is not the princess!' as he entered the room where we were being held.

He turned and asked who I was and what I was doing here. He didn't actually ask; he demanded. It was not an answer I was ready to give. I tried to clear my head and come up with any kind of plausible answer. I don't know where the answer came from. It just came out.

"I'm partner in a spice co-op in Sarat. They call me Lord Rudy, short for Rudolph."

He then demanded to know what this young woman was doing with me. Again, it just came out.

"She was a gift from my partners. They want me to be comfortable. And she is," I said.

My answer didn't surprise her at all. She looked at me as if it were true. That frightened me. They wanted proof. I held up my tied hands. They understood my meaning. As quickly as I could think, a knife came out and the ropes binding me were cut.

I stood and came up to my new mistress and slipped my hand under the cloth wrapped around her chest. I pulled out a silver rupiya and tossed it to the officer who was demanding proof. He caught it and looked at it closely. It surprised my little mistress. Her wide eyes caused the soldiers to laugh.

The man holding the coin said. "It's warm."

They all laughed again. My little mistress continued to stare in disbelief.

I almost laughed as well, she was so startled. Talking to her but loud enough for the soldiers to hear, I said.

"You think I only watch you undress? I always see you hide that piece of silver when you are dressing."

The soldier pocketed the coin and turned to leave the room. "Dispose of them," he said as he marched out.

Several soldiers followed him out, leaving four to guard us. As the last of the followers left the room one turned to the remaining guards and said, "Make sure they do not find the bodies."

One soldier had my hands tied again before I even had time to object. We heard several horses gallop off. They gave the four soldiers a task to kill us and dispose of our bodies. It was clear they were uncomfortable with this command.

One of them touched my little mistress and when I tried to object, someone hit me in the back with the butt of a rifle. It nearly knocked me down again.

"Let's kill them and be done," one soldier said.

"Let's have her first," another spoke.

"A terrible waste of flesh!" came a new voice from behind them.

All four soldiers turned to face a gray-haired man as he stepped into the room uninvited. His dark eyes peered out from behind an equally black scarf covering his face. He lowered the scarf. The accent was Persian.

He continued, "If you kill them, even if you have her before you do, you must dispose of the bodies." He paused a moment then continued, "I will give you 200 silver rupiya for her and 100 for him."

The four soldiers stood unmoving, not knowing what to say.

"The Ottomans will give me twice that for him and three times that for her. She will make a pleasant addition to a harem and he a fine galley slave."

They continued speechless.

The Persian continued, "You can take the money and each buy what you wanted from her and I will make my Ottoman clients very happy. You decide."

He turned and left us all alone in the room. One soldier finally woke up and grabbed me by the ropes on my wrists and dragged me out after the Persian. Another pulled my little mistress along.

"You Persians are at war with the Ottoman's, you would do business with your enemies?"

"Gold and silver are gold and silver, it matters not from whose pocket they originate."

The Persian was standing next to an enclosed cart pulled by two very stout horses.

The soldier holding my reins said, "300 for her and 200 for him."

The Persian looked me over closely and then went to my little mistress and looked her over closely and said, "300 for her, but only 100 for him. He is too badly hurt."

They exchanged the rupiya's, and lifted me up into the back of the cart. They were not gentle. I landed and groaned as I hit. Since they were certain my little mistress was not the princess, they tossed her up into the back of the cart with little care. Her landing was softer than mine. It was right on top of me. The door locked.

"How d'you know we had prisoners?" I heard a soldier ask the Persian.

"Been watching and following since you left Agra. I make a living buying and selling human scraps. Just thought, since you tied these two up, eventually they'd be disposable."

The cart rolled and my little mistress sat up and tried to get comfortable while the cart bumped and jolted. The movement of the cart told me the Persian turned it around and headed away from the soldiers. It was clear we headed in opposite directions.

I finally asked my fellow prisoner her name. She offered the name Adrina, but nothing more. My mind was no longer cloudy, yet I was confused enough with recent events I did not know where to start.

Adrina was just moments ahead of the soldiers. She sacrificed herself by trading clothes with Esther and was now being taken to the Ottoman slave markets to be sold. Is that what she agreed to do in trying to help the princess?

Ever since Moses told me the legend about the Snow Leopard and the mountain, I look at choices people make to see where they fit in the story. There always seems to be the immediate motivations to meet the wants and needs of the moment. It is not, however, clear how those immediate motivations may relate to the overall governing aim of one's life,—'The Mountain' as Moses put it. I've concluded that many don't even know or care about the mountain and are just valley dwellers, and if they knew of the mountain and the rewards of climbing it, they have no interest to do so.

I tried to stop thinking. All of this was too big for my mind to take in. Just then, the cart slowed and stopped. I heard the Persian step down and come to the back of the cart and unlock the door. It swung open. The wooden box I called the cart was too small for Adrina to stand up in, but she quickly rose and offered her tied wrists to the Persian. He cut the ropes as quickly as had the soldier back in the house. She hopped out of the cart and gave the Persian a hug.

Holding the knife out, the Persian waved it at me, inviting me to do the same. I climbed to my knees and scooted over to the door holding out my tied wrists. He freed them in an instant. As they came free, he smiled at me and said, "Dr. Alexander Hincher, it is a pleasure to meet you."

- Hinch

Forest's Edge - The Island - 1748

What Hunter would give for a carrier pigeon! He felt he would go crazy if he had to live on this island one more year. Why was he the only one on this island who wanted off? There wasn't a part of it he thought he didn't know. His failure to find anything convinced him it was not the *Fancy's* treasure island.

The whole reason Hunter elected to sail with the *Bringhurst* was because he suspected Glen was the link to a treasure Hassan spent a life seeking. Glen would lead him to the treasure, he had believed.

It had been nearly fifteen years since the fiasco in Newton Ferrers. Though he was half drunk that night, Hunter was certain Glen and the sailor were the same man.

Now, after two years on this island, he became equally certain Glen and the sailor were not the same man. Every day, he questioned if this island imprisonment was a just punishment for his mistake in judgment.

There is no one looking for the lost Bringhurst. Missing now for two years, even Hassan has given up. Even if he received the message sent by pigeon all those years ago.

The message to his employer expressed Hunter's certainty he found the sailor in Sheffield. As Hunter found reasons to await word from his employer, he made friends with the Sheffield residents, just as he did in every village he appraised for his employer.

Hassan's men had not responded when Hunter learned of the disappearance of three families.

Pausing now, he thought back to the morning he'd gone to see Glen. Hunter had found the door open and the shop empty. As he stood alone in the empty Checkmate, arms folded and wondering how a family could disappear, a naval captain tapped on the door as he also stepped into the vacant shop. This meeting was not meaningless to Hunter. He'd seen that face before; it was fifteen years younger when he did, but he couldn't doubt it. When he last met Captain Remington back in Newton Ferrers the morning following the fateful night, he was not drunk. This was the captain of the HMS *Kent*. The sailor's ship.

Hunter felt this was another confirmation that Glen was the sailor he had been seeking. At that moment as the two men looked at each other as if they knew each other but could not be sure, in-bounded Martin, a scruffy looking, wild-eyed young boy calling out "Lydia?" The empty room caught him by surprise too, and now the captain, Hunter, and Martin stood there awestruck.

The young boy finally broke the silence when he said to nobody in particular, "They did it. They left."

At that, he turned and readied to leave when the captain reached out and grabbed Martin by his collar, halting his exit.

"They left? Where'd they go?" he asked the struggling boy.

"Don't ask me. Why would I know?"

The captain didn't let go.

After a long pause there was a shrug. "Antigua I guess." Martin said, struggling to wiggle out of the captain's grip.

"Antigua? Why Antigua?" Hunter asked.

"Lydia said she was excited to go there one day." With that, he freed himself and scampered from the shop.

In his line of work, no one knew the port cities and coastal villages of Europe like Hunter. He knew if the West Indies or America were the destination, they would likely embark from Liverpool. It was close. Second only to London in size and popularity, Liverpool was a major trade port and easily the busiest slave port for all of Great Britain. Ships of every size came and went with every favorable tide.

There was no time to lose.

Hunter's plan was to contact Hassan's agent in Liverpool as soon as he found a ship bound for Antigua. He felt there was nothing to learn from the captain as the man was as bewildered with the disappearance of the family as he was. Hunter wished the captain a good day and left.

Standing on the newly built docks, Hunter stood in awe as he did each time he visited this bustling port. It took him two excruciatingly long days to arrive, and he hoped since he was traveling with his woman and no children, he would arrive before Glen and his family. He hoped they didn't have more than a day's head start.

Hunter lost no time inquiring of the various ships their destination and cargo, looking for a likely ship Glen and his family might use. They wouldn't be sailing with one of the dozens of slave ships, and certainly not a navy ship, which narrowed his search to about forty ships. Among those, nearly half were likely headed to one or more of the ports in the West Indies. Many of those planned to set sail with the tide in a few hours.

Hunter had nothing to lose except that he claimed to have found the sailor back in Sheffield. If he lost the trail now, Hassan would punish him handsomely.

Leaving the docks, he located his counterpart in Liverpool and sent another message. A terse note saying the family was sailing to Antigua. Upon returning to the docks, by chance, Hunter saw Glen and his family as the crew of the *Bringhurst* loaded several large crates onboard.

It was then Hunter made that fateful decision that landed him on this uncharted island. He chose to sail with the *Bringhurst*.

Hunter now doubted his conclusions. In all the years on this island, Glen gave no sign of treasure hidden here. Hunter was paid well when he led Hassan to Newton Ferrers those many years ago, as he was one of the few who had seen the young sailor when he met David Creagh in Newton Ferrers.

With a fresh pocket full of gold coins, he drank. Even the few drinks were enough to hinder his recall. The vague memory of the events later that night haunted him for years. Someone killed three of his employer's men, Creagh and the sailor disappeared, and Hassan fled, not wanting to have any entanglements with HMS *Kent*.

Once sober the next morning, Hunter, who was naturally observant, cunning, and had a keen eye for women, went back to work for the famed Persian slave trader Captain Ali Mutarid Hassan. Hunter's job was to come to a coastal village, assess its geographic layout, its population of young and potentially profitable women, and any resistance the captain and his men might encounter when they raided the village.

Using the pigeon network, he communicated back to the captain. Seldom would Hunter be in the village when Hassan's men attacked and kidnapped. It was during one of these fact-finding visits to Newton Ferrers, Hunter met Creagh and heard his story about the mutiny aboard the *Charles II*.

Pressure from the various countries' navies made it increasingly more dangerous for his employer to attack and retreat unscathed. Hunter became much more selective with his targets. One spy was foolish in recommending a village on Norway's western coast, not realizing the daughter of a naval captain lived there. Hassan took her as part of the prize. The navy captain tracked down Hassan's faster, smaller ship the Akbar, attacked and took it while it was in a port in Tunisia. Hassan escaped, but the navy captain captured many of Hassan's men along with his first mate. They were tried and hung, while the young Norwegian women was rescued. The ship was destroyed.

Hassan's spy was never heard from again.

Chapter Sixty

Our Persian liberator offered me a hand and helped me out of the cart. I wondered if this was how Persians treated galley slaves?

He gave me the traveling pack I had left at Bibi's and then handed me this journal. As he did so, he smiled and said, "Doctor, you've had quite an adventure. Welcome to the Mughal Empire and Safavid Dynasty."

He bowed and introduced himself as "Makhfi, the Invisible One".

He saw the multitude of questions in my eyes and spared me having to ask them. For the next few hours as we traveled north together, Makhfi told me of the intrigues of emperors, their ascent to their thrones, the battles, the murders, the enemies, the revolts, the betrayals, the assassinations, the jealousy, and the power.

This understanding made the pirates with whom I spent the past number of years seem like simple-minded thieves compared to the competition for thrones.

And I returned Esther to the middle of it all. He congratulated me for making it this far alive, then condemned me for making it this far at all, and bringing the princess back into danger.

He listed all the powerful people who wanted the princess dead. Who benefited from her capture by the pirates, who would stop at nothing to find her if they knew she was back in India, and those who wanted that dagger.

He was kind but deadly serious. He pointed out that the Maratha soldiers only spared my life initially because Adrina was willing to give hers to save the princess. He told me Adrina fully expected to be raped and murdered once they recognized she was not the princess. She offered to give her life for that of the princess. That is a bigger mountain than I'd ever climbed. I was only a casualty who meant nothing.

I looked at Adrina and wondered. She was beautiful, young like Esther, and now dressed like Esther, you could easily mistake the two. What would motivate a young girl to make that kind of sacrifice? I hoped to find out sometime. I could hear Makhfi speaking, but I was no longer listening.

This Persian, Makhfi, noticed my attention wandered. He snapped me back. "Esther is safe, and it is your responsibility to keep her that way." He said, emphasizing the 'YOUR RESPONSIBILITY' part.

"Can you ride?" he then asked.

I hardly noticed we arrived at a small corral where three beautiful horses stood ready. Feeling the bruised ribs, I asked, "Do I get to sit this time?"

He laughed and assured me I could. We mounted up and continued our journey toward Delhi. We headed into the mouth of the tiger.

- Hinch

Cliff's Edge - The Island - 1748

The man pulled out a large knife. Just as Jack thought he was about to face his second knife-wielding, wife-stealing, island resident, the stranger reached down and slit the hog's throat, quieting its squealing.

Elizabeth stood mouth open and speechless. As the man stood back up, wiping the blood off the knife with a large leaf from a nearby plant, he said to Jack, also standing speechless, "I'm Rags, who are you?"

Rags was still brandishing the knife, which had just proved to be very sharp and wielded by a man skilled in its use. Jack said nothing. Rags looked down at the knife and returned it to its sheath, then laughed out loud. Extending a blood-stained hand, he said, "Hello, I'm still Rags. Are you still deaf or just mute?"

This time Elizabeth came out of her shock first and took Jack's arm, lifting it so he could shake hands with Rags. As she did so, she said, "Not deaf, nor mute, just dumb."

Giving Elizabeth a scowl, Jack shook Rags' hand. "Jack, I'm Jack. And this is Elizabeth, my spokeswoman."

Rags chuckled, "Your wife, huh?"

"Not yet, but soon enough," Jack said.

Did I say that?

He took her hand, and though not obvious, made sure Rags saw the engagement ring on her finger.

"Hello, Jack-I'm-Jack, hello Elizabeth. Nice to meet you two. Sorry about him," Rags said as he pointed to the dead and bleeding hog. "Got away from me. They're stubborn; didn't want to join us for dinner tonight. Can you imagine such rudeness? I kindly invited him to dinner, and he took off complaining like crazy. Hogs can be that way, you know. Just passing through or here to stay?"

"Oh, I think he's here to stay," Elizabeth said, looking down at the hog.

"I think he's talking about us," Jack said, turning to Elizabeth.

"Well, if he invites us to dinner, we're accepting. Wouldn't want to be rude," she replied.

"I know most of the folks on this island, you must be new," Rags said. "And how did you get here? There's only one way to reach this island, and that's if a storm drops you here. There have been no storms for a while. How long you been here?"

Rags extended question gave Jack time to recover. "Yes, by table, and four days."

That quick response to the question caught Rags off guard, leaving him uncharacteristically speechless.

Jack reached out, shook Rags' hand again and said, "Let's start over. Meet Elizabeth. I'm Jack. Last week, pirates captured our ship, but we escaped before it sank. We drifted to the shore on the north side of the island. We were then captured by Glen and rescued by Rosemary. We are on our way to meet the others when we found this canyon and were so surprisingly greeted by your runaway hog."

"Well, if you're a friend of Rosemary, you're a friend of mine. Welcome. But it's not a canyon, it's a fjord." Rags said.

The three turned and stood looking across the chasm dividing them from the easier route to the plateau.

"Rags, I don't think you can call it a fjord. Glaciers create fjords and I am certain a glacier didn't create this canyon." Jack said.

"Call it what you want but I grew up with fjords in Norway and this is a fjord."

"You're Norwegian? Where'd you get the name Rags? Rags is not Norwegian. And you don't sound Norwegian."

Slipping into a very strong Norwegian accent, Rags replied, "Actually, my name is Ragnhild."

"Ragnhild? That's a girl's name," Elizabeth said.

"It vas a girls' name till I vas given it. Now it only belongs to the most masculine of men who'r proud of their manhood," Rags boasted.

"So they call you Rags out of respect!" Elizabeth said, bowing in jest.

"Precisely," Rags said, appreciating her bow.

"She's a smart one, Jack. And pretty too. Ya need ta keep 'r." Rags said, still with his strong accent. "Vell done, Elizabeth. Vell done. Ve vill be good friends."

Chapter Sixty~One

Journal Entry: May 1696 - Bageche Temple, Uttar Pradesh, India - Alexander Hincher -

The sun was just rising when we stopped at an abandoned ancient temple. We hadn't ridden fast in the darkness but after a long day and night; I found myself too tired to do anything but sleep.

I awoke in the late afternoon. My weary eyes fell upon the most beautiful sight I believe I've ever seen. The princess smiled and handed me a cup of hot tea.

Behind her stood Makhfi, talking with Moses and Rudy. They were too far away for me to hear what they were saying, but it was obvious they were planning a new adventure. I was close enough to see it in Rudy's expressions.

Esther told me how she slipped behind the sarcophagus just in time for the soldiers to take Adrina and me away. Once Adrina and I were gone, Esther snuck back to Bibi and told her what had happened. Bibi immediately put my rescue into action. Adrina saw the soldiers heading to the mausoleum and knew Esther was in trouble. She took a chance on her own.

"Who are these people?" I asked quietly. "Adrina, she gave her life for you. Makhfi, with no apparent concern for his own life, tracks Adrina and me, and pits his life against soldiers we know are murderous. What type of people do that?"

My question surprised Esther. She looked into my eyes for a long time and finally said, "Why did Rudy sacrifice himself to save Leilyn and myself? You bought his life from Avery for an untold sum. Why did you do that? What type of person are you?"

I am so naïve to have thought I would return Esther to her mother's loving care and protection. What could she do? She was a prisoner. Esther's question of 'what kind of man am I?' stabbed deeply into my heart. 'What kind of man am I?' A stupid one, motivated by honor? Maybe, but stupid? Certainly.

There was nothing I could say to that. She helped me up and as tender and sore as I was; it felt good to get moving. Makhfi, Moses, and Rudy turned my way and motioned for me to join them. I saw Adrina watching me with Esther. She and Leilyn and my harem were preparing something that smelled wonderful.

Rudy and Moses were trying to convince Makhfi we could free Esther's mother. They gave up the idea of killing Emperor Aurangzeb and putting Zeb-un-Nissa on the throne, though Makhfi admitted she would have plenty of allies to support her.

He waited until I joined the conversation before he continued. When he referred to Princess Zeb-un-Nissa, he used the phrase term "Shahdokht Joon." It was obvious I wasn't following, so Makhfi started over for my sake.

"The princess is being held under light guard in Salamgahr prison, part of the Red Fort. I doubt the rumors of Astrella's return have reached them. They will welcome her. Even though Zeb-un-Nissa is confined in prison, Astrella enjoyed relative freedom to venture beyond the fort as evidenced in her ability to make the pilgrimage to Mecca."

We all listened intently as we figured this information was setting the stage for the plan. Makhfi knew we already knew all of this.

"The reward offered for her return and the return of her grandfather's treasure would make you all wealthy beyond anything you can imagine," he told us.

"I've seen his treasure. I helped carry if off the Gunsway," Rudy said. "I don't need to imagine."

"Both treasures," I said.

"But you'll never collect the reward." Makhfi was very solemn. "You've met those men who want Astrella. There is nothing they won't do to get her. They didn't quit when they commanded your death."

We had a long and spirited debate but Makhfi prevailed in convincing us to let him take Esther and Leilyn with him to the Red Fort where tomorrow they will meet with his "Shahdokht Joon", Esther's mother, Zeb-un-Nissa.

I realize Makhfi has a deep respect for Zeb-un-Nissa. If I didn't know better, I would call it love. Actually, I do call it love. Who is this Persian? Esther never answered that question.

- Hinch

Canyon's Edge - The Island - 1748

Rags knelt, untied the rope from the hog's leg, and slit the underbelly from end to end. Blood and guts spilled onto the ground. Elizabeth stepped back and watched. Rags noticed the lack of any shock or queasiness in her reaction.

What held her attention was not the bleeding animal at her feet, but the majestic cliffs rising above the jungles. Here on the edge of the canyon, or fjord as Rags called it, she had a view unobstructed by dense forest. As it had earlier, the mountain range fascinated her.

"What's on the other side of those cliffs? More forest?" Elizabeth asked.

"More rocks. We've tried to climb 'em. They're too sheer. The only way to the other side is to swim. Built a raft once only to see there's nothing but rock."

"Where do you live?" Elizabeth asked, still looking up at the cliffs.

"On the plateau with the others. We all live there except for Rosemary's family and Hunter."

"How many others? And who's Hunter?" Elizabeth asked.

"There's me, of course. Louisa and Walt, you'll love 'em. There's the Adams, an old couple who just complain a lot. Ben and Susan are nice, though all they do is worry, but Susan is like Louisa; she can really cook and is a looker like you. Ben's afraid I'll steal Susan, so he keeps close tabs on her. It's Marge who's my favorite. Kinda old and probably a little crazy, but she wants to leave her husband and move in with me," Rags answered the question, never once looking up from his work on the hog.

"And Marge's husband, what does he think about her moving in with you?" Elizabeth asked.

"Oh, he wants her to. Wants to be rid of her. But I don't think I could take her snoring. Sometimes you can hear her all across the plateau."

"Oh, my," was all Elizabeth could say.

"Well, you gunna earn your dinner or not?" Rags asked, standing and wiping off the knife. He handed the knife to Jack. "Cut us a pole we can use to haul her to the plateau."

Jack stepped to a tree and quickly had a pole ready. He turned the knife over and over in his hands admiring it. A masterpiece. Even with smears of blood, it glistened in the sunlight. There he saw a familiar engraving: an elegant C accompanied by a W and a L. The knife evidently came from the same foundry and by the same cutler as Glen's machete. Maybe they came as a set. If he ever got off this island, he had news to share with his uncle.

Jack returned to where Rags and Elizabeth were waiting. Together they tied the hog to the pole and headed along the edge of the fjord. Jack just chuckled.

"Does Ben have anything to worry about?" Jack asked.

"Who?" Rags asked.

"Ben. You said Ben worried you might steal Susan. And if she's a looker like my Elizabeth here, I want to know if I need to worry," Jack said, as he gave Elizabeth a wink.

"Maybe. Me and Elizabeth, we're getting kinda close," Rags said.

"Can you cook?" Jack and Rags asked at the same time.

Elizabeth smiled and said, "When there's a reason to. Raised with a sister, my mother put us to good use."

"Elizabeth here's a teacher, if you can imagine that, Rags. She keeps children's minds from turning to mush."

"Nobody has any children here but Rosemary, maybe she can use help, but you better just settle down and have babies. We could use some more babies," Rags said.

Rags' matter-of-fact attitude was a bit startling for Elizabeth, and Jack smiled, waiting for her response.

"Babies?" she asked.

"Well, what else you two going to do on this island? You're stuck here. We can help you put up a house and you can get to work."

"Babies?" Elizabeth repeated.

"He's got a point," Jack said.

"Babies?" she said one more time.

"Why does she keep saying that? Makes it sound like you two never talked about it before getting married. You know how to make babies, don't you?" Rags asked.

Jack was working so hard to keep in the laughter he nearly dropped the hog. "Rags, we have talked about it and there's nothing I want more than to get to work. But you see, we are only engaged. Elizabeth here is only my fiancé."

"Oh, good. It worried me I'd have to teach ol' Jack here a thing or two about manhood."

Elizabeth's embarrassment took time to wear off, so Jack carried the conversation. "Glen tells us there's no way off the island. Does anybody want off the island?" Jack asked.

"How did you two get here again?" Rags asked, as if he didn't hear Jack's question.

"Pirates seized our ship, and we escaped," Jack answered.

"Did you say you floated here on a table?"

The question surprised Jack. He mentioned that fact earlier in such a commotion it impressed him Rags had heard it and remembered.

"You could use a good table in your new house. Where is it now?" Rags asked.

"On the beach where we washed up," Jack said.

"We all had dreams for the New World. Me, Glen, and Walt would start a business. Ben and Susan wanted a fresh start in the New World. Ben's our farmer and a good one. And Marge, oh Marge. She wanted to get her husband, Shel away from his friends, all drunks, sober him up and see if he could be worth something again." All this came flowing out of Rags, as natural as if he was teaching Sunday school class.

Elizabeth's embarrassment faded now they were talking about something other than her potential maternity. She squinted as she looked at Rags, as if she was trying to see inside him and figure out what made him tick.

"It worked, you know," Rags added.

"What worked?" Jack asked, saving Elizabeth the trouble. She was just as confused.

"Shel. He's sober." Rags nodded, "Not a drop on the island."

"Drop of what?" Jack asked.

"Elizabeth, I worry for you. This man of yours can't follow a simple conversation. Did he get hit?" Rags pointed to his head. "When you two escaped?"

"You have no idea. It wasn't trauma, I think he came that way," Elizabeth said.

"And you love him, anyway. You are a saint," Rags said. He continued on, as if he hadn't paused. "Rum. Ale. Whiskey. Anything good to drink. What they left of the stores on board was for the crew anyway, not the passengers. The *Bringhurst* was a merchant ship, not necessarily a passenger ship, so the stores of rum were small and didn't last long. So Shel is dry as can be."

"At least somebody got what they left England for. Marge got what she wanted.," Elizabeth said.

"I don't know. She's told me he was more interesting when he was drinking. When he took up hunting, he was pleasant for a while. Now he's back to being grumpy all the time. He has nothing to motivate him. It's like he's stranded on his own island, on a stranded island," Rags said. "So yes. We all want off the island."

Elizabeth felt like she just got off a carousel like the one she once rode patterned after the early jousting traditions, where knights would gallop in a circle tossing balls from one to another. She was getting just as dizzy the way this conversation had gone around.

This man was absolutely the most unique person Elizabeth ever met. He had answered a simple question with a simple answer—after an amazing journey of discovery.

Chapter Sixty~Two

Journal Entry: May 1696 - Bageche Temple, Uttar Pradesh, India - Alexander Hincher - Prisoner of worry

It's been days and no word of Esther and Leilyn, nor Makhfi. The plan was to learn if Esther and Leilyn could safely stay with the princess.

The life of a pirate is so predictable. Dangerous yes, but predictable. I always knew what those men wanted and what they will do to get it. They became disgustingly predictable. It almost became boring. In contrast, these past several months has been nothing but torture for me.

The difference is now I care. I never cared about my life and what might happen to me. I sorrowed for those whom my shipmates wronged, but I'd grown to face life without passion. I wanted to be free of those filthy men with their base motives of greed and loathsome passions. But I never recognized the difference between hating what I had settled for and living for something I loved. Despair and numbness swallowed my hopes and dreams.

I believe it wasn't until I cared for Rudy's torn flesh, which he sacrificed to save Esther and Leilyn, that a spark of humanity again ignited within me. Now that spark is a flame that will consume my soul. We have reunited Esther with her family. Why then am I so consumed with despair?

Makhfi promised to send word or bring word but we haven't heard. It's now a week since they left us. I broke our agreement to flee if there was no word after three days.

I refuse to run without knowing her fate. Yesterday, Adrina and Tanek took an insistent Rudy into Dehli to see what they could learn. Moses and I, along with the three remaining members of my harem, remain hidden here in this wretched old ruin, which serves more as a prison for me than a temple. I have second thoughts about Rudy and Moses' initial plan to storm the fort, free Zeb-un-Nissa, kill her father, and place her on the throne.

- Hinch

The Plateau - The Island - 1748

The trio finally arrived at the plateau after several dizzying conversations. Rags shared intimate and not so intimate facts about the island, the people, the trials, and the triumphs of their lives.

At one point in their journey, Jack happily set the pole down for a moment's rest. Elizabeth smiled. The two learned how Marge and Shel met after Shel was dishonorably discharged from the Royal Navy for drunken and disorderly conduct. He apparently insulted the admiral's daughter, calling her a strumpet. When she slapped him, he threw her overboard. She was a splendid swimmer, and they were in port, so it could have been more serious. They learned Shel was short for Shellie. According to Rags, having a girl's name was the reason Shel was so contrary. Rags would certainly know.

Shel was working as a smithy when a carriage pulled up to his shop. He stepped out to the carriage to see what they needed. When the coachman stepped down, two beautiful deep blue eyes captivated him. He was standing face to face with a coach woman, the first he had ever seen. Shel was accustomed to working with every sort of horseman. Never had he met a coach woman until he saw her; she fascinated him.

As Elizabeth absorbed the details of the story, she couldn't help but wonder how a second-hand story could have so much passion or detail. But she didn't complain.

Rags is a true romantic, she thought.

Shel re-shoed the horse, treated its lame hoof, and repaired a worn halter. When he finished with those, he looked for anything else needing repair, eager to keep this carriage and its coach woman from leaving.

Their relationship blossomed and he and Marge married. The relationship grew stale. His work become routine, there were no exciting challenges, and Shel returned to drinking. He lost his purpose. Nothing drove his passions; he'd become a man without a mission. Didn't feel like anybody needed him.

Finally, Marge convinced Shel it was time to start over in the New World, time to conquer again, and time to be a man again.

Rags said everyone liked Marge and Shel enough, but mostly they agreed with Rags; Shel was just a grumpy old sailor out of water and Marge was a little crazy. Fun, but crazy. Shel, Walt, and Glen explored various ways to get off the island, but without the tools, the three of them were without their trades.

As Rags, Jack, and Elizabeth continued their walk with the tied hog, they crested a ridge that provided a magnificent vista. Rags switched from Shel, and talked about Ben and Susan. That story got stalled. Jack and Rags put down the hog for another rest, and Rags began a tutorial on the geography of the island. He pointed out mostly what was obvious to everyone.

Elizabeth was still taken with the majesty of the mountain. They could see the wrecked ship in a small harbor about halfway along the shore. The island's abrupt shoreline was mostly rocky. Now they understood what Glen told Jack about their small sandy beach was probably true. It was among the only actual beaches on the island.

Elizabeth then pointed a distance beyond the small harbor to what Jack could faintly make out as a small community. It was situated on a small plateau. The plateau featured a few small homes, if you could call them that, surrounded by fields that looked like they were cultivated. The fields gave way to a thick forest which ended at the tall cliffs that ran the length of the island.

They looked down the expanse of the canyon, or fjord as Rags called it, and could see the mouth. If it weren't for those ragged rocks at the mouth of the canyon, Jack mentioned he thought this would be a perfect hideout for a ship and how appropriate it was people called the rocky entrances to a canyon like this skerries.

In her mind, Elizabeth compared the small lagoon where they saw the stranded ship high on the shore to this canyon where a ship in a storm would have been equally protected. Elizabeth wondered if Glen actually navigated to where he did or if he was just lucky.

Looking back the other way, the beach wasn't visible, but they saw where it would be, and how secluded the cove was where Glen and Rosemary now made their home.

"Rags," Elizabeth asked. "Why did Glen and his family build their home so far away?"

She knew he heard the question. He looked into nowhere, thinking. Elizabeth wondered what kind of journey this conversation might take them on before he shared the simple answer.

But shockingly, he said. "I don't know."

"Looks like we got a little walk ahead of us still," Jack said, eager to get moving. He reached to pick up his end of the pole supporting the hog. Rags didn't. He just starred back the direction the two had come. Jack put it back down.

"When we left the ship after the storm, we explored this end of the island. Finding the plateau, we were grateful for the groves of wild fruit trees. We were glad to be alive and with the ship careened, we got it ready to sail the next time the tide rose enough to float it again."

Elizabeth and Jack listened silently.

"We lived off the stores on board for weeks. We never thought to settle the island. We planned to sail again soon, we thought. Except Glen," Rags said. Then he went silent and stared into the distance again like he remembered something important.

"Did you know Guinea hens can fly?" Rags asked.

Elizabeth braced herself. *Here we go again.*

"Guinea hens?" Jack asked in total confusion.

"Ben's a farmer. Jack, you remember, his wife is the looker who can cook? Ben brought a few cages of Guinea hens and some of them got loose during the storm. When the storm ended, they somehow got off the ship."

"The other hens were getting restless, so I went to work making a pen for them up on the plateau where it was nice and safe."

Elizabeth knew what was coming and almost laughed before Rags finished his story.

"I took the other cages of hens and set them loose in the pens I built."

"I think I can guess," Jack said.

Rags gave Jack the look that said, okay guess.

"You learned Guinea hens can fly," Jack said.

"Those hens went everywhere," Rags said. "It took Walt and Glen both to keep Ben from killing me. Shel just laughed. It was one of the few times we ever saw him laugh. I guess it was worth it."

"You thought they were like chickens?" Jack asked, not really needing to.

Rags raised his eyebrows to confirm that to be true.

"Since you're staying around for a while, we'll probably have hen. You'll love the way Louisa prepares it. Susan's is good too, but Louisa does hens the best."

"My guess is, we'll be staying around a while," Elizabeth said.

"Good," Rags said. "It'll be nice having fresh folks to talk to."

Elizabeth was dying to see if Rags would circle around and finish addressing why Glen settled so far away.

Hearing Elizabeth and Rags conclude they weren't leaving the island soon made him anxious. Jack reached down, and picked up his end of the pole again. This time Rags didn't.

"Glen seemed to know we were staying. He spent his days exploring, went everywhere. A few times, he was gone for days. Made the rest of us nuts. Weeks went by and we realized we better at least make the best of it. Living on the ship was no good."

"What about the captain and the crew? Didn't they take charge? After all, it was their ship." Jack said.

"The storm killed the captain. We buried him the first day and the crew members who survived took the longboat and left. We were glad. Ben spent enough time up on the plateau hunting for his birds. By default, he chose the plateau as our settling place and we moved in."

"And Glen?" Elizabeth asked.

"Nope, he told us it would be safer down by the cove, but everybody liked it at the plateau better. So, we all settled," Rags said, as if the discussion was over.

Rags reached down and lifted his end of the pole. This time Jack didn't.

"And for all these years you've lived separated?" Jack asked.

"Why not?" Rags said, still holding up his end of the pole. The hog slid down toward Jack's end of the pole.

Jack picked it up, bearing the full weight. He let out a grunt. "It seems unsocial," Jack said as he jiggled the pole to get the hog back into the center. Jack and Rags were about the same height, so he had to raise the pole above his head to get the hog to slide toward Rags.

The word *settled* seemed to settle in Elizabeth's mind. It felt so heavy. So permanent and almost hopeless. For the next hour, the navigation over rocky terrain made conversation more difficult, which made Elizabeth grateful. Her mind was dissecting Rags' statement, "we all settled."

She heard her mother use that term when telling stories of her family carving their homestead out of a harsh mountain land and they settled the beautiful valley where Elizabeth's mother grew up. For her ancestors, settling their valley was triumphant. They conquered. They were proud of their accomplishment and as they lived, worked, and raised families, they were living their dream.

How different that same word sounded when uttered by Rags. The people on the idyllic island, which was far more hospitable and welcoming than her mother's mountain home had been for her parents and grandparents, these had settled not in triumph but in resignation. They settled in because they had no other choice. Their fate was selected for them.

The trio continued making its way in and out of thickets and groves and clearings, and Elizabeth's thoughts were doing the same thing.

One thought, which made its way out of the dense forest of her mind, was her fake engagement with Jack. What if they really couldn't get off this island? What if they lived here another four years? Or ten? Then, breaking completely free of any mental forests, Elizabeth asked herself, *Would I settle for Jack as a husband?*

Would Jack be like this island? Idyllic, but since he was not her choice, it would be settling. Could she be happy with something wonderful even though she had not chosen it? Would she always wonder if she could have chosen better if there were more choices? What if he was wrong for her? Would marrying him be right even though there was no other choice?'

Elizabeth's mind was more exhausted than her body.

"Here's the best thing on this island," Rags said as he set the hog down next to a short but very full tree, unlike the other forest trees.

"Cherimoya." Rags didn't just say it, he announced it, as if he created it.

Jack was glad to get a minute to rest his shoulder and back, which bore the brunt of the boar. Elizabeth was grateful her mind was being rescued. It began settling on children's names.

"Cherimoya?" Jack said, "Never heard of it back home."

"You wouldn't. It's tropical, but even on this island it's rare. Only a few on the island. A must taste," Rags said as he reached up and pulled the ugly green fruit from a loaded branch.

Out came his hog slaying knife and Elizabeth winced thinking she would taste blood tainted fruit. The skin of it looked like tiles of a roof. Already she was uninterested. Rags cut off a small tip of it and used the white flesh of this small piece to wash off the knife. Elizabeth gained a little respect for Rags for his thinking to clean off the remnants of blood. Rags then sliced the remaining piece in half and handed Jack and Elizabeth each a piece.

"Avoid the seeds or you'll end up like our friend here," Rags said as he pointed to the dead hog.

As he did so, Jack spit out one of the black seeds. They were both surprised. The fruit was smooth and flavorful.

"Glen says the cherimoya on this island are odd. Their season is off and we don't get cold enough, so we shouldn't really get fruit this good. We don't care what Glen says. We eat and enjoy," Rags said.

The two hadn't realized they were hungry. The fruit was very welcome.

How does Glen know so much about tropical fruit? Elizabeth asked herself.

"Not too far now." Rags said picking up his end of the hog pole.

Jack, doing the same, stepped in line and the convoy moved on. Elizabeth's mind, slightly rested, returned to its reflecting on the notion of settling in.

Had everyone on this island settled? Would she?

Then the memory of her grandmother Lillie's wit and wisdom brought one of her pet sayings to mind. Grandma Lillie would rattle off a whole paragraph; she had one for every situation. This time Elizabeth only needed a portion of one of these Grandma Lillie-isms.

Be grateful for what we have. It is enough. Gratitude gives us peace where we are today. It fuels our hope for tomorrow and shapes our vision of the future.

Elizabeth hadn't always understood the meaning behind each Lillie-ism, but she loved this one because she thought she knew what it meant. Today, stranded on an uncharted island, it meant a grateful person can be happy and fulfilled all along life's journey, even during the disruptions, detours, or waylays, and be satisfied with their progress without giving up on their dreams.

It meant she could enjoy this island, enjoy the people, be grateful for this opportunity, and still work diligently to get off it. So, she concluded, you can settle without settling and not give up your dreams. Her mind wandered to her sweet sister.

Did she settle? Where is she? Is she alive?

Elizabeth hadn't yet met everyone on the island, so she couldn't answer her earlier question: Are they settled, or have they settled? She left the other question unanswered—the one about Jack. And then Rags spoke up.

"So, how long have you two been engaged?" Rags asked.

This question brought a quick end to Elizabeth's mental journey.

"Um, a, oh—" Jack began.

"We've been together so long it seems like forever," Elizabeth answered.

That didn't satisfy Rags' curiosity. "When are you planning the marriage?" he asked.

Jack was out of his stupor this time and replied, "We are waiting until we return to England so we can be with family."

"Change that," Rags said. "We could be on this island a long time. We probably ought to make wedding plans."

Who is this guy? Elizabeth frowned. *We haven't even known him a day, and he becomes a wedding planner?* Maybe she didn't like him after all.

"With all my heart I'd like that, Rags," Jack said, "but I feel having her family is so important to Elizabeth, we need to wait and see what happens."

That was not at all what she expected. Was Jack actually a gentleman? Now it was Elizabeth's turn.

"You mentioned you were on your way to meet your fiancé when the storm brought you to this island instead," she said. "Tell us about her."

Chapter Sixty~Three

Journal Entry: May 1696 - Kanpur, India
Alexander Hincher - Bounty Hunter

After several nights of minimal sleep, I finally succumbed to the fatigue of worry. Adrina's tender but passionate plea gently awakened me.

"We've got to go. They've taken them, we must go. Now!"

Moses had the horses ready and the six of us were at a dead run within minutes of Adrina's return to our temple hideout. By mid-morning we caught up with Tanek and Rudy who were tracking the band of Santaji's soldiers.

As we rode, Rudy filled me in on the details of the kidnapping.

In a brutal raid on the fort by a rogue Maratha general by the name of Santaji, dozens were left dead and members of the royal family including Esther, her mother, and Leilyn are hostages. Rudy fears Makhfi is dead with the others.

The turn of events is mind-boggling. Zeb-un-Nissa is no longer held safely in prison under the watchful eye of a jealous, murderous, vengeful, emperor father. Our new aim is to rescue her from a rebel Maratha general, and some two hundred or more soldiers.

Our previous plan was the easy one. We were going to free Zeb-un-Nissa from prison. Escape north through Lahore, to Makfhi's hometown, where Zeb-un-Nissa, Esther, and Leilyn will be safe. Adrina and Tanek will return to Agra where Adrina and Bibi will help Tanek get back home. As for Rudy, Moses, myself, and my harem, we would decide where to go once we are safe in Persian territory. At least that was the plan.

I doubted anyone could answer my question of Santaji's motive, so I never asked. The Marathas have been at war with the Muhgals for many years. Santaji was once one of the Maratha revered generals. Now he is a rebel hated by both sides.

As we rested our horses tonight, Adrina took a guess of what we are up against. This man, Santaji, is at war personally with Aurangzeb. A few years earlier he attacked Aurangzeb's camp at Tulapur and with the help of his brothers and two thousand soldiers, cut the ropes of the emperor's tents, took the Imperial Golden Pinnacles, and fled. They killed so many in the royal tent; they assumed Aurangzeb died as well.

Later, Aurangzeb was found alive in Esther's aunt Zenat-un-nissa's tent. The success of Santaji's attack emboldened the Maratha fighters' dedication to throw off the emperor's grasp of the empire.

Adrina thinks this might be a similar tactic to embarrass the Mughal Emperor and thus stimulate their efforts to recruit more to the Maratha cause.

Moses vehemently disagreed with Adrina, which surprised all of us. He reminded us of the demands placed on Sangha to provide help in the Mughal siege of Jinji. Moses thinks this is a strategic distraction for Aurangzeb.

After Moses posed his opposing view of Santaji's motive for raiding the royal apartments in the Red Fort and seizing Salamanghr's prisoner, Zeb-un-Nissa, Rudy provided his expert opinion as well.

Rudy, Lord Rudy as he keeps reminding me, said Santaji had a falling out with the Marathas and is trying to get back in with them and so he wants to make himself look brave or clever to prove himself. Where he came up with that idea, I could never begin to guess. But I couldn't argue with any of the three conjectures.

Though Aurangzeb has been keeping his daughter in prison, her being kidnapped by his greatest personal enemy, is the ultimate insult to his kingdom. Zeb-un-Nissa is a pawn in a deadly chess match.

Adrina believes Santaji's men will go to Kanpur where they will rest their horses. Since Kanpur is a friendly Hindu town; she believes they will think themselves safe. We will try to get there first.

We can travel faster than Santaji's army as we have no wagons or footmen.

    - Hinch.

The Plateau - The Island - 1748

"Rags, you were telling us about Ben and Susan." Jack changed the subject, much to Elizabeth's appreciation.

"What was it Rosemary prepared when you arrived?" Rags asked.

"We had fish, some vegetable called pepinello and several different kinds of fruit," Elizabeth answered.

"Pepinello?" Rags said appreciatively.

"That's what Lydia called it. Tasted like a squash my grandmother used to make. Delicious," Elizabeth said.

"Pepinello is a squash, a chayote squash and nobody does the chayote like Rosemary. Next time ask for her boniato, her other specialty," Rags added.

"What's boniato?" Jack asked.

"That's all Ben," Rags said.

"Ben's a boniato?" Jack asked.

"As I told you, Ben's a farmer. Ben is the reason we eat so well. Walt can fish and it's Glen who knows how to catch the turtles."

"And you're the hunter?" Elizabeth pointed out.

"Yes, but it's the farmer that turned this island into a home. Ben and Susan wanted a nice big farm in the New World. Instead, they have a nice small one. Ben does amazing things on the plateau. He brought seeds, tools, and smarts," Rags said.

"How about Susan?" Elizabeth asked.

"Yes, he brought her too," Rags agreed.

Elizabeth couldn't tell if he was teasing her or if he was taking her literally.

"She loves it here as well," Rags said.

That wasn't what Elizabeth was asking, but she elected not to pursue the matter. She was grateful the answer was as short as it was. Besides, they had now reached the village. If you could call it a village.

Rags startled Louisa when he called her name. She spun to see Rags approach. Behind him were Jack and Elizabeth, but Louisa couldn't see them at first glance.

"Now, Rags dear, that is what I call a fine hog," Louisa said as they approached.

"Thank you. I believe he is. Name's Jack and his lady friend here is Elizabeth. Two strays," Rags said as he stepped to the side so Louisa could see who was carrying the other end of the pole. Then he let Elizabeth catch up and come into view.

"I was talking about the wild pig," Louisa said.

"So was I, his name is still Jack. Jack, meet Louisa," Rags said.

Louisa shook her head, raised her eyebrows, stood and took Elizabeth's hand.

"We don't get strays. Tell me you arrived on a ship powered by something other than wind." Louisa said.

"Yep," Rags said. "It's waiting for you down at the lagoon. If you hurry you might catch it."

Elizabeth explained how the pirates attacked the *Emerald*, how she and Jack escaped, their meeting Glen and his family, and how Rags escorted them to the plateau. Though she was disappointed Elizabeth and Jack didn't represent a way off the island, Louisa was very welcoming. She immediately put Elizabeth to work answering her multitude of questions about the outside world.

Rags and Jack set to work dressing out the hog.

Chapter Sixty~Four

When we arrived at Kanpur, we found a camp with provisions and horses ready for Santaji and his men. Santaji planned the attack and abduction well. He probably has camps like this set up every few days between the Salmanghar prison and what we estimate is Patna, which is probably two weeks away.

Rudy left to arrange supplies and fresh horses for us, in case we can't facilitate a rescue tonight. Without Makfhi we will have a more difficult time escaping to the north through Persian territory. Adrina is confident Zeb-un-Nissa will have enough friends to help us cross this country.

Even as I write, Rudy is back, not with a change of horses but a change of clothes. Camp organizers hired us as camp slaves. Even down to my harem and Tanek. Planning a quick communication system where we can alert one another once the camp is full of tired, hunted men, we changed into our new attire and are preparing to provide various services in the camp.

We don't know how soon Aurangzeb will know of the attack, nor how he will respond. All we know is they thought him to be at Bhopal at the time of the kidnapping. We can only guess he will not respond lightly. We have to find and rescue Leilyn, Esther, and her mother before Aurangzeb gets here.

- Hinch.

The Plateau - The Island - 1748

Once they prepared the hog and got it cooking, Rags led Jack and Elizabeth down to the lagoon to see the *Bringhurst* stranded high up on the beach.

As Rags and Jack were examining the hull, Elizabeth climbed topside to explore the deck.

"Glen told me there is no way off the island because of a lack of tide and currents, and that this island is uncharted for that reason. No ships will find it because the trade winds ships follow won't bring them here," Jack said placing both hands on the rudder and pushing it forward and pulling it back. *How did Glen use this to bring the ship safely here?*

Rags pulled the knife and scraped a flake of cracked paint from the name *Bringhurst* painted on the aft panel above the rudder. "Oh, there's a tide all right, but it's only high enough to make a difference a couple times a year, in the spring and fall. Even then, it's not enough to float the ship. Glen and Walt plopped it here when the storm gave the tide an extra twenty feet. Didn't need much repair, so we took the spare lumber that a ship like this carries in the hold to help build our homes. We figured it was of no use to leave the wood there. Glen said the only way this ship will ever sail again will be if a storm picks it up and carries it off. No one here is crazy enough to want to go get buried at sea."

Jack realized he was powerless to complete his assignment. It weighed on him. He became more direct with his questions.

"So nobody wants to be rescued? You're all happy living out your lives here? Glen says it's not possible. Walt says it's too dangerous to try. Louisa is so content. Ben and Susan are happy having their little farm, they never dream of ever having an estate or servants or cows?" Jack asked, knowing if he ever waited for Rags to run out of things to say, the conversation would wander endlessly.

"Oh, no," began Rags, "We all want off the island; we all have dreams. We're just realistic. We don't know the location of the island. If we got a ship and tried to sail away, the lack of wind would be our first issue. If we had enough strong oarsmen and a longboat, we could push out to sea. But what happens if nothing happens and there is still no wind? How far do we have to paddle till we catch the trade winds? And then, where does that wind take us?

"Jack, this island sits directly in the middle of nowhere, and because it does, we do. As for other ships," Rags continued, "they never come close. Once I saw sails on the horizon when I was on the top of the smaller cliffs.

But there's a thousand islands in these waters. Glen insists we are not on any trade route. No current comes close enough and there's no reason for anyone to chance getting out of the safe routes."

Rags loved having someone actually listening to him. So he never stopped talking. Jack found Rags interesting. A fountain of knowledge, no, more like a raging river of information, but one without clear banks, for the knowledge flowed in every direction, yet without direction.

"Has anyone been to the other side of the island? Other than just to float around it?"

Looking up at the majestic rise of the mountain behind them, Rags said, "We're sitting on a dormant volcano. Actually, not all that dormant, it puffed ash last year. We're also in the middle of the hurricanes' seasonal paths. It was a hurricane that brought us here. But it's that volcano that protects this side of the island."

"So how does the ship wreck on this side of the island?" asked Jack.

Chapter Sixty-Five

The camp is prepared for around two hundred men and horses. They assigned Rudy and Moses to the water carts, Tanek is with the horses, Adrina and my harem are with provisions, I hope only that, and I am with medical. Rudy saw to that, thinking I would have the best chance to access the prisoners. He also suggested I poison everyone and then we be on our way. If I had enough Yew, I would consider it. Better would be some Hyacinthus in the water.

Moses suggested Belladonna lily which paralyzes the legs. We're not in the jungles of Africa, I reminded him.

The advance party arrived and reported the army will arrive at sunset.

- Hinch

The Lagoon - The Island - 1748

"What's this?" Jack asked as he walked down toward a very large pole buried solidly about a foot away from the edge of the water, and nearly fifty feet from the wrecked ship.

About as proud as could be, Rags joined Jack and pointed to two marks he had carved into the pole.

"Right now we're at low tide. As you can see, the water doesn't even reach the pole. At high tide, about six hours from now, the water will reach this lower mark." Rags pointed to the mark that was about two feet above the sand. "All together we get about a three-foot tide. Glen claims that's not a tide at all, and as far as he's concerned, he's right. It will never be enough to float this ship."

"So what's this mark?" Jack asked as he touched a mark at his eye level.

"At the spring's high tide, the water will reach this mark. We get an additional four feet of tide. But as you can see by that short stake next to the hull of the ship, the water still never reaches where the ship stands grounded. Even with its shallow draft, we'll need an extra twelve feet of tide to get this frigate to make a move."

"So that's why Glen says we'll never get off the island. It's not the wind or the current, it's the tide, or lack of one. So why fix the ship if we can never get it to water?" Jack was mostly talking to himself. The reality of his being stranded and possibly never rejoining the *Kent* was finally sinking in. As Jack asked this question, Walt approached.

"You're asking, how did Glen ever park that ship that high on that beach? With a tide that only gets this high ever?" Walt went from pointing to the ship well up the beach to pointing to the high mark carved on the large post. Answering his own question he proclaimed. "A storm!"

A few seconds later, giving them time to absorb, Walt added, "Not just a storm, a hurricane."

"Exactly!" proclaimed Rags. "The way off this island is the same way we got here."

That was the question Jack wanted to ask ever since he and Elizabeth saw the wrecked ship. What kind of storm would it take, and what kind of skipper could navigate in that kind of storm to so safely land a ship of this size on that beach?

"Walt, you were on deck. You saw this whole thing play out. I've never sailed into a hurricane, nor captained a ship, but I don't see how you can find an uncharted island, or should I say an uninhabited volcano, come around from the windward side, and safely career that ship in what looks like one of the few safe harbors on its leeward side. All while caught in the middle of a hurricane," Jack asked.

"When you're in the middle of a hurricane, Jack," Walt said, "nothing makes sense. The fact we found land at all makes little sense, and yet this paradise? I thank the Lord every day."

"I don't see enough damage on that ship worthy of abandoning i," Jack continued. "If Rags is right, and a storm provides a tide wall high enough, couldn't we sail out of here?"

"We'd be back in the same fix as when we got here. We'd be in a ship in the middle of a hurricane looking for land. And who do you think would captain a ship in those conditions?"

Just then, Elizabeth approached and inserted a gentle question. "Don't you believe Glen could do it? Again?"

The four of them calmly stood there. No one wanted to answer that last question.

"So we're simply waiting for a storm?" Jack asked.

"We've had a few over the years. This is the season, but those cliffs knock the strength out of any would-be storm before it gets to us. Glen says it will take a full-on hurricane hitting us directly to bring the water up enough to sail the *Bringhurst* again." Rags said. "When it does, we'll at least get that ship to water."

"But we're on a tropical island, not a desert, which means we get rain and a lot of it, right? How do we get all that rain without storms?" Jack asked.

"Our rain storms are just rain. Light breezes bring the rain and light breezes take it away. Someday we'll get an actual storm," Rags said, pulling his knife to freshen the marks on the pole.

Carefully, Jack reached out and took the knife from Rags to examine it. It was beautiful. The handle was carved from an exotic wood Jack didn't recognize.

"Lignum Vitae." Rags said. "Native to the West Indies, but I'd never seen it before. The blade is crucible steel. Walt calls it Sheffield plate. He invented it. I thought he should have called it 'Walt's Wonder Steel.' Harder than any other steel. He was working in his brother's foundry and used coke to make the fire hotter. Glen was the artisan."

"What's this CWL?" Jack asked, interrupting Rags discourse on steel manufacturing, and running his finger over the flourish CWL on the blade. He lifted the machete and compared the two engravings. "I see it here on Glen's machete too."

"Glen's trademark."

"He has a trademark?" Jack asked.

"One day when I was in Glen's shop, The Checkmate…"

Jack's mind raced so fast he missed parts of Rags' documentary. The

Checkmate? Alex's Checkmate?

"… Glen was working on the governor's watch and I showed him how the new lever mechanism I created for Mr. Mudge could fix the movement. We were already good friends. Glen was friends with everyone. But after that, he and I spent many hours together with stuff like that."

"Rags, how did you come to join Glen and Walt?" Elizabeth interrupted.

"After we fixed the governor's watch, we devised a new timepiece that would be accurate enough to serve as a portable time standard to determine longitude with celestial navigation. The way it worked convinced Glen it would be a major technical achievement in navigation for long sea voyages. We call it a marine chronometer. Of course, I wanted to call it Rags' Celestial Compass."

"What did you do with it?" Elizabeth asked.

Jack's mind was off in another world again, putting puzzle pieces together as fast as his analytical mind could. He came out of his awakening in time to take part in the conclusion of Rags' enlightening revelation.

I need to go meet with Glen. We have got to get off this island.

"Well, we have one. We brought it with us. We only had time to make two before coming here. A Mr. Harrison who frequented Glen's shop, bought the other," Rags said. "John Harrison visited The Checkmate from time to time. He was Glen's source for Lignum Vitae."

"The same as your knife handle?" Jack asked.

"It's hard and self-lubricating, perfect for the marine chronometer."

How did Glen know so much about tropical woods? Jack asked himself. *A family man from England. Checkmate, Walt, and Lars? Not hardly! Cav, Walt and Lars. I've not only found the clues, I solved the puzzle.*

"Rags!" Walt called, "Louisa needs you!"

"The hog." Rags excused himself and he hurried up from the lagoon to the plateau

Chapter Sixty~Six

Even as a member of the camp medical team, I don't have access to the prisoners. They keep them under protection of an elite guard led by Santaji himself. We know which tent holds them, but tonight will not be a night of rescue. None of us can get close enough to even see how they are or alert them they have friends outside. Our goal now is to find a way to travel with the army tomorrow.

Rudy spent the night with Adrina scouring the village and countryside for the herbs and plants that might help us disrupt the camp. There is no way our small band can deliver our prize by force. Adrina reported several sexual advances she and my harem have narrowly avoided. Moses taught self-defense to my harem. He taught them well. Now I don't dare get close to them, even though they are mine. I don't know if I am more fearful of their skills or Moses. He has taken it upon himself to become their guardian.

Camp directors appreciate our service. They commanded even Tanek to join the caravan. We will follow the army to the next night's camp at least.

- Hinch

Clare's Tavern - St. John's, Antigua - 1748

"Well, well, well," Clare uttered as Remington and Lucas bounded through the door. The two took their normal place. Remington pounded a fist on the table. This gesture had become a private joke between Clare and Remington. Though to others it would seem a rude, demanding call for service, between Clare and Remington it meant "I'm back, did you miss me? Because I missed you!"

Wearing her customary grin, Clare waltzed over and plopped down two mugs of ale, Remington's favorite, "Do you two come bearing gifts, or just redundant, insufferable questions?"

"Just here on business. You know us, we're all about business," Lucas piped in sarcastically, to which both Remington and Clare rolled their eyes.

"Lucas, why don't you go find Amos and ask him about his latest journey to *El Dorado,*" Remington said.

Lucas shook his head in disgust and reached for the ale. He had to admit, Remington had a way of finding the best taverns, the best food, and the best drink in whatever port they visited. And they considered Clare's tavern the best from any port.

"Now that you mention it." Clare said, "Amos made some new friends the other day, three dark ones, not north Africans, but not Europeans either. One looked ancient and mean, the other two younger and better bred. Are you really here on business?"

"For once, yes," Lucas said, drinking his ale.

"We are meeting up with the *Emerald*. Some of their passengers are joining us from England. I'm surprised we didn't see it in the harbor. I figured it would beat us here. Their winds would be more favorable than ours," Remington said. "Did Amos tell you anything about them?"

"I never encourage Amos to tell me anything. His answers always find their way back to some ghost treasure. All I talk to Amos about is his going home so I can close up. But I heard an old man with a very strong accent I didn't recognize ask Amos about some 'Blade of Safavid'."

Clare barely got the words out when Remington jumped to his feet. "Persians, they were Persians! Where's Amos? We've got to find Amos!"

Ironically, just as he said those words, the simple-minded, considered insane by everyone, somewhat obnoxious yet lovable Amos innocently stepped into the tavern. All six lanky rumpled feet of him sauntered through the door and aimed directly toward Captain Remington, smile consuming his long whiskered face.

Turning back to Clare again, Remington asked in a panicky voice, "When were the Persians here?"

Quite taken aback by Remington's new found intensity, Clare squinted her eyes, begging answers as she provided one, "It was last night."

"What ship were they sailing?" Lucas asked, "There were no Persian ships in port."

"That was a mystery," Clare said. "When I asked Darby this morning, he said no ships had come or gone."

"Keep your eyes open!" Remington demanded to Clare as he grabbed Amos by the shoulder. "Amos, you're coming with me, we're going to find your ghost treasure!" He and Lucas bounded from the tavern, headed back to the *Kent*.

With Lucas keeping up and Amos eager to finally be of use, the three men rushed to the longboat and anxiously tendered to the *Kent*. Remington ran to his cabin, passing a crew who practically froze in place as they watched their captain fly across the deck.

His cabin door crashed open and he crossed to the desk in almost one large step. Frantically, he opened Cav's notebook and pulled a worn sheet of parchment from the back of it and folded it open. There, as clear as day but never before noticed, among the notes Cav had kept, was a manifest from the East India Company of the losses claimed by the Indian Mughal treasure ship. Listed was the "Royal Blade of Safavid," the one sacred artifact used for centuries as the sign of the rightful heir to the throne. Worth a fortune in jewels and gold—priceless in its importance to the Persian throne.

The words floated out of Captain Remington's lips, too quiet for Amos and Lucas to hear. "Cav wasn't looking for the treasure or a bounty on Avery. Cav was looking for the Blade of Safavid. And so are the Persians."

He plopped down on his chair and let his thoughts play out the discovery in his mind. This was a race, probably a race to their death. And whether Cav had met his fate at their hands or not, the Persians were following Cav's same trail, a trail that led them to these waters.

How sweet a prize, he thought. A race with the very ship Her Majesty's Service commissioned him to capture and destroy. The *Chawbuck*. It couldn't be any other. The HMS *Kent's* assignment and captain's personal mission were the same. He smiled up at the two standing in his doorway.

Chapter Sixty~Seven

Journal Entry: May 1696 - Madhya Pradesh, India
Alexander Hincher - Camp Support

As camp support, they assigned us to various parts of the caravan. They keep the prisoners in an enclosed wagon so we cannot see them, nor them see us. Rudy is traveling with the advance team and Moses with the main body. I kept close to Santaji. We traveled through some dense vegetation and each time we had an opportunity we gathered any plant that might help our aim of 'digestive warfare' as Rudy calls it.

- Hinch

Windward side of The Island - 1748

The *Sally* made good time on the early morning calm waters. By mid morning, Krist was certain the island was genuinely a twin. Scotty, the *Sally's* coxswain, stood at Krist's side and shared his glass.

"Captain, looks like another giant rock. No beach, no port, and no people. Wouldn't be a bad idea to move on. Seek a fortune on an actual island," Scotty said, uninterested in the idea of circling another rock.

Only three years Krist's senior, Scotty had been in his shadow ever since joining the crew when Krist's father attacked Scotty's ship off the coast of Malta. Scotty's ship, a competing slave ship, had been impeding on Hassan's monopoly. Hassan hung its captain, kept only a handful of the crew, took the slaves, and sunk the ship. Scotty betrayed his captain during the battle, which won him the loyalty of Hassan. The betrayal showed Krist he could never trust Scotty. Krist didn't answer. Krist noticed the slightest breeze, not enough to raise the sails but more than he had felt in two days.

Chapter Sixty~Eight

Journal Entry: May 1696 - Madhya Pradesh, India
Alexander Hincher - Camp Support

We have traveled eight days with the army. Day and night we watch, learn, gather, and plan for the opportunity to launch our digestive attack on horse and man.

On the third night, someone violently stabbed two men to death. Camp guards decided the two men got in a fight and killed each other. I thought it was curious how these two men were from the same section where Adrina and my harem are providing food, yet they claim no knowledge of the incident. I thought the wounds looked more like a master with a knife had his way with them. Moses won't talk about it.

We have enough supplies harvested, purchased, stolen, or confiscated to create serious havoc. Our plan is to launch an all out attack on the digestive systems of the captors—both man and horse. We feel confident we will have enough supplies and opportunity by tomorrow night.

We are two days away from the main Maratha camps, so tomorrow night may be our only chance. Besides, we will be near the Gomti River and will attempt to hide our trail in the water.

- Hinch

On the Trail - The Island - 1748

Lydia and Glen followed Jack and Elizabeth's tracks off the main trail when it reached a fork. "What is it?" Lydia asked.

"They went left," Glen responded. He knew that meant only one thing;

they went the long way. He wondered where they spent the night. Maybe Jack was more clever than he gave him credit for. Not a bad idea to spend another night in the jungle alone with a beautiful woman.

For the past many months, whenever Lydia was charged with caring for the twins while her parents were away, she told stories of a giant beast that would capture small children if they wandered off alone. Though Glen and Rosemary denied the truthfulness of Lydia's tales, the tales had kept the two youngsters somewhat close to the cove, and out of the deepest of jungles. Lydia never let up on the stories.

"The beast spooked em," Lydia offered.

"Probably."

Lydia and Glen eventually stepped out of the forest, following the trail left behind by Jack and Elizabeth. They guessed correctly; the couple had gone left, hit the canyon, and needed to follow it up and around. Lydia stood there looking at the pile of blood and remains of what was once a sizable animal. The remains were fresh. Glen thought he and Lydia might even catch up to the couple before they reached the plateau.

Glen sensed what Lydia was thinking.

"Looks like Jack put up a fight before the beast carried Elizabeth away." Glen said. "Looks, by these prints, that Jack's chasing it up that way."

She looked at the tracks.

"Well, should we follow or head back home and hide?" Glen asked.

"It's that hog Rags' been chasing. Looks like he finally got it," Lydia said.

"Looks like he had help," Glen said, pointing to the ground and noting the prints revealed three different kind of shoes.

Lydia stepped over to the edge of the cliff and peered down.

"Any bodies?" Glen asked. "The beast didn't get 'em?

With a smile and a shake of her head, Lydia turned and stepped back from the edge, satisfied.

"Where should we go?" Glen asked. "If you're convinced the beast didn't get them, we can return home or go on to the plateau and make sure Rags doesn't think Elizabeth and Jack are Visigoths."

"Or pirates!" she added.

With that, Lydia went charging up the hill, following the tracks that were pretty hard not to miss. Glen was a young forty-year-old and in superb shape. He had always been healthy and strong, but keeping up with a young, enthusiastic daughter took all he had.

They paused at each spot where the tracks showed the three people had stopped to rest. By the look of the blood where they found the remains of the hog and with Lydia's pace, Glen estimated they were only a few hours behind.

As they reached the small grove of cherimoya trees, the two noticed the remains of fruit. Glen could imagine Rags telling the couple all about the island, its special inhabitants, the food, and how they had survived. He smiled.

When they reached the main trail, Glen's slight head movement gave Lydia the choice to return to the cove or continue to the plateau.

"What do you want?" Lydia asked, more out of courtesy.

This time it was Glen who headed out at full speed toward the plateau, to Lydia's delight.

At one point early in their time on the island, they tried to map the island just to make it easy to discuss. Each of the residents offered their own way to measure, which made for a lively conversation, but they settled on using the English mile and concluded the length of the island was about twenty-five miles. It was harder to measure the width because of the mountainous cliffs, but having scaled some smaller cliffs and after floating around the island, Glen estimated the island was roughly 15 miles in width.

Of the approximately ten miles between the his cove and the plateau, Glen and Lydia were now only a few miles away.

Chapter Sixty~Nine

I spread out the various plants we collected and shook my head at the possibilities. I counted two hundred and eleven soldiers, their horses, and about forty camp followers, which includes us. We think there are between six and ten prisoners. We still can't get close enough to know for sure.

I have plants that kill quickly, slowly, painfully, quietly, and mercifully. I have plants that will cause all manner of discomfort internally and externally. I can make the horses crazy, kill them, or just loosen their bowels. I can make them impossible to saddle. But I don't have enough for all four hundred potential targets. Nor do I have a way to administer this mix efficiently in one night.

We can sabotage the water, the food, or the horses. But we can't get to all three to cripple the camp effectively. Moses shared a few ideas, and Rudy suggested we kill as many as possible, starting with Santaji. But it was Tanek who provided the solution.

In his village, they'd had an outbreak of illness and when one of the village leaders contracted the symptoms, fear traveled through the village faster than the illness. Tanek said the fear created more damage than the illness. The illness was over within a few days and not a single person died. But when a family panicked, and the father tried to escape what he feared was the plague, he ran over his children with a wagon. Two of the children died.

We have the perfect poison that will afflict almost every member of this camp. Fear.

I shared the idea of inflicting a few select members of the camp to create panic and the appearance of a plague. What better motivation to get a camp of tired soldiers to abandon their duty, than to get each fearing for his own life.

I went to work creating a series of poisons to inflict various segments of the camp in unique and fear inducing ways. I apologized in my heart for the innocent suffering I am about to cause, including the few horses that will sacrifice their lives for our cause.

None of our little band is eager to be included in our hoax. But we can't avoid it. I prepared an antidote for Adrina and Rudy, as they will be the worst off. I need Moses to be functioning fully and the rashes won't be as visible on his dark skin, so I won't poison him.

Tanek will afflict the horses and I need him to be careful with the tonic he will spread on their hair. But I have no antidote for the salve he will be using. If he is not careful, he will be in terrible pain.

We're not waiting until tomorrow night. The horror will start tonight. It will grow throughout the day tomorrow. I will administer my toxins in the food, the water, and the skin.

The risk I am most leery of is that the imitation plague must start in the prisoner's cart. If we are successful, I will apologize later. If we are not, I will probably not be alive to express my sorrow. They will be uncomfortable and terribly frightened, but they will suffer the least of any afflicted. But I must get them out of the wagon.

I anointed my scalp and arms and delivered the various blended toxins to each of our team. Water and food will become toxic by morning. By midday, the prisoner's wagon will be without horses and the chaos will begin.

In the chaos, our prisoners will make their escape. Tanek's selected the fourteen best horses and promises to have them ready for us to escape. Have them readied means their riders will not be in a condition to ride.

- Hinch

Lagoon's Edge - The Island - 1748

Jack stood staring at Elizabeth. A look of confusion, or maybe that of wonder, on his face.

"What is it?" she asked.

"Nobody seems anxious to leave. Am I the only one?"

Her head cocked; eyebrows raised.

Jack amended, "Sorry, are you and I the only ones?"

Elizabeth's expression relaxed. Her eyes accepted the apology.

"Rags has a fiancé, right?" Jack asked.

"That's what he says."

"If I had a fiancé," Jack paused, "actually, I do." He paused again. "I have two." He grabbed Elizabeth's hand and held it up, showing the ring on her finger. Elizabeth pulled her hand away and went to remove the ring. "No, keep it," he said, "At least until the other fiancé shows up and wants it back."

He continued, "If I was apart from my fiancé like Rags here, I think the motivation to get off this island would overpower all else. I would have built a boat, slapped a sail to it, and if that didn't work, I would swim across this ocean."

Jack's frustration turning to anxiety became exhausting. He now knew how it all fit together. He knew if there was any way to get his uncle and Glen… Cav back together, they'd complete their journey and he could get back to London and his comfortable life at the university and his fiancé, Anne. But right now there was nothing he could do about it!

Jack continued, "I understand how the others can be satisfied here. They have family, but Rags. He doesn't fit. I don't care if he is an English Norwegian from Ireland!"

"I like him," Elizabeth said, looking up toward the plateau.

"What?" Jack asked. Getting yanked from his anxiety filled mind was unsettling for him.

"I like him," Elizabeth repeated. "He reminds me of my father. My father could make the simplest answer an epic adventure. I like him. Hog, knife, mysterious fiancé, and all."

The door opened. In all the many exchanges he had with Elizabeth, he never asked about her family nor did she ever offer. It never mattered. Jack realized, for the first time, she wasn't intending to develop a relationship with him. He was only an acquaintance she'd made along the path of her journey. A journey he still didn't understand. In Jack's mind, his journey was simple;

make a few inquiries for his uncle and get back to his life in London. These few sidetracks, like getting shot twice, eluding a murderous band of thugs across England, and fleeing the law back home who wanted him for the killing of a half-dozen or so men and forcibly rescuing a beautiful woman from pirates, were simply an annoyance.

"Let's go," Elizabeth said, again pulling Jack out of his thoughts. She took him by the arm, pulling him toward the plateau.

"He's like your father?" Jack asked. Taking the hand she'd placed on his arm, he turned her back toward himself. "When you share this epic adventure with him, will I be a villain or a hero?"

"I don't know yet. It could go either way," she said.

For the moment, her smile seemed to lean toward hero he thought. Yet, her resolution was firm.

Elizabeth continued, "But it may be a long while before I share it with him. Pirates killed my father in an attack off the coast of Libya while returning from an expedition to Surat."

"I am so sorry."

Jack said it so sincerely Elizabeth's boldness softened.

"He worked with a family who had roots in India. Together they developed trade with a prominent merchant there, a Lord Rudolph."

"Lord Rudolph. Sounds English, not Indian," Jack said. Immediately he realized he could open or close this door that was so long in opening. "Sorry," he said.

"I knew little about the business or the relationships. I was still a young girl when he died. What I later learned was that my father, even though he had no title, no fortune, and no status, was loved by everyone who knew him." Elizabeth spoke with such reverence, Jack expected a tear or two.

She paused, her face tightened. "Pirates killed him on board the galley ship, the *Lost Dutchman*. When they captured the ship, they plundered it. Although the captain surrendered, they killed him and three others. There were several women on board who they took captive as well."

Elizabeth paused just long enough to catch her breath, then pushed forward with the story. "Those who tried to protect the women were shot and thrown overboard. My father was among those, and died. However, two others shot, survived. A fishing boat picked them up and the men brought my father's body back to us."

"I am so sorry."

"Thank you, but don't be sorry. Though my father attained no prominence in the eyes of the world, and he died at the hands of barbarians, he was one of the greatest men who ever lived. Yes, he may have followed none of his pursuits to a successful completion. He even got stranded on a couple of his own uncharted islands along the way, but he cherished my mother. He loved my sister and me, and taught us how to live, how to dream, how to love, and how to…"

While she paused, Jack waited. Her tough exterior might soften, he hoped. As Elizabeth talked of her father, Jack watched as her countenance transformed from love, to compassion, to anger and hate, and then to sorrow, returning to determination.

Elizabeth continued, "He taught us everything. What did he get for it? Well, me. I'm all that's left."

"You're all that's left?" Jack didn't know what else to say. It just came out. She'd shared the most intimate words he ever heard her say. If he could take them back, he would. He quickly tried to recover.

"Your sister and mother are no longer with you?" he asked, much more tenderly and respectfully.

She softened, but only slightly. "We lost them tragically a few years before they killed my father. Yes Jack, I'm all alone." Silently, Elizabeth turned and headed back up the beach to the plateau.

Another ball in the chest couldn't have taken his breath away with more impact.

Chapter Seventy

Journal Entry: May 1696 - Madhya Pradesh, India
Alexander Hincher - Camp Doctor

Commotion started early as the horsemen prepared the horses. Several horses appeared to have gone mad. Foam lathered around the mouth and their wide, wild eyes frightened the soldiers. They found three horses lying on their sides motionless.

After eating and breaking camp, soldiers complained of stomach pain. Horses rebelled against their riders. Santaji and his captains realized something was wrong. Terribly wrong. Other men of medicine attended to the ill. I joined them and attended to a soldier who displayed terrible blisters on his arms, hands, and neck.

After attending to him and providing no relief on purpose, I returned to the other doctors, displaying terrible symptoms that looked far worse than they really were. This instilled the fear that this plague was contagious. Since the doctors had no way to treat this malady, they hesitated to even attempt to provide relief.

We contaminated enough of the food and water, and afflicted enough of the horses that a general panic ensued. Then two of the four horses that pulled the prison wagon bucked, flailed, and died. My heart broke for having done to these horses what needed to be done.

With the panic in full swing, the army made little progress once it started leaving camp. The sick, both horse and man, were strewn along the few miles we traveled. Those still in their saddles were frightened enough they refused food or water, and I estimate nearly a quarter of the soldiers fled, abandoning the camp all together.

When the prison wagon was forced to stop and the doors opened, the guards stepped back in horror. Santaji was so shocked he refused to approach. The other doctors refused to come in contact with these prisoners. Since I afflicted myself and looked equally ill, they allowed me to escort the prisoners from the wagon. The guards kept their distance but remained at their posts.

Esther carefully helped her mother, the Princess Zeb-un-Nissa from the wagon. Behind her stepped Leilyn helping Makhfi who was not only nursing a grotesque rash, but a badly bandaged arm and leg. It overcame me with relief he was still alive.

I decided I would never reveal that I had caused this fake plague—even to Esther. I reached Esther first and whispered for her not to recognize me and that this was an escape. This message made it to Leilyn and Makhfi and the princess.

As I provided a calming salve antidote for the rashes, which were far more visual than painful, the four prisoners listened as I shared our plan. It had to change slightly since we had a crippled Makhfi to care for.

"Can you ride?" I asked quietly.

"If you can get me on the horse," he said.

All the while I was attending to the prisoners, the horses that were pulling the wagon were being replaced with four fresh ones. Tanek made sure these were among those planned to rebel this afternoon.

Santaji, ordered me to ride with the prisoners and care for their illnesses. I requested leave to go gather the rest of my supplies; he sent a soldier instead and insisted I get in the wagon immediately with the prisoners. One of his captains, one also afflicted, joined us as well.

His presence prevented me from continuing our discussion, and with me a prisoner there was no way to carry out the rescue.

- Hinch

Onboard HMS Kent - St. John's Harbor, Antigua - 1748

"Captain," Amos said as he and Lucas stood just inside his cabin, "it's the Blade of Safavid, isn't it?"

Nodding, Remington turned the East India Company loss manifest around, showing it to Lucas and Amos. "Why didn't I see it?" Remington asked himself.

"Excuse me, Captain, but why would some Persians sail halfway around the world looking for a dagger?" Amos asked, "What is it, solid gold?"

"For the last two hundred fifty years, it's been the key to who rules the entire Persian Kingdom," Remington flatly stated. "Since its disappearance, the Safavid dynasty has been in continual strife."

"A knife holds a kingdom together?"Amos whistled, "Must be some knife."

"This is no time for a history lesson. Amos, what else did the Persians tell you, ask you, or you told them?" Remington jumped to his feet, "No time to waste."

"They were the first to take me seriously in two years. It felt good. Do you know what it's like to act the crazy man? The guy off kilter? The one taken to be touched in the head?" Amos asked.

"Amos!" Remington slammed his hand down on the manifest, "This is not an employment review. We are not renegotiating your employment. I simply want the information I have paid you to gather. I pay you to sit around, snoop around, and hang around the finest tavern in the New World! Now, about the Persians!"

"It has been a good job, thank you."

"AMOS!"

"No one saw their ship. I don't know what they're sailing. They're slavers, pirate slavers. They're not alone. I think they have a fleet, maybe three ships. Each of the three men I met captain his own ship, so there are at least three. They have a base of operations on one of the thousand islands scattered around here. I think they are combing every island. When they came here, they were just fishing for information about who and what comes and goes."

After thinking a moment, Amos added, "They are not afraid to fight. One of them mentioned a ship they recently attacked, and the passengers kidnapped, on their way back to somewhere."

"The *Emerald*?" Lucas asked Remington, almost in a whisper.

"I'm afraid that's likely."

Amos held up a coin, "They paid with this at Clare's last night."

"They're either foolish or cunning," Remington said as he held the coin in his fingers, turning it to look carefully at the markings.

"They have a private pirate island as their base. They have slave ships probably sailing between here and a home somewhere in Africa, bringing black slaves here and returning with white slaves back to the markets. My guess is northern Africa," Amos said.

"We've got to find that island. They probably have quite a business transporting and must have partners here," Remington said.

"The Persian Gulf is a long way away," Lucas said.

"My bet is they take the white slaves to the Barbary Coast. They're sold and distributed from there. That's where they pick up the African slaves to bring back here," Amos said.

The men continued to suggest possibilities but Remington was no longer listening.

We have got to find that island. They are carrying on a business while looking for the blade. Smart. If they took the Emerald, some dear friends of mine, very important friends of mine, are soon on their way to very harsh servitude. It's time for me to take the next step, Captain Remington thought.

Chapter Seventy~One

The wagon stopped a short time later, and they ushered me out. My salve had done wonders. It was clear I was curing the plague. Though the army was decimated, losing nearly half of its soldiers and horses, Santaji kept control of his army.

Santaji's chief captain escorted me throughout the camp, as I treated the remaining soldiers suffering with the 'plague.' Rudy and Adrina's antidote worked sufficiently, that it was unnecessary for me to treat them.

Fear worked, but only among the weak. The remaining soldiers were the more loyal. Even though many of them were afflicted, it became clear in working through the army that Santaji's followers were typical. Some of his soldiers followed out of trust; they believed in his vision. Others followed out of false hope and fear, the rest out of pure greed. The fearful and greedy were the first to run.

Our plan failed because I didn't know the army well enough. I killed innocent animals and tortured the very people we were attempting to rescue. What a fool I am. Though we executed well, we miscalculated the effectiveness of my toxins against the loyal soldiers. I hope no one suspects I was the cause.

Santaji recruited this army with a single vision of glory and fortune. Why didn't I realize he is just a pirate on horseback? Instead of the sea, he has a countryside vast and wide. His army is just like a ship's crew, each with their own motivation for being onboard.

This was not an army of loyalists fighting a common enemy for family and home. They were privateers gone rogue. Pirates. Santaji promised reward and glory when they arrived at the Maratha stronghold with the Mughal Emperor's daughter as captive.

All we accomplished was to help those motivated by fear and greed to turn their loyalty to themselves and run. At least with a pirate captain, the weak and the afraid seldom jump overboard and swim away.

The partial remaining army motivated by trust and vision will be as effective as the larger army with mixed motivation would have been. We didn't even strike a blow. I fear we may have strengthened Santaji's position. What a fool I am. It was Rudy who rescued Esther and Leilyn from a disgusting crew of pirates on board the *Fancy*. And I delivered them back.

Tonight, they have summoned me to the prisoner wagon. Tomorrow we reach the Maratha stronghold in Maharashtra.

- Hinch

Trail Summit - The Island - 1748

Glen and Lydia reached the small summit that overlooked the plateau. The sweet aroma of a roasting hog drifting up through the trees.

"Rags finally got that hog. Hope he's willing to share," Glen said.

"I know he'll share with me. You can have some of mine if he's still mad at you," Lydia said.

"That's kind of you. You think he's still mad?"

"I would be if you told me the hog was smarter than I was."

"All I said was that hog seemed to always outsmart him."

"Same thing."

"No, it isn't. Rags refuses to use one of Walt's crossbows, says it's not sporting. Says he needs to give the hog a fair chance at life. I simply said the hog was too smart to be given a chance."

"Same thing. I'm just saying if you can't outsmart old Rags, I'll share with you."

Glen winked at Lydia, and they headed toward the plateau.

Chapter Seventy~Two

Journal Entry: May 1696 - Lost, India
Lord Rudolf - New Author

Whoever reads this journal, you need to know I'm not Hinch. I'm Lord Rudy. Hinch is gone. Aurangzeb has him. What Hinch wrote is not what really happened. He's too modest. If he never writes in this journal again, we did not get him back and he's dead. Sorry.

- Lord Rudy

The Plateau - The Island - 1748

Glen and Lydia made good time crossing the island. They arrived at the plateau just in time to join the group feasting on Rags' hog.

"I knew if I killed it you would be here to enjoy it," Rags said.

Jack and Elizabeth were excited to see Glen and Lydia. The conversations included Lydia talking about the flying beast, what Elizabeth learned from Rags, the escape from pirates, and on it went. Glen didn't join the conversation.

Something more important distracted Glen's attention. He felt an unusual breeze. He excused himself and left the group. Once out of view, his casual pace turned to a full out run—up the plateau towards the cliffs where he could get a view of the eastern horizon. At a full run, it still took him over an hour to reach the pass through which he could ascend to the tops of the cliff. He cut through the pass and climbed.

The wind wasn't enough for the others to notice. Slight winds were common and always welcome, but they seldom became anything of consequence. Walt, the resident weather expert, was certain the island was located just outside the path of the seasonal storms common in the West Indies.

They had only experienced a few sizable storms since arriving on the island, and the massive rock wall protected them from the fury of the storm. Each time a storm threatened, Rags was eager to prove his inventions to get the ship off the beach. However, the storm surge never rose the water enough to lift the *Bringhurst*. Being careened there, the men had repaired all the damage to its hull just in case. All they needed was water.

Completely out of breath, Glen reached the summit and saw the white cirrus clouds on the horizon. He stood there and just watched. Still no waves of consequence, but he could feel it. How long, he wondered. Could this be the storm he had prepared for? Instinctively, Glen knew that if it was, he had maybe twenty-four hours, thirty at the most, to get everyone ready to get off this island. Any longer and they would miss their chance. They had to be ready to sail the minute the storm passed. If they left beforehand, he knew he couldn't outrun the storm, but as soon as it passed, he would ride its tail out to sea.

He hiked down the windward edge of the cliff to a hidden lagoon where he and Walt had spent the past two years preparing for this storm. He hoped he was ready. Pride filled his breast as he admired the *Rosemary*, a patched-up frigate some unlucky sailors stranded during a previous hurricane. They would find out if Walt's and Sal's shipwright skills were good enough. This looked like the storm they were waiting for.

He was still planning on sailing the *Bringhurst* if the hurricane was head on. If not, the *Rosemary* was the safer choice. Only a full-frontal hurricane could get the *Bringhurst* off this island. The *Rosemary* only needed a brush with one.

Glen left the lagoon and hiked around the rocks that hid his private little harbor to see if any waves would validate his hope for an upcoming storm. As he stepped down onto the smallest of the rocky beaches, fear replaced hope.

A small galley ship was hoisting sails.

Chapter Seventy~Three

It's still me. It's not my journal, but we're all going to die trying to get Hinch and Esther's mother back, so I think you should know how this ends.

Whoever finds this, we died trying to do something good. At least we thought it was good. If you do something you thought was good, but it was dumb, will God forgive the dumb thing because you were doing it for a good reason?

I'm not talking about making half the camp sick and killing a few horses. That wasn't dumb. That was funny. It was miserable because Adrina and I nearly scratched ourselves to death before the antidote helped. I almost killed Moses he was laughing so hard.

The dumb thing was letting Hinch convince us to bring Leilyn and Esther back home to a mother in prison, surrounded by a family who all want her dead. Everyone knows that's dumb. But Hinch kept making us think it was noble to bring them back here.

Is nobility, even in the face of danger dumb? I think this journal must be cursed. I read what I just wrote. I'm sounding like someone who thinks too much.

We were about to make new plans when Santaji's captain summoned Hinch back to the prison wagon to check on the prisoners. I wanted to see how Leilyn was doing so I followed him.

Just as Hinch entered the prison wagon, two soldiers ran past me, slammed the door locked, and the wagon charged off in an absolute run. Chaos hit the camp.

The camp was under attack. Hundreds of soldiers on horseback stormed out of nowhere. The battle lasted only minutes. They slaughtered man and horse. I was out of sight following Hinch, so I was out of the line of fire. I stayed out of the way. It was dark, nobody saw me. There was nothing I could do anyway.

After the army finished slaughtering Santaji's camp, they returned the way they came. They captured the prison wagon, and when it passed me, I saw about a dozen soldiers on foot tied to the back of the wagon.

I couldn't count the attacking force in the dark, but there had to be hundreds. I stood there in the darkness and wondered what I was doing in the middle of a battle zone watching the only honorable man I had ever known being hauled away in a prison wagon. My only friend, a big dumb African tribal chief was probably lying dead with the rest of a Maratha army.

I about jumped out of my skin when what I thought was a ghost broke the silence. "That was Aurangzeb." It was Adrina's voice.

- Lord Rudy - still

Onboard The Sally - Windward side of The Island- 1748

"No, we keep going."

Krist knew Scotty well enough to know his recommendations were founded in nothing but his own selfish pleasures. Scotty wasn't loyal to Hassan's quest. He was loyal to his desire to pursue his own ambitions. If he could, he would visit a few islands with a bounty of women and return to the island feigning exhaustion for so diligently seeking the Avery treasure. So when Scotty recommended they forget this island and move on, Krist didn't even consider it.

But now, Krist wasn't looking at the massive rock standing before the *Sally*. He was looking at the white mass of cirrus clouds appearing on the eastern horizon.

"Aye, sir," Scotty replied and signaled for the oarsmen to continue.

While the sudden, yet slight wind, should have felt like a blessing, Krist knew it meant only one thing. "Hoist sails," commanded Krist. He knew he couldn't outrun a storm in the *Sally*. He had to get to land, and this rock wasn't what he considered land. They at least had to get to the leeward side of this rock if there was to be any hope.

The *Sally* continued around the island. This rock looked to be more sheer, more uninviting, more formidable than its twin. As they rounded the island, to their shock, the massive rock immediately gave way to a lush jungle. Surprised beyond measure, Krist couldn't decide whether to cry or cheer. On this side of the island, the wind weakened enough they struck sails, and the oarsmen took over, powering the *Sally* again.

He was looking for a small harbor. Even with limited beach on this side of the island, the water looked too shallow to risk a landing. As they moved along its shore, they noticed a small inlet. The *Sally* dropped anchor, and they lowered the longboats.

Chapter Seventy-Four

When Adrina scared me out of my skin last night, Moses laughed like the fool he is. There he stood along with Adrina, Tanek, and Hinch's harem. When Aurangzeb's soldiers attacked, Moses quickly got them all into the trees.

We're not so good at rescues. They have our leader and we're now facing an entire empire's army led personally by the Mughal Emperor. We're only six nobody's trying to do a dumb thing for a good reason.

Leilyn and Esther are home. We did our job, maybe we should go home too.

When I proposed we go home, Adrina asked if I could leave Hinch. Of course we couldn't. But we couldn't just march up to Aurangzeb and say we captured your treasure ship and took all your treasure and kidnapped your granddaughter, had second thoughts so we brought her back, and by the way we tried to rescue your daughter from you and escape through Persia and live happily ever after. Oh, and by the way, sorry about your treasure. You'll never see it again. Will you please let our friend go home with us?

Looks like Moses put on his tribal chief hat. His tribe of six is ready to challenge a tribe of millions. Why not? We're in the doing dumb things business.

We waited until it was light and walked through the camp strewn with the dead. You will not find a young boy wear his pride as well as Tanek did when he exited a large grove of trees leading fourteen beautiful horses. He chose these to serve in our escape—the failed escape. We will not be on foot. Adrina and the harem gathered uncontaminated food and water while we surveyed the remains of the Maratha army.

We don't know which of the Maratha army they took prisoner, but since we did not find Santaji among the dead; we assume he was one of those left alive and taken prisoner.

Moses mounted a beautiful light brown Marwari and explored the surrounding area to be certain we were alone. He returned, we mounted up, and headed back into the lion's den.

I now see Hinch's passion for keeping this journal. Regarding his memory, in case he's dead and probably he is, I won't write what I want to write. With this exception, I think Moses wants the three tribal princesses, who Hinch refers to as his harem, for himself. I just think that's obvious. That's all I have to say about that.

Santaji is going to assassinate Aurangzeb. How do I know? Because Esther told me so. Yes, that Esther.

- Lord Rudy

Mountain Pass - The Island - 1748

Exhausted following his push up the cliffs and back down its windward side, Glen began the reverse journey. Torn between detouring to the cove to warn Rosemary or hurrying back to the plateau where Lydia and the others would be the first to encounter the visiting ship if it should make landfall, Glen put his trust in Rosemary's inspiration to hide herself and the kids if there was any sign of trouble.

Had the approach of an uninvited ship not consumed his mind, he would have been eager to tell Rosemary to pack up and ready the family to go home.

This very reason was why he chose to live in the cove. He had seen firsthand what brutality and evil accompanied these uninvited ships and their crews. Many a time had his assignments in the Royal Navy onboard the HMS *Kent* taken him to a coastal village where corsairs had landed, raped, pillaged, and looted a town. Taken their women, killed the men, and left it in flames. The horrors of evil were clearly etched in his memory. This was another reason he had selected an inland town like Sheffield, far from the raiding hoards.

All of this coursed through his mind as he again reached the summit of the island's enormous cliffs. He looked back towards the horizon where the clouds were quickly gathering. He felt the air pressure changing. Yes, within one or two days this storm would be upon them.

He caught his breath and began the trek back towards the plateau, fearing he would not beat the strangers to it. Glen was in good shape, but this was a big island. If only he could warn them.

Chapter Seventy~Five

Before Aurangzeb's attack, two of Santaji's elite guards took Esther from the prison wagon for Santaji to have his way with her. When the Aurangzeb army attacked, Esther escaped her captives who fled into the forest along with Santaji.

Esther remained hidden throughout the night as Santaji and his guards searched for her. As they were close enough for her to hear their plans, she heard them swear to avenge this attack and kill Aurangzeb and take his head back to the Marathas.

She thinks Santaji gave up looking for her and headed to Aurangzeb's city of tents, a mobile capital of his armies where Santaji hopes to get lost in the crowds. Esther describes the camp as a city with thousands of tents, hundreds of bazaars, and tens of thousands of camp followers.

We're going there too. Mostly because we don't know where else to go. We don't know if Aurangzeb will return the captives directly to the Red Fort or keep them with his army.

When she believed Santaji was no longer looking for her, Esther felt safe returning to Delhi to find the prison wagon and start over. She captured one horse left for dead. She followed us for three days when Moses noticed a lone rider keeping its distance for the good part of our fourth day.

That night he backtracked and found the lone rider was the princess. She was unsure who we were and was afraid we might be part of Santaji's scattered army.

- Lord Rudy

The Plateau - The Island - 1748

"Thank you, Louisa. I never expected this fine a meal on an island with no market," Elizabeth said.

"To Louisa, the entire island is her market," Walt proudly proclaimed. "You can see it was not just her beauty that attracted me to her," he continued as he patted his rounded belly.

"Yes, I can tell you, he is a victim," Louisa said.

"I can see the men on this island don't go hungry," Elizabeth said as she motioned ever so slightly with her eyes towards Rags, who was now on his third serving of wild pork.

Rags felt all eyes on him, which they were. He looked up, and with a mouth full, uttered, "Whaaat?"

"Lydia, where did your father run off to in such a hurry?" Elizabeth asked. "He didn't even finish, and I can't imagine he didn't appreciate Rags' fine catch."

"I thought he'd be right back," Lydia answered with a question in her tone.

Walt recognized the slight breeze and felt it was accompanied by an almost imperceptible change in air pressure. He suspected since Glen didn't return within minutes, it would be several hours before he did. Even longer if he swung by the cove to tell Rosemary to get prepared.

Walt thought he'd best get ready for a new journey, just in case Glen returned with the news he was hoping for.

"Would you two run down to the ship? There is a small box of tools I left on the binnacle. It's about the size of Rag's head," Walt said to Elizabeth and Lydia.

"I'll be happy to go help," Jack said, quickly standing to join the girls.

"Thanks, Jack, but I need your help with some other tools." Then looking at Rags, still eating, he added, "And Rags... when you're done, will you help Louisa?"

Chapter Seventy~Six

We took another week to reach Aurangzeb's encampment. Esther was right. It is a giant tent city. It's supposed to be mobile but nobody's moving this thing very fast.

Adrina found a bazaar where we got new clothes. We shed the Maratha Hindu camp look for the Mughal Emperor camp look. I can't tell the difference. But even without princess clothes, Esther is regal.

She and Adrina are roaming the camp looking for friendly faces they can trust to help us get close to the royal tents. We have the horses stabled and a makeshift place to lodge for a while. We have two targets. Santaji and Zeb-un-Nissa and we hope to find one of the two before they find each other.

Tanek disappeared once he got the horses stabled. I'm not looking for him. If he gets lost, I'll miss him, but not enough to risk looking. He shouldn't have run off.

Moses stays close to the harem. It's clear nobody knows how to write their names, even them, that's why Hinch calls them his harem. I'll do him the favor. His three princesses are Muhumzingha, Seh-Dong-Hong-Beh, and Nyabinghi. Since names always mean something, I suppose these names combine to mean, Englishmen can't write African names. My grandmother would be sad to know I still spell words my own way. Since these remarkable princesses and Moses don't read or write, I can write their names anyway I want, though they deserve more respect than that.

We wandered the tent city for three days with no success. We've circled the royal encampment and see no tactical way to enter, then find Hinch, and then escape. Still no Tanek. Esther and Adrina are like sisters. No trustworthy allies yet.

- Still, Lord Rudy.

The Plateau - The Island - 1748

As the girls left and stepped over the small footbridge, they passed Hunter heading up to the plateau. When he reached the dining table and saw Rags there alone, finishing off the remnants of wild pork, he sat, and without invitation took a piece of pork and began eating.

"This is quite a feast, Rags, where'd everybody go?

Rags looked up, acknowledged Hunter with a slight nod and shrugged his shoulders.

Chapter Seventy~Seven

The tent city never quiets down at night, there's always activity somewhere. Tanek slipped into the tent just as I was turning down the lamp. He was badly hurt.

I didn't know if I should be angry or grateful he is back. Esther quickly attended to his cuts and bruises. Moses threatened to avenge his little friend's injuries. Tanek said it was a horse.

Adrina prepared some food. Tanek ate as if he hadn't in three days, which was probably the case. He said a mad horse kicked him. Tanek was cutting through a bazaar when three men leading their horses passed by him. He recognized Santaji. Carefully, he tried to follow, but when one horse saw Tanek, he reared up and kicked him. It knocked him down and tried to stomp him to death. Its master got the horse under control and was leading him away when Tanek recognized the large scar on the horse's back. A scar caused when Tanek had sabotaged the Maratha camp.

That horse recognized Tanek and wanted no more of him. Santaji didn't, so Tanek kept his distance but followed. He said he could lead us there in the morning.

Esther, Adrina, and I followed Tanek to the bazaar, hoping to find Santaji and his men. Working our way through the mass of people, we approached a large crowd gathered to watch a procession of horses enter the camp.

We got closer and Esther quickly ducked behind me to hide.

"Follow those horses," she told us. She didn't have to whisper; the crowd was noisy. We did.

Aurangzeb's vizier, who we met while traveling with Sangha, led the procession. He was returning Esther's uncle to Aurangzeb.

The procession passed through a blockade of soldiers and into the royal encampment. We watched them dismount and escort Esther's uncle into the largest tent in the center of the collection of royal tents.

Santaji was also in the crowd. Tanek pointed him out. Adrina and Esther stayed hidden and Tanek and I followed Santaji as the crowd dispersed. Once we found his tents, we came back here.

There are five prisoners we know of—Esther's mother, her uncle, Hinch, Leilyn, and Makhfi. We thought they killed Makhfi at the Red Fort when Santaji kidnapped Esther and her mother. They beat him badly and broke his leg, but Hinch re-set it and felt it might heal if they all live that long.

Esther says her grandfather will probably behead the prince for betrayal. And while he's at it, he'll likely execute Hinch for attacking his treasure ship. Adrina and Esther fear more for Makhfi than Hinch. He is a Persian who just won't die. Esther said her grandfather has ordered his death so many times, but never seriously enough for him to ever be beheaded. Too many friends. And it was him who saved the emperor during a recent attack by Maratha assassins. It was Makhfi who staged the false royal caravan where the decoy emperor was savagely killed, saving the emperor's life.

It's my turn to plan a rescue.

Makhfi's plan to rescue Zeb-un-Nissa failed and only got himself, Esther, and Leilyn captured. Hinch's plan to rescue Makhfi, Zeb-un-Nissa, Esther, and Leilyn traded himself for Esther and landed them all in Aurangzeb's personal care. Now we do things my way.

I proposed we join Santaji and kill Aurangzeb, then kill Santaji and put Zeb-un-Nissa on the throne. Moses thought it was a good idea. Then he pointed out that during all that killing, Santaji would probably kill all of us because he is a better killer than we are.

I'll think of a better one.

- Lord Rudy

On board the Bringhurst - The Island - 1748

"Hunter gives me the creeps," Lydia said as soon as they were safely out of earshot.

"Me too. What's his story?"

"I don't know. He just seems to haunt the island."

"He's a ghost?" Elizabeth said looking back to see if he was hovering behind them.

"An evil ghost maybe. The devil maybe. Just creepy. I hate him."

"Why is he here?" Elizabeth asked

"Back home he just showed up one day," Lydia said. "Lots of people visited Sheffield. Mother and I often visited The Checkmate, my father's shop, to bring him lunch. Sometimes we met some of his customers. They were fun. They all loved my father. Everybody loved him. One day, Hunter came in while we were having lunch. It was like cold air came in the door with him. When he left, Mother asked who he was. All I remember is that Father said he was just another visitor. Mother was kind but said she didn't like the feeling he gave her."

"But he wasn't visiting?" Elizabeth asked.

"No. He stayed and nobody liked him. He acted friendly, but he was creepy. My friend Martin wanted to take cow pies and stick them on his porch and light them on fire."

"Oh my," Elizabeth said.

Lydia laughed. "We couldn't find enough dry cow pies."

Elizabeth laughed with her, then asked, "How did he live? What was his job?"

"Nobody knew."

"Was he rich?"

"Didn't look rich."

The girls reached the lagoon and began crossing it towards the ship. That's odd. Elizabeth thought, the water level seems higher.

They made their way up the beach and climbed into the ship looking for Walt's tools. Again Elizabeth thought, if only they could get it to water, this is a seaworthy ship.

"Then one day," Lydia continued, "I heard them talking about him and I thought I heard mother tell daddy she didn't trust Hunter, that there was something wrong."

"Oh?" Elizabeth's eyes opened wide.

"He told her not to worry. That it'd be ok and not to tell anyone our plans."

"Plans?" Elizabeth asked.

"Plans to come here. Well, not here but, you know, plans to come to the New World, to Antigua. They wouldn't tell me anything, I was just a "child" but I wasn't dumb. They didn't like Hunter either, I think they were just too nice to tell the devil to go back to hell."

"Lydia!" Elizabeth exclaimed, "You really don't like him, do you."

"I hate him. I'm not alone, nobody likes him. Not even his wife."

"He has a wife?"

"Yea. She's nice enough, but she never comes around. Mother says she's embarrassed for her husband."

"So how'd they end up here with you?"

"That's creepy too. My parents were planning to leave Sheffield for a long time, I never knew why or when. But they promised me in our new home we would have a piano. I had a violin that I loved. Father made it, and I wanted music lessons. That's all I cared about.

"Then one day, father came home from the shop, said let's go, we packed up that night and put everything in a wagon and left our life behind, without ever saying goodbye to any of my friends. I cried all night."

"I can't imagine how hard it would be to leave your friends without even saying goodbye." Elizabeth's heart was breaking.

"I wasn't crying for my friends, I was crying for my violin. I let Martin take it to show his mother so she would get him one."

"Oh my. Who's Martin?"

"He's my friend. He said we were going to get married. I told him one day we were going to Antigua to get me a piano and he said he would sail around the world to find me."

"Martin sounds a bit romantic. How old was he?"

"Oh, he was older, he was ten."

Elizabeth just smiled thinking back at how romantic people can get, even if they know little about romance, or love or anything.

"I wonder what Martin thought when he brought my violin back and I was gone?" Lydia said, snapping Elizabeth back to their conversation.

"Surprised, certainly. I am sure his folks told him you were moving to the new world."

"Nobody knew. That's why we left in the middle of the night. It was a secret. Only Walt and Louisa. They knew because they came with us."

"You said Martin would sail the world to find you in Antigua, so he must have known."

"I told him I heard my folks talk about my new piano in Antigua, but even I didn't know we would sneak out in the middle of the night."

"So why did you bring Hunter and his wife along?"

"That's what's so creepy! When we got to Liverpool and they were loading our things on the ship, I thought I saw Hunter on the docks. I told mother and she said I must be mistaken. But when we set sail, he and his wife were on the ship."

"I see what you mean!"

"I have never seen my father afraid of anything, ever, but when he saw Hunter on the ship, his face went white. Then it went red. I thought he was going to explode!"

"Oh my," was all that Elizabeth could muster.

"Here they are," Lydia said as she held up a small leather wrapped box. Elizabeth stepped over and opened it to see which tools Walt might be looking for.

"That's odd," she said. "An astrolabe, a back staff and an octant? Is Walt going someplace?"

"What are these?" Lydia asked, looking into the box.

"These are navigation tools. Not much good unless you're going somewhere," Elizabeth said. Goose bumps went up Elizabeth's back. Something was amiss. Elizabeth had now been on the island only a few days. It had been a continuous adventure but even she could tell things were not normal.

"Let's go," Elizabeth said. Chills ran up her spine.

As she turned, she stood face to face with Hunter.

"What do you got there?" Hunter asked, reaching for the box.

"Something for Walt," Lydia said as she pulled it close.

"Here, I'll carry it for you," he offered.

"Thank you, but no," Lydia said, surprising Elizabeth with the calm in her voice.

After the recent discussion about Hunter, it surprised Elizabeth the younger girl hadn't thrown the box in the air and run screaming. In fact, Elizabeth wouldn't have been surprised if she had done the same.

Hunter didn't move out of the way, but he also didn't insist or grab for the box. He stood still with a look that illustrated exactly what Lydia had described. It was more than a look of lust. It was a penetrating glare, a hunger, an evil. The goose bumps went from bumps to mountains. Elizabeth was in awe that Lydia could hold it together. This was the devil.

"Excuse me," Lydia said as she stepped around Hunter, box in hand, and climbed down the ladder.

Elizabeth quickly followed this brave, though terrified, young girl. Elizabeth felt like a parasite feeding off the courage of a young twelve-year-old child. Lydia was becoming her hero.

"How does she do it?" Elizabeth asked in disgust once they were a distance away.

"Who?" Lydia questioned.

"His wife. You said he had a wife?"

Lydia's attention left the box in her hand. She squinted up into Elizabeth's eyes. "Joanna?"

Elizabeth stopped. Chills froze every living cell in her body. In that instant she recognized perfectly the feelings she'd felt those many years ago. The image of the men carrying away her screaming older sister. As vivid as if it were the very moment, she remembered that face, that face hidden in the recesses of her young terrified memory. Hunter's face. That horrible face, that face that made her skin crawl just moments before.

"Joanna? His wife's name is Joanna?" Elizabeth wasn't sure if she thought those words or screamed them. "Where is Joanna now?" The heat of hate melted the stone-cold chills. Just as quickly, hope pushed the hate aside.

Lydia stood stunned by the intensity of Elizabeth's questions.

"She lives beyond the plateau—"

No time for words, Elizabeth grabbed Lydia's arm and practically dragged her around the ship heading back down past the water and up towards the plateau.

Again they came up short. Wide eyed, they faced a dozen men, pistols and cutlasses at the ready.

Chapter Seventy~Eight

I'm now a prisoner and will be executed tomorrow. I write on this piece of parchment so generously given me by Princess Zeb. I write these last words so someday in the future when a young man wants to become a pirate, he will know it's a dumb idea and if he becomes a pirate, the Grand Emperor of India will eventually execute him.

I now tell the events that sealed my fate. When Esther told us how Makhfi used a decoy to preserve the emperor, I got an idea. We dress Moses up as the tribal chief he claims he is. He visits the Mughal Emperor bearing three gifts, Hinch's harem. Once inside, I, who, posing as a slave to Moses, sneak away and help Hinch, Leylin, Makhfi and Princess Zeb escape while Aurangzeb is busy with his new gifts.

Moses said he had a better idea. He proposed he takes me in chains and trades me for the lot since I was none other than Henry Avery.

Adrina suggested we alert Aurangzeb to Santaji's plan. If we help Aurangzeb prepare, he catches his personal enemy and in gratitude he releases his prisoners and at worst he exiles his daughter and sets the rest of us free.

Adrina's smart.

We couldn't get past the gate into the royal compound. The soldiers forbade our entry. We waited until night to try again.

Tanek led us through the camp and past the guards. He was watching and found a section guarded by inattentive soldiers. In the darkness we crossed to the emperor's tent and were about to enter when we heard a commotion inside. We quietly opened the tent door but we were too late.

Santaji beat us to the emperor.

Taking a javelin from a dead guard laying inside the tent door, I hurled it at one at Santaji's soldiers. Though it missed by nearly 10 feet, it distracted Santaji who had not seen us enter. In that moment Aurangzeb freed himself. Two of Aurangzeb's guards who saw Adrina and I enter the tent, came charging in to stop us. When they entered the tent, they knocked her aside and me to the ground. When Santaji saw the guards enter, he tried to kill Aurangzeb rather than take him hostage. Wounded, Aurangzeb fell, but before Santaji could strike another blow, the guard was on him. Other guards entered and killed Santaji's men. Adrina ran to help the emperor who lay bleeding on the ground.

I went to help Adrina with Aurangzeb. In one last attempt at him, Santaji threw a knife which missed him but hit me. Santaji fled, chased by Aurangzeb's guards. He escaped… again.

Aurangzeb's injuries were not so serious that he couldn't immediately take control. He commanded and demanded. I saw the power of this man. I don't like him. He scares me. I sacrificed my hip to save him and though Adrina tried to help him; we are still his prisoners.

When the guards arrested Adrina and me, they brought us to the prison tent where we found the princess and Makhfi. Leilyn and Hinch escaped during the attack. But I got to meet Princess Zeb, Esther's mother. I like her. I really like her.

Princess Zeb told us a young boy slipped in and urged them to run. The princess refused because Makhfi couldn't with his leg so badly broken. So Leilyn and Hinch escaped and promised to return.

I think I'm ready to go back to pirating. It was so much easier. You always knew who the enemy was—the pirates—and I was one of them. My pirating days are over, my rescuing days are over and tomorrow all my days are over. Farewell to the world.

- Lord Rudy

The Lagoon - The Plateau - The Island - 1748

"Who have we here?" asked the tall, well-dressed stranger.

His smile was almost too big for his face and he stood several inches taller than any of the scraggly men following him. Elizabeth couldn't consider any of the men clean or welcoming, though she couldn't be judgmental. She hadn't had a change of clothes or bathed in a week after floating on the open sea and trudging through jungles, but there was a difference between this man and the others.

He looked from the two young women to the ship stranded up on the beach, and then back to the girls. Weathered, but still easy to read, the *Bringhurst* was painted on the bow of the ship. His smile never wavered.

As Hunter stepped around the side of the ship, he caught the pirates' attention. Elizabeth took advantage of the distraction and grabbed Lydia by the arm. The two of them charged up the hill.

† † †

Jack's eyes widened as Walt opened the large locker revealing a cache of weapons.

"May I?" Jack asked as he reached and pulled a magnificent crossbow from the top of the stack. Beneath it were at least two others and a collection of fine tipped bolts. Next to the bolts were knives and swords. Covered in a fine cloth he saw the outline of at least one musket and a few pistols.

As Jack handled the crossbow, he showed a wicked smile to Walt.

"You've handled one of those before," Walt said. He watched how Jack held the weapon and how much respect he showed it.

"Not one like this."

"Glen's design. My metallurgy. Rags' modification to the trigger mechanism makes is easier to load and fire. One reason we invited him to be part of our enterprise he so eloquently shared."

Jack noted the elegantly carved 'CWL' on the stock. The same symbol he saw on Rags' knife and Glen's machete. He stroked his fingers over it.

Cav, Walt, and Lars.

The crack of a pistol echoed through the trees. Both men flinched and looked toward the source of the sound.

"Who carries a pistol?" Jack whispered.

"Not anyone friendly."

† † †

The two girls froze as the ball struck inches from Elizabeth's foot.

"The next one won't miss," the stranger shouted. He motioned for his men to retrieve the two girls.

Hunter also froze. He waited to catch the captain's eye and carefully motioned not to reveal Hunter's identity. Hunter played the victim also, raising his hands and slowly stepped down to join the captured girls.

† † †

Walt reached for the musket, tossing the cloth to the side. It was just a glance, but Jack noticed the prettiest musket he'd ever seen. With no time to admire, he gathered a handful of bolts and set through the trees like a deer, bounding up and over plant, rock, and log.

Walt followed suit. He left the musket and elected for the other crossbow and a handful of bolts. There would be no time to load and reload a musket.

Even at a full run over uneven ground, Jack loaded, cocked, and readied the crossbow. "Rags is a genius," he shouted to the trees, flying past them as fast as he could run. A traditional crossbow would never load and cock this fast.

† † †

Lydia held her tongue and glared. For Elizabeth, this was the second time in a week someone was attempting to take her captive.

Where's Glen when you need him? Or Walt? Or Rags? Or even Jack? And why did Hunter give up so easily?

"Where's the captain?" the pirate demanded, motioning toward the *Bringhurst* with his head.

"Who are you?" Lydia calmly asked.

"No one for you to trifle with, miss!"

"The captain's dead! And if you hurt us, you will be too," she said.

Elizabeth stood in awe of the strength of this little girl who was growing in Elizabeth's estimation by the minute.

The pirate holding Elizabeth slapped Lydia so hard she flew out of the other pirate's grasp and crumbled to the ground. Elizabeth slipped free and jumped to Lydia's aid, taking her in her arms.

"Scotty, that's enough!" he bellowed.

Scotty! Elizabeth turned her hate to the man.

The slap was so hard it left an immediate mark and cut Lydia's cheek, leaving a ribbon of blood. Elizabeth noted the collection of rings on Scotty's fingers. Perfect for cutting the flawless face of an innocent, precious little girl.

As quick as a cat, Elizabeth lurched up and raked her fingers across Scotty's face, drawing immediate blood on his own face. Scotty screamed in pain, though it didn't stop him from knocking Elizabeth back to the ground.

Had the captain not quickly intervened, Elizabeth and Scotty would have continued their brawl.

Hunter stood still, arms raised, mustering just as much cowardice as a man possibly could. Elizabeth hadn't expected Hunter's help, but his lack of even a hint of courage confirmed she was right. He was of the devil and these were his fellow minions.

"Who else is on the island?" the man asked, this time to Hunter.

"Only a few families. But one of those families is the one you're looking for," Hunter said.

"And the captain?"

"Captain Krist, she's right, he's dead. Died in the storm. It's this brat's father you're looking for. He's who we've been chasing for fifteen years," Hunter added.

"Let's go get him," Scotty growled.

"You two," Krist said to two of his crew. "Do you think you can get two little girls to the boats? And keep them quiet?"

Hunter looked over to Scotty, and making sure Krist heard his rebuke, said, "he will not be easy to get!"

"Where is he?" Krist asked annoyed that petty bickering could continue between these two even after years apart.

"He left the plateau a couple hours ago, heading who knows where. Probably back to his side of the island. He doesn't live with the others here."

"How far?"

"A few hours if you run, all day if you walk," Hunter said.

"We don't have all day or even a few hours. I can't get the *Sally* in here out of the storm and I can't leave it out there," Krist said, his annoyance growing.

"A storm?" Hunter asked.

"Where do we find an inlet where we can wait out this storm?"

"This is the only one on this side of the island. I don't know the windward side," Hunter admitted.

"What do you know?" Scotty snapped.

"I know I've been sitting on this godforsaken island, babysitting your prize for two miserable years while you've been off raping villagers," Hunter spit back.

Elizabeth and Lydia, still within earshot, couldn't believe what they heard. Maybe, Elizabeth thought, Scotty hit me harder than I realized. This can't be true.

The two pirates dragging Elizabeth and Lydia away, had just witnessed the fire lit inside these two girls. They held tight. Just as quickly as Scotty had knocked Elizabeth to the ground earlier, the pirate dragging her to the boat dropped lifeless to the sand. A small drop of blood lay next to his head.

There was no gunshot, no sound at all, just a thud and the man hit the ground. Without warning, the second man holding Lydia also collapsed. When the first man fell, the second one took a tighter grip on Lydia, so when he fell, he took the girl to the ground with him and landed squarely on top of her.

Hunter, Scotty, Krist, and the remaining pirates heard the thuds, they turned and headed toward Elizabeth, who was trying to get the fat, disgusting man off Lydia.

† † †

Jack reached a small clearing at the edge of the beach giving him a view of the lagoon. In the distance, he saw Rags, quick as lightning, dash from a thicket and throw the dead pirate off Lydia.

As a pirate raised his pistol toward Rags, Jack aimed and launched his first bolt, missing by nearly six inches. The pistol sent another echoing boom across the lagoon. Rags fell motionless.

Walt joined Jack just as Jack launched his second bolt. Now familiar with the new weapon, Jack's next bolt met its target, dropping the pirate standing next to the man who fired the pistol. The rest of the unwelcome visitors rushed toward the spot where Rags collapsed, oozing blood. They didn't realize another pirate had fallen. Walt was now ready and Jack had a third bolt cocked and ready to fire.

Standing between Jack and a clear shot at the other pirates, ran the fool Hunter up the beach toward the ship. Jack leaped over a small pile of rocks and bounded down the beach toward the pirates to get a better shot. As he cleared another large rock, a pirate turned and took aim at Jack. Jack loosed his bolt and caught the pirate squarely in the neck. The pistol fell to the ground, followed by a dead pirate.

† † †

When Scotty reached Rags, he holstered his pistol, looked into the fallen man's eyes, examined his face and smiled. "It's you. You cost me my shares when you stole that wench from me at Salcombe. I swore if I ever saw you again, I'd kill you."

Rags searched into Scotty's eyes as if he was memorizing them.

Scotty kicked Rags in the face and all went black.

"Now I have!" Scotty said.

Krist rolled each of his men over, only to find a walnut-sized rock planted deep in each of the two men's foreheads.

"We need to get that ship safe and we need to get her father. Can you find him or not?" demanded Krist, looking for Hunter and not finding him.

A bolt tore through Krist's shoulder, knocking him to his knees. A second one entered the neck of a pirate standing next to Scotty. A third arrow struck Scotty's thigh.

"To the boats!" Krist yelled.

In the commotion with fallen and wounded men, Elizabeth helped Lydia to her feet and the two ran up the beach toward the ship. Nearly clearing its bow, Hunter, who'd slipped away during the shooting to light a small fuse, hit Elizabeth with a fist, sending her tumbling over an outcropping of rocks. She lay still.

Lydia jumped to Elizabeth's aid but got yanked onto her back, Hunter holding her single long braid in his hand. He scooped her up and bounded down the beach.

Limping and bleeding, the pirates fled from the lagoon headed toward the longboat they'd pulled on shore.

A shrill scream echoed up the beach. "Elizabeth!"

† † †

Elizabeth sat up, her head dizzy and eyes unfocused from the hit she received from Hunter. Her name screamed by an innocent, helpless young girl was enough to refocus her. She recognized the scream; it was the kind of scream she had never forgotten.

"Sorry Joanna. I tried." Elizabeth took one look toward the plateau, caught a glimpse of Jack and Walt getting weapons ready, and charged back down the beach.

† † †

Jack readied another bolt. Walt put his hand on Jack's arm.

"No, you might hit one of the girls," Walt said.

Jack winked at Walt and let the bolt fly. The last pirate was about to leap into the longboat as he readied to push it off the sand. He fell limp into the water, blood spilling into the rising tide.

As another sailor hopped out to push the boat, Elizabeth reached it and climbed over him while trying to get to Lydia, plunging him backwards into the water. When he stood, a bolt caught him in the back. But it was enough momentum for the boat to become free of the sand. Oarsmen dug deep, escaping the deadly lagoon.

As the boat set back into the water, an explosion rocked the lagoon. The *Bringhurst* would never sail again.

Chapter Seventy-Nine

I am grateful Lord Rudy took such care of this journal.

Our reunion may be the best story this journal contains.

Our fear inducing digestive warfare was not a total failure. It got me into the prison wagon. Had I not, Makhfi would be crippled for life. Although I am not convinced his life will be a long one. He is an enemy to Aurangzeb but a friend to the princess. Aurangzeb was undecided whether to execute him or exile him again. Which was rare. He seldom hesitated to execute an enemy, or a perceived threat.

As we traveled together, the education I received from my fellow prisoners is priceless. No university in the world could give me the education and understanding I received from the Princess and her companions. This journal is not expansive enough to contain it all.

The Princess's concern for her daughter was palpable. Just as Makhfi rebuked me so soundly for bringing Esther back into all this trouble, the Princess poured out her gracious gratitude for having rescued Esther from Avery and a tragic fate among pirates.

She shared stories of Esther's childhood, her triumphs and missteps. We laughed together and cried together. None of us knew what our future held. The Princess is a religious woman with faith in a God whom I am certain knows her and answers her prayers. I had the chance to converse with her and Makhfi as I had with Sangha. I cherish those days in captivity.

I may share those thoughts and feelings when I can do them justice when we are not running for our lives.

Princess Zeb-un-Nissa's brother was returned to the royal encampment by her father's vizier. They brought him to the prisoner tent where he and the Princess embraced as a brother and sister who cared for each other. Her father entered the tent later that afternoon and demanded answers why this son would betray his father. The emperor demanded an immediate execution. That is when I saw the power the Princess held over her father. It was magical and ironic.

Her majesty was on full display. Remember, this daughter is the heir to two empires, imprisoned now for over fifteen years by her father, the Mughal Emperor. He had his own brother executed. He also executed his father and countless others so he could retain his own power and control. He now ordered the execution of his youngest son for treason. This daughter gently stood and with a voice of unspeakable love and compassion pled for the life of her brother.

This brother is not even the son of Zeb-un-Nissa's mother. He was the son of a mistress.

Zeb-un-Nissa with such grace and nobility, practically transformed her father from a tyrant to a father, right before my eyes. He embraced his wayward son and forgave. I witnessed the Princess save his life.

That moment of humanity we saw in Emperor Aurangzeb was only a short moment. Almost embarrassed for his self-perceived moment of weakness, he turned and marched from the tent.

None of us spoke for a long time. It was that night, Tanek slipped into our tent and urged us to follow him. He told us that Adrina and Rudy were waiting outside to help us. Finally, when the Princess and Makhfi insisted Leilyn and I flee, we followed Tanek and easily slipped through the darkness and returned to where Esther, Moses, and my harem were waiting. We saw no signs of Adrina and Rudy.

It was the next day we learned of Santaji's attack and the capture of Rudy and Adrina.

As I read what Rudy wrote in this journal, I laugh because he was right. None of us are good at rescues. It's more like a game of trading hostages.

We've decided to make one more trade. Santaji's head for the freedom of our friends and Esther's mother, the Princess Zeb-un-Nissa.

- Hinch

The Island - 1748

Even miles away, Glen felt the shock of the exploding powder barrels. His racing heart was now breaking.

The blast threw Walt and Jack to the ground. Any hope of overtaking the pirates before they got the boat to their ship vanished with the blast. It took several minutes before their dizziness subsided and the men got back to their feet. By the time they did, they saw the long boat reach the *Sally*.

Helpless, they watched as the pirates lifted Elizabeth and Lydia on board, raised the long boat and hoisted sails.

It had only been a few hours since Walt and Glen recognized the small breeze and felt the pressure in the air changing. Now, Jack too recognized it.

An experienced mariner recognized the signs of an approaching hurricane days before the storm would hit. If possible, the pirates would find a safe harbor and hold tight. Walt stood and seemed to look into nowhere, assessing.

As Jack's mind cleared, he hustled over to Rags. He was still breathing, though his body and head were a bloody mess.

"Is he...?" Walt began.

"Breathing? Yes. But for how long? This is bad!" Jack uttered. "How's your surgery skill?"

"That's Glen's expertise. We reserve my needle and thread for sails."

You mean that's Alex's expertise, or how about Cav's? Where did he learn it? Jack touched his shoulder remembering how quickly and completely he had recovered. *So that's where Victoria learned it.*

Louisa arrived on the bloody scene. "Look out," she said, tearing open Rags' shirt revealing a large hole which hadn't stopped bleeding. She ripped off a chunk of her dress and plugged the hole to stop the bleeding. She took Jack's hand and placed it over the makeshift bandage.

"Hold that there."

She handed Walt another torn piece of her dress. "Get that wet from the stream, then get me some hot water from the fire."

Both men followed orders. Before long, the three were rinsing Rags' blood from their hands in the rising water of the lagoon.

"We have to move him. The storm tide is rising fast," Walt said.

They were only a few feet from Rag's tide pole and the water had already risen past his high tide mark.

"This is the storm we've been waiting for," Walt announced to the rest of the island's residents who'd arrived to watch the flames consume the last of the *Bringhurst*.

Chapter Eighty

Journal Entry: June 1696 - Madhya Pradesh?, India
Alexander Hincher - Bounty Hunter

Santaji and his men are no longer in the camp. Aurangzeb practically has his entire army looking for him. There is no way Santaji could stay around.

Starting at the bazaar where Tanek first spotted Santaji, we organized our own manhunt. Tanek thinks if he finds the horses, we'll find Santaji. Tanek shared the story of his bruises with other stable boys and described the horse that caused them. Several remembered seeing the horse. One young boy witnessed the horse kick and try to stomp Tanek. The boy also remembered the rider was mean. He led us to the stables where he'd seen Santaji and his men come and go.

We learn that not everyone in Aurangzeb's camp is loyal to the Mughals and Aurangzeb. Nor do they support Aurangzeb's enemies. Mostly people are loyal to themselves. There are many Maratha loyalists we find, also individuals with a personal vendetta against Aurangzeb or against the Marathas. Our success depends on finding someone we can trust.

Tanek found one of the stable boys whose mother hated Santaji and is angry with her husband for helping him. When Tanek took me to meet her, she feared my loyalties. Esther, dressed as a peasant, revealed herself as the emperor's granddaughter. She agreed to talk with Esther. Moses stood nearby ready to protect if needed.

This woman refused to share her name, but told us Santaji killed her brother. She said her sister's husband served both the Marathas and Aurangzeb. His deceit disgusts her. Her sister lives near the forest of Karkhala and sometimes Santaji will hide out there.

- Hinch

The Vista - The Island - 1748

Glen reached the vista, the halfway point between the cove and the plateau. He paused not only to catch his breath, but to take in the scene. He first examined the galley ship he saw hoisting sails on the other side of the island. It was now at full sail, running for its life.

He had seen few galley ships in the West Indies. Mostly they served in the Mediterranean where navigating calm waters was more common. They were unnecessary here. The plentiful and favorable winds met most shipping needs.

Unless you were hunting for lost islands in the calm seas.

This thought filled Glen with fear. The one relief was that the ship was on a course away from his cove. Rosemary and the children were safe.

The smoke rising from the water's edge confirmed his suspicions that the explosion was the gunpowder stored in the hull of the *Bringhurst*. They worked hard to keep it dry all these years. Well, they succeeded. The smoke also confirmed and predicted the approaching storm. The way the smoke rose and seemed to chase the ship told Glen he was wrong about his timetable.

Since he was a boy, he was sensitive to the air pressure. The winds, the shifts in temperature—he could feel changes in climate. Glen spent days and nights watching storms build and collapse, attack and fizzle. Cloud formations and their unique characteristics became a childhood fascination. Living in the Scottish Highlands, learning weather patterns was one of the few oddities his folks knew Glen loved. When his father took Glen on his first ship, he carried this fascination with him. Oh, how he loved the sea. He wanted to be a sailor when he grew up. Why his father so feared the sea was always a mystery to Glen. Their home was as far from the sea as they could get without nearing the island's other coast.

When he felt the breeze earlier, during dinner on the plateau, Glen knew. When he confirmed the cirrus clouds on the horizon as he reached the cliff summit and the speed of the dropping air pressure, he had calculated the eye of the storm reaching them within 48 hours. But now, with the clear wind pattern visible from the rising smoke of the *Bringhurst*, he knew the storm would be on them by morning.

This would be a long and busy night.

Chapter Eighty~One

Journal Entry: June 1696 - Forest of Karkhala, India
Alexander Hincher - Bounty Hunter

The woman from the camp told Esther where her sister lived and who we should be wary of and who we could trust. She warned us to use great caution.

We are looking for the home of this woman's sister. Her husband is a Maratha general, but serves Aurangzeb, she thinks. She said her sister hates Santaji and is afraid to have him near their home.

Not knowing where we are, and as we are not safe, Esther and Leilyn are traveling as peasants, with my harem and Moses as my slaves. Mostly we want to be invisible.

We passed several small villages as we traveled to the forest where we hoped to find the home.

Tonight we are staying in a small inn. We learned Santaji, once a successful and feared Maratha general, has many enemies.

I don't understand why he would feel safe hiding out here. It's desperation that encourages us we might have success finding him. Our fear is that someone might recognize us as Mughals rather than Marathas. If anyone suspects Esther, we are doomed.

- Hinch

Onboard the Sally - Open Sea - 1748

Once on board, the captain gave sharp orders, and the men had the ship at full sails almost immediately. As she watched the sails fill with wind, Elizabeth thought of Glen and his claims of no wind. Now he had no ship. She shook her head at the irony. Elizabeth sat with Lydia in her arms and played the scene through her mind repeatedly.

Pirates come to the island looking for something or someone. It has to do with Glen. Or it is Glen, and Hunter knows it? Hunter knows the pirates. Did he bring them to the island somehow? Is Hunter's Joanna, my Joanna, my sister?

Elizabeth had crossed the oceans and by providence came within minutes of possibly reuniting with her sister. The thought of losing that chance tore at her heart. She left everything behind to find her Joanna. Now just as Elen had warned, she sat at the foot of the monster. In her arms was another one of the dragon's victims. Behind them, stranded on an island, was another destroyed family. Could she be strong enough, could she, like Elen had, cut the claws off this monster?

She looked across the busy deck and saw Hunter standing next to the captain and felt the urge to throw up. The man made her sick. He was no captive; he was an accomplice. He was the monster. Could she kill the very monster possessing her sister? How had he abused Joanna? She turned to the side and shared her wild pork dinner with the roughening sea. The only peace Elizabeth could find was the fact he could no longer hurt Joanna, no matter whose sister she was.

What kind of man lives with others for years and maintains such an enmity for them that at the first sign of trouble, sides with the enemy? No. He is the enemy. He was always the enemy. He is still the enemy.

And what kind of man, armed with only a sling and a few rocks, gives his life to save two helpless females, one which he's only known for a day? Elizabeth's mind raced. It was all too much to take in, to process. Of the million thoughts and feelings that raced through Elizabeth, one that returned over and over was her love and respect for this little girl she held in her arms. Tears trailed down her cheeks. This little Lydia stood up to twelve pistol wielding, cutlass brandishing pirates. Dirty, stinking, evil pirates.

"You're amazing," Elizabeth whispered to Lydia's small form.

There were now several questions holding Elizabeth's attention. What makes people do the things they do? What makes them say the things they say? What keeps them from doing or saying what they should or shouldn't do or say?'

These questions were not foreign to Elizabeth, but at the moment, the contrast between the actions of people made them much more visible.

Rags gave his life to protect two girls. Hunter let others die to protect his own.

"If you hurt us, you'll die too!" Those words from a child who had full confidence in the protection of her father penetrated Elizabeth's heart. Glen had been over protective all these years. Elizabeth began piecing this puzzle together. Glen settled within the cove because he knew this day would come and he wanted to protect his family.

But why were these pirates looking for Glen? How did they find this island? Who is Glen?'

These pirates are smart, she admitted to herself. The only hope of leaving the island was now burning up. Storm or not, Jack, Glen, Rosemary, Walt, poor Rags, her sister Joanna who she came so close to finding, and the rest would not be leaving that island soon. Their only means of escape was sending a thick cloud of smoke up into a very turbulent sky.

The island grew smaller and smaller. The feeling on deck was one of being anxious. Elizabeth was no expert with ships, but her thoughts turned to this one and its crew. She watched and listened. Her mind always drifted when she was in the company of mariners as they talked about ships. Though as a young girl, her father did teach her, all she cared was if it got her where she needed to go. She didn't care if it was a sloop, a schooner, brigantine, or a frigate. She didn't care about the draft, the mizzenmast, the jibs, or the helm. What she knew was that the *Emerald of the Sea*, a large frigate, didn't get her where she wanted to go and this much smaller ship was going as fast as it could to where she knew she didn't want to go.

It had three masts and all the sails they could put on those masts. And they were each full of wind. There was at least one deck below the main deck where she and Lydia sat. When they were lifting her on board, she saw the lower deck was made for oars. She didn't count, but she thought it might be ten or fifteen oars on each side. She reasoned that's how it navigated these normally calm waters to find the island.

If they went to that much work hunting for Glen, he must be somebody of importance or have something they want very much. She figured they took Lydia, thinking to trade her for Glen or for something he had. The thought she and Lydia might also be merchandise for sale didn't escape her either.

The captain, who she learned was Captain Krist, stood at the helm, but he would not stay there long. The bolt that pierced his shoulder was broken off but not removed. It was still bleeding. The blood patch was growing. It was obvious to Elizabeth he was growing weak.

The crew on deck were too busy at their stations to pay attention to her or Lydia. Hunter wandered off somewhere and Scotty went below immediately after coming on board, his bleeding leg left a trail of blood across the deck—a blood trail the storm would soon wash away. Elizabeth hoped he bled to death. No, she hoped he had it cut off, then died a slow death from the infection that would creep over his body.

Lydia's sobs ceased. "Sit right here. Nothing will happen to you, I promise. I will be right back," Elizabeth whispered. She slid Lydia off her lap and knelt close brushing the wet hair from her young friend's face.

Could she promise, though? She'd let them take her sister. But she was so little then.

No, I do promise!

Through the howling wind from the rising storm, Elizabeth couldn't make out what the men were yelling to each other. The ship was pounding through the waves. Sprays of water splashed over the railings. The deck lurched and the sea water washed from starboard to port and bow to stern.

Elizabeth, bracing against the storm, stood and carefully worked her way towards the captain, intending to request a more appropriate place for her and Lydia. Whatever made her think that would matter to these men who had treated them so roughly and had cruelly killed Rags? She prepared for him to hit her again when she asked.

As she reached the captain, he slowly looked her way with wide, un-focusing eyes and fainted. She caught him as he fell and both tumbled to the storm drenched deck. She now sat holding the captain instead of Lydia.

The ship pushed wildly with no one at the helm, which eventually brought attention to the crew. A tall red-headed man wearing only water drenched trousers and an open vest took up the helm and steadied the ship back on course.

Nobody seemed to care about the captain in her arms. It at least appeared that way.

Chapter Eighty-Two

Journal Entry: June 1696 - Forest of Karkhala, India
Alexander Hincher - Failed

Again, I caution the reader who may find and read this journal. We failed one more time. We are not so good at rescuing. Are we good at anything?

Last night Tanek found out Santaji was at someone's home. After dining, Santaji went into the forest to wash. Tanek came and told Moses and me the direction he went. We quietly went out to look for him. Tanek assured us he was alone. He was bathing in a small river when we saw him in the moonlight. This was our chance. Moses was quick with his knife and after a short struggle Santaji lay dead.

Using Santaji's own sword, Moses severed the head, and we wrapped it in a bag. I returned to retrieve Esther, Leilyn, and my harem. When we met back with Moses and Tanek, Santaji's head was gone, and Moses lay motionless on the ground, an arrow protruding from his chest.

I was attending to Moses' wounds when Tanek returned. He tried to see where the attackers had gone. Moses' wounds did little damage. They knocked him out from a hit on the back of his head. I removed the arrow, which had barely entered his rock-solid chest.

We were not the only ones on Santaji's trail. What we don't know is whether it was Aurangzeb's men or Maratha's that now have a head start on us. Forgive my attempt at humor. We now have no items to trade, if you can call a severed head an item. We gathered our horses and will return to the camp.

- Hinch

The Plateau - The Island - 1748

Walt and Jack carried Rags up to Louisa's small house. The bleeding returned in earnest as Louisa pulled the temporary plug from the hole in Rag's chest. Walt answered the questions she didn't need to ask. He told her how though Rag's risked his own life, they took Lydia and Elizabeth anyway, and that his sacrifice was in vain. With a motion of her eyes and head she asked about Rags' bloody face. Walt went on how he hadn't seen well enough from his vantage point but assumed following what looked like a brief interchange between Rags and a pirate he was kicked hard in the face.

Louisa was grateful Rags was unconscious as she worked through the bleeding hole to retrieve a ball that fortunately missed vital organs. Jack held Rags as she dug. With one hand he tried to mop up the blood as it oozed from her digging site.

Content the removal of the ball permitted her to close the wound in his chest, she sewed the hole closed in a stitch pattern Jack recognized. He smiled. She then turned her attention to Rags' bloody face.

A small lantern lit the room. Outside, the wind blew across the plateau, and the small home provided some protection from it. Gusts of wind buffeted its walls; everyone knew they did not construct the house as a storm shelter. Upon cleaning up the bloody mess, Walt and Jack left Rags lying peacefully with Louisa and returned to the burning ship.

The sun had set by the time Glen returned to the plateau. With the approaching clouds, the post-sunset light was disappearing fast.

Glen stepped inside the house, and seeing Rags lying there motionless, bluntly asked, "Is he dead?"

"Nearly," Louisa said. "Should be anyway."

"Can we move him?" Glen asked.

"Can we move him?" Louisa repeated. "Why? You want a sleep over?"

Louisa was like that.

"Of course we can move him. He'll die in the process, but we can move him!" she snapped. After a few moments of silence, she continued. "Why?"

"If we're going to have a sleep over, it will be at my place," Glen said as he gave Louisa a faint smile that tried to keep the seriousness of the situation light.

"I know you believe in Rosemary's nursing skills, but I've done a good job here. He's got a hole in his chest, a smashed in face, and he's unconscious. You wake him and the pain alone will kill him."

"I wasn't challenging your nursing skills. If there was someone I would want patching me up, it'd be you. I admit, I'd rather it be Rosemary because she cares if it hurts."

"And I don't?" Louisa challenged.

"I didn't mean it that way. I mean when you stitched up my back when Rags' paddle broke free and cut me open, it hurt like the devil. And you digging around inside trying to pick out the slivers and me without a thing to drink, well…"

"Did it heal?"

"Well, yes."

"Did it get infected?"

"Ah, no."

"Then quit your bellyaching and leave Rags' care to me. When he's well, you can ask if it hurt. Until then, go join Walt and Jack and cook something over the bonfire, those savages started before they took Lydia and Elizabeth and ran."

"They got the girls?" Everything went fuzzy. Blood rushed to his face blurring everything. The loss of the ship was unfortunate, the approaching storm was critical but his daughter, his Lydia. It was too much. For what seemed an eternity he stood frozen. Finally, he thawed. Glen flew out the door and raced down to the lagoon.

"Glen, they took Lydia," Walt yelled as he saw Glen bounding down the hill toward them.

"Elizabeth went after her, they got her too," added Jack. "And practically killed Rags."

"Yea, I saw Rags. What happened?"

"I'd sent the girls down to the *Bringhurst* to pick these up," Walt said, holding in his left arm the box of tools Lydia dropped when the pirate hit her. "I figured this might be the storm, and we'd need 'em. Jack and I went up to the keep to pack up the weapons." Walt held the crossbow in his right hand and motioned to its equal in Jack's hand.

"Did they get hurt?" Glen interrupted.

"Well, yes," Walt answered. "Jack killed those two and got the captain in the shoulder. I got this one and his mate in the thigh."

"Don't forget the two in the lagoon," Jack added. "But not before Rags killed those two with this." Jack held up Rags' sling with his other hand.

"Not the pirates! The girls!" Glen growled.

"We don't know that. Didn't seem to, not permanently. They were both on their feet when they got to the ship," Jack said.

"We were up at the keep when we heard a shot. Jack here took off like a deer. We circled back toward the ship and saw who we guess was the captain pull Elizabeth off the mate. When he did, the mate was ready to shoot her. Blood was pouring down his face."

"The girls!" Glen interrupted.

Jack took over. "Lydia was on the ground. We couldn't see if they hurt her or not, but Elizabeth was, as Walt said, furious, so I assume they had done something to Lydia to ignite Elizabeth."

Walt turned to Jack, "Did you know your fiancé had that kind of fury in her?"

"The girls!" Glen interrupted again his voice now raging.

Walt continued, "The captain then turned to Hunter and said something that made Hunter relax a little."

Glen cut in again, "Hunter was there?"

"Yes, he stood there motionless with his hands raised like a baboon."

"Where's Hunter now?" Glen asked, growing impatient with how long this story was taking.

"They took him as well."

"Why didn't you say that earlier?"

"Well, actually, we were glad he was gone," Jack answered. "The captain sent two of the men with Elizabeth and Lydia towards the boats while he and the others continued to talk with Hunter."

Breaking in, Walt added, "Suddenly the first man escorting the girls," he pointed to the body on the left, still there on the beach, "the one holding Elizabeth dropped like a rock to the ground. Just as suddenly the second one fell, but this time he took Lydia with him and landed right on top of her."

Jack took up the story. "With that commotion, the pirates turned just in time to see Rags run out of those trees and throw the dead man off Lydia. As he helped her up, a shot echoed through the lagoon and Rags dropped."

"That was our cue." Walt pointed to dead pirates. "We came charging from our cover, and Jack here sent a bolt through this one's neck and another through his body. I got the one that shot Rags. I must be getting old. I hit him in the hip. Jack's next bolt missed the captain's heart and only got his shoulder. With that, they scrambled to the boat. Jack killed two more, but when the *Bringhurst* blew, well, they got away."

Glen reached down, picked up the half of a broken bloody bolt and held it up. "You got five of them?" He looked at Jack. "A researcher? Does your fiancé know this side of you?"

"But only four are dead and they still got the girls," Jack said, slowly shaking his head in disappointment.

"What are they looking for?" Walt asked no one in particular.

Glen and Jack just looked out to the sea and chose not to answer that question.

After a few seconds, Glen said, "I can see why they elected not to wait the storm out here, but why wouldn't Hunter direct them to my lagoon? He knew my lagoon would be unprotected. And the draft on that galley is shallow enough. With oars they could have easily navigated in. That doesn't make sense."

"Glen, I am sorry to say, but I fear they're just hoping to outrun the storm, a risk I don't think I would have taken. That galley is no match for this kind of storm," Walt said.

Jack added a thought. "Maybe Hunter didn't want to risk your family's safety."

Both Glen and Walt gave Jack a squinted look accompanied by shaking heads.

"There are only two chances to get off this island. One is in flames. We better be ready for the next one," Glen said. "We all need to get to the cove. This will be a long night." He turned, and Walt followed.

Jack looked to the sea where the galley was now well out of sight, then over to the smoking timbers that were once the *Bringhurst*. Just a few hours before, Rags talked about the day the storm would come and raise the water to the high-water mark. When it reached that mark, there would be enough water to float the *Bringhurst* once again. It was then his pulley system would work, and hold the ship in place so they could attach his paddles and paddle the ship home.

The water was now well past the high-water mark and was dousing the remaining embers of the burned-out hull. Rain fell.

Jack headed back up the hill to join the others.

Chapter Eighty-Three

When we returned to the camp a few days ago, rumors raced through the tent city that Aurangzeb's cunning spies tracked and killed Santaji and retrieved the head.

Moses is furious. They brought his prize, the head of Aurangzeb's enemy, into camp this morning. There is sure to be a great celebration and we will make one more effort to free our friends and Esther's mother.

- Hinch

The Island, West Indies - 1752 -

Jack approached Louisa's and Walt's house, which was more like a hut with makeshift panels and logs. Compared to Glen's home, it was much less substantial and surely less wind proof.

As he entered, a heated discussion was underway.

"Glen, you can't move him while he is in this condition and in the dead of night? AND may I add, during a storm." Louisa was not budging; she was not about to give in.

"Louisa, our best chance to weather this storm is in the cove. The storm will sweep this plateau clean! And I'm not a bully!"

"You want Rags dead?"

"Of course not, you know that," Glen said. "Walt, you know what's at stake and our timetable. Speak with your wife."

Walt smiled, winked at Louisa, and spoke for the first time during this stubborn exchange. "What would Rosemary want us to do?"

"Don't bring Rosemary into this!" Glen said and dropped his head. He was beaten.

Rosemary was like Louisa in several ways, but Glen knew exactly what Rosemary would want. She wouldn't take sides with anybody. She would take sides with what was right. Rosemary would risk losing everything else if that was required to protect someone she loved. And they all loved Rags.

The woman had a way of influencing Glen to make the right decisions. Persuasion, long-suffering, patience, and kindness were Rosemary. Louisa was opinionated, persistent, stubborn and downright blunt. The problem wasn't the end result or even the style differences. Well, actually, Glen thought, style was the problem. When Rosemary prevailed, he felt they had made a good decision. When Louisa prevailed, he felt he had lost.

Glen had to step outside to cool down. Bringing Rosemary into this argument was unfair. What would Rosemary want us to do? She would make him calm down and consider the whole picture, not just what he wanted.

Glen sat under a small covering that hardly kept him from the rain. He began reasoning to himself, asking and answering his own questions as he considered the right thing to do. There was more to consider than just what he wanted, he admitted to himself, but this was their chance to get off the island. And maybe their only chance. More importantly, if he waited, he might not ever see his little girl again.

Their safety in the storm, the post storm winds, Rags' safety—why did the pirates show up today?

Two years of preparation couldn't be wasted now! Finally after grueling self-assessment, he asked himself, "What do you really want?"

"I want Lydia to be safe. I want off this island and I want to kill those men who hurt my daughter. If I can't get off this island now and track them down now, I may never see my precious baby girl again and I will go mad!" Then his mind went racing again through the possible problems in getting this mob safely to their back-up plan, a second ship stranded as was the *Bringhurst* in some other storm countless years ago—a ship on the other side of the cliffs.

† † †

Jack stood in the doorway holding the door closed against the gusts of wind which had just tore the latch free. His attention was on the careful bandaging and care Louisa gave Rags. The light provided by one small lamp felt puny compared to the work expected from it. Jack nearly flew across the room when Glen, calm, resolute, and full of fury, threw open the door and took command of the island.

"We will go rescue my daughter, kill some pirates, get Jack's fiancé back, and then go home! And we're starting right now!" Glen said with as much power as the pounding rain outside. He then turned to Louisa and with kindness back into his voice, added, "Without killing Rags! You know how we've worked salvaging one of the ships in the graveyard, we've done better than that and soon we'll know if we can go home."

"Walt, take everyone up to the keep. I don't have to say it but I will. Be careful with Rags."

The keep was a small structure they'd built shortly after settling the island. It was like a small storage building built into the side of a hill constructed out of lumber from the salvaged ships. Glen knew they could all crowd in if they had to. It was not as secure as the fort but it might withstand the storm better than the homes on the plateau.

Glen continued giving directions, "Don't forget Joanna, I want her here with us."

A soft voice interrupted Glen's instruction. "I'm here. Thank you for wanting me," Joanna said.

Her kind voice was one more weight added to the yoke he felt responsible to carry in getting these people off this island. Possibly it was one of the sweetest weights after the terrible burdens she had to carry living with Hunter. Tears found their way down Glen's cheek as he looked up and saw her tender face. His demands softened.

Jack looked up, captivated by the source of the delicate voice. He never even saw her there. If he'd been sitting on a chair, it would have flipped over.

"We all want you, Joanna," Glen said. "Will you please help Louisa with Rags? He'll need care all night. In the morning, I will be back and together we'll cross this island for the last time. For now, I need Rosemary. Jack, when you get back to the classroom, make sure your students know evil can run, but it will never escape," Glen said, pushing the door closed behind him only to have it blow open before Jack grabbed it again.

† † †

"It took Elizabeth and I overnight to cross this island. Granted, that was getting lost, and with Rag's commentary. Glen will cross it and return by morning?" Jack asked. "In a hurricane?"

"When you're motivated, a man can do superhuman things," Walt said.

"Superhuman?" Jack asked.

"You are familiar with Greek mythology? Zeus, Apollo? They're gods," Walt said.

"So Glen is a god?" Jack asked. It was more a sarcastic statement.

"Sometimes he thinks so," Louisa said.

Walt just looked at her and smiled, then shook his head.

Jack turned back, unable to take his eyes from Joanna, who gracefully slipped down next to Louisa at Rags' side. The hair was darker but the nose, the cheekbones... he waved an open palm toward her and scanned the room with his eyes. The resemblance was too close! Didn't anyone else see it?

I think I know why Elizabeth risked her life.

Chapter Eighty~Four

Our pursuit to free the Princess Zeb-un-Nissa is now over. We failed again. Failure seems to be the theme of this journal. We are in Lahore in the care of one of the princess's dearest friends, a poet they call Razi.

Esther is so heartbroken she is almost beyond reconciliation. Rudy is doing his best to shine a favorable light on our plight. He and Moses are healing, and considering we are still alive, in the middle of a Persian dynasty in turmoil, and a Mughal Empire fighting for its life, Rudy thinks we won.

Esther, however, lost.

During the great celebration among Aurangzeb's camp, they paraded Santaji's head from one end of the camp to the other. We took that opportunity one last time to free our friends. Tanek led us back to the same area of the Imperial camp where, this time, there were no guards. Esther and I made our way to Zeb-un-Nissa's tent, still heavily guarded. Esther approached the guard, revealed her identity, and requested an audience with her mother. Assuming Aurangzeb had approved, the guards ushered us in. We told the captives we had horses ready, and we prepared to escape just as soon as we distracted the guards. The distraction was Moses's job.

I opened the tent door just as a flaming cart pulled by a team of frantic horses came charging at the guards. It was time to run. And we did. All of us cleared the guarded tent and arrived where Tanek had our horses waiting and ready. Just as we mounted, Moses rounded a tent at a full run and yelled for us to go, go, go. Our horses lurched forward. A wounded Rudy needed help. Moses practically jumped on his horse.

Just as he did, arrows flew.

Horsemen charged from around a large tent that sat between the prison tent and the stables. The flaming cart hadn't distracted everyone.

An arrow struck Moses in his bottom that almost caused him to fall from his horse. With arrows flying and a cavalry charging, hope was gone.

When Tanek secured our twelve horses back in Santaji's camp weeks ago when Aurangzeb's army swept through, Tanek outfitted each with the weapons he gathered from fallen soldiers and their horses. We were each riding well-trained and experienced war horses. But even so, we were no match for a professional cavalry.

Makhfi turned his horse and charged the approaching soldiers, scattering them. He pulled a sword and began a work of death I would never have imagined from the man I'd taken for more a diplomat than a warrior.

He left body after body dead or too wounded to continue the pursuit. With the cavalry in chaos, the archers turned their attention from us to him, and yet because of his quickness and agility they failed to knock him off his horse. Zeb-un-Nissa halted just in time to turn and watch him fall from his horse, having finally been struck by enough arrows he could no longer hold on. She screamed and charged back into the fray. We watched as she leaped to his aid.

Esther turned her horse and was about to return as well.

When her mother saw Esther about to join her, she cried out words I will never forget.

 "Take my aziz-e delam, my Astrella. Take her somewhere safe. Take her away from here."

One last glance and we galloped away, leaving Makhfi bleeding in Princess Zeb-un-Nissa's arms. The last thing we saw were Aurangzeb's soldiers surrounding them.

We took several weeks, traveling quietly and mostly at night. We followed Makhfi's instructions and found our way here to Lahore. We know there is no going back. No going forward either. Without Makhfi, we will never make it through Persia alive. Esther's Persian brother will undoubtedly have heard that she is no longer with Avery nor the *Fancy* in the new world.

He will have placed a bounty on her head. We also learned that the Shah imprisoned a Captain Ali Mutarid Hassan for having lost his ship in Bourbon. I would feel remorse for his punishment if he hadn't been sent to kill Esther. I disrupted a fratricide.

These friends of Makhfi are well informed.

- Hinch

Onboard the Sally - Open Sea - West Indies - 1748-

Elizabeth wanted with all her heart to put this poor man bleeding to death in her arms out of his misery, but she didn't have a pistol. She also wasn't strong enough to strangle him to death, nor was she strong enough to simply snap his neck. It would have been easy enough. Everyone on board anxiously attended to the ship's flight from the storm. The wind was increasing; the ocean was more turbulent. The spraying sea soaked everyone above deck, especially her, she thought.

Instead, she betrayed her feelings, and tore the sleeve from his shirt. Elizabeth peeled away his vest to reveal the splintered edges of an arrow protruding from his shoulder. Blood still oozed and inside his vest was a mass of red sludge. It was immediately clear why he fainted. She kept an eye on Lydia, who was watching intently. With the slightest motion of her head, Lydia was up and over to Elizabeth's side despite the rolling of the ship. Together, they fussed enough to stop the bleeding and waited for someone in charge to give them directions. No one was in charge.

Finally, a large African man came up from below decks and walked over to where Elizabeth and Lydia were caring for Krist. Without a word, he reached down, picked Krist up, and carried his limp body back the way he came. Nobody objected, so Elizabeth and Lydia followed.

Below decks, Elizabeth thought she saw Lydia break out of her shock. Her head and eyes seemed to notice everything. Elizabeth did the same. She wasn't consciously thinking to notice, but Lydia appeared to be capturing every detail.

Two rows of black slaves, one on the starboard and one on the port side of the ship held tightly to the oars. She didn't stop to count, but at a glance figured nine on each side totaling about eighteen men. This was a big ship, she thought. The slaves were shackled in place.

The waters were rough. The ship would pitch up and down, giving the galley slaves reason to hold tight. Then she noticed she was doing her best to stay upright. Is this what Lydia experienced when they were on the *Bringhurst* in the hurricane? She saw there were two large doors at the aft of the galley slaves.

She and Lydia followed the captain, still in the arms of the large African. He entered a room finely appointed with intricately carved furniture. Polished swords hung on the walls. Curtains covering the open window was that of a fine cloth. However, they were soaked and dripped water on the enormous bed. She concluded this must be the captain's cabin.

The large man carrying the captain tossed him roughly on the bed. He turned to leave and only then realized the two women tailed behind. Quickly they stepped to the aid of the captain where his bleeding began again. The man turned to stop them, but halted when a harsh voice called him back.

"Leave them, Caesar. I will deal with them."

Until then, she didn't notice the table behind them. It was Scotty. Slimy, nasty and disgusting. At his side stood Hunter. Elizabeth feared she had just led Lydia into the viper's pit. She wished she'd stayed above decks where the rocking of the ship was the only cause of her nausea. Down here it was the company.

Caesar left the cabin, slamming the door behind him.

"Is he alive?" Scotty demanded. Elizabeth glared.

"Not for long," she finally said.

"Hunter, take those two to the aft hold and be sure it's locked," Scotty barked over the noise of the raging storm outside. "I need to get us out of this storm."

Hunter stepped over and tried to act submissive to the command, not knowing that the two captives heard everything on the beach, and knew full well Hunter was one of the captors.

"You're disgusting," Elizabeth said as she spit in Hunter's face. Her spittle contained the remnants of the loss of Rag's hog dinner.

Hunter slapped Elizabeth so hard she crashed against the foot of the bed and fell to the floor. This time, Lydia jumped to her aid.

Scotty stood from behind a large table, revealing the growing patch of blood where the arrow had penetrated his thigh just below the hip. Scotty's movement was slow and deliberate, proving the bolt had caused serious damage and the mass of blood revealed a hasty and insufficient bandaging job.

"Leave them here," Scotty commanded as he limped past Krist's still body. "Send Caesar back to throw this corpse overboard."

Hunter wiped the spittle off his face, glared, and stomped out. Scotty followed slowly, giving his painful limp due attention. He locked the door behind him.

Elizabeth and Lydia had a decision to make. Did they prefer as their captor the captain, who would soon get thrown overboard, or Scotty and Hunter? It was not a hard decision.

They hastened to the captain and removed his vest and shirt. Together, they cleaned off the blood. Plenty of water had entered the cabin through an open porthole. The soaked curtains became makeshift rags to clean the matted blood off the wound. They both noted the knife in the captain's belt when they removed the shirt and vest. Taking the knife, Lydia looked to Elizabeth for permission and together without a word agreed to go to work. He was unconscious anyway, they reasoned.

Lydia, with masterful dexterity which denied her twelve years of age, dug the arrow from the captain's shoulder. She plugged the ragged hole with the cleanest piece of cloth she could find, a worn purple cotton bandana she wore around her neck.

Elizabeth tore strips from the only dry section of the curtains and they wrapped the freshly cleaned wound.

As they finished, the door clicked open. Caesar entered, prepared to bury the captain at sea. It was clear, Scotty was perfectly happy for the captain to die and for himself to captain the *Sally*.

"Caesar," Elizabeth said assuming he understood, "You have a choice. Scotty wants the captain dead so he can command this ship. The captain is not dead. As you can see, he is sick and may die, but right now he is alive. Can you wait until he dies?"

"Captain Scotty commands this ship. Mr. Krist may die or he may not. He is no longer in command. I obey my captain," Caesar said.

Elizabeth knew she was asking a lot of a man who had little experience thinking for himself. Caesar was an obedient slave who knew who was in charge. Making decisions was not part of his skill set.

"What did Captain Scotty command you after throwing Mr. Krist into the storm?" she asked.

"I will lock you in the cargo hold," he answered.

"Please lock all three of us in the cargo hold?" she asked.

"I must throw the body overboard," he said.

"Take us to the cargo hold first and bring the body," Elizabeth pleaded.

Caesar picked up Krist and ushered the two women out of the cabin. They walked past the oarsmen to the aft of the ship. This time Elizabeth was more conscious as she noted practically everything. The musty smells, the submissive look on these slaves' faces, the scars on their backs, the heavy chains that held them in position. As the ship rocked, Elizabeth and Lydia struggled to keep their balance. Caesar remained sure footed, which, of course, he would, so accustomed to life at sea.

When the ship pitched, it threw Lydia into the lap of a galley slave. It surprised Elizabeth to see Lydia showed no fear. He was gentle; he helped her to her feet as much as his chains allowed. He shared a kind smile which revealed beautiful white teeth. She said nothing, but mouthed the words 'thank you' as she looked into his eyes. Elizabeth's stomach filled with empathy. She had no personal experience with slaves but had heard plenty from those who did. She knew she hated it.

Caesar pushed the door open to the small cargo hold, releasing a smell Elizabeth recognized as the ship's pantry. It wasn't the fresh cool earthy smell she loved when she visited her grandmother's root cellar. This air was warm and musty, but still told her the room was full of food, particularly fresh fruits and vegetables. There were also casks of what she assumed was fresh water, other foodstuffs, which accompanied remnants of a bail of cloth, ship's supplies and other probable pirate plunder. Several discarded sacks which had been full of food of some sort lay discarded on the floor. This gave Elizabeth an idea.

"Please give us a few moments alone to prepare the body for burial. He deserves that much respect."

He laid the body down and Elizabeth quickly picked up a sack and began filling it. She threw in a bundle of rope, a couple other discarded bags, several coconuts, a large piece of torn canvas which looked like a piece of a damaged sail. It soon looked like they had stuffed a body into the sack.

Elizabeth knew this was a decision Caesar was not prepared to make. She stared at him, eyes pleading for understanding. He understood and made what she thought might be the biggest decision he had ever made.

Caesar picked up the sack, and holding it as if it were a body, stepped out of the cargo hold, locked the door, passed eighteen watching slaves, and went above decks.

Chapter Eighty~Five

Journal Entry: August 1696 - Lahore, India
Alexander Hincher - Sojourner

We awaited news for several weeks. It finally came.

This morning, messengers arrived from Aurangzeb's camp. Princess Zeb-un-Nissa has been returned to Salmangahr as a prisoner. In his anger, Aurangzeb executed Makhfi. This time Esther's mother didn't have influence enough to persuade her father to spare a life. Esther has spent countless nights crying herself to sleep in my arms. None of this surprised her, but knowing she'll never see her mother again and such a dear friend Makhfi giving his life for hers, is overwhelming.

The messenger personally gave me a note sealed with instructions not to share with anyone until we were safely out of Persian or Mughal controlled territory. It may remain sealed for some time.

- Hinch

The Plateau - The Island - 1748

Rain was common on the island, but now it was accompanied by a very uncommon wind. With its growing intensity, Glen estimated the optimum time to catch the trailing winds of the storm could be anytime between tomorrow and three days from tonight. He did not want to miss it. He'd been waiting and preparing for this storm ever since they landed on this island.

It was impossible to have foreseen the destruction of the *Bringhurst*. It sat prepared for this storm these two years. Yet he wondered why he felt it so important to prepare a backup plan. He now knew why, but could only thank providence for the feelings.

In perfect conditions, Glen could travel from the cove to the plateau in just over two hours, which was at almost a full run. It would take the rest of the island's residents six to seven hours under good conditions at a somewhat aggressive pace. In a storm and with an injured Rags, they would need much more than that.

Granted, they were not going all the way to the cove, but they would traverse rough terrain to get up to the fort. It would probably be an even trade in time required.

All of these calculations pushed through Glen's mind as he ran toward the cove. This was now his fourth journey across the island in the past twelve hours. And it wouldn't be his last.

He was grateful his mind was engaged in these tactical calculations. Each time his mind wasn't busy planning their escape, it fell into the dark thoughts of what might happen to his Lydia. The only comforting thought he had was the pirates would be too busy outrunning the storm to be doing the girls any immediate harm. He hoped they were competent mariners and would find a safe harbor to wait out the worst of the storm. Glen was certain this storm would show no mercy to land or sea.

The unknown piece of the storm puzzle was how much the cliffs would protect this leeward side of the island once the storm's fury was upon them. If it stalled or paused even slightly, once it was over land, it could bring the winds in such a direction that would easily cripple the *Rosemary* —the backup plan.

There was too much to think about and Glen was growing weary. The last hour of his return to the cove was a blur. When he reached the cove, Rosemary and the kids were gone.

Chapter Eighty~Six

Esther and I are back on board the *Caspara* heading home to Scotland. I am again a ship's surgeon. The crew are my former mariner slaves. Though no longer slaves, in the many months they worked on our spice plantations they gained skills. It was Lord Rudy's promise they receive ownership as they exercised responsibility.

Our cargo, besides myself and Esther, comprises precious East India spices and remarkable silks.

Rudy calculates that if I am more competent in the Indian spice and silk business than I am in the rescuing business, he will eventually make up for the financial losses he incurred when he purchased Esther and Leilyn from Avery and the crew of the *Fancy*. He conveniently forgot to deduct the share I paid for his life. Regardless, we are confident there is a future for our little Indian spice and future silk business.

It's not safe for Esther and I to stay anywhere near India or Persia. Rudy and Leilyn remained in the Indian village now called Rudyshijan.

Moses was very gracious in accepting the charge to care for my harem in my absence. And since my absence will be permanent, I expect he will create a new tribe. Rudy scolded me for my disrespect referring to these three tribal princesses as my harem rather than sharing their names each time I mention them in this journal. When I asked him to spell their names the same way twice in a row, he settled down. I do however owe them much. They were never treated as a harem, they are independent, wise and delightful friends. And in respect, I went back several pages and honor them with the same spelling so creatively made up by Rudy. Muhumzingha, Seh-Dong-Hong-Beh, and Nyabinghi.

Adrina promised to help my new little son Tanek return to Tonk. He insists it would be him who helps Adrina to Agra.

Moses remained in Rudyshijan with Rudy. Those two are like brothers almost in every way. Good and bad. Rudy plans to expand into silks. He claims it will be a good venture.

It has not been an eventless journey, however. The *Caspara* is a quick ship and with favorable winds we outran the several ships wanting to add our cargo to their plunder. With few stops we will reach home within a matter of weeks.

- Hinch

Onboard the Sally - Open Sea - West Indies - 1752-

Weak and tired, Scotty was at the helm. Darkness set in. Pre-hurricane winds made for very full sails.

Typically, they would be favorable winds, but with each passing hour they increased. The *Sally* was not equipped with storm sails. It was not intended to be out in storms. It was merely a search vessel. Scotty smiled as he watched Caesar carry a large sack above decks and toss it over the port bow.

Scotty consumed a bottle of rum to help him endure the pain of his damaged thigh. He knew if they didn't spot land soon, they risked spending the night in the open sea. He knew he couldn't keep the ship at full sail much longer. The power of the wind would destroy the sails and topple the masts. They were reaching thirteen or fourteen knots, which was more than this galley, more than any ship, was built for. Just as he called to lower the aft sail, he spotted a small island ahead.

As they approached, he recognized this island. With sails now lowered, Caesar took control, directing his oarsmen to bring the *Sally* safely into the small harbor.

They might survive this storm. The crew set anchor and Scotty, his strength spent, struggled below decks to Krist's cabin, now as captain, it was his cabin. Protected in the small harbor, the night and possibly a day or two would pass in relative safety. Scotty collapsed in exhaustion.

† † †

The cargo hold held only one small port hole which offered just enough fresh air and light to sustain its new residents. In the darkness, the violent pitching of the ship ceased. They finally found safety for the night, Elizabeth thought.

Elizabeth and Lydia made a small bed for the captain behind the storage casks. He was still unconscious, but was at least breathing. Leaning against Elizabeth as the two rested next to the captain, Lydia's breathing became rhythmic and smooth, that of a deep sleeper.

There was too much to think about, and sleep was impossible for Elizabeth. What had she done? She just saved the life of an evil man who had taken the two of them captive and who intended to capture Glen, and who knows what else. She saved the life of a dragon.

She thought of the discussion she had with Jack about her family. Her sister was within reach. She couldn't even think of what she had done to follow Lydia and abandon hope of finding her sister, let alone why. Then saving her captor? What did she expect to gain from that or the costs involved? What would the captain do when he woke? If he woke? What would Scotty do when he found Caesar didn't throw him overboard? If the captain died, could Elizabeth and Lydia fit his body out the porthole?

If it was Scotty who fainted in her arms rather than Krist, would she have saved his life, or would she have finished him? He killed Rags after all.

Why hadn't she thought through all of this at the time? How could she protect Lydia in the morning when everyone was sober and rested? How long would the storm last? Where were they going? Why did they want Glen? How did they find the island?

Somewhere amidst all these questions, sleep finally overtook Elizabeth, and for the second time in days, she slept cuddled up with a stranger.

Chapter Eighty~Seven

Loch Linnhe is now in sight. We are home. We will make Fort William our base of business, and from here I hope to take our cargo to London and visit my father. I now feel safe enough to open and read the sealed letter I have been holding for these many months.

This is how it reads.

> *My dearest Dr. Alexander Hincher,*
>
> *If you followed my wishes, you are reading this letter in safety and peace. You are no longer running for your life. God willing, and I believe He is, my beloved daughter Astrella is with you.*
>
> *I thank you as only a loving father can, for your love and care for her. I chastised you for attempting to bring her back to her family. If you recall, I also praised you for that effort. Now I thank you with all my heart. I give you my blessing to share this letter with her and to share your life with her. You have earned my devoted honor.*
>
> *In a world where a father will imprison his favorite daughter, execute his brothers and father and sacrifice the lives of countless thousands to retain a power that can only be maintained by blood; I want you to know there are also fathers who will give their lives to protect, teach and provide for those they love.*
>
> *There is no way you cannot have seen my love for the Princess Zeb-un-Nissa. Though Aurangzeb always suspected I was the father of his granddaughter, the*

*political advantage he realized with the world believing
the deception of Shah Suleiman I as the father and
Shah Husayn as Astrella's brother minimized the threat
Aurangzeb felt from me.*

*Though Esther's actual father was not the Shah of Persia,
and the current fool is not her real brother, do not
minimize the royal blood that flows in her veins. You need
to know that I am the grandson of Safi Mirza, crown prince
of the Safavid Dynasty under his father Shah Abbas the
Great. My father had me secreted away before his father, the
Shah could have us assassinated as he did to 4 of his sons
and two of his grandsons.*

*You can see how if Astrella ever claimed either of the two
thrones of which she is a rightful heir, she would never live
long enough to reign.*

*I don't believe I will ever meet you again. Know that I have
no regrets. I will die with the peace knowing my azizam
Astrella is cared for. What more can a father want?*

In your eternal debt, Makhfi

- Hinch

Glen's Cove - The Island - 1748

Glen smiled an exhausted smile. She did it. I knew she would.

He thought he could rest in his home there in the cove for a few minutes to gather enough strength to climb to the fort. He pulled the door closed tight, laid back on his bed and closed his eyes just for a few deserved moments. Then he would seek the protection of the fort with Rosemary and the children.

It was daylight when a fierce gust of wind blew open a window and a falling branch crashed into the side of the home. Glen woke so suddenly when he sat up it took him a few minutes for his head to clear and to get his bearings. Both hands clung to the bed.

His mind raced from the people on the plateau holding up in the keep, to his sweet Lydia in custody of wicked men, to his Rosemary, who he hoped was at the fort, to his other *Rosemary* which he hoped was safe in its own harbor. He cursed himself for falling asleep.

Glen rose, still mostly wet from the night's rain. He gathered up some dry things and went outside into the pounding rain. He searched a hidden compartment built into the base of the stone oven, only to find it empty. One more thing to give him great concern. When constructing his stone oven, he crafted the base of it in such a way as to provide a place to secretly protect precious possessions. Those possessions were now gone.

He threw a pack over his shoulder and began the trek through the storm up to the fort. The storm winds and rain were increasing, just as he thought they should. Glen didn't know if it was his mind or body that would succumb to complete exhaustion first. He reached the fort, as they called it, and pounded on the outer door.

The fort was a large hidden room partially carved out of the hill and the surrounding stone and trees. Its earthen walls were overgrown with ferns and native grasses. If not looking specifically for it, you would walk past and never know it was there. Which was its purpose. Created not just as a storm shelter, Glen knew the day would come when the visitors who had come, would come.

Glen couldn't let the despair of his failure to protect Lydia overcome him. He had to keep pushing forward. He readied to knock again when the door cracked open and a familiar voice called out.

"Who is it?"

"Why don't you open up and find out?" Glen asked.

The door burst open and Rosemary pulled Glen inside out of the storm. He was too weak to resist, nor would he have done so. Rosemary's embrace practically healed every muscle. She could heal every hurt.

"Rosemary… they have Lydia," Glen said, still in Rosemary's embrace.

She pulled away. "Who has Lydia?"

"I don't know yet. Ten or twelve men landed in the lagoon. Came on a galley. Walt thinks they were hunting for this island. When they tried to take Lydia, Rags killed two of them. Walt and Jack were up at the keep. When they heard a shot, they ran to the lagoon. They killed another five and severely wounded two others with the crossbows. Elizabeth tried to save Lydia, and they took her too." Glen let it all pour out.

The twins were still asleep, but the baby fussed. Rosemary released Glen, who picked up the baby. Glen took her in his arms and gently rocked her. His mind went immediately to his failure to protect Lydia. This was killing him.

"Glen, we have to get Lydia!" Tears and fear filled Rosemary's face and voice.

She could see the anxiety in Glen's face and knew he understood even more than she did the urgency of her request.

"Is this our storm?" Rosemary asked.

"Looks like it."

"Then we've got to get to the *Bringhurst*." She said as she started to gather things, preparing to leave.

"They shot Rags," Glen said. "He's bad, but Louisa and Joanna have him up in the keep with the others out of the storm."

"Let's go. Glen, we've got to go," Rosemary said, anxious to get on their way.

"They blew up the *Bringhurst*, Rosemary. It's not going anywhere. Burned to the ground."

"That's what that was." Rosemary sat back, deflated. For several minutes, she stared at Glen. It was an empty, hollow stare. Her mind turned to Rags. Hopelessness filled her.

"Will Rags live?" she finally asked.

"I wanted to bring him with me last night, but Louisa refused me . . . wisely."

"Why here?"

"Looks like the storm is coming right over this island, probably hit tonight. I want everyone safe, and this is the safest place on the island. I will go get them. Can you get the fort ready for visitors?"

"You know I can," she replied.

Glen quickly changed his clothes, even while knowing it made no difference. Rosemary noticed he was looking around as if he was searching for something. As he readied to leave, Rosemary held up a journal.

"Looking for this?" she asked.

Glen looked at the journal, then at Rosemary.

"Who are these people?" she asked. Her eyebrows raised and lips went firm. Glen knew she wouldn't wait patiently for this answer.

"You read it?" he asked as if surprised it held interest for her.

"Reading it," she answered.

"When this is over, I'll tell you all about it," he promised. "We'll be back tonight. Keep that," he said, and pointed to the journal, "and those," a gesture to the twins, "safe."

Glen hurried out and into the storm and closed the heavy door behind him.

Chapter Eighty-Eight

Onboard the Sally - Secluded Harbor - 1748

When Elizabeth awoke, Lydia was standing, looking out the porthole. Though the storm was raging outside, the inlet appeared to provide relative safety. Elizabeth removed the captain's arm from around her. He wasn't dead, she noticed. During the night he got a little close. Krist looked much better. He was still pale, but his breathing was easier.

Several hours passed before they heard keys unlocking the large wooden door. Caesar stepped in and collected supplies obviously meant for preparing food for the crew. He said nothing but attempted to locate the captain and see where they had hidden him. After looking him over, he permitted a slight smile, and with the wooden box full of supplies, stepped out of the cargo hold and locked the door behind him.

Elizabeth and Lydia checked out the rest of the supplies in the hold and enjoyed the clean water to drink and freshen up. They then went to work on the captain. They gave his upper body a bath, removing the dressing from the night before, and replaced the bandaging. Elizabeth noticed that Lydia was quite adept with bandages.

When she realized how Elizabeth was watching, she simply said, "I learned it from my father."

The girl tore bandages from a bolt of cloth, probably the remnants of a pirate booty. She tucked clean packing into the hole, which bled again. As she cleaned around it and gently wrapped him up again, she said, "and this from my mother."

Elizabeth smiled. Naturally the basic difficult task, stop the bleeding, and who cares if it hurts that was Glen, and the gently clean and wrap, that was

Rosemary. This was a very lucky young woman.

Throughout the morning, they heard noises and commotion as they assumed the oarsmen were being fed and allowed personal care. The *Sally* remained anchored but still rocked and rolled as the wind and rain howled around them. It wasn't until late in the afternoon when the door was unlocked again and in stepped Scotty, flanked by Hunter.

There was no pretense any longer that Hunter was a fellow prisoner. Scotty glared at the two women. If they thought Hunter had an evil look, Scotty put him to shame. His wicked smile almost made Elizabeth throw up again. They said nothing, turned, slammed the door, and locked it. The prisoners could hear laughing and talking on the other side but couldn't make out what they said.

Goosebumps returned in majestic fashion. Elizabeth and Lydia were grateful the two vipers didn't snoop around to find the captain. It was clear they didn't suspect he lived. When the door closed, Lydia carefully put the captain's knife back in her boot. Elizabeth smiled.

"Who's the master archer?" Elizabeth asked. "Somebody knows their way around a bow. I saw Jack and Walt at the edge of the jungle. No way that school boy Jack could shoot like that."

"You never saw your fiancé shoot?" Lydia asked innocently.

Elizabeth shook her head.

"Probably Walt then. He's tried to teach me, but the bows are too big for me. He and my father are proud of them. They're beautiful."

Elizabeth thought of the scene of two dead pirates, killed with a rock to the head. Dead and wounded pirates from crossbow bolts. What a unique little army.

"Lydia?" Elizabeth started, "Please tell me about Joanna."

"Hunter's slave wife?" Lydia said with disdain.

"You don't like her?"

"I hardly know her. Never joins in. Hunter keeps her away from us. Mother and father try to be friendly. She's like a ghost. A friendly ghost, I guess, but never happy. I never saw a smile."

"Young or old?" Elizabeth asked.

"Mother says she looks older than she is. Probably older than you. Not as pretty. Has long dark hair." Lydia paused, looking around the room to refine her memory of a person she'd never really talked to. "Maybe, if she cleaned up, dressed up, she might be pretty.”

What else could Elizabeth expect from a young woman with so little experience, so little interaction with Joanna. What were the chances she would search the world over for ten years and find her sister by accident on a lost island? It was so long ago, and Elizabeth was so young, would she even recognize her own sister?

Yet, a woman, an unhappy woman, was under the thumb of evil. Did Hunter buy her? Steal her? Could his Joanna be her Joanna? She hoped that now, this Joanna, whoever she was, could remain free of the loathsome Hunter.

Lydia spent much of her day watching out the porthole. The two talked very little. Finally, Lydia asked the question they both wanted to ask.

“Why do you think they are looking for my father?”

That was the question Elizabeth was afraid to ask such a tender young girl. Even though this tender young girl was proving to be not all so tender.

“Tell me what you remember about Sheffield. You were born there weren’t you?”

Lydia shared stories about what she remembered. She told about the friends she had, her schools, and her love for music. She told how the family traveled the countryside. Elizabeth thought it curious Lydia said they never went to the sea. Other families visited the shores and even London, yet her family never did. The family visited Scotland frequently and Lydia loved the Highlands.

As they spoke, Lydia shared her excitement to go on a ship. It was her first time, but Hunter ruined the excitement. When she brought up Hunter, the opportunity opened for Elizabeth to ask more questions about him.

“Did you ever see his wife in Sheffield?” Elizabeth asked.

Lydia shook her head.

† † †

A rustling noise behind the water casks interrupted the conversation. The two quickly silenced and checked on the captain, who was now awake. The three of them stared at each other. The captain looked from the two girls to his bandaged shoulder.

“You did this?” he asked.

Elizabeth nodded.

"Why?"

Elizabeth shrugged her shoulder showing she wasn't sure.

"Thank you," he whispered.

Lydia pulled out the knife and pointed it at the captain. He smiled and tried to pull himself up into a sitting position.

"Am I a prisoner?"

"Yes, and no," Elizabeth said. "It's complicated."

"We're all prisoners," Lydia said.

"Is this still my galley?"

"I don't think so," Elizabeth answered.

"Is it yours?" he asked.

"Actually, Scotty took it from you when he threw you overboard. So I guess he thinks it's his." Elizabeth said.

"He threw me overboard?"

"Actually, he had Caesar throw you overboard," Lydia said.

"Was I dead?"

"No."

"Did he think I was?"

"No. But he wanted you to be, and he wasn't about to wait around and let you get better."

"I swam in this condition, in a hurricane? Who'd they throw overboard?" Krist asked.

"Four coconuts, a large rope, and an old canvas sail," Lydia said.

"Caesar made it look convincing," Elizabeth added.

"Who knows I'm alive?" he asked.

"The three of us and Caesar," Elizabeth answered.

Lydia remained in place with the knife pointed directly at Krist. She maintained a firm scowl that Krist obviously took serious.

"May I repeat an earlier question?" He asked.

A nod.

"Why?"

Elizabeth and Krist stared at one another for a long time while Elizabeth tried to fashion an answer that would make sense to him and to her, as to why she would save the life of a dragon. What had motivated her to keep him alive? A hundred possible answers raced through her mind, but none of them rang true. A hostage? No. Compassion? No. Leverage? No. Practice? No. Fear? No. Hope? No. Charity? No. Attraction? Certainly, no. Ok, maybe. He was quite ruggedly handsome, and there was something amiable in his eyes.

It was Lydia who finally broke the staring contest. She knelt closer to him and kept the knife out of his reach, but close enough to remain threatening.

"Why are you hunting for my father?"

Krist had no personal reasons to harm her father. There was no conflict between them. He was following the orders of his father to find the man his father had been chasing those many years. Because he was not personally invested, he answered truthfully and dispassionately.

"Many years ago, a pirate named Henry Avery captured the Mughal Emperor's treasure ship. Among the vast treasure were two items of great value. One was the emperor's own granddaughter, the other was the Blade of Safavid, a priceless and sacred relic belonging to the heir of the Persian Safavid Dynasty."

There was no way Elizabeth could have prepared for this revelation. The intersection of facts, the blade, pirates, Joanna, ol' Denn, Jack, Glen, the island. What else would life expect her to process? Again, she had to calm her racing mind and force herself to breath.

Krist continued to speak. "My father was sent by the Shah to recover both. He failed. He believes the pirate ship's surgeon stole his ship. My father believes this surgeon had possession of both the granddaughter and the Blade."

"You're looking for the wrong man. My father is not a surgeon, nor a pirate. Believe me, he never captured a treasure ship, nor kidnapped a princess," Lydia said.

Krist chuckled at her claim, which, of course, was true.

"The Shah imprisoned my father for over twenty years for his failure. Since then he has dedicated his life to finding that pirate. Unless your father is an ancient man, no, your father is not that pirate."

"Many years later, a young sailor and my father met in a tavern. It became evident they were both looking for the same pirate, this ship's surgeon. The sailor escaped, along with the evidence of the pirate's whereabouts. It is that young sailor my father is hunting."

"You are still looking for the wrong man. My father is no sailor. He has stayed away from the sea his whole life. He hates the ocean," Lydia said.

Though captivated by the story, Elizabeth was being Elizabeth and a thousand questions begged an answer. Only one came out. "Where did your father and this sailor meet?" Elizabeth asked.

Lydia turned an eye to Elizabeth's question. A look that clearly said: What does that matter? She asked a question of her own. "So why did you kill Rags and take us prisoner?"

This conversation was taking its toll on Krist. He slowly and painfully laid himself back down. Lydia did not relax her intense grip on the knife, and both Krist and Elizabeth noticed her serious glare.

"Instinct," Krist finally said.

"Instinct?" Elizabeth asked. "You naturally just kill innocent people and take women prisoners?"

"Sadly, yes," Krist answered.

Elizabeth could see and feel the pain in his response. It was full of remorse, almost a genuine regret. It completely caught her off guard, yet she noticed Lydia was unaffected.

"Everyone on this boat thinks you're already dead. You want to hurt my father. You killed my best friend. You kidnapped two innocent women. Please give me one reason, good or bad, why I shouldn't carve you up and stuff you through that porthole," Lydia said.

Krist looked at her, almost pleading for her to carry out her threat.

"Newton Ferrers," he said and closed his eyes.

Chapter Eighty~Nine

Onboard the Sally - Secluded Harbor - 1748

At the sound of a key unlocking the door, the girls sprang over the casks and sat calmly as the door swung open. Caesar entered again, this time with bowls of hot soup, bread, and cheese. More than enough for two. He set the food down without a word, quickly glanced behind the casks, caught Krist's eye and left the room locking the door behind him.

They said nothing more while the three ate. The *Sally* continued to rock back and forth but not furiously; the storm was not pounding this small island.

"There is no reason for you not to finish what Scotty tried to do, which by the way, began on the island by somebody with a superb aim," Krist said touching his bandaged shoulder.

"Walt," Lydia said. "Father said he can put the eye out of a seagull in flight. He must have missed. You still have both eyes."

It amazed Elizabeth how Lydia kept so focused on her hostility toward this helpless man. Of course she would, he threatened her family, she's held captive, and Rags is dead. Why didn't I let them throw this man overboard? She still couldn't answer the question.

"You are wrong about my father, but why take Elizabeth and me and run?" Lydia asked.

"And why did you blow up the *Bringhurst?*" Elizabeth added.

"The *Bringhurst* was Hunter. A good idea. It will keep your father from following us," Krist said.

"If we could sail the *Bringhurst*, we would have already," Lydia said.

Krist disagreed. "The storm was raising the water, if it hadn't blown, the

Bringhurst would be afloat, your father would race after us, and would have sunk in the hurricane. Hunter probably saved your father's life. And everyone else's."

Elizabeth hated the logic of that.

"He would have caught you. Walt would have finished his job," Lydia said.

If Elizabeth could read minds from a startled expression, she'd think Krist was as amazed at this young girl's tenacity as she was. She thought about her fiery attitude back on the beach while at gunpoint. He had to respect that.

"I thought you said your father hated the sea and stayed away from it. You believe he would risk his and everyone else's life in a wrecked ship, in a hurricane if he wasn't a sailor?" Krist asked.

This question stopped Lydia. Glen landed the ship safely in a hurricane and seemed to know a lot about ships and tides and currents. Was he the sailor they were looking for? Elizabeth wondered if Lydia recognized his logic.

Krist continued, "All my father wants is to know what your father knows. All he wants is to learn what that surgeon did with the Blade and the princess."

"And the surgeon?" asked Elizabeth.

"Well, if he is still alive, my father wants to kill him too."

"Will you help him?" Lydia asked.

"Kill the surgeon?"

Lydia nodded.

"No, he does his own killing. He knows I won't."

"Scotty kills for you?" Elizabeth asked.

"Nobody kills for me."

"What do you do?" Lydia asked. "Steal women?"

Keys rattled again and Lydia and Elizabeth hurried into position just as the door opened. Caesar stepped in followed by a badly limping Scotty and Hunter. Elizabeth's stomach turned, and she worried Lydia would hurl herself at him knife first. Glancing at Lydia's hand, to her relief she saw it empty.

"Ready to earn your passage?" Scotty asked, reaching toward Elizabeth.

"Are you ready to die?" Lydia asked.

Elizabeth looked again to see where the knife might be hidden. But she also couldn't help but see the massive blood stain on Scotty's fresh pair of pants.

She hoped he would bleed to death.

"Careful, little one. The only reason you're alive is to get your father to tell us what we want to know." This time it was Hunter speaking.

"He's coming for you right now!" Lydia shouted.

"Oh? In what?" Hunter smirked. "I blew up the Bringhurst. When we get back to the island, we'll be prepared to make him talk."

Elizabeth put her hand on Lydia's arm to calm her. Then, looking between Scotty and Hunter, she planned. "You harm either of us and we'll kill ourselves rather than get used. Mr. Scotty, sir, you killed your captain. You touch either of us and it's as good as killing us too. When you get back to our island, no matter how many of your kind you bring with you, you will learn nothing from her father and certainly you'll be sent running like a wounded dog, just as you were a few days ago."

Scotty reached out to slap Elizabeth. Caesar got in the way, a bit obviously, which infuriated Scotty.

"Out of my way, you fool!" Scotty yelled at Caesar.

But the look Caesar gave him was enough to hold the pirate back. Although Caesar now answered to Scotty as the captain, Caesar knew the true captain was only feet away behind the casks hearing everything.

"When we deliver you to Hassan, he will give you to me as a reward. When I am done with you, no one will want you," he spat at Elizabeth.

"What will he do when he learns you killed his son?" Lydia asked.

"Even if he believed that, he wouldn't care. All he wants is your father," Hunter said.

Caesar gathered the remaining evidence of the food as he ushered the men out of the room and locked the door.

The two girls stood there for some time before they climbed back to where Krist had been listening to the entire conversation.

"May I ask another question for the second time?" Krist asked.

"Why not? Which one?" Elizabeth answered.

"Am I a prisoner?"

"I answered that one already. Yes, we all are." Elizabeth answered.

"Let me be more specific. Am I your prisoner?"

Out came the knife. Lydia was quick with it, which surprised both Krist and Elizabeth. Then she set it aside.

"You saved my life," he touched his shoulder, then waved his hand indicating his current bedroom. "I doubt you will chop me up now."

"Scotty's plans don't include you. You're in more danger than we are," Elizabeth said. "We can't keep you hidden forever. They will find you."

"Not till we make landfall at my father's island," he said. Pointing to the back wall of the room, Krist continued, "Push the top panel of that wall."

Lydia stood and pushed the panel. A section of wall opened, revealing a small compartment loaded with fabrics and barrels of gunpowder. There was a small porthole which let in enough light so they could see it was surprisingly clean. There was also a breeze that flowed out into the room, which provided a nice airflow.

"Make room for me in there. For the few days it will take to get to my father's island, I will be safe enough," he said.

"And for us?" Elizabeth said.

Looking at Lydia now, he said, "Keep that knife handy. I feel confident, should the time come, you will be quite handy with it."

"What is this hideaway for?" Elizabeth asked.

"Hidden treasure."

"Women?"

"Those I tried to protect," he said.

As things were moved around in the hideaway, they realized the space was sufficiently large. Then Elizabeth noticed something she hadn't seen in many years. A pair of spectacles and a Bible.

Spectacles and a Bible that looked uncommonly like some that belonged to her father.

Chapter Ninety

The Fort - The Island - 1748

Rosemary recognized that Glen pushed through the storm just to warn her of the weather and ensure she and the children were safe. There was no way he could not tell her about Lydia's abduction, but he must have known how it would make her crazy with worry. She appreciated him more than her words could tell. She felt, however, she may have been better off to simply wonder how Lydia and Glen were doing in the storm. She was certain he would protect Lydia, whatever the storm. He was an overprotective father—most of the time. Why not this time?

Where was he when the pirates arrived? Why didn't he protect her? What were they going to do with Lydia? Too many questions. The only comfort was she knew Glen loved Lydia enough that if someone could do something, he would do it. He was doing it, she concluded. There wasn't a storm on this planet that could stop him. He set the *Bringhurst* safely on this island in this same kind of storm. She knew he knew what he was doing now. And there was nothing else she could do for the time being. The twins were still asleep, and the baby needed feeding. She would get ready for company later.

As Rosemary sat down to feed the baby, she picked up the journal and looked over at the ornate wooden box from which it came. Last evening, as she was packing up to leave the cove, the rushing waters flooded down past the stone oven Glen so carefully built. The water eroded away some of the dirt, exposing what looked like an opening between two stones. She knelt and pulled a stone free, revealing a small, tightly crafted box. She pulled it out and tucked it under her arm, then ushered the children up to the fort. Once inside and safe, she fed and prepared them all for bed.

For the children, this was an adventure. They came to the fort many times, sometimes just for fun and other times as a drill, until Rosemary and Glen were certain they could tell the children to go hide in the fort and they could do so all by themselves. They stocked it with enough food to last them more than a week. The children rested peacefully. They did not understand this was not a drill. After they were all sleeping, Rosemary opened the box, removed a journal, and read until darkness set in. She hadn't expected a visit from Glen, so she wasn't ready to ask all the questions she had the night before.

Now as Glen was heading back to the plateau, and as the storm raged outside, Rosemary opened the journal and continued to read. She hoped it would take her mind off the kind of worry only a mother can have for a child in distress. She read:

- From the journal of Alexander Hincher - ship's surgeon - August 1695

It was nearly eighteen hours before I awoke. I learned they left the survivors aboard their emptied ship, which the pirates set free to continue on their voyage back to India. Evidently, the treasure satisfied the crew's greed, for they pursued no other of the Indian fleet.

Once I returned to the deck disgusted and sick to my stomach at the sight of these barbarians, I saw we were at full sail, heading south as far as we could get. The crew now busied themselves counting and glorying in their treasure.

While the Fateh Muhammad's treasure of some £50,000 to £60,000 was enough to buy the *Fancy* fifty times over, it was the treasure of the *Gunsway* that had everyone's attention.

I noticed that we were sailing alone and so assumed that while I was unconscious they divided the treasure between the *Pearl*, the *Portsmouth*, and the *Fancy*. I still don't know the truth of it, but it appears that the *Portsmouth* did not join in the battle. So, Captain Faro's crew received none of the treasure. Captain Mayes and the crew of the *Pearl* parted company with the *Fancy*, they having received a sum of coins purported to be the fair share. I am certain Avery used his profound negotiating skills to take advantage.

When all was calculated, the loot totaled somewhere around £600,000. Avery and his crew are easily the richest pirates in history.

Any words of rebuke or disdain would fall upon deaf ears, so I elected not to share my feelings. I had sailed with the crew for two years; they know my feelings, my lack of approval, my utter disdain for piracy, but as a surgeon they know my dedication to their well-being. That dedication is now gone. I swore I would get off this ship at the next port.

And then it got complicated.

Rosemary tucked a small leaf between the pages to keep her place, closed the journal, and whispered to herself, "Yes, it gets complicated."

Chapter Ninety~One

The Plateau - The Island - 1748

This was the storm Glen planned and prepared for. Ever since they landed on the island, he and Walt calculated what it would take to get back to civilization. In the past few days, fate, or maybe providence, added several unexpected variables into the original equation. Two visitors drifted in, cutthroats discovered the island, Lydia and Elizabeth were kidnapped, Rags was shot, and it all happened right when the storm hit.

Glen knew a hurricane would come. As a young sailor, he spent enough time in the West Indies to become intimate with these tropical storms. He outran them, hid from them, weathered them, and fought them. The latter landed them on this island. The one thing he didn't do was fear them. Respect them, yes, but fear them, no.

Glen fought his way across the island. It did not surprise him at how the wind changed directions so quickly. He knew the worst of the storm would hit the windward side of the island and he estimated that would happen around midnight.

Both Sal and Jack were outside the keep preparing a wheeled stretcher for Rags when Glen arrived. The stretcher was basically a cart with a piece of sailcloth suspended between the two side rails, keeping him from feeling the inevitable bumps and jolts. This would give him a slightly safer ride. But nothing about this journey would be comfortable for any of them, especially Rags, if they made it at all.

They prepared packs for everyone. Ben gathered what he could and loaded it onto a small cart Rags and Sal crafted for him to use in the fields.

Glen spent only a moment or two with these men before entering the keep to check on Rags, who was now awake.

"Well, looks like Louisa here didn't kill you after all," Glen said as he sat down next to the makeshift bed. "How are you?" he asked.

"If I wasn't engaged, I'd marry her," Rags mumbled between the bandages on his face.

"She's ornery enough. Walt'll probably let you have her," Glen said.

"If we move him, we'll undo all the good we did last night. Can we wait one more day?" Louisa asked.

"Rags, this might be your lucky day. We're leaving here. Louisa wants to stay here with you. What do you say about staying here with her alone on the island?" Glen asked.

Looking at Louisa and barely audible, Rags said, "You're not leaving either of us here. I can make it."

The sound of the wind and rain continued outside. Glen turned to Joanna, who sat on the edge of the makeshift bed.

"Joanna, you ready to care for this patient? It's going to be a harsh day. But I promise if we get to the fort, we can safely wait out the storm," Glen said. "I'm sorry about Hunter."

Joanna lowered her face and closed her eyes, then slowly looked back up into his eyes. Her gentle smile accepted his expression of sorrow. He paused, looking deeply at her face. There was not only a sense of relief, there was a new familiarity. A smile crept across his face.

There could have been an argument for staying put in the keep, except the winds had loosened one side wall and water sprayed in each time the wind changed. A few more big gusts and this place would be gone.

"We're all with you. We'll get him through. Louisa's been keeping those herbs she chews fresh inside that wound. He's doing real well," Joanna said.

"And Marge and Susan?" Glen asked.

"Ready when you are," Marge said, stepping into the keep.

With the four women, Rags and Glen inside, it was cramped.

"We'll be ready soon," Glen said, stepping back outside into the storm.

Minutes later, the cart was ready. It was too big to go inside the keep, so it remained outside until everyone was ready. They loaded Rags onto the stretcher, secured him with a couple of ropes, and set off for the fort. If they were fortunate, they could arrive by dark. Within minutes, all were soaked to the bone.

Chapter Ninety~Two

On the Trail - The Island - 1748

The storm's intensity increased by the hour. They quickened their step. At times, Rags took a beating between the rocky ground and the powerful wind gusts. His closed eyes and clenched jaws were evidence of great pain, but he never complained. The trail was wet and slippery and there were several times they had to stop and help one another up when they slipped off the trail.

With everyone's clothing soaked through, Glen wondered how much the inevitable chaffing, blistering, and fatigue would eventually dampen the eagerness to press forward. It never came. Not a single murmur was made, at least not one that could be heard above the howling of the wind. Glen was proud of these island-mates. It surprised him that no one challenged his statement they were getting off the island.

This dedication to cross the island in the heart of a hurricane could only be attributed to the motivation of self-preservation. The hurricane had not yet triggered the anticipation of actually leaving the island.

The *Bringhurst*, their hope of escape, was destroyed. They all knew of the progressing efforts to build a seaworthy vessel from scraps of the old ships in the graveyard. Only Glen, Walt, and Sal knew about the *Rosemary*.

For now, there was only one immediate aim—to get to what they called the fort. Everyone had been to the fort during their years on the island and they all knew it would provide safety during this storm.

Concentration on the trail ahead demanded his attention, but he couldn't help but often wonder why when he announced they were leaving the island, no one demanded details.

He thought back to how after months of exploring the island, Glen discovered the graveyard, as he called it, where unfortunate ships had drifted and been gently deposited over the past century. Most of the island residents knew of the graveyard and several had taken the risky hike up and over the cliffs to see it.

Glen and Walt proposed building a small vessel from the remnants in the graveyard, but efforts continued to come up short.

Hunter balked at the thought of a backup plan to the Bringhurst. He refused to take part, yet he watched and scoffed. If a storm ever came, "what was wrong with the *Bringhurst*?" Hunter said.

The *Bringhurst* didn't sustain substantial damage when Glen landed it on the shore. Within a few weeks after the storm, Walt and Sal had it ready to sail again, if it could ever get to water.

Accident only discovered the second secluded and hidden lagoon when Glen and Walt were at the graveyard assessing if it were possible to resurrect any of these ships. Glen watched a large piece of driftwood float in and then float back out of the entrance to the graveyard being urged by the slightest current. He entered the water and floated with it for several hours as it made its way around a massive sea cliff.

Just as he was about to turn and swim back, he saw what might be an opening between the cliffs. He couldn't wait for the drifting log and he swam between the cliffs to find another small, protected lagoon. The entrance at water level was too small for any size ship to enter or exit, but despite that fact, there sat a frigate badly damaged but calmly lying on its side, waiting to be found and liberated. The water was so shallow Glen walked around the ship, examining the damage. He scanned the surrounding cliff walls to see if there was any overland route to this lagoon, and couldn't immediately see one.

He plunged back into the water and swam back the way he came. The current was so slight it didn't put up any resistance, and within an hour, he entered the graveyard where Walt impatiently waited with worry.

Glen knew Walt was a good enough swimmer, but knowing he preferred not to swim, it took a strong persuading to get him into the water. They stepped up out of the water, examining the stranded frigate.

"We can make this one seaworthy," Glen said.

"Possibly," Walt said. Then turning to the small opening to the lagoon, "But we'd have the same problem as we do with the *Bringhurst*. Water'd have to rise thirty feet to get it past those cliffs."

"I'm certain that's how it got in here," Glen said.

"By accident?" Walt asked.

"I think they were escaping a storm. When they found themselves trapped as the storm ended, they panicked and fled on their longboats. But where to? I couldn't guess," Glen said.

"How seaworthy can it be?" Walt asked. "It's probably been here at least fifty years."

After the two men examined the ship inside and out, they returned to the graveyard and spent the next number of months discussing and debating the value of pursuing the repair of the ship. Glen proposed calling it the *Rosemary*. He called it that so many times Walt gave in and the project ship became the *Rosemary*.

During one of the many visits to the ship, Glen found a small gold coin on the gun deck. The gun deck fascinated him the most. There sat forty-six rusted cannons, one even fallen through the rotted floor. He brushed off the coin and slipped it into his pocket. When back up above decks, he shined it on his pant and held it in the light. He recognized the image. He knew enough to read Aurangzeb 1674.

Several months later, they let Sal in on their secret ship project. They needed his muscle and skills as a smithy. He thought them nuts to even consider preparing a second ship. There was no logical reason to spend energy preparing a ship for sea if they could never set it free to sail. And why would they? The *Bringhurst* was in fit shape as soon as they had the water level to float her.

But the idea that they needed him intrigued him. These two men, Glen and Walt, who could do anything, needed him, Sal, a mere smithy. The fact this particular ship was a secret mission made it even more intriguing.

It was never articulated, but the real purpose of the project's secrecy was their lack of trust in Hunter. Each of them felt if Hunter knew, it would undermine the success. There was nothing good about Hunter.

Glen knew Sal looked forward to the surprise when these people realize Glen was dead serious about leaving the island. He turned to see if Sal was smiling. The rain was too strong to see frown or smile. His only worry was now getting Rags to the fort and then over the cliff and down to the ship.

Chapter Ninety~Three

On the Trail - The Island - 1748

Joanna tried to stay at Rags' side as much as the trail allowed. Mostly the path was so narrow she stayed just ahead or just behind Jack and Walt who managed the narrow cart.

The group approached the part of the trail Glen feared the most. Above them two of the sheer rock cliffs appeared to come together as they formed a narrow canyon. The rain falling on the rugged rocks collected in a small valley carved over the centuries. With this harsh rain, Glen knew it was only a matter of time before that small valley filled and discharged its concentrated accumulation of water in a torrent through the narrow canyon and down this hill.

Above the cry of the wind and rain, he felt the earth move. His cry of warning lost in the wind, he planted his feet as best he could in the slick mud.

The deluge surged down the hills onto the path directly in front of Rags and his cart.

Glen watched in horror as the water washed sections of the path away with it.

Unable to react, Jack's feet slipped with the mudslide, tearing him away from the cart and down the hill.

At the other side, Walt hung on with every ounce of strength, but it was obvious his grip was slipping, both on the cart and the remnants of the muddy path.

"Hold on!" Glen shouted, though his words were largely lost in the roar of the wind. Feet slipping clumsily he tried to get back to help.

Louisa and Joanna both scrambled over the flooded earth to reach Rags' stretcher as it tipped down the hill with the flow of the water.

Joanna made it first, getting a solid grasp and footing. She pulled it back onto the path. Glen breathed out in relief.

Too soon. The moment he turned back toward Jack to help him up the hill, another torrent of water swept the path, this time washing out both Walt and Joanna.

It was like living a nightmare where everything seemed slow. Walt skidded down the hill. The cart tipped. The water and sliding earth took both Rags and Joanna over the edge. Thrown from the cart, Joanna grabbed Rags and held him close, tumbling end over end.

Their plummet stopped when Joanna's thin body slammed into a tree, cushioning Rags from the impact.

"Joanna!" Louisa called. "Rags!" More words lost in the storm.

Walt crawled back up to the path, coated in mud.

"Where are they?" he asked. "Are they okay?"

"They went down hard and far," Louisa answered in a pitch that was markedly higher than her usual.

"Tie the rope to that tree!" Glen shouted, as he tossed one end to Walt.

Slipping and sliding down the steepest part of the muddy hill, Glen didn't keep his feet. He slid down on his backside.

Glen reached the wreck of the cart, which fortunately landed on top of the two, the pocket of air it provided saving them from drowning. He pulled it free as the flood of mud continued to pour down the hill then quickly lifted their heads out of the torrent.

Joanna coughed and took in a breath that was a bit too shallow. It was a breath, though.

"Rags?" she asked, no sound coming from her, but he read the name on her lips.

The hurt man moaned a bit, but didn't move at all.

"Alive!" Glen called back up the hill. "Hurt, but alive!" No one heard him but the wind.

Sliding down the secured rope, Jack arrived, taking Joanna into his arms and securing himself against another tree. The continued flow of mud and water pinned him in place. The small tree wouldn't hold long.

Glen pulled Rags up out of the flow. Walt arrived tethered to a second rope. Step by miserable step, Glen and Walt climbed and secured Rags back up onto the trail. Louisa and Ben cleared the mud from his face, and with a makeshift umbrella held over him, Rags breathed evenly again.

Sliding back down the hill, Glen and Walt extracted Joanna from Jack's clutches just as the tree gave way to the flood, washing Jack and the tree further down the hill. With free hands, Jack grabbed another tree's limb just as it also gave way to his weight. As he slid, bouncing from tree to rock, he painfully worked his way across out of the main current. He raised his face to the pounding rain to wash away the mud holding his mouth and nose hostage.

Joanna was limp in their grasp. She was breathing but was badly hurt. Neither of them could get a secure footing. Losing ground with each step they trudged down through the torrent until the broken mountain let go. Without the ropes all three would have been washed away. As gently as possible, Glen and Walt worked their way back toward the path as the mountain continued to cascade away. Joanna was dead weight. Both men knew she could easily be lost. When they finally made it to solid ground, Glen's strength was spent. Louisa attended to Joanna's bleeding head and arms. The bones between her knee and ankle broke clean. Her foot and ankle dangled loose. It would be a long time before she walked again.

Glen held Joanna in his arms until she was breathing evenly. She probably had several broken ribs as well, and likely more he thought. Joanna's sacrifice saved Rags but at what a cost! How he wished he had his pack full of medications. The rain continued to pound, and the wind made it impossible to speak or call for help. As Glen tried to stand, Louisa placed her hand on his shoulder for him to sit back down. Louisa pulled a small cask from her shoulder bag and held it to Joanna's lips. The injured woman took a sip, and within a few minutes, her muscles relaxed. The sedative took over, and the pain was gone.

Louisa helped Glen up, carefully now with Joanna in his arms. Jack and Walt carried Rags cradled in the sail fabric rescued from the shattered cart. United again, the group continued their trek. No one questioned they had to get to the fort before nightfall. The storm's intensity continued growing by the minute. No one talked. None of them had the strength. Their voices wouldn't carry in the wind, anyway. Hour after hour they trudged forward through the wind, rain, mud and exhaustion.

As darkness completely obliterated the trail, a light moved back and forth, waving well out ahead of them.

That light was enough to give the group a sliver of hope as they trudged one foot ahead of the other seeking to find solid ground with each step. The door to the fort opened and the group saw its light spilling out to guide the last few steps safely out of the storm. Once everyone was inside, Rosemary pulled the door closed and the group collapsed with exhaustion.

Rosemary immediately attended to Joanna, while Walt and Louisa attended to Rags. As Sal assessed the two invalids, he wondered how they were going to get them off the cliffs and down to the *Rosemary.*

The fort proved to be the lifesaver they built it to be. When the door was opened in the morning, the hillside was completely destroyed, wiped so clean they could see clear to the lagoon past where Glen's home once stood. The only thing still standing was his stone oven. They pulled the doors closed. The eye of the storm gave them a brief window to make the next leg of this journey.

Joanna was now conscious. She refused more of Louisa's elixir, insisting they keep what was left for Rags. He, too, was conscious, but considerably quiet. Though Joanna took the brunt of the fall, Rags sustained considerable bruises and a few cuts. While Joanna was unconscious, with Sal's and Jack's help, Glen did his best to set and splint her leg. Her many bruises frightened them that there might be more damage they couldn't see.

Rosemary provided a lifesaving broth and breads the night before and now they were eating dried fish and coconut milk from the fort's stores.

Glen stepped outside one more time, this time with Sal and Walt. They assessed the storm and decided it was time to go. The front of the storm passed during the night and if they were going to chase this storm, now was the time.

"Let's go home," Glen said. "If we want off this island, now is the time."

The thought was hopeful and frightening to the group.

"The *Bringhurst* was plan A. The *Rosemary* is Plan B. You know, we've been working on a backup ship in the graveyard," Glen said. "You've all been to it."

"We're sailing that thing in a hurricane? Wouldn't swim be a better word than sail?" Ben asked.

Glen smiled, appreciative his, Walt's and Sal's other efforts on a second back-up plan remained somewhat covert.

"Ben, you couldn't be more right," Glen said, "but if you continue a couple hundred yards around the windward side of the island, there's a tiny lagoon. Trapped inside was a three-masted frigate, severely damaged and stranded. Undoubtedly during a similar storm as this, its captain sailed it into the harbor for protection only to find, once the storm water receded it stranded them as it did the *Bringhurst*. Only a major storm will free it from the lagoon. Just like the *Bringhurst*."

Walt interjected a few word to complete Glen's statement. "We've spent months repairing it. Glen named it the *Rosemary,* and it's ready to sail."

Glen continued, "We have to get to it and get out of the lagoon before the storm surge subsides and leaves it imprisoned once again. I am sorry, Joanna and Rags. It is going to be painful when we lower you over a cliff and swim you to the ship."

He stopped speaking and the fort was quiet.

"You named a ship the *Rosemary?*" Rosemary whispered to Glen. "Why not the *Marge* or the *Louisa?*"

Glen shook his head in disbelief. We're getting off this island, it will probably get Rags and Joanna killed, the storm will likely sink the ship, and we'll all drown, and the name of the ship was all she wondered about?

He smiled and answered, "let's go home."

They packed up. Fresh packs Sal created for each of them were stored in the fort. There were harnesses to be connected to the large rope he fashioned to raise and lower certain supplies down the cliff. During the many months of repair, Walt, Glen and Sal transported most of the physical materials they scavenged from the ships in the graveyard using a small barge they built. With the barge, they floated those materials around the cliffs to the lagoon.

There was no way they could transport people in the stormy ocean that same way. They knew when it was time to go, it would be during a storm and over the cliffs.

Sal crafted the harness system using pulleys and jibs from the ships in the graveyard. The challenge was the reliability of the many aged weather-worn ropes they'd spliced together in order to reach the water from over the cliffs.

The group made its way toward the cliffs. Instead of its fury increasing by the hour, the storm seemed at rest for the moment. The eye of the storm, they thought. After several hours of climbing, they reached the cliff's edge. The eye passed. Howling winds returned, silencing the collective gasp as the group looked into the lagoon and saw the *Rosemary* sitting majestically anchored in the middle of it. Looking down at the sheer rock surface, fear replaced the soreness, the discomfort, and the discouragement.

Sal took charge and began lowering supplies and bodies over the edge. Glen went first. He made it look easy as he splashed into the lagoon and connected the barge to the ship with a large rope. Rosemary clasped the baby as they lowered her off the cliff. There was no beach. The storm erased it when the water level rose, lifting the Rosemary from its sleep. When she reached the water level, the small barge met her and the baby. Glen helped her and the baby on and pulled it to the ship's edge. She carefully climbed the wooden ladder fashioned from stairs taken off a Dutch schooner.

Before signaling Sal to raise the rope, Glen checked the whipping and splices. So far, so good. None of the ropes from the *Bringhurst* or the remnants of any ship in the graveyard were long or strong enough to give Glen certain confidence in their splices. As any of the splices passed through the pulleys, he feared their loss of strength would multiply with each additional pass.

Next came Jack and Joanna. Jack held her close, trying to keep himself between her and the cliff wall. Occasional gusts slammed the passengers against the cliff. The wind was too strong to let the grunts and groans be audible, but they certainly were there. Only once did the wind spin him before it pounded the two against the rock; Joanna taking the brunt of the blow.

Glen had the barge ready when they reached the water and the two men swam the barge to the ship. With Rosemary's help, they lifted Joanna to safety.

When they began the evacuation, the lagoon was somewhat calm for being in the middle of a hurricane. The cliff walls provided considerable protection. But now, the sea in the lagoon was experiencing the wrath of the storm. The water became more turbulent.

Again, Glen inspected sections of the ropes as he could. He regretted he was the first person down while the ropes were at their best.

The twins came down with Louisa and Marge. The two women took the bumps and slams with courage. With Jack's help, they quickly made it onboard. Glen climbed up the rope to test a splice he'd considered the weakest. It showed its wear. Ropes were not his only concern. The platform supporting the pulleys was secured with sturdy ropes tied to stakes pounded into seams in the stones. He knew as the wind twisted and pulled on each passenger; the ropes, the stakes, the pulleys, and the platform itself would be tested.

Ben and Susan, not large people, came next with no complications. Only a few expected bumps and bruises. The test was now to come. They hadn't tested for two full size men, especially if one were as robust as Walt.

Just as the turbulence in the lagoon increased, blinding wind at the top of the cliffs forced Sal and Walt to hold tightly to the platform to prevent being blown off the slippery stone. The platform shifted from its place on the edge of the cliff. Stakes held it from plummeting over the edge, but nothing held it from sliding back towards the stakes. There was no time to waste.

Walt readied to take Rags down. Sliding over the edge the full weight of the two men pulled the platform back into position at the edge of the cliff, straining the grip the ropes had on the stakes. Sal gave all his strength to keep the two men from plunging down. A support beam holding the pulley cracked. Sal couldn't hear it over the wailing wind and rain but he saw tension in the ropes struggle to tear it loose.

The wind and rain obscured Glen's vision of the landing at the top of the cliff. He knew Rags and Walt were next. This was the test. He had Jack pull the barge back to the ship in case the ropes failed and the two men plunged into the water.

The two men came into view, as did the failing splices of rope. Between bursts of wind and rain, Glen watched as Walt repeatedly slammed against the rock wall. Sal designed the double harness to hold an adult and a child, not two adults. Glen knew that if they took any more furious slams against the rock wall, if they made it at all, their bodies would either be mush or broken fleshy lumps. They continued down.

As the two men neared the water Glen signaled to Jack, and the barge came over to carry the two to the ship. Rags proved to be more challenging than Joanna. Though he had the frail use of legs, his weight and size demanded everything a bruised and exhausted Walt and Jack had to give.

Sal was left alone on the cliff's edge. One more man, Glen pleaded to heaven. One more man.

Sal would come down on his own power. They'd practiced a few times but never in the wind and rain, and only with fresh ropes. Glen floated, struggling to keep his head above the turbulent water, he hoped, and prayed, while waiting to pick up his last passenger. The rope began to move. Though Glen couldn't see past the storm to the top of the cliff, Sal was on his way down. Hope increased.

After several smooth minutes, the rope stopped moving. Through the rain Glen spotted Sal about halfway up the cliff wall, his descent stopped. Glen tugged on the rope. He couldn't be heard, so he didn't even try to yell up to Sal. After a few minutes, he assumed the rope at the top of the cliff jammed. Sal could climb down the rope, Glen knew, but if he were attached to a harness, it would be extremely difficult to get out without falling. To climb to his aid would strain the ropes to complete failure. The turmoil in his head was as violent as the turbulence in the lagoon. Glen decided to try anyway.

Hand over hand with bare hands and slippery feet, Glen inched up the rope. When Sal recognized Glen was coming to his aid, he tried to wave him off.

A sudden jolt dropped both men about four feet. Glen slid back down the rope a dozen feet before his grip held. It wasn't the ropes, he realized, it was the platform supporting the pulleys. Sal was trying to get out of the harness before the platform failed, but with the wind pounding him into the cliff walls, it was difficult holding onto the rope with one hand and fighting the harness with the other.

His weight did not help. Glen had to let go. Too late, the platform holding the pulleys cracked free, releasing the ropes, the pulleys, the jibs, and shattered beams, all of them chasing Sal and Glen into the sea.

Sinking to the bottom of the lagoon, Glen caught his bearings and pushed to the surface. He was breathless, but couldn't leave Sal tangled on the bottom. A big breath and back down he went.

Tangled in ropes, Sal wrestled to get free. The harness he so cleverly designed held him captive. The tension held him fast to the ocean floor. The ropes and pulleys provided no buoyancy. The breath he took before the plunge was spent, as was his strength. Looking to the surface one last time, he saw one more splash. Like in a dream, Sal saw, knife in hand, a virtual mermaid cut the harness loose, slice through the tangled ropes, and pull him free of the fetters. Just as Glen arrived to help, the last rope denying its captive freedom was severed. As the three men reached the surface gasping, Jack sputtered, "Now we can go home."

Chapter Ninety~Four

Onboard the Sally - Secluded Harbor - 1748

Elizabeth froze in place. A thousand emotions flooded through her.

She reached for the spectacles, and taking them in her hands, brushed the dust and rolled them over and over in her hands, absorbing every detail. She opened the Bible to a page bookmarked in St. Matthew, Chapter 5 Verse 44.

> "But I say unto you, Love your enemies, bless them
> that curse you, do good to them that hate you, and pray
> for them which despitefully use you, and persecute you."

Her father gave his life protecting women, on a galley ship off the coast of Libya. This was that ship, she realized.

"What is it?" Lydia asked, noticing the color drain from Elizabeth's frozen face.

Despite the passage of scripture her father underlined in the Bible, she yanked the knife from Lydia and practically pounced on Krist, knocking the breath out of him as she held the knife to his throat. This time Lydia was wide eyed, shocked at Elizabeth's reaction.

"Where did these come from?" Elizabeth said, holding the spectacles in front of Krist's eyes.

"Maybe a previous passenger? I wouldn't know," he said.

"How did you get this ship?" she asked, digging the blade into his throat. Small drops of blood seeped from around its tip.

"We traded cargo for this ship. We didn't seize it."

"What was its name?"

"The Lost Dutchman," he coughed.

"What was the cargo?"

"Slaves. What is this all about? You are about to either lacerate my throat or puncture a lung." He tried to breathe as Elizabeth knelt on his chest.

"What happened to the passengers and crew?" She did not get off him.

"Some stayed with us, others went ashore," he exhaled.

"Nobody was hurt?" she demanded.

"There were three. They objected to our trade."

"The trade?"

"We kept two female passengers."

The blade drew more blood.

"A man and two others objected. My father shot them and threw the bodies overboard," Krist choked out under Elizabeth's threat.

"That man was my father! Yes! You are my prisoner."

With that, Elizabeth slid off him, and with both hands, shoved Krist into the small compartment and slammed it closed.

She jammed the knife into the compartment's door. It hung there shaking as Elizabeth struggled to calm her breathing. Lydia sat frozen, staring.

Chapter Ninety~Five

The Hidden Lagoon - The Island - 1748

Broken up by the towering cliffs, the winds inside the lagoon gusted in every direction. As the *Rosemary* jerked under the power of the chaotic wind, it lurched forward and backward and leaned starboard and port like a small rodent trying to outmaneuver an attacking predator. Only its anchor kept it from crashing headlong into the sheer rock walls.

They waited. Hours passed. The storm raged. Outside the protection of the lagoon, the gale force winds could easily destroy the weathered sails. Jack wondered what Glen wouldn't give for a crew large enough and experienced enough to man the ship. Soon enough, he'd test the condition of the half-rotted ship and his little band of sailors. Jack knew a ship this size could easily keep a crew of a hundred men or more busy, especially if the guns were ever required.

As he walked the main deck it was evident to Jack the modifications performed by experienced shipwrights converted this ship to be fast and nimble. This was becoming more of an adventure than he'd had in any summer spent with his uncle. Once he got below to the gun decks, a giant smile spread across his face at the realization.

A pirate ship, this is a pirate ship!

The small crew stood ready. Sal assured them the repair and rebuild of the *Rosemary* was as solid as they could make it with such limited resources. Everyone knew Glen was anxious to pursue the ship that took his Lydia. They recognized his experience with the storm that landed them on this island, justified his current caution. There was no reason to escape the island, only to find a watery grave. In their preparations, Glen and Walt calculated the point where the receding storm surge demanded action. After several anxious hours, the water reached it and they pulled anchor.

At the helm, Glen navigated between the two stone towers and immediately called to reduce sails as they became free of the prison the *Rosemary* inhabited for so many years.

The small crew proved to be quite adept. Jack climbed, tied, pulled, and descended the ropes with such agility, he knew it betrayed the innocence-at-sea image he tried to project. Glen smiled as he watched. Even Ben showed promise as a sailor. The years of preparation, instruction, and hope now produced fruits of its labor. The island soon disappeared behind them.

They were off the island! That relief was short lived. Glen was on the immediate lookout for signs of any island where the galley ship may have taken refuge from the storm.

Powered by the tail of the storm, the *Rosemary* sailed at half sail most of the day. Waves and rain pounded the ship. By nightfall, the storm edged off to the west. The winds and surf lessened enough, Glen called for full sail and the *Rosemary*, at about nine knots, sailed due north. A large crack became evident in the foremast with the first gust against its sails. He immediately lowered its sails.

A break in the clouds allowed a sliver of moonlight to penetrate the darkness.

The lack of conversation, the lack of questions, the lack of concern, the dedication of each passenger to their duty onboard absolutely fascinated Jack. It was as if they had all trained for this day. Louisa and Marge took turns caring for Rags and Joanna, helping on deck as well. Rosemary kept the children safe and Susan worked alongside Ben as a deckhand.

"You've been here before," Jack said as he approached Glen at the helm.

"So have you." Glen said.

Jack's eyes, which were barely discernible in the near darkness, questioned Glen's statement.

"I estimate this is about where they captured the *Emerald*." Glen said. "If I'm right, and this wind holds, we can reach Antigua by nightfall tomorrow. Isn't that where you were headed?"

Jack never discussed their destination and so was very interested in how Glen would know.

"Did you ever see your captors?" Glen asked.

"No, actually I didn't."

"Could they be Persian?"

"Persian?"

"Just a hunch."

Jack stood there in awe. Captain Remington may have underestimated his sailor friend, he thought.

"Tell me what the pirates looked like. The ones that took my Lydia and your Elizabeth."

"Well," Jack reflected. "They looked like any other sailors, dirty, ugly, and dangerous. You saw them. Six lay dead back in the lagoon."

"Not them, their captain. Nothing stood out?"

"Their captain held himself with confidence, the others with arrogance and hate. A subtle difference maybe. Actually, he looked like you, except with pistols across his chest and a cutlass instead of a machete."

"He looked like me?"

"Well, lighter hair, different complexion, same build though, but younger. Just as confident. Hair was longer. I guess we didn't get close enough to see much detail, but I did look twice to make sure it wasn't you."

Jack remembered how he thought the ship that attacked the *Emerald* was Portuguese with Middle Eastern engravings. But the galley that took Lydia and Elizabeth was not the same ship that attacked the *Emerald,* he was sure of that.

"I feared the captain might be Persian." Glen said. "When we find them, and we will, we'll find out how much you love Elizabeth. Even if you've only been tangled up with her for a week."

A week? Try a summer, a torturously painful summer!

"How?" Was all he got out before Glen continued.

"The only ship that could find our island is a galley. With little wind, no current to speak of, they're hunting. Think. Why would pirates be hunting for an uncharted island? No ships would be out here. It was a man-of-war that took yours last week, not that galley. Why was that galley out here?"

"Well," Jack started. Again, Glen continued before Jack could get a whole sentence out.

"They're hunting for two things. Jack, they're hunting for the same thing you are."

"I'm hunting for something?"

"We all are, Jack. You're not a sailor. You're smarter than any I've sailed with. But you've studied. My guess is you have been taught. But you came down here looking for something."

Jack couldn't believe this man could guess so well.

"What are you hunting for?" Glen asked.

Jack figured there was no reason to hide his past, nor his present.

"It's a who, not a what." Jack said. "And right now, I think 'was hunting' is more accurate."

"I thought so," Glen said. "Who's payroll are you on? There's only two I can think of. One kidnapped my daughter and your fiancé. The other is the East India Company who still wants to find Avery and his treasure."

"There's a third," Jack said.

"A third?" Glen asked.

"Captain Remington of the HMS *Kent.*"

"He's looking for me?" Glen asked, grinning. "I should have known."

"We were supposed to meet in Antigua last week," Jack said.

"So he's down here in the West Indies? Now that's great news," Glen said. "We will need his ship."

The wind and water were still violent, but not so much so that Glen needed to cut back on sails. His target was Antigua. A friendly and familiar port. Most importantly, the track of this storm appeared to be to the west of Antigua.

Nearly two years late, they would finally make it.

Chapter Ninety~Six

Onboard the Rosemary Open Sea - West Indies - 1748

As the seas calmed ever so slightly, Rosemary made her way on deck.

"So this is the other woman in your life?"

"You like her?" Glen asked proudly.

"She's beautiful. A woman could get jealous, you know. Her man spending so much time with another woman."

"That's why I named her the *Rosemary*. Only one woman for me."

"What about Sal and Walt? Don't you think Marge and Louisa object to their husbands spending so much time with the *Rosemary*?"

"Sal thought 'the *Marge*' sounded like a barge and 'the *Louisa*' was ok but didn't have the romance that the *Rosemary* had," he said somewhat unconvincingly.

"We're renaming this ship. If we ever arrive anywhere calm and dry," Rosemary said without a question in her voice. "Maybe, *'The Shellie.'*"

"We'll be calm and dry by tomorrow night," he promised.

"You continue to amaze me! But I don't want calm and dry. I want Lydia back!"

"That, I promise!"

"Then, I have a few questions about a journal, and in particular, an entry on its last page," Rosemary said. "And this ship. Have I read about it somewhere?"

Chapter Ninety~Seven

Clare's Tavern - St. John's, Antigua - 1748

"If the *Emerald* was out in that storm, I wouldn't plan on seeing it again. And if it wasn't, we have other troubles," Lucas said as Remington entered Clare's tavern.

Lucas got up and stepped outside. Remington took his seat.

"Have you ever sailed through a storm like that?" Clare asked.

"A few, but not in the heart of one. We lost a ship anchored in harbor when one passed right over us," Remington said. "They're merciless."

"I am sorry," Clare said to Captain Remington. "The storm missed us and it still did a lot of damage." She was cleaning up debris that blew through a smashed window.

"Did we learn anything more about Amos' friends?" he asked.

"I haven't seen him since before the storm," Clare said.

"He sailed to St. Martin to meet friends," Remington said thoughtfully. "I thought he'd be back by now. Have you been through a storm like this one?"

"This is the worst I've seen personally. The last big one devastated the whole area just before I arrived," Clare answered.

"If we don't have word of the Emerald within a few days, we'll consider it lost," Remington finally said with a sigh of resignation, his head shaking lightly.

"Who is on the *Emerald* you're waiting for?"

"An agent."

"An agent for HMS or for you?" Clare asked.

Over the past two years, every time the HMS *Kent* came to port, Clare got a visit. A bit of His Majesty's business and then the captain would meet with his agents to see if they'd learned anything about his personal mission. With the *Emerald* lost, he hoped Jack kept his word and stayed put in England. But he couldn't give up on Jack bringing him the information gathered from the old man in the Nookery.

"Is your agent an HMS agent or a Remington agent?" she asked again.

Captain Remington was accustomed to Clare's frank approach, but she had never inquired about his official business and little about his personal business. She knew he grew up in the Royal Navy and was a very respected captain. His beautiful wife, as he described her, bore him three lovely daughters.

One of his daughters was engaged to marry a naval officer. Another, according to the captain, "Was too much like him and had the mind to wander the world." She planned to live in America when she became of age. The third studied at Oxford, interested in law. Other than this bit of personal knowledge, all Clare knew about the captain was that he loved her cooking. And bless his soul, he told everyone about it.

"Both," Remington answered.

Just as Clare was about to pry more, Lucas re-entered the tavern, announcing the arrival of the *Hopwell* in port. Remington jumped up. He and Lucas charged out toward the wharf. There wasn't much happening in the tavern, so Clare joined them.

The sun hung lazily in the late afternoon sky as the *Hopwell* was tied up at the wharf and Amos quickly disembarked. The captain and Lucas met him immediately. Only then did they notice Clare right behind them.

"My news is not good, and surely not for everyone's ears," Amos said, motioning to follow him back to the tavern.

As they turned to leave, the captain saw a speck on the horizon. He stood motionless and watched as the speck grew. It was a race between the sun setting and a ship reaching the harbor.

"Amos, did you have bad news for me?" he asked as they stood watching this mystery ship take shape on the horizon.

"A Persian Man-of-War captured and sank the *Emerald*," Amos said.

"The same one we've chased across the globe?"

"Likely."

"We guessed right, it's coming to these waters."

"Slavers?" Clare asked.

Remington nodded.

"Fate of the passengers?" he asked.

"Unknown. But it's likely they're now merchandise," Amos said.

"Anyone know where they are?"

"Rumor has it an island west of Montserrat."

"Can any of your friends take us there?"

"None have been there. The location is a guess."

Through the choppy interrogation, Remington's eyes never left the mystery ship as it approached the harbor. As it got closer, he squinted to make out the sails. Something seemed familiar.

"What is it?" Lucas asked.

"Something I haven't seen in a long time," the captain said almost reverently. "The foremast must be broken. The captain's favoring it. A skill rare among sailors."

"Even I know not to put stress on a damaged mast," Lucas said. "What's so special with this one?"

"The bowsprit. Look how it's set upright and tied to the stump of the original mast. Those knots, the way the makeshift stays and shrouds support the jury mast, I've only seen that once before." Remington's smile covered his face from ear to ear.

The ship rested right behind the *Hopewell*. Two men jumped off and tied it up. By the time the ramp was in place, Remington, Lucas, and Clare stood alongside.

Remington, in uniform and though he had no port authority, approached the men tying off the ship.

"What ship is this?"

"The *Rosemary*."

"From where?"

"Hell."

"Who is the captain?"

"Captain Glen," Walt said.

"Who's asking?" bellowed the captain standing at the top of the ramp.

For what seemed like a lifetime, Glen and Remington stood smiling at each other. Finally, Remington bounded up the ramp and took Glen in an embrace twenty years overdue.

As they released the embrace, another passenger caught Remington's eye. Jack smiled at his uncle. A smile conceding to his uncle's earlier insistence that Jack wasn't made for the academic life.

"I should have known," Glen said, watching the two embrace.

"How?" was all Captain Remington could ask.

All the passengers on deck watched this reunion.

Tipping his head toward the HMS *Kent* sitting at anchor in the harbor and interrupting the reunion between Jack and his uncle, Glen asked, "The *Kent's* still yours?"

Remington nodded affirmatively, releasing his embrace.

"I need it," Glen said, just as casually as if he were asking for a refill of rum while the two played a friendly game of whist.

Remington was about to answer when Rosemary, the baby in arms and the twins at her side, stepped up to Glen's side.

"You two friends?" Rosemary said.

"Does she know?" Remington asked.

"She's about to," Glen answered.

"Glen sailed the world with me before you caught him," Remington explained. Then turning to Glen, added. "She's beautiful, and three beautiful children. I don't blame you for abandoning me."

"Thank you. And four," Glen said.

"Four?" asked Remington.

"Four, and that's why I need the *Kent*," Glen said firmly. "They took my Lydia."

"And my Elizabeth," Jack said.

"Elizabeth?" Remington asked, turning to Jack.

"Elizabeth," Rags said. "You will love her."

Joanna sat with her broken leg propped on a barrel tipped on its side. At Jack's mention of Elizabeth, which was the first time his fiancé was spoken of by name in her presence, Joanna leaned into the conversation and repeated the name, "Elizabeth?"

Both Glen and Jack turned their attention to her pleading eyes. As much as this reunion surprised everyone, there was urgent business at hand. Rosemary gently placed her hand on Glen's arm and pulled him back into the urgency of her daughter. "Glen... Lydia."

Glen turned squarely to Captain Remington. "Half a dozen men took my daughter and Jack's fiancé Elizabeth..." he looked back to Joanna, validating her question, "...sailing a galley just before the hurricane hit. We've got to find them."

Jack interjected, "My guess is it's captained by your Persian."

"Let's get all these people settled and we can talk—it's a long story," Glen said anxiously.

Chapter Ninety~Eight

St. John's Harbor - Antigua - 1748

"Lars?"

A scream brought everything to a halt. Everyone turned.

Clare crossed the deck and in one bound took Rags in her arms, yanking him from the support provided by Marge and Louisa. He winced as she hugged him. She was so animated to find him alive, she didn't notice. In the few short days since the attack, he'd healed enough to walk with a little support. His face was still badly bruised.

She finally let go and pulled away to look at him.

"You're late!" she said, and squeezed him again.

The pain forced a groan.

Louisa came to his rescue.

"I hope you're Clare. Rags is still tender."

"Rags?" Clare lightened the grip and took another look at him. "You look like a rag. What happened?"

"He sacrificed himself protecting Elizabeth and Lydia," Marge said.

Clare tilted her head, and squinting one eye, asked, "Did he tear off their dresses?"

"What?" Louisa asked.

"That's how he saved me!" Clare said. "He's like that." She took him again in her arms.

Ben and Susan helped with Joanna, and Clare, with Rags in tow, carefully led everyone to her tavern.

They entered the tavern. The rich textures of the window coverings featured patterns from Ireland. Rags smiled. Heavy wooden tables filled the large open room. A small fire burned in the large hearth under an enormous kettle hanging from an iron hook. An intricately carved frame wrapped around the large mirror above the fireplace made the tavern look more spacious.

"This is yours?" Rags asked.

"Ours," Clare said proudly.

As everyone settled, Clare brought food. Despite all the catching up taking place with long-awaited reunions between former shipmates, a bride and groom to be, uncle and nephew, the one reunion that took center stage was between Remington and his spy, Amos.

Amos described the governor of a small island west of Montserat by the name of Ali Mutarid Hassan.

Almost in sync, Jack, Captain Remington, and Glen said: "Nakhoda."

"He has a small fleet of ships, a productive plantation, and profitable slave business," Amos said.

"The *Chawbuck*," Captain Remington said.

"And a galley," Amos said. "Reports are the man-of-war captured the Emerald."

As Amos shared what he learned from his fellow spies, questions were raised and answered. The scene took shape, much like it would if a painter were creating a great masterpiece.

"Is the *Kent* ready to sail?" Glen asked. "How many men do you have?"

"Not so fast, my dear friend," Remington said.

"That galley took my daughter," Glen said.

Rags was part of the discussion, but didn't contribute much. Mostly he asked the obvious questions no one else was brave enough to ask. The question about what the pirates were looking for was yet to be considered. This was where Rags excelled.

"Glen, they came to the island looking for you. Why?" Rags asked.

Everyone turned to Rags, then to Glen. The question was kind, but challenging. Coming from Rags, it was innocent enough, but Glen knew someone would eventually ask it. "Bless your heart, Rags," Rosemary said.

For years, Glen avoided answering similar questions. For a few years, his hidden past was a point of contention between him and Rosemary.

He was preparing to tell Rosemary everything before it all came apart at the island. She now had the journal, and knew there was much more to Glen than she ever knew before. But he didn't have to share it all. Yet.

Though this consideration took only seconds in Glen's mind, everybody waited without a sound. It was Remington who broke the awkward silence.

"Cav, it's the Blade of Safavid isn't it?" Remington asked.

Glen looked around the tavern. Each of these people knew a piece of the puzzle. So, how much to tell? he wondered. "Many years ago, a pirate fleet captured the Mughal Emperor's treasure ship," He began. "Captained by Avery in the *Fancy*. You all know the story. Even after a worldwide manhunt, only a few of Avery's crew were ever captured and tried. Their testimonies didn't provide clues to find the treasure or Avery.

"For fifty years, treasure hunters from scores of nations scoured these islands in search of Avery and the Mughal treasure. At one point, I was one of them. I had the benefit of sailing with one of His Majesties' finest Naval Officers, Captain Joseph Remington."

"That's where you learned it," Sal muttered.

"Right when I thought I was on the trail, I encountered a competitor in Newton Ferrers. A brutal competitor, a Persian by the name of Ali Mutarid Hassan. His trade? White female slaves for the harems in the Ottoman empire. I watched him kill innocent people to get the information I had. That's when I abandoned my quest. That night I chose to disappear."

"How did that stop his killing or slaving?" Clare asked.

"It didn't. But I knew he would follow my trail, leaving behind death and destruction wherever I went. Some of those victims would be people I loved. No treasure was worth that. I had to vanish and stay away from ports he might visit," Glen said.

Walt sat motionless, elbows on the table, fingers cupped over his cheeks, hands supporting his jaw. The story enthralled him as much as anyone.

"And you came to Sheffield to build musical instruments?" Walt said, shaking his head. And weapons, he thought, but didn't say. "What a career change."

The baby was fast asleep in Rosemary's arms and the twins were surprisingly engaged with their father's revelation. Glen knew they likely didn't understand the importance of all this, but they always loved listening to the wonderful stories he told them at bedtime. Bedtime stories that included heroes and rescues and daring sailors in exotic ports around the world. Rosemary whispered to herself, "Those bedtime stories were true."

"What about Hassan?" Ben asked.

"He never gave up his quest," Glen said. "I failed. He has my daughter."

"How old would he be?" Jack asked.

"By now… seventy? Eighty?" Glen answered.

"Seventy or eighty? The pirates that took Lydia and Elizabeth were too young to be him," Jack said.

"It's him," Glen said. "That was his galley. His men."

"And now he's got Lydia and Elizabeth," Rosemary said, almost in tears. "Why did we leave the safety of Sheffield?"

This was a question he wanted to answer in private, but he knew her heart couldn't be held back any longer. A filthy pirate who sells young white girls to wicked men kidnapped her daughter. She was being torn apart. If he answered honestly, it would destroy another heart.

Another answered instead. "Hunter," Joanna said.

Joanna wasn't much of a talker. For two years on the island, she was part of only a handful of conversations. She was likable enough, somewhat attractive, but lived as alone as she could. Her alleged husband, Hunter, was disliked by everyone. Because she knew it, it was too uncomfortable to be part of the small society on the island.

Glen was always kind and Rosemary went out of her way to have a relationship with Joanna, even though it was difficult. Rosemary was the only one who knew she and Hunter were not actually married, and Joanna's fear of him angered Rosemary. Joanna never talked of being abused, but Rosemary knew otherwise.

More than once Rosemary invited her to leave him and join them in the cove. She always refused. Many times, Rosemary shared her feelings with Glen about Joanna. She hated what fear did to people. She felt that fear was like the brakes on a wagon, like shackles on a horse, like a cage for a bird. Fear kept people from becoming what they could be. She knew Joanna had great talents, talents that would be appreciated by everyone on the island. She could contribute so much. She knew Joanna would love to contribute. It was fear that imprisoned her.

"Hunter?" Louisa asked.

Joanna was in tears, but continued, "You left Sheffield because of Hunter. You all knew there was something wrong. Hunter is a spy for Hassan." Joanna, with her broken leg up on a chair and leaning on Marge, wiped tears from her cheeks. Nobody spoke.

"I didn't know," Joanna continued. "I didn't know why we left Sheffield so suddenly. When I saw all of you on the *Bringhurst* in Liverpool, it scared me. That is when I realized who he was spying on. My heart was sick. For days, all I could do was cry and pray."

"When I went to tell Glen, Hunter threatened me that if I did, he would hurt the children. I couldn't let him do that. And now he has your Lydia." She buried her face in her hands. Her shoulders shook as she wept. When her breathing calmed, she again wiped tears from her cheeks, and with reddened eyes, turned to Glen and said, "I am so sorry. You must have suspected him, or why else would you run?"

Glen's eyes were fixed on the woman. "When Hunter arrived in Sheffield, we knew our time there was limited. Walt and I talked about the New World and Rags here brought an inventive mind that assured success in our new business venture. When I realized Hunter was communicating with other spies, I knew we had to go. I wanted to be wrong. I don't know how he knew we left, or where we'd gone." Glen said. "Until the storm, all I did was worry about how to get away from him. Once we were on the island, there was no way to communicate with Hassan, so I left it in God's hands."

"Was Hunter the reason we didn't know about the ship you found, the one you call the *Rosemary*?" Joanna asked.

Glen nodded his head. "I suspect he blew up the *Bringhurst* to keep us on the island till the galley could return."

"When was the last time you slept?" Remington asked.

Glen looked at him, realizing his energy was spent.

"The *Kent* will be ready to sail tomorrow. It will be nice to have you back," Remington said, standing up and ushering everyone to rooms Clare had prepared.

"Do we know anything more about this Blade of Safavid?" Jack asked his uncle as the two left the tavern, heading to the *Kent*.

"Blade of Safavid?" Remington repeated, "What's this about a fiancé?"

† † †

Glen and Rosemary retired to the room Clare prepared for their little family. No windows, but a vent in one wall let in fresh air. The air was filled with a spice she didn't recognize. Rosemary's questions she wanted answered denied her the opportunity to appreciate the beautiful flowered Irish quilt covering the first bed she would sleep on in years.

The twins were too excited to settle down, so Susan volunteered to accompany them for a few minutes to get their energy spent. Rosemary was mindful of Glen's need for sleep, but the question couldn't wait. She set a beautifully crafted, but well-worn leather box on the bed. She could tell it was once adorned with jewels, which had long been missing. She lifted the lid. She removed the journal.

"Tell me about this."

"It's a long story."

"I know, I read it. Why do you have it?"

"That is the long story."

"Is this why he's looking for you?"

Glen nodded.

"He thinks you have the Blade of Safavid?" she asked. "Do you?"

He shook his head no. "I quit my quest so nobody would have reason to hurt my family."

"What is the rest of the story? This journal ends." Rosemary held up the journal. "Is there another volume?"

"That's all of it. It ends," he said, ending the conversation.

Chapter Ninety~Nine

Onboard the Sally - Open Sea - West Indies - 1748

Elizabeth stood and watched out the porthole. The Sally pulled anchor, leaving the safety of the lagoon. The storm lightened; they were soon at full sail heading to what Elizabeth assumed was Krist's father's hidden island. Little was spoken over the next two days. Caesar provided food, and Krist's dressings were changed, yet Lydia did most of the work.

Within Elizabeth's power was the man responsible for her capture, her father and Rag's death, and she hated herself for not being able walk over and slit the monster's throat. When he claimed he wasn't the killer, she believed him. But he tolerated killing. He never stopped it. And his life's work was the slave trade. A work Elizabeth loathed. And apparently they traded in white female slaves. Which meant only one thing. Harem building.

How many in his harem?

Interaction with Hunter and Scotty was minimal. Only once did Caesar spend more time delivering and recovering their food than absolutely necessary. That was to check on the captain and when he did, the two spoke too quietly for either Elizabeth or Lydia to hear.

Finally, Elizabeth could not suppress her questions. She opened the hidden compartment and saw Krist sitting up, looking well.

He meekly spoke, "I haven't stood and walked for days. If you want my help when we arrive, I must use my legs. May I?"

He gingerly climbed out of the compartment and stood stretching. His legs were weak, but he flexed and stretched as best he could. All three of them realized doing anything rash right now would benefit no one. That didn't keep Lydia from keeping the knife close.

"Why do you do this? Too much of what you've said tells me you're in the wrong business. Unless you are a superb liar," Elizabeth said. "Which wouldn't surprise me."

"Family."

"Are you afraid of them or love them?"

He paused for a while before answering. "Both."

"I don't understand how someone can remain in a position, a business, a relationship, anything they dislike, and not do something to change it. I don't care if it is family," she said.

"Duty."

"Oh, that sounds noble."

"I'm serious. Haven't you ever continued at something simply because it's your responsibility to do so?" he asked. "Life isn't free of unpleasantness."

Elizabeth pondered his words for a few moments. Her short adult life was dedicated to finding her sister and avenging the wrongs perpetrated on her family. So yes, she understood responsibility.

"Killing, kidnapping, merchandising females, that's a responsibility?" she finally said. "You owe it to your family to follow in that trade?"

"Is there a difference between the white female slave trade and the black African slave trade?" he asked.

"No," Lydia answered. "They are both wrong."

"Is slavery ever right?" he asked.

Both women thought about that for just enough time for Krist to continue. "Hard question? Is there ever anything that is always right or anything that is always wrong?"

Both women were thinking on that question.

"Yes," Elizabeth answered.

"And who determines that? You? Governments? Preachers?" he asked. "You can't determine what's right or wrong for me any more than I can for you. Governments change. Laws change. Who says it's wrong to kidnap young white women and sell them to rich Ottomans? The same people who say it's ok for one black African to kidnap the men, women, and children in a neighboring tribe and sell them to the white English plantation owner?

"If you're offering a better motivation to life than duty, I'm your willing student," he said.

Elizabeth didn't hesitate. "There's got to be some foundation to start with. A fundamental right or wrong." Her eyes were as fiery as her words. "You talk about duty. You feel that to follow your father is your duty. There has to be something in it for you, a reward."

Krist sat down. His legs weren't ready for a lecture.

Elizabeth didn't care. He asked for it, he gets to listen. "Your father is looking for a relic?" she asked, rhetorically.

Krist nodded.

"Will recovering the relic, the Blade, undo the punishment he received?"

"No. That can't be undone."

"And the Shah, who meted out the punishment, what happens to him?" she asked.

"He was overthrown and is dead," Krist answered.

"So then, what is his reason?" Elizabeth pressed. "Is there a financial reward for its return?"

"No, the Safavid dynasty has fallen," he said. "It's personal."

"It usually is. And the princess?" she continued.

"What about her?"

"What does he do with the princess if he finds her? She's probably too old to sell." Elizabeth couldn't help herself.

Somewhat embarrassed, Krist lowered his head as he answered. "She would be killed. She was her brother's threat sole threat to the Safavid throne."

Elizabeth asked one more question. "You're not afraid of one little knife. Why are you still our prisoner?"

This change in direction caught Krist and Lydia off guard. Krist pondered for a moment, raised his head back up, and answered. "Are you asking why the cold-hearted captain of a pirate ship allows two little girls to hold him hostage on his own ship, while one of those girls lectures him on the virtues of freedom and tries to convince him of right and wrong?"

"Actually, that's exactly what I asked," Elizabeth answered. "And we're not little girls."

"Could it be you saved my life?" he said. "And maybe I'm not the cold-hearted killer that a pirate captain should be?"

"Your men are," Lydia said.

"Yes, they are."

"What now?" Elizabeth asked.

Krist reached down and pulled a second knife from a boot. The girls hadn't seen that one. He handed it to Elizabeth. Lydia still had hers at the ready, even more ready once she saw he held its twin.

"I don't know what will happen. I don't know what decisions I will make—duty and all. But you've given me a reason to choose wisely. Keep those handy and hidden."

He stood slowly and stretched again, giving each muscle a chance to flex and relax. He stepped over to the hidden compartment. As he climbed in, he looked back, and with all the sincerity a cold-hearted pirate captain could muster, said, "I am truly sorry about your father."

He looked at Lydia, "I don't yet know what I can do for your father. For sure, I don't know what I will do for my father." Krist pulled closed the secret door behind him.

Chapter One Hundred

Onboard the HMS Kent - St. John's Harbor, Antigua - 1748

Glen breathed deeply, chest filling with the cool morning air. It felt good to be back on the *Kent*. It was an older ship, in service well over thirty years. He remembered it vividly. He and Remington traversed the globe with her. Compared to larger war ships which sported up to a hundred twenty guns and required crews of many hundreds, the *Kent* was a dangerous foe because of its agility and speed. Its two gun decks sported only forty guns, the smallest of which were twenty-four pounders giving the *Kent* considerable fire power. The *Kent* was not built as a line battleship; it was a hunter and protector.

Rigged with three masts, each supporting square sails, the *Kent* was a beautiful ship with a large open main deck and more comfortable living quarters than a typical naval vessel.

"What's this all about?" Glen asked as he stepped on deck and saw Walt, Sal, Jack, and Rags playing a game of whist.

Rags looked at Glen and said, "Winner gets to kill Hunter. Want in?"

Glen smiled, but the surprise on his face showed he wasn't sure if Rags was kidding.

"We're doing it for Joanna," Rags said.

A night's rest had done wonders for Glen's feeling of hope. The captain stepped up and welcomed his old shipmate on board.

"Shall we go hunting for pirates?" Remington asked.

"Nothing I'd like more. There's a lot of ocean out there."

The men circled around the large map in the captain's cabin. Jack pressed out the creases, attempting to help it lay flat. The map had spent years folded in the back of Cav's notebook. Glen looked at the map, Remington, and then to Jack. He smiled.

"You kept my map?" Glen asked.

"It's more accurate than the cartographers."

Remington pulled Glen's notebook from a drawer and handed it to him. Glen hadn't seen it for many years. He turned it over and over.

"You kept this?"

"It was the only hope we had to find you," Remington answered.

Glen unfolded another map and placed it over the map on the table. Glen's map was smaller and crudely drawn. One additional island stood out, one which was not on the larger map. Jack immediately recognized it as the one they'd just escaped. Glen started the discussion by pinpointing exactly where he thought his island was located.

Jack smiled. *I knew it.*

"We sailed three days at nine or so knots to get here." Glen said, pointing to their current position on the map. "The galley was two full days ahead of us, but I hope they found an island somewhere around here to wait out the storm."

"If they encountered no problems, and Amos is right, and the pirate island is somewhere out here, they could still be at sea. I can't imagine that galley kept up nine knots like we did," Glen continued.

"Where is Amos?" Clare asked.

Rags was getting along well for his condition, but it didn't hurt to have Clare at his side. She insisted on joining the party when Rags refused to stay in port and convalesce.

"Sent him to talk with the men on the barque that anchored early this morning," Lucas answered.

Jack stepped away from the map and looked out the starboard window at the large ship anchored only a few hundred feet off the starboard bow. It was a large three-masted barque. Jack noted the sails and deck structure. "Dutch," he muttered.

"Even if we knew which island we're looking for, and the *Kent* maintains nine or ten knots, without a storm providing the extra boost of wind I don't think we plan on beating the galley to the island," Remington said.

"We don't have to," Glen assured his friend. "We have to get there before they leave. Their first goal is to get a heavily armed crew back to this island." He pointed on the map.

"Thanks to Hunter, they think we're stuck there," Walt added. "They'll take their time."

"That's true. They don't know the island's deserted," Jack said, stepping back to the table.

"That old dog won't waste any time. If he is looking for me, which I am sure he is, he's getting old and anxious," Glen said. "This may be his first break in years."

"The question is whether he'll take the girls back with him, or leave them on his island as hostages to get you to come along," Walt said.

"Or sell them," Rags added.

They all turned his way.

"It's possible," he said.

Everyone turned as Amos stepped into the cabin.

"Their captain was on shore already, but his mate said they spotted what they thought was a galley yesterday. Wondered why they'd need a galley in these seas. They followed for most of the day. Said neither they nor the galley seemed to be in any hurry."

"Where was the galley headed?"

"Around here." Amos pointed to an area on the map the men already identified as the targeted area.

Jack looked at Glen's crudely drawn map. When Amos pointed, Jack's eyes widened. He pulled in closer, and rotated Glen's map, which aligned it slightly off the original map pulled from Glen's notebook, made decades earlier.

All eyes focused on Jack's intensity as he lined up three irrelevant landmarks which to the group drew no interest. In a show of triumph, Jack pulled from his vest pocket a small oilcloth pouch only a few inches square. He pulled it open and extracted a tightly folded weathered paper. He carefully unfolded it. Three shapes crudely hand drawn were all it contained. Shapes that meant nothing on their own. Jack laid it over the now repositioned maps. Each way Jack turned the tattered and worn paper from ol' Denn, two marks could possibly relate with known islands, the third never did. Yet each time Jack rotated the small paper to line up two marks against known landmarks, the third consistently hung free.

Jack looked into each of the men's eyes, hoping they saw what he saw.

Captain Remington shook his head in disbelief. "I guess this is what you call research?"

Jack smiled. "The old man from the Nookery. Ol' Denn gave it to me as he lay dying in my arms. Somehow, he knew we'd be here and needed help to get here." Jack touched the exact spot everyone stared at. "It was a legend, not a map he gave me."

"Glen, or Cav, whoever you want to be; you said you failed to protect your daughter. Ol' Denn made me promise to keep Elizabeth in England. I failed. How about we go get our girls?" Jack said.

They headed above decks.

Captain Remington called up the anchor and the HMS *Kent* set sail.

Chapter One Hundred One

Onboard the Sally - Open Sea - West Indies - 1748

The door opened and Caesar entered, this time alone, empty box in hand, to gather food and supplies. Just as before, he leaned over the barrels communicating something to Krist. They spoke softly. Caesar gathered vegetables, beans, a large cask of water, and left, locking the door behind him.

Hunter accompanied Caesar from time to time, and each time he looked like a hungry animal surveying its prey. Each time they left, Lydia asked if she could please put her knife to good use.

The *Sally* made good time; the winds were favorable, the sea relatively cooperative most of the day.

"The crew is on edge," Krist told the two girls. "We've had a shadow most the day; a Dutch barque."

"Pirates?" Lydia asked.

"Not likely. They don't advance or retreat, just follow us. No one knows our precious cargo, nor would they care about it. The lack of any clear objective frightens any captain being followed by another ship," Krist explained.

"Can't two friendly ships just be sailing the same direction using the same winds?" Elizabeth asked.

"Ours isn't a friendly ship." Lydia said.

She was looking out the porthole trying to see another ship, but only saw the vast ocean.

Krist carefully stood stretching his legs. As he reached his arms to stretch he winced as the stretch pulled against his healing shoulder.

"Have you and Caesar finished your plan to help us escape, figured out a way to blame it on Scotty and Hunter so your father kills them, and then take back your ship, help our people off the island, and retire with your mother's family in Iceland?" Elizabeth asked.

Krist sat there in such amazement at this question, he couldn't quite decide if she was serious. After a few moments, he answered.

"No, but it appears like you have. Care to share with me the details?" He asked, smiling.

"You're the captain. Or were the captain. The details are your responsibility," Elizabeth said.

"Are you tutoring me again on my responsibilities?"

"Someone needs to."

Krist sat there wondering how a prisoner, a future member of an Ottoman Sultan's harem, and one that would bring a considerable price, rather than trembling with fear for her fate, would lecture her captor about his responsibility to not only free her and her companion, but to quit his career as a slaver and rescue her friends and family from an uncharted island.

He chuckled at the thought of the Sultan demanding his money back after tiring of his precious lover lecturing him on his responsibilities as a sultan. Krist liked this woman. There was something very attractive about confidence. Fear was a different characteristic all together. Krist had seen and sold many a young woman, most crying in fear and terror. He hadn't realized how unattractive that made them. He was not immune to a woman's beauty, but he had never been personally attracted to any of the slaves. They were merchandise.

Many times, the thought made him hate this life, but he resigned himself to his duty to his father and family.

"Who are you?" Krist finally asked her.

Elizabeth couldn't even look at him.

"Tell me about your father."

"He's dead. Your father killed him."

"I am sorry. Please tell me about him."

"Why?" she asked.

"Maybe so I can better appreciate your hate!" Krist said.

Her glare helped him appreciate the hate. His 'sorry' began its journey to sincerity.

"You wouldn't understand!" Again, her animosity held firm.

"Probably not," he conceded, but didn't lose eye contact. He leaned back and sat on the edge of a barrel. He carefully folded his arms prepared for a story or more likely a lecture.

"He was an ordinary man," she said. "A man wishing to raise and provide for a family. A man whose life was cut short by another father who claimed he was raising his family."

"Please," Krist begged. "My father spent his life seeking revenge for a wrong he suffered. I know nothing of a father who spends his life caring for others."

Elizabeth tried to pull back the hurt. "You said they punished and imprisoned your father for losing his ship while in the service of a shah," she asked, looking for confirmation.

"The Shah Sulton Hosayn, who sent him to recover the Blade of Safavid and his sister, the Princess Astrella," he answered, confirming her statement.

"Was it his fault for failing?".

"Does that matter? He failed."

"What do you do when two responsibilities or duties clash? When your duty to yourself clashes with your duty to the family, which do you choose? What of when your duty to your community clashes with your duty to family or self?" Elizabeth asked. "Where does right and wrong enter the equation?" She continued, "Does duty overshadow right? What is your duty to truth? When does one duty have more power or importance than another?"

"I wanted to know about your father. He must have been very patient." Krist said.

In disgust, Elizabeth turned from him, ending the conversation.

Krist pondered upon his mother, whom he never met. He concluded that she must have been like Elizabeth. Not only attractive, but confident. Was his father attracted to her confidence like he was becoming attracted to Elizabeth's confidence?

This whole confusing conversation caused him to change his mind. He needed to talk with Caesar again before making landfall at his father's island. He hoped they would reach the island at night, and from the information provided by Caesar, he was certain they would. He doubted Scotty would dare navigate the ship into the harbor in the dark. He would likely anchor just outside until daybreak. That would be perfect for his new plan.

The *Sally* came to rest. They arrived outside his father's harbor. Around midnight the *Sally* dropped anchor. Krist figured that in the morning, Scotty would bring the *Sally* into the harbor, a champion for having found the one person Hassan sought for decades. Krist knew Scotty planned to express his great regret for losing his son, but be the hero for having taken Glen's daughter in the fight. Scotty and Hunter would return with Hassan and storm the island.

Except that's not how it will be. Krist smiled. He and Caesar had spoken.

Caesar, accompanied by both Hunter and Scotty, stepped past the opened door to take one more glare at their prisoners. Krist remained in hiding and Elizabeth and Lydia cowered in faux resignation of their fate. Defiance appeared gone, but not the hate. Not much interaction took place, just evil sneers. The door closed and locked. This time Caesar gave the keys to Scotty.

"I'll be busy in the morning," Caesar said.

When all was quiet, the secret compartment opened and Krist invited Elizabeth and Lydia into the small hidden chamber. He was grateful Elizabeth didn't put up a fight or finish him off with his knife. She looked in to see Caesar bidding them to crawl through a small opening that led to the longboat he was standing in. This small compartment had an escape hatch.

"Quite clever if you need to drop into the ocean. Or launch a rescue," Krist said.

Krist locked the secret compartment door behind them and the three settled into the longboat. Caesar closed and secured the outer compartment, keeping in the shadows cast by the moon over the lowering sails of the *Sally* as he quietly rowed them to shore.

Chapter One Hundred Two

Hassan's Private Island - 1748

Caesar stepped off the bow and pulled the boat onto the sand. Extending his hands he helped Lydia then Elizabeth onto the shore. Favoring his wounded shoulder, Caesar helped Krist to his feet and onto the sand, which was lit by a waning moon. Caesar quietly pushed off and rowed back to the *Sally*.

Krist turned to the two, quietly and firmly giving instructions. "This trail leads around the plantation and down to a small lagoon. The vegetation there will provide enough cover to keep you hidden. When Scotty finds you have escaped, there will be a full-scale manhunt, or should I say woman hunt, until they find you. And they will find you."

"Where are you going?" Elizabeth asked.

"To create a way to get you off this island, before they find you."

"What about you? Are you going to tell your father about Scotty?" Lydia asked.

"He knows Scotty. And he knows Scotty is the only one who can lead him to your island. He won't kill him for losing you two until he gets what he wants."

"But he'll be happy you're alive," Lydia said. "You can talk to him."

"My father is not like your father. Your father is probably swimming here to save you. My father is sorry I am dead because I'm a good sailor. But he won't waste time mourning. As soon as they find you or your dead bodies, they will be on their way to your little hidden island. I cannot stop them."

Krist paused and pondered for a moment.

Lydia and Elizabeth wondered if he was listening for something, so they strained their ears in case there was something they should be hearing.

"Take off your clothes," Krist said, breaking the silence.

"What?" Elizabeth protested.

"I knew it," Lydia said, her feet not budging an inch, but a hand reaching for her knife.

"No, I didn't mean it that way. Stay right here!" Krist said.

Krist hurried up the shore and into a small building. The only thing audible were the calm waves lapping against the shore. Within a few minutes, he returned and handed rough and worn trousers and shirts to Elizabeth and Lydia.

"Put these on, and give me your clothes," he said. "Hurry."

The two women just stood there looking at him. With open palms shaking impatiently, he encouraged them to hurry. They didn't move. He dropped his hands, shook his head muttering something neither could make out, and turned around. They quickly changed and handed him their clothes.

Krist gave them a quick look and approved. "You even make those rags look good."

"What do you know?" Elizabeth said. "It's dark."

"You think you're the first women I've seen in the dark?"

Krist regretted saying that the second it left his lips. There was no way to take it back, and he knew no matter what he tried to say to explain it, they would take it wrong. Which, of course, he knew a woman always would.

He continued his instruction. "When the sun comes up, make sure you are hidden, and do not surface until I come for you, or someone I send. If I have to send someone else, they will wear a yellow bandana."

"What are you going to do?" Lydia asked.

"Find me two dead bodies," he answered, and then he worked his way up towards the plantation, wishing he'd stretched and exercised more in the tiny confines of the ship's storage.

Lydia and Elizabeth followed the trail along the shoreline for nearly an hour before it ascended up through a thick bush. As the trail got steeper, the vegetation lessened, and soon they were walking on slick rock. It was hard to see if there was a trail at all. They walked across an expanse of smooth stone. Where the stone ended, they met an abrupt line of small, waist high brush.

"Did we miss the trail?" Elizabeth asked. "Krist never mentioned this." They wandered back and forth along the rock where it met the brush.

Finally Lydia said, "Here it is."

"I don't see anything."

"This brush is disturbed. More than one person came this way," Lydia said.

"You can see that in the dark?" Elizabeth asked, impressed once again.

"My father may not really be swimming to rescue us, but he taught me a few things about survival. Following a trail is one of those things."

I wish he'd taught Jack how to follow a trail.

The two worked their way through the brush and eventually over a summit and back down to what they thought might be the back side of the island. Not knowing how large the island might be, or how far the lagoon Krist described was, they were careful to follow the trail as it practically disappeared from time to time. Elizabeth gave the teenager, the tracker, the lead.

They finally reached water. The last of the moonlight reflected on the lagoon giving a peaceful calm to the jungle. They settled into a grove of palms and hoped when the time came, they could see out well enough to spot danger and stay hidden. Huddled together, they soon fell asleep, unaware of the large nocturnal eyes curiously watching.

Chapter One Hundred Three

Hassan's Private Island - 1748

Krist quietly stepped into the small hut and placed his hand over the mouth of one of the few slaves on this island he trusted, or that trusted him actually. Mereday opened his eyes wide and tried to stand but relaxed as soon as he recognized it was Krist. His woman, lying next to Mereday, remained motionless as he slipped off the woven mat serving as a bed. He and Krist quietly slid out the door and away from the hut.

"Mereday, we have trouble." Krist whispered. "I need two dead bodies, female. Have any died recently? White if possible."

"Not since you gone, Masta Krist." Mereday said.

"What can we find?" Krist asked.

"Must dig. Masta Krist," Mereday said.

"Help me. We also need crocs, where have you seen them recently?"

"In you lagoon."

Horror struck Krist. Did he just send Elizabeth and Lydia to their death? The crocs that plagued the island came and went as if there was a migration. There were seasons with no sightings or encounters, then without notice, crocs reappeared and the shorelines became deadly. These saltwater crocs were certainly not native to the West Indies, Krist only guessed they got to these waters carried accidently by some ship traveling from their native shores in Africa or Asia.

Krist's urgency increased. He led Mereday through the plantation fields to the small graveyard. Mereday pointed out the two most recent burials. They dug and readied to pull two partially decomposed bodies from their final resting places. Krist knew Mereday was disgusted with the violation of the dead.

Mereday was a highly religious man. He and his family lived on the island since before Krist's father had conquered it, killing the interlopers who had settled here. Krist was kind to the slaves and over the years became close to many of them. Krist knew Mereday did not approve of the life he and the other slave owners led. He was not afraid to say so, at least to Krist. Krist knew he was right.

Maybe that is why he trusted Mereday. The two men were completely honest with each other.

"What can justify this violation of sacred rest? You violated these in life, why do so in death, Masta Krist?"

Krist quickly explained what happened aboard the *Sally* and how he helped the captives escape. He told Mereday where he sent them to hide. Krist knew Mereday hated Scotty, and he also knew Scotty would eventually find the girls.

He smiled at Krist's plan.

"Leave the dead to rest. Come, Masta Krist," Mereday said as he covered the graves and headed toward the small corral.

Mereday was not young, but he hopped the fence like a young man. A small squeal filled the still air and silence returned. He handed a limp hog over the fence to Krist. Krist's shoulder was not yet up to the weight of the hog and it fell to his feet. In the darkness Mereday hadn't seen Krist's wound.

"Crocs want blood. They are like white men, Masta Krist," Mereday said.

Krist followed Mereday down to the shoreline where he tossed the hog into a small boat. "I protect your women, Masta Krist," Mereday promised.

He rowed out of the harbor and along the shoreline. The large ship barely cast a shadow as the waning moon called it a night. Mereday saw it but paid it no attention.

By the time Mereday entered the lagoon, the light of morning was silhouetting the rugged mountainside.

A scream shattered the peace of the tropical morning air.

Chapter One Hundred Four

Onboard the Sally - Anchored in Private Harbor - 1748

Morning came early. Caesar unchained the first row of the *Sally's* galley slaves to take them ashore. They'd been in chains for nearly three weeks.

Left onboard between the last two journeys, it was time to put them to work on the plantation and replace them with a fresh crew.

"Caesar! Leave them, we will not be in port long enough," Scotty yelled.

Caesar refashioned the irons on the slaves he had freed. As soon as the *Sally* dropped anchor Hassan rowed out to the *Sally* and now stood on deck. Scotty shuttered at the sound of his voice. He knew Hassan was more interested in how they fared in the storm than their success with the hunt for the mysterious sailor. These hunting journeys always failed. He barely hoped for success anymore.

"You survived the storm," Hassan said.

"Captain," Scotty began.

"Where's my son?" Hassan asked. Demanded more than asked.

"Captain, we return with grave news." Scotty said, faking humility. "Captain Krist was successful in finding this man you've hunted these many years. Someone had prepared them for us. When we made contact, they ambushed us from the jungle and they killed your son."

Hassan looked at Scotty suspiciously but noted his blood-stained pants and obvious limp.

"Even with this," pointing to his bloody hip, "I got the rest of the men back to the Sally. The storm came so quickly, we had to flee the island. But with the help of your spy, Hunter here, we did not leave empty-handed."

Hunter stepped forward when Scotty mentioned his name, bowing respectively to Hassan.

"You're not dead nor a traitor." Hassan said, "So you brought me the Blade?"

Scotty knew better than to expect any show of gratitude from this man. He demanded, and rewarded or punished. Both rewards and punishments were lavish. Gratitude was not. Scotty also expected little remorse for losing his son if the journey was successful. Hassan did not surprise.

Scotty and Hunter explained how Hunter was a valiant spy for leaving Sheffield to follow Glen and his family. He added how the hurricane left them stranded two years, and how Hunter's quick thinking destroyed the *Bringhurst,* guaranteeing the island residents remained stranded. Sharing how the attack on the island forced them to flee into the storm, and how capturing the two girls would guarantee Glen's cooperation, they waited, then expressed their deep sorrow for Krist's death.

The three men marched below decks, past the chained oarsmen to the locked room. Scotty was deliberate with his limp. When he reached the door, he pulled out the key, turned the lock and pushed the door open. There stood an empty storage room. Hassan was slow and careful as he looked around the room, then turned back with raised eyebrows to Scotty for an explanation. No words were spoken.

Horror filled Scotty's face. Hunter immediately scoured the room, looking under, behind, and above every cask, crate, and box.

Hassan waited.

Chapter One Hundred Five

Hassan's Private Island - 1748

The coati lay dead, a knife buried deep in its heart. Lydia stood next to Elizabeth still shaking. When Elizabeth opened her eyes face to face with a curious coati, her scream threatened the large cat-like animal, it bore its sharp teeth in defense. Lydia didn't give the coati nor Elizabeth a chance to stare each other down. In a quick reaction to the scream, her knife founds its mark.

Mereday was quietly searching the areas around the lagoon when the scream woke the large croc he was side stepping. In a few quick bounds, he avoided the croc's snapping jaws and stood alongside the girls. He was quick enough and lucky enough that Elizabeth was not as adept with a knife as was Lydia. They both jumped when he stood beside them.

"Masta Krist sent me," he said as he placed his hand on Elizabeth's arm to calm her.

The yellow bandana around his neck helped her relax.

He held up their clothes and shared the plan. The dead coati was a bonus. He dressed the dead coati as Lydia, and returning to the boat, the hog as Elizabeth. Not knowing where the crocs would care to have breakfast, he wiped enough of the animals' blood on torn scraps of their fabric and placed them along the shore.

When offered the fresh meat for breakfast, the crocs tore the animals to shreds. A small fight broke out between the three crocs and made for a brilliant display.

Mereday left the boat on the beach, hoping when Hassan's men came searching, they would find the bloody scene. Carefully covering his tracks away from the scene of bloodshed, Mereday led the girls up and away from the shore. He helped them to a safer hiding place near a small spring that provided the girls fresh water and a clear view of the lagoon.

"I bring food. Stay here. Please," he said. "No scream."

Mereday left the girls and disappeared into the jungle.

A few hours later a small boat entered the lagoon. Rowed by one who looked like Ceasar, they saw two men approach the abandoned boat Mereday left on the beach. When they saw the blood and messy scene of a croc attack, they quickly paddled back out of the lagoon the way they came.

Several hours later the boat returned. This time they recognized Scotty with a much older man they assumed was Krist's father. Elizabeth and Lydia knew it must be him by the feeling of evil that drifted up the small hillside to their hiding place. Elizabeth wondered how Krist, so fair, was the son of a father so dark. She hoped his mother's contribution to the making of this young man went beyond just the physical appearance.

Like the first search party, these men checked out the scene from the safety of their boat. As if trained to help in the charade, one of the crocs was laying in the sun a few feet away from the crime. The few fragments of the girls' clothing strategically placed by Mereday, were convincing enough to put an end to the search.

It was now late in the afternoon. Though they had water, hunger plagued the two and Lydia stood to look for something she might find to eat. She wasn't interested in killing anything she'd have to cook. But there had to be a coconut or banana or papaya in this jungle.

Then she saw it, but she'd have to leave this hiding place to get it.

Chapter One Hundred Six

Onboard the HMS Kent - Open Sea - 1748

As the *Kent* sailed, the old shipmates caught up on the events of the past twenty years beginning with the day Glen went ashore in Newton Ferrers to meet David Creagh. They laughed, teased, and planned. Jack finally got the whole picture of what made Glen tick. Walt filled in some embarrassing holes Glen wasn't eager to share, but they all laughed hard when Glen told the truth about Elizabeth's kiss saving Jack from Glen's machete.

What unified this team against the common enemy the most, not that any unifying was needed, was when Rags gave details of who shot him and kicked him unconscious when he was trying to help Elizabeth and Lydia.

In the two years they were on the island, Rags never told the whole story about his rescuing Clare from pirates. When he identified that pirate as Scotty, Rags got very serious.

"You can all kill whoever you want . . . but I want to look Scotty in the eye when I thank him for giving me Clare," Rags said with a tiny teasing smile and pulled her close.

Rags said this so somberly and threateningly, they all expected a grand promise of violent and bloody revenge.

"Then you can kill him however you want. As long as he's completely dead when you're done killing him," Rags added.

Following hours of banter and discussion, Jack finally asked the one totally unimportant question that had bothered him all night and day. He turned to Rags.

"What is your name?"

Clare smiled, Glen laughed, and Rags started into a story that was so confusing about how his friends teased him about one name, his mother called him another name and his teachers another. With such confusion, Rags decided on Rags, a variation of his first childhood girlfriend's name, Ragnield. When they were young children, he teased her with that name and when she moved away he missed her, yet liked the name so much, he took it as a nickname.

"Lars Fredrik Gustoff Adamson," Clare finally said, ending Rags' discourse.

"Rags will do," Jack said, eyes darting from person to person confirming they all agreed.

Captain Remington then turned to Glen to ask a similar question. Glen didn't let him complete the question.

"Cav was the nickname my friends used when we enlisted. It sounded good for a sailor. When I got respectable, Glen sounded better."

He winced, thinking about how much he would need to share with Rosemary when they got back together, after all, he wasn't really wanting to talk about the journal she found. He prayed Lydia would be with them when he did.

Chapter One Hundred Seven

Hassan's Private Island - 1748

Lydia climbed from where she and Elizabeth were safely hiding to reach the freshly fallen coconut. However, the coconut wasn't what caught her eye. She brushed sand and leaves away to reveal a small worn leather covered box. Where several jewels had probably once adorned the box, holes filled with dirt remained, with the exception of one small opal. Someone carelessly left the box, she thought. They probably took the other jewels and had no use for the opal. After brushing it off, she opened it and found nothing but rotted velvet lining the inside.

The rotted lining exposed the workmanship of the wood. She recognized beautiful craftsmanship. She saw it every time her father created musical instruments. She didn't recognize the wood. She could barely make out some carved characters on the inside lid in a language she had never seen before.

She slipped the box under her arm, picked up the coconut and hurried back to where Elizabeth carefully kept a lookout.

Chapter One Hundred Eight

Hassan's Private Island - 1748

Kirst watched all day as they provisioned the *Sally* for sailing. His heart ached for the galley slaves who remained onboard. How could he help them? he wondered. How could he keep the *Sally* from sailing? And how could he get the girls off the island?

The search for the missing captives first tickled Krist. From his hiding place on the shore he watched his father tender out to the *Sally*, then return to shore angry. He watched Scotty and Hunter leave the Sally and recognized the fear in their faces.

Krist wondered, Why didn't I just kill Scotty and Hunter, take back my ship, and return the girls to their island? He asked himself this question all night, never finding a satisfactory answer.

Caesar made several trips back and forth to the Sally until it looked like they sent him with a small group in his longboat. He rowed several men out of the harbor in what Krist assumed was a search party around the island.

If they circled the entire island, it would be a long journey. Krist knew they would enter his lagoon first, and hopefully not finding anything would continue around from inlet to inlet and lagoon to lagoon until they returned to the harbor. At any rate, he hoped that was the case. Then the *Sally* couldn't leave until tomorrow. He knew they wouldn't sail without Caesar.

Other search parties were sent, and some returned, but all were empty-handed. There seemed to be no success. Hassan appeared from time to time to meet with men along the shore. Krist could only imagine the frustration his father was experiencing. So many times he had come so close to finding the next clue, only to be denied. His father did not take denial well.

Then, with some excitement, Caesar returned. He obviously did not circle the island. A man jumped out and ran up to the manor house. Followed by Hassan and Scotty, he returned. They all boarded the boat and rowed out of the harbor.

They found the girls. Or at least what he hoped Mereday's deception led them to believe was the girls. Time would tell.

The waiting drove Krist crazy. He couldn't figure out how to intervene. That was what concerned him the most. He did not know what to do next.

His father's boat finally returned and even from the distance Krist saw the anger in his father's face and the fear in Scotty's. They took the bait. The search was over.

Caesar must be exhausted, Krist thought, but the man returned to provisioning the *Sally*. Then provisions were taken to the *Chawbuck*. His father would take both vessels. Likely, they would sail in the morning. With the girls gone, they would take the island by force. They had nothing to negotiate with. Krist assumed his father would take full crews on both ships. When they got to where the winds would leave the *Chawbuck* powerless, he would trade his fighting men for the galley slaves so when the *Sally* reached the uncharted island, he would have force enough to take on the small group of innocent residents.

Krist realized Hunter knew the island only had a few residents, but he and Scotty would never admit to being defeated by a handful of farmers. And Hassan would take no more chances.

Somberly, Krist knew he had to sail with the small armada. The girls would be safe enough remaining on the island in Mereday's care. There was much to think about, but his mind was exhausted, his body was exhausted. He couldn't think anymore.

Chapter One Hundred Nine

Onboard the HMS Kent - Open Sea - 1748

A strong wind favored the *Kent* most of the day. Small islands came and went.

Jack's confidence in ol' Denn's paper was enough to persuade the experienced sailors of the existence of a mystery island. That confidence waned as the day wore on. Yet, the hand-drawn map Glen produced wasn't complete enough either. It was a leap of faith and hope.

Several of the men commented they were in awe that pirates could keep an island so hidden.

As evening came, they circled an island they thought looked possible.

"This isn't it," Glen said.

The winds picked up slightly and before total darkness set in, they spotted another island. Through the glass they saw lights. As they approached, it was evident these were lamps, probably oil lamps. They decided this was an island with potential. It was either the pirates' island or else the residents could give them information where the island might be. Either way, it felt like a worthy place to anchor.

Captain Remington brought the *Kent* as close as he felt he safely could; not knowing any shoals or reefs that might protect what they thought to be a deep harbor. They spotted the masts of two ships.

Glen pushed a sailor lowering the long boat aside. The sailor was far too slow. The sailor on the other end was no faster, and the boat nearly flipped upside down when Glen let the ropes free. Finally, despite his impatience, Glen had one of the two longboats in the water right side up before the crew finished lowering the sails and dropping anchor. Glen's persuasion to have Captain

Remington sail right in failed, and they anchored well outside the harbor.

Remington left the *Kent* in Lucas's care. He, Glen, and Walt took one boat and tendered through the moonlit night. Jack, Sal, and Amos took the other. They supposed this to be a simple exploration mission to identify who or what occupied this island. Could it be one of the two islands unique to Glen's hand-drawn map? It was not on any of Remington's maps.

Each of the men watched for the same things, somewhat subconsciously. With what light they had from the waning moon, they looked out for reefs or shoals that might be an obstacle to bringing the *Kent* into the harbor. They also scoured the hillside, looking for any battlements and trying to get a feel for the possible size of this community.

As they entered the harbor, Glen was the first to recognize the *Sally*. He practically jumped out of the boat and swam to shore, he was so anxious. It took everything Walt and Remington had to keep him calm. They'd never seen Glen like this.

Voices indicated there was activity on the *Sally*. Both boats slowed and stayed in the shadows as they approached. Men were loading provisions. The conversations made clear the plan was to sail in the morning.

This was the island, and with no word, the men knew they had only tonight to find and rescue Lydia and Elizabeth.

On shore, another boat loaded and headed toward the large man-of-war anchored next to the *Sally*.

Remington whispered, "The *Chawbuck*. Glen, do you remember this ship?"

"Should I?" Glen asked.

"It anchored next to the *Kent* the night I lost you. I've been chasing it for twenty years."

"You remember ships in a harbor from twenty years ago?" Glen asked.

"When we entered the harbor at Newton Ferrers, the *Kent* was one of only two or three ships. Later that evening, the *Chawbuck,* this ship, docked alongside us. You had already gone ashore. Just before dawn the *Chawbuck* sailed, and I never saw you again. Confusing stories have always circulated about this ship. Owned by a Persian merchant but rumored to be a slave ship dealing with the Ottomans. Glen, these are bad people," Remington warned.

"Their business with the Ottomans is over. Once I have my Lydia, this ship never sails again," Glen said. Then looking at Remington, added, "And your soon to be niece."

There was just enough moonlight they had to be careful. The men drifted back away from the two ships and made a plan.

The second boat with Jack, Sal, and Amos pulled up alongside. None of them knew the island, and in the darkness, did not know if there were any friendly people on the island, or where they might find the girls and what kind of guard could be protecting them. They sent Jack, Sal, and Amos around the island to see if there might be other inlets or other settlements, or even a safer approach to the settlement over land.

Remington dropped Walt and Glen at the shore away from where the supplies were being ferried to the two ships. Soon after, Remington returned to the *Kent* to prepare, in case either of these two ships tried to sail.

† † †

Krist realized he hadn't eaten in nearly two days. His strength was gone. A quick bite to eat and a short nap was all he needed. Something caught his eye. In the faintest of moonlight, an unfamiliar boat reached the shore far to the left of the docks. Two men climbed out of the boat. Then the boat, with what appeared to be a single oarsman, headed toward the mouth of the harbor. Where had it come from, and where was it going? he wondered. *Who are these men invading my father's island?*

No time for food or rest.

Krist knew his father made scores of enemies over the years, some of them very nasty enemies. He could think of any number of them who might risk a night visit. But they had been so careful to never divulge the location of this island. Besides, if someone ever asked, they rumored the island's governor was no one to trifle with.

The present conflict expanded, how to protect the two young women from his father, how to protect his father from these two invaders, how to protect himself from Scotty and Hunter, and how to remain faithful to his father while being true to his own conscience? A conscience which had just recently been awakened by a bright, beautiful and captivating captive. He was too tired to add one more conflict into the mix.

Chapter One Hundred Ten

Hassan's Private Island

Remington pushed off after leaving Glen and Walt on shore and returned to the *Kent*. It was time to reposition the *Kent* where it would best serve in the morning.

Under the watchful eye of Scotty, Caesar finished loading provisions on the *Sally* and then slipped below decks and quietly unlocked the slave's chains. He gave quiet instruction to the slaves to stay in their places until he returned. Krist's instructions had been brief. He told Caesar he wanted the option to either stall the Sally from leaving or hasten its retreat if needed. Caesar didn't know when or where he might get the word from Krist but he figured if he stayed close to the arms bunker, Krist would eventually contact him. After unlocking the galley slaves, he went ashore.

Hassan was so angry with the loss of the two hostages he commanded Scotty to stay onboard the *Sally* and Hunter stay onboard the *Chawbuck*. On this rare occasion, he elected to sleep on shore. Earlier, Krist watched him leave the shore and make his way up to the manor house. Which is exactly where the two intruders appeared to be headed.

Captain Remington climbed back onboard the *Kent* and pulled anchor. With just enough breeze, he urged it forward, and the *Kent* lowered anchor squarely at the mouth of the harbor. No ship would slip by tonight without a fight.

With persistent urging from Clare and Rags, Remington permitted them to take a longboat and head to shore. He knew Glen would argue that choice, but

Glen was not the captain of the *Kent*.

† † †

Krist headed to the armory for weapons. He found Caesar waiting for him. He took two loaded pistols, a sword, and replaced the two boot knives he had given to the female captives.

"Are my galley slaves unlocked?" Krist asked.

Caesar nodded in the affirmative and gave a questioning look at the weapons Kirst was preparing.

"We have intruders and they're heading to the manor house where my father is."

"I will stop them," Caesar said.

"No, it's my responsibility. Don't let the *Sally* leave without me. Go to Mereday and make sure he keeps my prisoners safe. He knows where they are."

"They are dead. Crocs," Caesar said. "Bloody Crocs."

"Convinced you?" Krist smiled. "Blood was a hog. Mereday set it up."

Krist left the armory. Though exhausted and sore, he made his way toward the manor house. As he reached the short wall surrounding the large plantation-style manor house, he wanted to hop over it as he had so many times. He didn't have the strength. Instead, he carefully climbed. As he did, he glanced back toward the harbor, and his heart practically gave up. The HMS *Kent* sat majestically silhouetted in the moonlight of the harbor's mouth. These two intruders were just spies. Even if he could stop them, the Sally and the *Chawbuck* would not be sailing as planned. Krist hoped Caesar noticed the ship blocking the harbor and would keep the *Sally* ready to escape if occasion permitted.

† † †

Glen and Walt kept an eye out for any movement. They knew the activity on shore was to prepare for the two ships to sail. Likely to return to their island. They tried to stay in the shadows. When they reached a clearing and looked back, the sight of the *Kent* comforted them.

The crew necessary to man the *Chawbuck* and the *Sally* could be formidable and likely were trained for battle. Glen and Walt were not looking for a fight, they were looking for two young female hostages. Unlike other prisoners, they calculated these two would be under personal lock and key as opposed to being held with other human merchandise. As they passed other buildings, they noted both crew and slave quarters.

As Walt slipped over the short wall, Glen followed. As he did, a knife was thrown and caught Glen in the leg just as he landed on it. The leg gave way and Glen collapsed on the ground. Walt turned and loosed a bolt from his crossbow, catching its victim in the shoulder. Krist dropped the pistol he was about to fire and laid motionless.

Glen pulled the knife from his thigh. He removed his belt and stuffed the hole with the sleeve he quickly tore free and stopped the bleeding. Walt stepped over to Krist, picked up the pistol, and aimed it at his head.

"Get up. You're going to help us," Walt said.

Krist didn't move. He couldn't be dead, Walt thought. Walt leaned down and checked.

A shot rang through the air, and Walt dropped to his knees. A second shot followed, and Krist lay still.

Chapter One Hundred Eleven

Outside the Manor House - Hassan's Island - 1748

With bleeding temporarily stopped, Glen limped over to Walt and tried to help him to his feet. Walt's shirt was covered in blood. Glen tore it open to reveal a nasty hole. He hoped the ball missed essential organs, but it was spewing enough blood that if he didn't get it stopped, it wouldn't matter what organs it missed.

Glen was again plugging a bleeding hole. Doors opened and voices sounded from buildings surrounding the manor house. Within minutes, angry, heavily armed men surrounded Glen and Walt.

Caesar ran to the scene, arriving just as Mereday did. With the two intruders surrounded by Hassan's men, Mereday and Caesar went to work and stopped Krist's bleeding.

Hassan hastened out of the manor house and rushed down to investigate. The silhouette of the HMS *Kent* standing guard at the entrance of his harbor stopped him in mid-stride. After a few moments, he continued to his men.

"Bring them inside!" he bellowed. He then turned to see Caesar and Mereday attending to another man laying still. "Who's this?" he asked.

"It appears to be a ghost," Caesar answered.

"It's your son." Mereday said.

"Is he dead?"

"No, Captain, not yet. But close."

"Bring him too."

The men pulled Glen and Walt into the manor house, while Mereday and Caesar carried Krist. Hassan stood staring at the *Kent,* arms folded, head cocked, contemplating his next move.

Once Krist was stable, Caesar slipped away to make sure the *Sally* couldn't leave without Krist. As he left the light of the manor house and saw the *Kent* standing guard, it confirmed his decision to strand the *Sally*. It was in no condition to fight.

Caesar slipped down to the shore and rowed out to the *Sally*. There, Scotty stood trying to see what the limited light allowed.

"I heard shots. What happened?" he asked as Caesar scaled the ladder and stepped up onto the deck.

"A mistake. Someone saw a ghost," was all Caesar said.

Caesar went below decks and Scotty heard him open and close the crew's quarters' door. Hunter shouted from the *Chawbuck* to Scotty still standing on the deck of the *Sally*.

"What's happening up there?" Hunter yelled.

Scotty didn't answer. He climbed into the longboat and rowed to shore. Thinking the same thing, Hunter joined him onshore, and the two scrambled up to the manor house.

Caesar led the galley slaves out the back of the ship where they quietly slipped into the water and swam to shore.

He joined them in their swim, leaving the *Sally* alone in the moonlight.

† † †

As Rags and Clare stepped from their boat to the shore, men climbed out of the water. Surprised, Clare jumped back, stumbling into Rags and causing both to land flat on the sand. Each man looked at the two stunned visitors on the ground as they left the water but didn't slow, and disappeared into the field that ran along the shoreline.

"Galley slaves?" whispered Clare. "Escaping?"

Rags nodded and whispered back, "But why? Where could they go? They're on an island."

It piqued Rags' curiosity. He stepped back into the boat, but before he pushed off, Clare joined him. They quietly rowed back to the *Sally* and standing as tall as he could, Rags took hold of the edge of the open compartment and tried to pull himself up. His wounded chest wouldn't let him. He settled back down into the boat, checked the contents in his pocket and whispered to Clare.

"I want to get inside."

Light from the approaching morning turned dark silhouettes into discernible trees, buildings, and people. Inside the manor house, Krist opened his eyes. The pain was unbearable. A new hole in his abdomen, not fatal, yet, combined with the bolt protruding from his other shoulder, gave him reason to consider a return to unconsciousness to lessen the pain. He recognized Mereday attending to the hole caused in reprisal to his shooting the intruder. He should have aimed better. But how could he with a new bolt in his good shoulder?

He looked closely at the bolt. As his eyes focused on it, he realized his other shoulder had met its twin only a few days earlier.

"What have I done?" he muttered to himself.

$\mathcal{C}$hapter $\mathcal{O}$ne $\mathcal{H}$undred $\mathcal{T}$welve

Hassan's Private Island - 1748

Jack, Amos, and Sal entered the small lagoon, hoping it would give them a back door to the plantation. They rowed up alongside the boat Mereday beached there. The splash of a croc waking and entering the water gave them pause.

Elizabeth and Lydia woke to the sound of the distant gunfire. In the moonlight, they saw three men carefully climb on shore and quickly retreat from the water's edge.

Mereday came over the hill, nearing Elizabeth and Lydia's hiding place when he saw the small boat reach the shore. He watched as the three men cautiously climbed up the small hill.

Lydia was first to have her knife at the ready. Elizabeth followed with hers in hand.

The faint light revealed only the men's silhouettes. As they passed the two knife wielding women in hiding, Elizabeth sensed something familiar.

Mereday watched as the men passed where he left the women hiding. As they got close, he stepped from the darkness and pushed a large machete tightly against one's neck.

"Before I slit your throat, tell why you sneak around my home," Mereday said.

Jack felt the man was strong enough to carry out his threat. He lowered the crossbow he'd held at the ready.

Amos and Sal froze, not knowing if they could overpower this lone man in the darkness without getting Jack's throat slit. Amos opened his mouth to speak when the knife in his back sucked the words back. Sal froze when he felt a knife cut through his shirt and touch his bare skin.

Jack stumbled to utter the words.

"We're friends, looking for two young women brought here in the past few days."

Elizabeth recognized the nervousness in that voice. She couldn't decide if she should let him suffer or if Mereday had the same sense of humor as Glen. She chose not to take the risk. She removed the knife from Sal's back.

"Sorry," she whispered to Sal. Then she heard Jack continue.

"One of them is my fiancé." Jack struggled to say without causing the blade to sever his throat.

"Mereday, I am his fiancé. He is harmless enough," Elizabeth finally said.

Mereday released Jack and lowered the machete. Elizabeth threw her arms around Jack.

Sal took Lydia's shoulders in his hands. "Oh, you're safe!" he said. It was more tender and kind than she'd ever heard him speak.

Lydia asked questions so quickly, it took Sal a few moments to calm her and get the first answer out.

Mereday spoke up.

"Captain Krist sent me to bring you to your ship. Your friends are hurt. Captain Krist worries what will happen if he dies before your father and his friend know you are not dead."

"What's happening?" Lydia asked.

"Your friends invaded the island. Captain Krist crippled one with a knife and shot the other," Mereday answered.

"What? Why would Krist do that?" Elizabeth asked.

"Who?" begged Lydia.

"Two strangers at night. I did not know." Mereday said.

"Walt and Glen," Jack said, "They're looking for you."

"We must get you to the ship," Mereday repeated.

"What ship? How did you get here?" Elizabeth turned to Jack.

"Later," he said. "Right now we need to get you two to the HMS *Kent*." Jack wished he could see the reaction on her face. It was still too dark to appreciate it.

"You said Krist will die. Why?" Elizabeth asked, turning back to Mereday.

"Your friend hit Captain Krist with a bolt and a ball."

"How serious is he?" Elizabeth asked.

Jack listened to this interchange and noticed the slave referred to the man as Captain Krist and Elizabeth referred to him with less formality, eliminating the 'captain' as if they were close friends. *Does Elizabeth really think I am harmless?* he wondered.

"Who is Captain Krist?" Jack asked.

"Back on the island, he's the leader Walt shot in the shoulder. He's captain of the *Sally.*" Elizabeth answered.

Walt? But I hit the captain … and three others. Jack shook his head.

"Where is he?" Elizabeth asked, turning to Mereday.

"At the manor house. Captain Hassan believes you two dead. Captain Krist and your friends need to know you are safe if there is hope for them." Mereday continued, "You must go to the ship. I will tell the captain you are safe."

"The ship isn't safety," muttered Amos. "That *Chawbuck* easily out-guns the Kent."

"Then we disable the *Chawbuck,*" Jack said. He turned to lead the group back to the boat on the beach.

Without a word, Elizabeth and Lydia charged up the path toward the manor house. "Not again," Jack muttered, lowering his shaking head. Jack wanted to charge after Elizabeth and Lydia. He now knew better.

"Thank you," he said to Mereday. "Please look after those two."

The three men ran back down the beach. Sidestepping a sleeping croc, they jumped in the boat and rowed back toward the *Kent*.

As they approached the harbor entrance and started toward the *Chawbuck,* they first reached the *Kent,* which Remington had prepared for a fight. They rowed up alongside it.

Jack quickly scaled the ladder and told his uncle the girls were safe. Remington shrugged when he heard Walt and Glen were injured and held captive in the manor house. A problem and a blessing. "Do you know where?"

asked Remington.

"Now what?" Remington asked, mostly of himself. The agreed upon signal telling everyone the girls were safe, would be a shot from the *Kent's* long gun at the manor house.

The plan was clear. If Glen and Walt found the girls and could rescue them, they would. If they couldn't rescue, they'd return to the *Kent* and get the help they needed. If they needed help and couldn't return to the *Kent,* they'd start a fire as a signal for Remington to send in help. If someone found the girls safe elsewhere, Remington would hit the manor house with a ball from his long gun and the two men would retreat to the *Kent* under the diversion of the manor house's explosion.

Hitting the manor house could create enough distraction and chaos to facilitate a safe retreat back to the *Kent,* they thought. That plan made Remington smile. A smile of irony. The girls were safe elsewhere on the island, and Glen and Walt were now the ones needing rescue in the manor house.

From the vantage point on the deck of the *Kent,* the growing light of early morning revealed scores of men pouring out of various buildings. They headed toward the shore where longboats would take them to the *Chawbuck.*

"Jack, use your schoolboy smarts and neutralize that ship," Remington said. "Or we will have our hands full."

Jack hurried back down the ladder and jumped back into the longboat. He, Sal, and Amos rowed quickly toward the *Chawbuck*. It was a race.

Chapter One Hundred Thirteen

The Manor House - Hassan's Private Island - 1748

Hunter's face went white when he stepped into the room. There Glen was holding Walt up, while the two were surrounded by a half dozen guns. He turned to leave so quickly it caught everyone's attention. However, all Glen and Walt saw was a shoulder disappear.

Figuring the two were spies from the *Kent*, Scotty stepped up and demanded to know who they were, as if he were in charge. "What are your lives worth to the captain of that ship blocking our harbor?" Scotty demanded.

Walt recognized Scotty from the island. His severe limp favoring the hip both pleased and disappointed Walt. How did I miss? Walt wondered. That bolt should have hit the heart. He gave Glen a slight nod, confirming Scotty as one of the men responsible for his daughter's disappearance.

Glen and Walt were in no position to react rashly. It took uncharacteristic control for Glen not to come off the bench they sat on and break Scotty's neck.

He composed himself. "A business opportunity," Glen said, answering Scotty.

"Business?"

"You deal in human flesh; we want to be partners," Glen said.

"Partners?"

"Nobody suspects a ship of His Majesty's Navy would be carrying human cargo to the Eastern Mediterranean. Can't pack hundreds like you do, but we can safely sail where you can't. We can also deliver the precious cargo in better condition."

"We both win," Walt added weakly, holding a bloodied hand to his abdomen.

"We don't transport cargo," Scotty said.

“Oh?”

“No.”

Glen tilted his head, motioning toward the buildings outside the manor house wall and asked, “They all work the plantation? Even the white women?”

Hassan entered the room, leaving Krist alone and cut Scotty’s interrogation short. “What are you doing here?” he asked, looking Scotty right in the eye.

“They pretend to be interested in business,” Scotty said. His boldness and confidence slipped under Hassan’s commanding presence.

“Pretending? They are not pretending. They are here on business. Serious business. If anyone here is pretending, it’s you.” Hassan said.

Scotty, along with everyone else in the room, was stunned with the power of his denunciation.

“Step through that door and you will understand,” Hassan said.

Five minutes earlier, as the only person who could lead Hassan to the island, Scotty felt confident. Only he could lead Hassan to the clues Hassan hunted for two decades. Reluctantly and confused, Scotty walked toward the door. He looked from Glen and Walt to Hassan and back. He turned and stepped into the adjoining room. Krist looked up and gave a pained smile to his former first mate.

Scotty had one choice. He made that choice and ran headlong to the harbor. Jumping into the longboat, he rowed to the *Sally*. Reaching it, he bounded up the ladder and shouted to Caesar to hoist the anchor and get his galley slaves to put the *Sally* in motion. HMS *Kent* or not, he had to leave the island.

Remaining on the island guaranteed a painful death. He preferred to die escaping. The *Sally* remained motionless. Scotty yelled again. Still nothing. Angry, he stomped down the steps and where only a short time before sat eighteen galley slaves, Scotty stood facing a Norwegian and the beautiful redhead he’d tried to kidnap just five years earlier in Salcombe.

Scotty reached for a pistol which was not there. In his haste, he hadn’t armed himself.

They stood staring at each other. Finally, Rags broke the silence.

“I owe this to you,” Rags said, pointing to the remnants of a badly bruised face. “And this I owe to you,” he continued, revealing a large bandage on his chest where a ball had barely missed his heart. “And this I owe to you,” Rags finished, as he reached his arm around Clare and pulled her close. "For her, I thank you and forgive you."

Scotty stood there in shock. Staring, just staring.

"Did you know on this island cowitch grows freely? Your slaves know. They never touch it," Rags said.

"So what?" Scotty demanded.

"So, once on your skin, there is no hope without the antidote. Within minutes, its oil penetrates the blood system, shutting down the nervous system. It starts with an itch. Then turns to a painful welt. And soon becomes open sores. Assassins have known how to use this cowitch with great accuracy and efficiency for centuries."

Scotty looked at his hands, which began to itch.

"Let's talk about Elizabeth and Lydia," Rags said.

"I don't know where they are!" Scotty said.

"Is that a rash I see?" Rags asked. "You seem very uncomfortable."

"Somehow, they got off the ship, escaped. When we came into port they were locked safely in that storage room," Scotty pleaded as he pointed past where Clare and Rags stood.

Scotty became very agitated. Persperation soaked his clothes.

"You're not looking well," Rags calmly said. "Where would we find my two young friends?"

"I swear, I don't know. Somehow they got off the ship, and we never saw them again!"

"Two little girls outsmarted a ship full of pirates? Pirates feared the world over for kidnapping young girls?"

"Please! I don't know where they are! Give me the antidote and I will help you find them," Scotty begged. "You said you forgave me!" Scotty became frantic as his hands began itching feverishly.

"Yes, I did say that, and I do forgive you." Rags said.

"But I don't," came a voice from behind them.

A shot rang through the large galley before Scotty could turn. He dropped to the floor, blood rushing from his chest.

Clare and Rags turned; fearful they would be next.

"For what he's done? There is no forgiveness."

Clare and Rags stood frozen, looking at a large, black muscular giant of a man. Dripping wet. He dropped the pistol to his side and with a surprising smile asked, "You poisoned him?"

"He and I have a history with poisoned skin. It didn't take much to convince him."

"A history with skin poisoning?" Clare asked.

"Remember the rash that brought us together?" Rags asked. "I shared that same rash with him and his men while I was saving you. They suffered for weeks thinking a sick, infectious, dangerous tramp infected them. When I came back down the stairs behind you, I poisoned the railing."

Clare smiled up at him and gently kissed his cheek.

"Can you help us find our friends?" Rags asked.

"They saved Captain Krist's life. We got them free. They are safe."

"Can you take us to them?" Clare asked.

"Who are you?" Caesar asked.

Chapter One Hundred Fourteen

Inside the Manor House - Private Island - 1748

"I am sorry for this unfortunate way we finally meet, I had envisioned this opportunity much differently," Hassan said.

"I understand," Glen said.

It was clear Hassan knew who Glen and Walt were and why they came to the island. Scotty never met either of them and didn't know why they'd come. There was no sense keeping up any pretenses now.

Glen knew exactly who he was talking with. Though it had been some twenty years, he recognized that face, even though they had only met once in Newton Ferrers, in the dark.

"I will punish that man for what he's done," Hassan said.

"I imagine you will," Glen said. "That is your business. I am here about my business."

"I am sorry about taking your daughter and her friend. He will die for letting that happen."

"Letting that happen?" Glen said. "Your men stormed my island, shot my friend when he tried to protect my daughter from your men, and then carried her and her friend back to this island. Your island. Nobody 'let that happen.' You made that happen. You are responsible. Not 'that man'."

Hassan remained calm. "I'm not convinced you have what I'm looking for, but I hope for your daughter's sake, you can help me find it."

Hassan calculated that Glen and his companion didn't know crocs killed and ate his daughter. He knew there would be little chance of negotiating if he did.

Glen said, "I am certain you have what I am looking for and we won't talk about what you're looking for until you deliver her to me."

"You are not in a position to negotiate," Hassan said, looking at the two wounded, unarmed, and surrounded men.

"Oh, I don't know. My daughter and I will leave this island together or we will die trying. That puts me in a good position. Are you willing to give your life for your child? Because I am," Glen said.

Hassan's response was about to be the most important thing Krist would ever hear. When Scotty dashed from the room, he left the door open and Krist was listening to every word of the conversation. Glen didn't disappoint at all. The little he learned from Elizabeth and Lydia about Glen the past few days gave Krist the image of a man so courageous, so confident, so almost superhuman, Krist hadn't let himself believe a person like that lived.

But why was he being so stupid? Doesn't he know my father will just as soon kill him as not?

The silence between Glen's question and Hassan's answer said more than did the response. Krist knew his father's desire to find the man who stole his ship and to recover the Blade of Safavid meant more than Krist's own life. With that level of hate and passion, people meant nothing to him.

"That's not even a question needing an answer. I won't make that choice," Hassan said. "We both followed the same trail that led us to Newton Ferrers twenty years ago. David Creigh told you about the ship's surgeon. You bounded from the tavern. All I want to know is where that information led you."

"What I learned led me to Sheffield. You found the same information, or you would not have known where to send your dogs to find me. Where did he run off to now? A dog so cowardly he disappeared, tail between his legs."

Glen continued as Hassan glanced around. Hunter was there only moments before.

"Have you been trolling these waters the whole time we were stranded on that island?" Glen asked. "It must frustrate you now to learn that what you thought you were hunting is what we found and left behind right there in Sheffield."

"It was your lap dog, Hunter, who drove us away. You should have hired someone with a heart. Maybe then you would have avoided all this disappointment."

Hassan had kept a calm, cool expression, but now it was filling with anger. With so much hate for so many years, anger came naturally to him. But he needed more answers. There were no other leads, no other clues, no other chances and very few years left.

"Are you telling me I must go to Sheffield to get what you left behind?" Hassan asked.

"Oh, you won't find what you're looking for there. I was looking for the last few pieces of a puzzle. The piece I found in Newton Ferrers fits a very different puzzle than the one you're trying to put together," Glen said.

"And what kind of puzzle do you think I'm trying to put together?" Hassan asked.

"Someone wronged you when you lost your ship. Knowing Persians, likely they punished you for it. You failed to return this blade they talk about, which is said to have been taken by the pirate Avery when he looted the treasure ship. You failed to rescue the Mughal Emperor's granddaughter from Avery."

Hassan's lack of interruption confirmed Glen was on the right track.

"You wanted revenge for your failures. I understand that. And I don't fault you for it. Records from the Old Bailey led you to believe a ship's surgeon was responsible for your loss and that there was a chance Avery didn't have everything you wanted. I followed those same clues. Now you were hunting for more than a pirate and his treasure, in fact, I don't believe the treasure was ever your aim and you would have left it buried if you found it."

Hassan's slight nod confirmed that.

"You think I learned where to find the surgeon, the princess, the dagger, or the treasure. Maybe all four, there in Newton Ferrers. But I wasn't looking for any of them. Not the surgeon, the princess, a treasure, or even some relic of a dagger. Those were never my aim. Yes I was curious, even anxious for resolution to the mysteries of the Avery legend."

Hassan just stared at Glen. The two men's eyes were locked. After a few deep breaths, Glen continued.

"You hope the puzzle piece you find will complete a map that will lead to the satisfaction of getting even. Revenge. The Mughal's lost their hold on the empire. The Safavid's have fallen. You don't need a treasure. I know how life becomes personal. Bring me my daughter and what I know I will share. It won't help your puzzle, but at least you can continue searching in the few years you have remaining. I won't stop you."

Hassan had no leverage, he never had with people who didn't fear him.

He had killed men like this Glen. Good, fearless men had died at his hand for decades. But none of them had what Glen had - the missing piece to his puzzle.

† † †

The sun was about to rise and in the early morning light they saw a few men standing on the edge of the *Chawbuck's* deck, busy looking toward the shore. As Jack, Sal, and Amos feared someone would notice them, they slipped out of the boat and into the cold water, leaving the boat to drift.

"You can swim?" Jack asked his two companions.

"A little late to be asking," Sal said.

The three men split up and swam to their respective positions. Amos reached his assignment first. The rudder. Quietly, he submerged climbing hand over hand pulling himself down the blade of the rudder below. He then jammed the oar between it and the keel. This wouldn't disable the ship completely, but might make it difficult to maneuver in a battle.

Sal and Jack swam to the chain securing the ship to the anchor. Jack climbed. He reached the opening where the chain entered the ship. He was relieved it was large enough that he could make it through. He removed the crossbow from over his shoulder and tucked it through the hole and then squeezed through himself.

Jack hoped Sal and Amos could fit through this opening. Sal was larger around the belly and Amos didn't appear to be as agile as Jack.

The *Chawbuck* was a large ship. Jack didn't have time to search it and look for any other crew remaining on board.

Looking out one of the open holes on the gun deck, Jack saw several boats leave the shore loaded with Hassan's men heading for the ship.

No time to wait for Sal and Amos, Jack thought.

As quietly as he could move on a creaky old ship, Jack climbed above decks. He saw three men standing together on the main deck, watching boats leave the shore. Another was atop the mainmast, with a fifth on the upper deck. Both appeared to be intent, also looking toward the shore.

Jack had bolts enough, but five men would be a challenge. The man on the upper deck was first. He fell to the deck with a grunt, a bolt in his neck. The noise caught the attention of the three men on the main deck. As they turned, looking to the upper deck, a man fell from the mainmast dead, a bolt in his back. Each man turned frantically, looking for the source of the bolts.

Jack loosed one more as the sailor closest to the railing spotted him. Too late. He toppled overboard and splashed below. A shot rang out, and the crossbow shattered in Jack's hands.

He now faced two armed pirates with only Rags' knife in his belt. He ducked behind the mainmast as another shot missed his head by inches.

How fast can they reload? Do they have more than one pistol?

A third shot caught Jack in the upper arm, tearing through the shirt and skin. That answered his question.

He ducked down as a fourth ball shattered the edge of a stack of crates, sending splinters into his cheek.

How many shots do they have?

Jack pulled his knife and crawled carefully around the crates and stood. The pirate reloading a pistol looked up just as Jack's knife caught him in the stomach, causing him to drop the pistol. Jack's eyes searched for the other man, then crumbled to his knees as a plank shattered over his back. Jack crawled forward quickly and tried to stand to face his two hopefully unarmed foes. Pain pounded through his back and bleeding arm. But his arm worked.

† † †

Glen knew the man would kill him, Walt, Lydia, and Elizabeth when he thought the negotiations were over. In his heart, he was praying for Jack, Sal, and Amos to find the girls before Hassan made his final judgment and concluded this negotiation. Glen had worked with bullies plenty of times and he knew just how to keep them thinking they were in control as they lost their influence.

One signal Glen and Walt were waiting for was a cannon shot aimed at the manor house. He hoped Remington's gunner would miss so as not to kill him and Walt. This would let them know to wrap up the negotiations and get free. He had to keep the bully talking.

"Unless you can bring my daughter, I believe we will have a difficult time coming to an arrangement satisfactory to both of us." Glen said.

"Again, you are not in a position to negotiate." Hassan said.

"Unless you know something I don't, with a navy ship out there, there's not a very easy way for you to get out of here alive without letting us go, with my daughter."

Hassan stepped to the window and motioned to a guard standing outside.

† † †

On deck of the *Chawbuck,* the roar of a cannon blast shook the air. Stunned, all three turned to see Sal reloading the deck's swivel gun. Jack didn't wait. He plunged his shoulder into the man, pulling his knife from the man's stomach. Surprised, the man lost his balance and Jack cracked him into the wall. The knife fell to the deck. Jack grabbed him by the lapels, keeping him off balance and pushed him over the rail into the harbor.

Jack turned to face the last man. The echo of a second shot from the swivel gun rang across the deck. The last sailor and Jack were both stunned as the blasts and smoke filled the air. Catching his breath, Jack readied for another fight. The sailor jerked forward, fell to his knees, then to his face. Behind him stood Amos, the stock of a broken crossbow in his hands.

Harmless? Did Elizabeth say harmless? Jack wondered.

Joining Sal, Amos and Jack saw the approaching pirates were not deterred. They kept coming.

Sal reloaded and turned to Jack. "Want a turn?"

Jack smiled like a child with a new toy. He swiveled and aimed toward the lead boat. This small four-pound cannon was surprisingly loud. Jack's aim was dead on. The first boat ripped in half, launching sailors into the water.

† † †

When the sound of a cannon shot echoed up the plantation to the manor house, Hassan smiled directly into Glen's eyes.

"That was my *Chawbuck,* warning the *Kent* to stay out of our business. Yes, I know that ship well. It's never stopped me yet, nor will it." Hassan said. "We're ready for occasions like this. My *Chawbuck* out-guns your *Kent* by three times. You know that."

Seconds later, a second cannon shot was followed by a third.

† † †

"Can you two keep this up?" Jack asked.

Sal looked at the old crate holding a small pile of balls and a satchel full to the top with gunpowder.

"All morning!" he said with a chuckle.

Jack quickly snatched up his knife and threw himself over the railing.

The shortest distance to shore was cut off by pirates, confused as to which way to go. With his damaged arm, he struggled to swim around them. Finally he climbed up onto a patch of rocks. Shaking off the water, he rushed toward the manor house. All he knew was Glen and Walt were hurt, the girls were chasing headlong into the trouble, and chaos kept the harbor busy.

† † †

Hassan stood feeling confident he was in control. He recognized those shots were from his deck gun.

A second later, a ball from the twenty-four-pound long gun of the *Kent* with a range of well over 1500 yards tore through the western wall of the manor house, shaking everything in the room where negotiations were taking place.

When things settled, Glen said, "that was the *Kent,* politely saying, this is our business."

† † †

Hunter's only hope for survival was to catch up with Scotty and escape with him. If Hassan prevailed in the negotiation, Hunter was doomed, if somehow Glen triumphed, Hunter was doomed. Scotty was his only chance.

He dashed through a hall, out to the yard, hopped over the small rock wall and halted face to face with Elizabeth and Lydia.

Lydia pulled her knife so quickly both Elizabeth and Hunter took a step back.

The feeling of repulsion, of fear, of evil was gone. Hate smothered them out.

Elizabeth hated Krist's father for what he did to people, especially to his own son. She hated Krist for his cowardice. She wanted to hate this man who stood in front of her for what was done to her family. She could then unleash that hate once and for all. She pulled the knife Krist gave her back on the Sally.

"Tell me about your wife," Elizabeth said.

Lydia's head turned to Elizabeth so fast she nearly lost her footing.

Hunter glared at the ridiculous question.

"Tell me about your wife, your Joanna," Elizabeth repeated.

"That tramp. Who cares about her?" he said.

"I do," Elizabeth lifted the knife a few inches.

As if this grown, evil man thought two women, one only a child, could threaten him into fear. Elizabeth would have laughed if she wasn't so determined to see justice.

"Where is she from?" Elizabeth asked just as firmly as she had her previous question.

"What does it matter. She was a gift. Taken from some coastal town. She was young, pretty, and once I taught her to obey, she served my needs. Nothing more than a loyal dog."

His disdain for life, for love, and possibly for her sister so repulsed her, the nausea nearly crippled her resolve.

"Your Joanna is somebody's daughter. Taken by force, abused, and discarded. You're not even human." Elizabeth regretted she didn't have words to express her disgust, her hate for his kind. She thought back to the conversation with Elen and Elen's admonition.

"The men who took your sister are animals. They've lost their claim on humanity. They're unworthy of forgiveness. There's no reconciling their actions with mercy. Are you ready to confront that fact if you eventually find the monsters that took your sister? Are you ready to be the judge, the jury, and the executioner? You will not be able to walk away. It will be you or them."

The words came back to Elizabeth's mind so vividly.

"You will yield to their power. You will become their victim with a similar fate as your sister, or you will yield to hate that will drive you to destroy them."

Could she kill Hunter? Yes, and she must. She remembered vividly her response to Elen.

"Someone must stop them! Justice must be satisfied! Civilization demands it."

The battle in Elizabeth's mind ended. Yes, she must destroy this man. She adjusted her footing, secured the knife in her grip, and readied to plunge the knife into his heart.

She gritted her teeth, pursed her lips and the passage from her father's Bible pushed it all aside.

"But I say unto you, love your enemies, bless them that curse you, do good to them that hate you, and pray for them which despitefully use you, and persecute you;"

Tears rolled down a cheek. The battle she'd prepared for, she'd hardened herself for, she'd given her life for, was ripped from her.

"Your wife, your loyal dog as you called her..." but Elizabeth couldn't move, she froze. Knuckles white, cheeks trembling, legs shaking, she cried, "...is somebody's sister!"

Then she lunged.

Hunter's hands were too quick, and he knocked her arm away, pushing her to the ground, then turned to Lydia so fast he knocked her knife to the ground.

Elizabeth's shock of failure stunned her ability to react. Hunter grabbed Lydia. "You're my passage off this island."

For the third time in her life Elizabeth saw the same nightmare playing out before her eyes. Horror washed over her.

Just as fast, the nightmare ended. Hunter released the struggling Lydia, who stumbled to the ground. He looked to his chest and saw protruding from it a majestically carved handle.

"Not this time."

Hunter dropped to his knees, reaching to pull the knife from his chest. As his hands reached it, his body dropped, plunging it deeper.

The morning light highlighted Jack's brow. He lifted Lydia to her feet, bent to help Elizabeth to her feet, then kicked the bleeding body of evil over and pulled his knife free.

† † †

Hassan quietly stood and attempted to end the conversation by inflicting the greatest pain possible. A pain a parent will suffer more than if a child were dead.

"If we are at an impasse, which you tell me we are, there is no use to continue this conversation. You said you would leave this island with your daughter or you wouldn't leave it alive. You made your choice. Here you will die. I can't threaten to hurt your daughter to get you to share with me what you know, because she never made it back to this island. Fools should have brought her to me, but made the mistake of sending her with the others.

"Your daughter is now bound for the Eastern Mediterranean. I can stop that, if you give me what I want. If not, I may never realize the profit she will bring. You and I might both be dead. But you may be sure the pleasure she will provide my customers will be worth the price you pay.

"You've put an end to my journey," Hassan said, turning and stepping among the fragments of wall and glass that fell when the cannon hit the manor house. "You asked if I would give my life to save my family? No, but I will die to destroy yours!"

He reached for a pistol, one of two remaining that hung on his coat.

"No, father, I am sorry but you won't," Krist said, weak and leaning against the door's opening.

Krist was holding a pistol aimed at his father. Hassan hadn't yet pulled his pistol. He paused and looked at his son without fear. Glen and Walt were still under guard.

"Father, this man does not have what you want. Nobody has what you want. You want something no man has ever had. You want the peace that will come once you have revenge," Krist said. "That peace does not exist. That is the piece of the puzzle they found and left in Sheffield. That is the peace that will never fit into your puzzle."

Hassan reached for his pistol and Krist fired, grazing his father's neck and putting a hole in his father's collar. Hassan stopped and glared at his son in shock.

"I didn't miss father," Krist said as he dropped the empty pistol and transferred a second pistol from his left to his right hand. "You taught me well. I've just never needed to kill anyone. I am prepared to do so now."

"You couldn't," Hassan said.

"This man's daughter and her friend are not on a ship. That is a lie. They were not eaten by crocs, that is a lie. You will never hurt them, that is not a lie. You will let these men go. If not, I suppose that ship out there will level this house and sink your precious Chawbuck, right where it sits. And we all die. Let them go. Have your revenge on me for destroying your last effort to get that elusive revenge which you so proudly used to destroy lives. Then you and I can die together."

Everyone in the partially damaged main room waited and watched. The cannons from both ships were silent. The next decision Hassan made would determine who would die first. Glen was trying to absorb the news that Lydia was still alive. The cannon blast told him they found Lydia, but the confirmation from Hassan's own son confirmed his prayers were answered once again. He wanted to ask how, but he knew this was now between a father and his son.

After staring in disbelief at his son, and risking his son wouldn't shoot, Hassan reached for his pistol. A shot echoed through the room. Hassan lurched, but didn't fall. He placed his hand over his stomach. Blood oozed through his fingers. He looked to Krist, who still held a loaded pistol.

Behind Krist stood Caesar. Behind him stood an out-of-breath Mereday.

Seconds later, Jack, Lydia, and Elizabeth rushed in.

Surprised, Krist turned and looked at Caesar holding the smoking pistol.

"Why?" The word barely audible.

"Because you wouldn't," Caesar said. "Go home, Captain. It's time for you to go home."

Hassan dropped to his knees and Krist tried to cross the room. He was far too weak and stumbled to the floor. Elizabeth slipped past Mereday and helped Krist crawl to his father. Lydia ran to Glen. The guns were no longer aimed at Glen and Walt. During the exchange between Krist and Hassan, the guards changed their allegiance.

Krist was too weak to help his father as they both lay bleeding on the floor.

"I'm sorry, Father. I'm sorry for the life you thought you had to live."

Hassan said nothing. He looked at his son, to Elizabeth, and back to his son. He closed his eyes and took one last difficult breath.

Chapter One Hundred Fifteen

Onboard the HMS Kent - Hassan's Harbor - 1748

Captain Remington and Lucas watched the retreating pirates scramble from their longboats back on shore. The manor house was under attack, the *Chawbuck* was under control by the pirates' enemy, the pirates had no place to go.

"Whatever happens in that manor house, you've got decisions to make," Lucas said to his captain. "There's a hostile force to deal with."

Captain Remington gave Lucas the orders to keep the guns prepared and the crew ready. He was taking a small force with him and going ashore. If he met resistance, Lucas would send a few shots strategically placed to establish who was now in command.

† † †

Word came from the manor house that Captain Hassan was dead and that Captain Krist commanded they lay down their arms. The pirate crew put up no resistance. Once ushered back into the barracks, Remington placed guards to keep them there.

He made his way up the hill, and with a few men, entered the manor house. Surveying his damage, he congratulated himself. "That's a good piece of firing."

"Not if we'd been on that side of the room." Walt said.

Lydia helped Glen up, and together they attended to Walt's wound. After some painful poking around by Glen, still bleeding a bit himself, Glen pronounced the prognosis.

"Well, Walt my boy, Louisa won't kill me for making her a widow."

Mereday, Caesar, and Elizabeth helped Krist back to a bedroom adjacent to the main hall. They cleaned the blood and applied clean bandages. Mereday insisted

on some ale to soften the pain. Krist refused.

Jack stood in the doorway, watching as Elizabeth helped care for Krist.

The feelings he felt shocked him. He reflected back on the first time he really met her. It seemed bandages were always needed. Who is this mystery woman? Besides Joanna's sister.

"Can I be of help?" Jack asked.

Elizabeth turned and welcomed him with a smile.

"On the other side of the island, you asked who this Captain Krist was," she said. "Meet Captain Krist, both our captor and liberator." Then turning to Krist, she continued, "Captain, meet Jack, my fiancé."

Captain Remington stepped up to where Glen was attending to Walt's bleeding chest. It wasn't so bad he was critical, but Glen was careful to get the bandaging right before they moved him around.

"What do you propose we do with an island full of cutthroats?" Remington asked.

Caesar was watching all of this and gave instructions to servants to remove Hassan's body. He then stepped over to the men and repeated himself.

"It's time to go home. Take your family home. The worst are dead. Everyone can go home." Caesar said.

Mereday entered the room. "This is our home. We will stay here."

† † †

At Krist's direction, Captain Remington, Caesar, and Mereday spent the day assessing the needs and desires of the island's residents, including Hassan's crew. The conclusions confirmed Caesar's proclamation that the worst were dead. For the next few days, the men convalesced, and they made preparations to transport those who wanted to leave the island. For those who wished to remain behind, Krist organized the new management of the island's affairs naming Mereday its new governor.

Captain Remington took control of the *Chawbuck* renaming it the *Kristan*. On the third morning, all three ships sailed with the tide. The *Kent* was under Glen's command. The newly named *Kristan*, with a crew of men having sworn allegiance to His Majesty, was under the command of Captain Remington. Caesar took command of the *Sally*, and with a galley empty of slaves but manned by freemen, they escorted Captain Krist to a home he hoped to find in Iceland.

Chapter One Hundred Sixteen

Clare's Tavern - St. John's, Antigua - 1748

The children finally slept. Rosemary quietly closed the door and walked down to the common room where Ben and Susan finished closing down Clare's tavern for the night. They said good night and Rosemary sat alone with the single lamp illuminating the small corner of the room.

She opened the journal and re-read the last page which contained the letter from the Princess Astrella's father to the ship's surgeon, Dr. Hincher.

My dearest Dr. Alexander Hincher,

If you followed my wishes, you are reading this letter in safety and peace. You are no longer running for your life. God willing, and I believe He is, my beloved daughter Astrella is with you.

I thank you as only a loving father can, for your love and care for her. I chastised you for attempting to bring her back to her family. If you recall, I also praised you for that effort. Now I thank you with all my heart. I give you my blessing to share this letter with her and to share your life with her. You have earned my devoted honor.

In a world where a father will imprison his favorite daughter, execute his brothers and father and sacrifice the lives of countless thousands to retain a power that can only be maintained by blood; I want you to know there are also fathers who will give their lives to protect, teach and provide for those they love.

There is no way you cannot have seen my love for the Princess Zeb-un-Nissa. Though Aurangzeb always suspected I was the father of his granddaughter, the political advantage he realized with the world believing the deception of Shah Suleiman I as the father and Shah Husayn as Astrella's brother minimized the threat Aurangzeb felt from me.

Though Esther's actual father was not the Shah of Persia, and the current fool is not her real brother, do not minimize the royal blood that flows in her veins. You need to know that I am the grandson of Safi Mirza, crown prince of the Safavid Dynasty under his father Shah Abbas the Great. My father had me secreted away before his father, the Shah could have us assassinated as he did to 4 of his sons and two of his grandsons.

You can see how if Astrella ever claimed either of the two thrones of which she is a rightful heir, she would never live long enough to reign.

I don't believe I will ever meet you again. Know that I have no regrets. I will die with the peace knowing my azizam Astrella is cared for. What more can a father want?

In your eternal debt, Makhfi

- Hinch

- From the journal of Alexander Hincher - Finally home.

Just as she did the first time she finished the journal, Rosemary turned the next few pages hoping to find more. The pages were blank. As Glen confirmed earlier, the story ended.

Chapter One Hundred Seventeen

St. John's Harbor - Antigua - 1748

During the absence of the others, Rosemary took the twins and Lizzy down to the harbor to watch for the returning ship each morning and evening. Rosemary did her best to tell them bedtime stories, but she couldn't match Glen's passion and enthusiasm when he described the many adventures of the heroes he called 'Hincher and the Princess.'

Having finished reading the 'journal of a ship's surgeon,' she realized many of the stories he told over the years were based on characters and events he took from the journal. She wondered if the other stories he told the children weren't actually from his own life. There would be time enough to find out when he and Lydia returned and the family reunited, she hoped.

Nearly a week had passed. Rosemary and the children took a meandering walk through the hills where the children loved to explore. Like every other day, the adventure ended down on the water's edge. The sun hung lazily along the early evening horizon. Rosemary squinted against its brightness, focusing on the sails of two ships that broke the line between sea and sky. The anticipation was palpable. She called to the children and together they all stood and watched as the ships sailed closer and closer. Finally, she identified the *Kent*. Her heart told her all was well, but it could hardly handle the feeling of gratitude when she spotted her precious Lydia standing as tall as she could on the port bow, waving as hard as she could.

As the gangplank lowered, the twins were up and in their father's arms before the ship was secured to its moorings.

Lydia rushed down into Rosemary's arms, practically squashing little Lizzy. "You're ok?" Rosemary cried squeezing her tight. With help of a cane, Glen shuffled down to his wife and daughters. The twins, following the quick reunion with their sister and father, began their exploration of the new ship.

Walt, with Sal and Amos mostly carrying him, met Louisa's disapproving glare at his bandaged chest. "What is this?" she demanded.

"You can thank Glen and Lydia." He said, "I got shot."

"Glen and Lydia shot you?" she asked.

"They patched me up," Walt chuckled, wincing in pain.

She looked at the bandaging and back at Glen. "I'll forgive the bandaging job since he's alive." Louisa accompanied Walt toward Clare's tavern, which served as home base since arriving in Antigua.

Noting the excitement down at the docks, Joanna, aided by a pair of homemade crutches and Ben's shoulder, shuffled from the tavern toward the water. Anticipation that she might have a sister provided a new hope for a life unfettered by humiliation, pain, and anguish. She clung to Rosemary's belief that she could have a younger sister. The recent visitor to the island carrying the same name as her younger sister, and as Rosemary proclaimed, "whose likeness was too profound to dismiss," gave her a hope she hadn't experienced for years.

That very hope alone returned a light to Joanna's countenance, that Rosemary confirmed was the same she'd seen in Elizabeth.

Joanna halted in mid-hobbled-stride as a beautiful woman bounded down off the ship to the shore. Visions of her mother pulsed through her mind. The walk, the way the long reddish blond hair hung over her shoulders, the squint in the eyes and the tiny, crooked smile confirmed instantly this stranger was indeed family. It was as if her mother was charging toward her to the rescue. She blinked to clear the flooding tears away and confirm it wasn't her mother. For nearly fifteen years, the horror of the attack haunted her waking and sleeping hours. With her mother murdered and father away, she made her baby sister, not yet a teenager, promise to stay hidden no matter what. Was it possible the same little girl who tagged along everywhere Joanna went when they were young and free, was now a grown woman? Could it be possible that little sister was fulfilling a promise made as a frightened child those many years ago? The words were so vivid in Joanna's memory. "I will find you! I promise!"

Joanna had long ago buried that promise and smothered that hope. How could little Lizzy ever find her? Alone, hidden, frightened? How many times had Joanna wondered, prayed and hoped her little sister was even alive? And what of her father? But there she was. All strength left Joanna. Without the crutch and Ben's firm grasp, Joanna would have collapsed to the rocky ground. She hung on his support.

Looking past the crowd reveling in the reunion, Elizabeth sighted her sister. She turned from the group and stared. Her legs felt like lead. Though her heart and mind urged them to run to Joanna, her legs only permitted deliberate steps. One agonizing step at a time, her mind memorized every inch of this other woman. How many times had she dreamt of this moment, the reunion she'd given her life to pursue? A thousand possibilities, countless dreams, and now she was just feet away from the reality. Nothing measured up to the emotion overtaking her soul. She jumped the last few feet and took Joanna in her arms, pulling her so close she practically hung in Elizabeth's embrace. Both women shuddered as tears drowned the years.

No one dared move. Even the twins hanging off the edge of the railing were captivated by the moment. Watching from the bow of the *Kristan*, formerly the *Chawbuck* as it pulled up behind the *Kent*, Jack's tears rolled off his cheeks watching the reunion resulting from the drama into which he'd painfully and unintentionally been plunged.

By the time Remington's men secured the *Kristan*, the island's triumphant visitors were drying tears in Clare's tavern.

Rosemary curiously watched Jack enter with his uncle, Captain Remington. The story Lydia briefly told of his saving her and Elizabeth's lives from Hunter, included enough clues she wanted to confirm if the proposal of their engagement at the point of Glen's machete only weeks ago, stuck. Apparently, it did.

Jack spotted Elizabeth immediately and nonchalantly sat near where Joanna and Elizabeth continued drying tears.

The twins hung on every word Lydia tumbled out as she told about the hurricane, the ship, the galley slaves, saving Krist, being saved… the story went on and on.

Marge, Susan, and Louisa put on a welcome feast that gave Clare some concern she'd have competition. Though, not enough concern to drag her away from Rags' side. His story about Scotty's permanent retirement was one for the annals of history, Rosemary thought.

This is right. This is how it's supposed to be. Rosemary felt it in her bones and in her heart.

Captain Remington announced that since fulfilling his quest to find his sailor Cav and his commission from His Majesty to find and destroy the *Chawbuck* and its captain, he expected to be rewarded with a boring, unfulfilling assignment which he'd likely turn down in exchange for a position where he could finally be a father and a husband, since Cav made it look fulfilling enough.

† † †

After a few weeks catching up and convalescing, it was time to move on.

Walt, Glen, and Rags invited Sal to join them in their new venture, but when he heard it would be in New England, he didn't know if he could stand the cold winters. Once they reminded him that New England was outside hurricane paths, he accepted. After all, they couldn't do without him.

Captain Remington in the *Kent* and Captain Lucas in the *Kristan* escorted the *Rosemary* as far as New York before returning to England, where Captain Remington planned to return to the colonies with his brother's and Elizabeth's family for a New England wedding.

Chapter One Hundred Eighteen

Boston Harbor, Massachusetts, America - 1748

The *Rosemary* dropped anchor among a dozen other ships in Boston Harbor. Its passengers tendered ashore and settled comfortably in an inn overlooking the mouth of the Charles River. Walt and Louisa were as giddy as the children. Sal and Marge tried to act mature, but they too were overwhelmed with excitement at the prospects they were ready to start a new life.

Rags and Clare planned to remain in Antigua until spring. They stayed to help Ben and Susan learn to run Clare's tavern before they moved to Boston. Clare was excited to bring her new Caribbean flavors to the north.

At first, both Lydia and Joanna resented Jack getting in the way of their relationship with Elizabeth, but Jack grew on them and they became fast friends. The twins kept Jack busy enough the women had plenty of female time together.

Once settled, Glen was eager to explore this new port town with his family. He invited Jack, Elizabeth, and Joanna to join his little expedition.

The hired carriage stopped in front of a beautiful home.

"What's this?" Rosemary asked.

Glen smiled, stepped from the carriage, and helped her down. The twins jumped out and Lydia handed the baby down to Rosemary. Jack helped Elizabeth and Joanna and the group stood there all looking to Glen for some kind of explanation.

"I want you all to meet someone," he said, stepping through the gate and up to the door. He knocked gently.

An old gentleman opened the door, smiled, and gave Glen a hug that shocked the group. Rosemary stepped back in surprise. She didn't know who this old man was holding her Glen, but her tears threatened as she witnessed the loving embrace.

Elizabeth recognized him at once.

The old gentleman welcomed them inside and ushered them into a beautiful library where they each took a seat on very comfortable furniture. Glen walked over to an exquisite pair of chairs and invited Rosemary to sit. As he did, he ran his fingers over the armrest with a delicate, almost reverent touch. Rosemary couldn't figure out what was going on in Glen's head, let alone what they were doing in this elegant home.

It had been a very long time since this kind of elegance had surrounded her. She couldn't help but worry if the twins would get restless and break something. Turning to Glen and wondering what he was doing, she broke the silence.

"What is it?" she asked.

Reverently, he continued admiring the craftsmanship of the chair.

"I built these chairs," he finally said. "They were the first real furniture I ever built. They kept them." He continued, "You kept them," he turned looking toward the old man.

"Yes. Why wouldn't we? They're beautiful," the old man said. "Will you please excuse me? I need to get my wife, my princess."

Rosemary thought that it was sweet of this old man to refer to his wife as a princess. She wondered how Glen would refer to her when the two of them were this old.

"We know him," a stunned Elizabeth whispered to Joanna.

Joanna sat wide eyed.

After a few minutes, the old man escorted the most beautiful woman any of these visitors had ever seen into the room. Though by her movement she was obviously about her husband's same age, she looked more vibrant and regal. Her tears chased each other down her cheeks. Everyone stood in reverence, yet none of them knew why. She took Glen by the hand and kissed his cheek, and turned immediately to Rosemary. After a few seconds of just peering into her eyes, she took Rosemary in her arms and held her tight.

As they released the embrace, Glen took Rosemary by the hand.

"I want you to meet the Princess Astrella. Heir to both the Safavid Persian

Dynasty and the Mughal Empire," Glen said as he bowed.

Everyone stood frozen in complete silence and awe. Even the twins and the baby in Elizabeth's arms remained silent in the moment.

Then, with his arm on the shoulder of the old man who stood alongside the princess, Glen continued the introductions. "And the famed ship's surgeon, Dr. Alexander Hincher Cavanaugh."

The shock of meeting the very characters she'd read about from a place far away and time long ago stole her strength. Rosemary reached out and held tightly to Glen's arm. One of the twins burst out, breaking the reverence.

"That's our name!" little Jessie said.

"Yes," Glen said. He pulled the children close. "I want you all to meet your grandparents. Mother, Father, meet your grandchildren."

Glen continued the introductions, first with Elizabeth still holding the baby. "Miss Elizabeth Farrow visited our island in search of family and willingly chose to sacrifice her own to protect mine. A debt I will never be able to repay."

"I know you," Elizabeth said reverently. "Dr. Cavanaugh, you..."

"Please, to my friends, it's Hinch," he said.

"Mr. Hinch," she continued, "you were in business with my father. I was a child but I remember you. After our family was destroyed, you came to help me to my grandparent's home. My father loved you."

"You've grown to become a beautiful woman. I loved your father. I wept when I learned of his death. Is this your sister? I never met her." He took Joanna by the hand with great gentleness and respect. "Your father was a great man and an honorable business partner. Lord Rudy, my good friend, trusted no man more. Not even me."

"Father, meet Mr. Jackson Remington, Lord Remington's son from London. He so kindly escorted Miss Farrow to our island, leaving a trail of bodies and an appointment to Cambridge University's hallowed halls behind to do so."

"Your father is a fine man. One of the few deserving the title of His Lordship," Hinch said. I met him once when Esther and I visited in London. He was instrumental getting my son assigned to serve with your uncle, though Captain Remington never knew it was his brother who recommended him so highly.

"You're friends with my uncle?" Jack asked.

"I never met him. I simply trusted the recommendation of your father, and was never disappointed."

Watching all of this, Rosemary nearly fainted at the irony of it all. Glen's giant smile told her everything.

Lydia finally asked, "Grandmother, are you really a princess?"

Astrella nodded.

"Does that make me a princess? A real princess?" Lydia asked, growing jubilant.

Hinch took her by both hands, and slowly bending down, looking her straight in the eyes said. "Yes, it does. But you are more than a princess."

He released her, slowly stood back up, shuffled over to a cabinet and removed a remarkable leather box with gemstones beautifully placed around its edges. He opened it and lifted out a dagger of exquisite beauty.

"Princess Lydia, may I present to you the Blade of Safavid." He bowed in reverence to a sovereign queen.

She took it, eyes wide, and held it like a delicate newborn baby.

"Not just a princess, you are an empress," he said bowing again.

"We have a box like that!" Jesse said.

Rosemary had that very thought but hesitated to take this moment away from Lydia. She might be a daughter and a sister, but if this was not a dream, which she feared it was, her daughter was indeed an empress.

Hinch turned to Glen, "you have a box like this one?"

Glen nodded.

"So do I," Elizabeth said.

Glen and Hinch turned to Elizabeth, expecting her to tell more. She did.

"On the island. While in hiding, Lydia dug up a box just like that one, but rotted and worn. Of all the jewels, only an opal remains," Elizabeth said.

Hinch turned back to Glen with the same expectation.

"While searching for a secure hiding place on our island, I found that same box. The jewels were also missing," Glen said. "It seemed the perfect container for your journal, by the way."

Rosemary knew this was the very Hinch, the ship's surgeon, the one who rescued and married the princess, but when Glen pronounced it so boldly, she shivered at the realization. Goose bumps textured her arms.

Esther chuckled. She stepped over and took the box in her hand.

"There were three boxes like this made. Each housed one of the Safavid Dynasty sacred relics. This one holds the Blade of Safavid, which is the emblem of rights-of-political rule. The two others, rights-of-religious and rights-of-economic rule. The emperor retains the blade and appoints the other two."

Jack gently took the box from Esther, examining it inside and out.

"When Captain Avery plundered my grandfather's ship, all three were taken, but we only saved this one. Lord Rudy tried to rescue the other two but couldn't get to them before we escaped the *Fancy*," Esther said.

"Avery had all three boxes?" Jack said. "But Rudy saved only one?"

Everyone thought the same thing. Everyone but the twins; they were thinking about climbing the beautiful winding staircase. They had never climbed real stairs before.

"What else did Avery hide on those two islands?" Rosemary finally asked.

One of the great advantages writers of historical fiction have, is the credibility of the world from which they establish the settings for their stories. As writers of fiction, they can then cast and direct their fictional characters to weave in and out of history in a world they can bring to life. They have the freedom to bend and shape stories to create images and emotions to influence their readers. If done well, history can come alive for their audience.

Yet they have the challenge to preserve historical integrity as they bend and shape their characters and the events they share.

In the Blade of Safavid, great effort is taken to keep the events possible within the settings. The fictional characters have been cast to tell the actual stories here. The facts surrounding Captain Henry Avery are as close to historical fact as possible. Though told by the fictional ship's surgeon Dr. Alexander Hincher - 'Hinch'; Captain Avery's story is as real as real can be, considering there was no real journal kept, he never posted on his blog or other social media, and historians of the day (300 years ago) recorded the history from legend, hearsay and rumor. The actual testimony from the trials of the few eyewitnesses may be all that credibly exist.

The non-fictional Mughal and Safavid characters are as true as possible. That one of the Mughal Emperors family was kidnapped during the pirate attack is among the historical facts alleged to be true. Thus Astrella could be a real character. Let's pretend she was. - after all, that is what fiction is all about.

In the following pages, you will find both fact and fiction. From here, simple research will help you know the difference - that research can be almost as fulfilling as is this fiction.

I thank the many contributors to the many online blogs, articles, white papers, wiki postings and theses that gave me plenty of historical facts from which to weave my fiction.

More is available at: www.kentmerrellauthor.com

Historical Lines of Succession

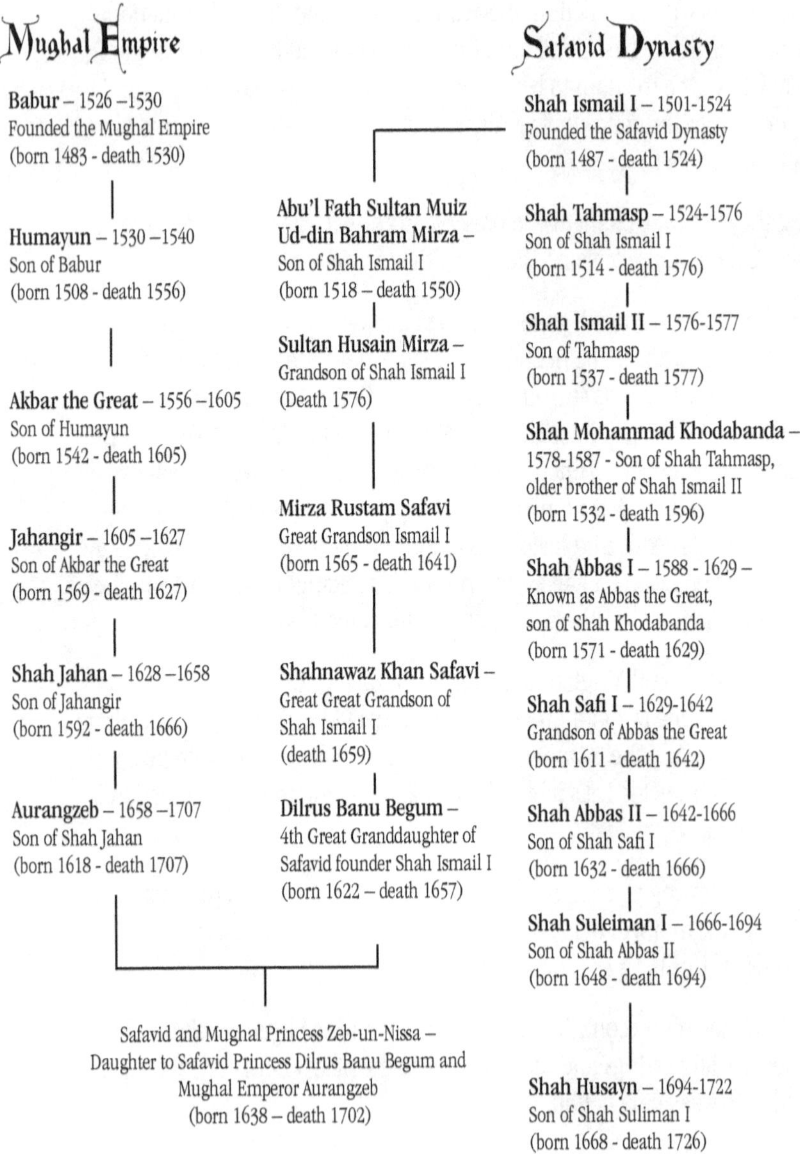

Mughal Empire

Babur – 1526 –1530
Founded the Mughal Empire
(born 1483 - death 1530)

Humayun – 1530 –1540
Son of Babur
(born 1508 - death 1556)

Akbar the Great – 1556 –1605
Son of Humayun
(born 1542 - death 1605)

Jahangir – 1605 –1627
Son of Akbar the Great
(born 1569 - death 1627)

Shah Jahan – 1628 –1658
Son of Jahangir
(born 1592 - death 1666)

Aurangzeb – 1658 –1707
Son of Shah Jahan
(born 1618 - death 1707)

Abu'l Fath Sultan Muiz Ud-din Bahram Mirza –
Son of Shah Ismail I
(born 1518 – death 1550)

Sultan Husain Mirza –
Grandson of Shah Ismail I
(Death 1576)

Mirza Rustam Safavi
Great Grandson Ismail I
(born 1565 - death 1641)

Shahnawaz Khan Safavi –
Great Great Grandson of
Shah Ismail I
(death 1659)

Dilrus Banu Begum –
4th Great Granddaughter of
Safavid founder Shah Ismail I
(born 1622 – death 1657)

Safavid and Mughal Princess Zeb-un-Nissa –
Daughter to Safavid Princess Dilrus Banu Begum and
Mughal Emperor Aurangzeb
(born 1638 – death 1702)

Safavid Dynasty

Shah Ismail I – 1501-1524
Founded the Safavid Dynasty
(born 1487 - death 1524)

Shah Tahmasp – 1524-1576
Son of Shah Ismail I
(born 1514 - death 1576)

Shah Ismail II – 1576-1577
Son of Tahmasp
(born 1537 - death 1577)

Shah Mohammad Khodabanda –
1578-1587 - Son of Shah Tahmasp,
older brother of Shah Ismail II
(born 1532 - death 1596)

Shah Abbas I – 1588 - 1629 –
Known as Abbas the Great,
son of Shah Khodabanda
(born 1571 - death 1629)

Shah Safi I – 1629-1642
Grandson of Abbas the Great
(born 1611 - death 1642)

Shah Abbas II – 1642-1666
Son of Shah Safi I
(born 1632 - death 1666)

Shah Suleiman I – 1666-1694
Son of Shah Abbas II
(born 1648 - death 1694)

Shah Husayn – 1694-1722
Son of Shah Suliman I
(born 1668 - death 1726)

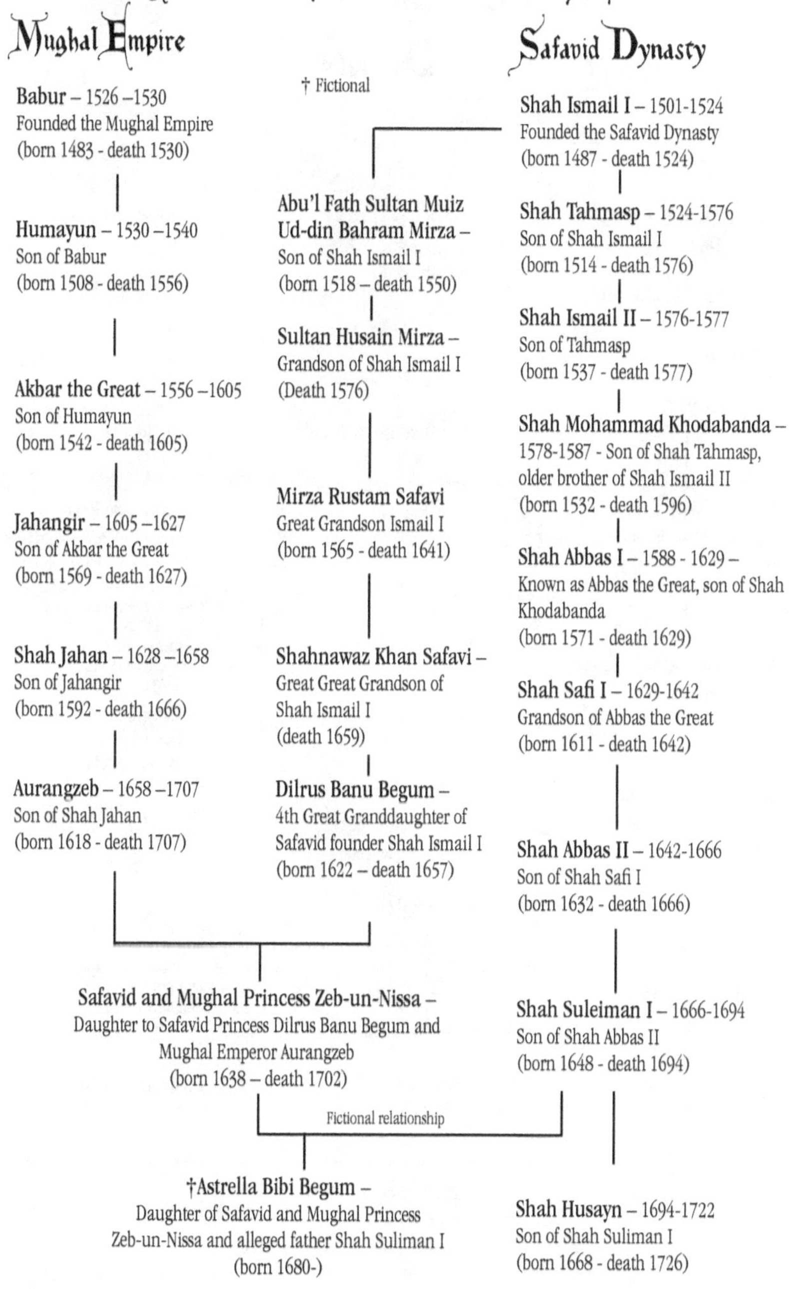

Historical Blended with Fiction

Mughal Empire

Safavid Dynasty

† Fictional

Babur – 1526 –1530
Founded the Mughal Empire
(born 1483 - death 1530)

Humayun – 1530 –1540
Son of Babur
(born 1508 - death 1556)

Akbar the Great – 1556 –1605
Son of Humayun
(born 1542 - death 1605)

Jahangir – 1605 –1627
Son of Akbar the Great
(born 1569 - death 1627)

Shah Jahan – 1628 –1658
Son of Jahangir
(born 1592 - death 1666)

Aurangzeb – 1658 –1707
Son of Shah Jahan
(born 1618 - death 1707)

Abu'l Fath Sultan Muiz
Ud-din Bahram Mirza –
Son of Shah Ismail I
(born 1518 – death 1550)

Sultan Husain Mirza –
Grandson of Shah Ismail I
(Death 1576)

Mirza Rustam Safavi
Great Grandson Ismail I
(born 1565 - death 1641)

Shahnawaz Khan Safavi –
Great Great Grandson of
Shah Ismail I
(death 1659)

Dilrus Banu Begum –
4th Great Granddaughter of
Safavid founder Shah Ismail I
(born 1622 – death 1657)

Shah Ismail I – 1501-1524
Founded the Safavid Dynasty
(born 1487 - death 1524)

Shah Tahmasp – 1524-1576
Son of Shah Ismail I
(born 1514 - death 1576)

Shah Ismail II – 1576-1577
Son of Tahmasp
(born 1537 - death 1577)

Shah Mohammad Khodabanda –
1578-1587 - Son of Shah Tahmasp,
older brother of Shah Ismail II
(born 1532 - death 1596)

Shah Abbas I – 1588 - 1629 –
Known as Abbas the Great, son of Shah
Khodabanda
(born 1571 - death 1629)

Shah Safi I – 1629-1642
Grandson of Abbas the Great
(born 1611 - death 1642)

Shah Abbas II – 1642-1666
Son of Shah Safi I
(born 1632 - death 1666)

Safavid and Mughal Princess Zeb-un-Nissa –
Daughter to Safavid Princess Dilrus Banu Begum and
Mughal Emperor Aurangzeb
(born 1638 – death 1702)

Shah Suleiman I – 1666-1694
Son of Shah Abbas II
(born 1648 - death 1694)

Fictional relationship

†Astrella Bibi Begum –
Daughter of Safavid and Mughal Princess
Zeb-un-Nissa and alleged father Shah Suliman I
(born 1680-)

Shah Husayn – 1694-1722
Son of Shah Suliman I
(born 1668 - death 1726)

Historical Lines with Fiction

Safavid Dynasty

Shah Ismail I – 1501-1524
Founded the Safavid Dynasty
(born 1487 - death 1524)

Abu'l Fath Sultan Muiz Ud-din Bahram Mirza –
Son of Shah Ismail I
(born 1518 – death 1550)

Sultan Husain Mirza –
Grandson of Shah Ismail I
(Death 1576)

Mirza Rustam Safavi
Great Grandson Ismail I
(born 1565 - death 1641)

Shahnawaz Khan Safavi –
Great Great Grandson of
Shah Ismail I
(death 1659)

Dilrus Banu Begum –
4th Great Granddaughter of
Safavid founder Shah Ismail I
(born 1622 – death 1657)

Safavid and Mughal Princess Zeb-un-Nissa –
Daughter to Safavid Princess
Dilrus Banu Begum and
Mughal Emperor Aurangzeb
(born 1638 – death 1702)

Shah Tahmasp – 1524-1576
Son of Shah Ismail I
(born 1514 - death 1576)

Shah Ismail II – 1576-1577
Son of Tahmasp
(born 1537 - death 1577)

Shah Mohammad Khodabanda –
1578-1587 - Son of Shah Tahmasp,
older brother of Shah Ismail II
(born 1532 - death 1596)

Shah Abbas I – 1588 - 1629 –
Known as Abbas the Great, son of
Shah Khodabanda
(born 1571 - death 1629)

Shah Safi I – 1629-1642
Grandson of Abbas the Great
(born 1611 - death 1642)

Shah Abbas II – 1642-1666
Son of Shah Safi I
(born 1632 - death 1666)

Shah Suleiman I – 1666-1694
Son of Shah Abbas II
(born 1648 - death 1694)

Shah Husayn – 1694-1722
Son of Shah Suliman I
(born 1668 - death 1726)

† Fictional Character

Five Sons of Shah Abbas I:
(Abbas I had his 5 sons and one
grandson killed)

- **Safi Mirza** - Crown Prince
(born 1587 – killed by father 1615)
Safi Mirza had three sons:
  1. † Sultan Abu Hassan Mirza -
     Crown Prince secreted away.
  2. Sultan Abul-Naser Sam Mirza,
     succeeded as Shah Safi I
  3. Sultan Suleiman Mirza
     (killed 1632)
- **Sultan Hasan Mirza**
(born 1588, died as child 1591)
- **Sultan Mohammad Mirza**
(Born 1591, killed 1632)
- **Sultan Ismail Mirza**
(born 1601, killed 1613)
- **Imam Qoli Mirza**
(born 1602, killed 1632)

Safi Mirza's oldest son, the crown
prince †Sultan Abu Hassan Mirza,
born 1610, was secreted away for
protection from his grandfather. His
son †Mohammad Ismail Mirza born
1632, had one son, †Mirza Akhbar
Fikhr born 1652.

†Mirza Akhbar Fikhr - executed
by Emperor Aurangzeb in 1696.

† Astrella Bibi Begum –
Daughter of Safavid and Mughal Princess
Zeb-un-Nissa and Safavid Prince Mirza Akhbar Fikhr
(born 1680-)

Meet the Characters:

If you've ever felt like you've been called every name in the book, well you haven't, not from this book anyway. I once read that Brandon Sanderson named over 1500 characters in one of his epic fantasy series. Well, I'm not Brandon Sanderson, yet. So, if I ever wanted to grow up and become like him - and by the way I do - think about it - he's creative as heck, has a ton of fun making up worlds, is a nice guy who loves his wife and kids and he's mostly normal, ok and he sells millions of books - why wouldn't I want to be like that - so I was not afraid to give a name to practically every character in the book. And it was fun. Some of them are actual historical characters and others are fictional (†). (organized somewhat in order of their appearance or location)

Though the book may not include their full name, or their name at all, just as when I write advertising copy I imagine a person I'm writing to. In The Blade of Safavid I tried to visualize the character, even if just in passing and if I didn't dwell on describing them in the book, I did see them in my mind and I hope you can envision them in yours. I did try to keep names appropriate for the time and country and I thank the internet for the many sites I visited, including my own family tree, to help assure I wasn't too far off base.

Spoiler alert - if you read all these before you read the book you may loose the charm of the surprises. Ok, I left some details out just in case you cheat. *Remember † means fictional.*

From the world of Henry Avery's Mutiny

Henry Avery: (1659–1696 or 1699) Captain Avery was an English pirate in the Atlantic and Indian Oceans and made one big score: the treasure ship of the Grand Mughal of India. After this success, he retired. Little is known for certain of his ultimate fate. He was a slave trader, a sailor with the Royal Navy.

† Alexander Hincher: Known as Hinch, the author of the journal, is a young medical school graduate employed as a ship's surgeon on a privateering mission. His personal journal is what drives much of the story.

(an actual ship's surgeon was on board)

Admiral Sir Don Arturo O'Byrne: An Irish nobleman commanded the Spanish expedition's convoy of four ships.

Flag captain, John Strong: He died while the ship *Charles II* was still in port.

Captain Charles Gibson: He replaced flag captain John Strong. Was allowed off the *Charles II* following the mutiny.

Captain Humphreys: Captain of *James* who tried to stop Avery during the mutiny

David Creagh: the former second officer of the Charles ll, David Creagh, one of the only officers who refused to take part in the mutiny in 1694.

John Sparkes: 19 was from London. a testimony of John Sparkes, one of the 6 members of Avery's crew eventually convicted and executed during the trial held at the Old Bailey – (Central Court of England and Wales)

Joseph Dawson: One of the six members of Avery's crew captured and tried. The only defendant to plead guilty, was granted a reprieve.

Edward Forseith: 45, One of the six defendants indicted on charges of committing piracy on Gunsway.

William May: 48, One of the six defendants indicted on charges of committing piracy on Gunsway.

William Bishop: 20, One of the six defendants indicted on charges of committing piracy on Gunsway.

James Lewis: 25, One of the six defendants indicted on charges of committing piracy on Gunsway.

John Dann (Avery's coxswain and one of the six): He had sewn £1,045 in gold sequins and ten English guineas into his waistcoat, which was discovered by his chambermaid, who subsequently reported the discovery to the town's mayor, collecting a reward in the process. In order to avoid the possibility of execution, on 3 August Dann agreed to testify against other captured members of Avery's crew.

Captain Tew: Captain of the pirate ship Amity, a sloop-of-war with a crew of about 60 men. His previous success in the Arabian Sea helped lure Avery to the area. Part of the six ship flotilla sailing together prepared to attack the Mughal treasure ships. Captain Tew was killed in the first attack.

Captain Joseph Faro: Captain of the ship Portsmouth Adventure with a crew of about sixty men. Part of the six ship flotilla sailing together prepared to attack the Mughal treasure ships.

Captain Richard Want: Captain of the ship Dolphin with a crew of about sixty men. Part of the six ship flotilla sailing together prepared to attack the Mughal treasure ships.

Captain William Mayes: Captain of the Pearl with a crew of between thirty and forty men. Part of the six ship flotilla sailing together prepared to attack the Mughal treasure ships.

Captain Thomas Wake: Captain of the Susanna with a crew of seventy men. Part of the six ship flotilla sailing together prepared to attack the Mughal treasure ships.

Captain Muhammad Ibrahim: Captain of the Ganj-i-sawai, (Gunsway) a fearsome opponent, mounting eighty guns and a musket-armed guard of four hundred, as well as six hundred other passengers. His poor leadership is credited for the loss to the pirates.

Abdul Ghaffar: Abdul Ghaffar is reportedly Surat's wealthiest merchant. He was so wealthy he drove trade equal too the English East India Company. It is estimated he would fit out more than twenty ships between 300 and 800 tons.

† **Lord Rudy:** Rudolf - a young sailor pirate onboard the fancy joins with Hinch.

† **Esther:** Kidnapped granddaughter of the Emperor Aurangzeb and Safavid Princess Dilrus Banu Begum.

† **Leilyn:** Esters childhood friend and companion.

† **Black Moses:** A tribal chief, captured and sold as a slave several times until he becomes Hinch's property.

† **Kibo** (19340 ft.), **Mawenzi** (16896 ft.), and **Shira** (13000 ft.) Names of the three princes in Moses' legend, they are the names of Mt. Kilimanjaro's three extinct volcanoes:

† **Princess Muhumzingha:** One of Chief Embattu's daughters given to Hinch.

† **Princess Seh-Dong-Hong-Beh:** One of Chief Embattu's daughters given to Hinch.

† **Princess Nyabinghi:** One of Chief Embattu's daughters given to Hinch

† **Chief Embattu:** Tribal chief whose favorite wife and daughter are healed by Hinch.

† **Aadarsh:** Aadarsh is the village guru who leads Hinch's group overland to Sanga's elephant caravan.

† **Kairah:** A young woman in the village helping to care for the children attacked by tigers.

† **Valen:** Valen is the Maharaj Kumar son of the Maharaj, Maratha King.

† **Sangha Singh:** Sanga was the mahout (keeper and trainer of elephants) of a powerful herd of elephants.

† **Maneet Bhatt:** Owner of the Livery in the town of Tonk, his son Tanek accompanies the group through the adventures.

† **Tanek Bhatt:** Maneet's young son up for an adventure. The son of a livery owner has a great hand with horses. Is about 12 years old.

Bibi Hafiza Mariam: A guardian of Princess Zeb-un-Nissa and tutor to Esther.

† **Adina:** Daughter of Bibi and dear friends with Princess Esther.

† **Makhfi:** Dear friend and consort of Princess Zeb-un-Nissa.

From the Imperial Courts

Emperor Aurangzeb: Father to Princess Zeb-un-Nissa and grandfather to † Princess Esther.

Dilrus Banu Begum: Zeb-un-Nissa's mother, a direct descendent of the first Shah of the Safavid dynasty, Shah Ismail I.

Zeb-un-Nissa: Esther's mother, daughter of Emperor Aurangzeb. Put in prison by her father. The actual first born to the Mughal Emperor.

Razi: Real person and a great poet and friend of Princess Zeb-un-Nissa. She shelters Esther and team when they escape.

Safavid Dynasty

Shah Ismail I: 1501-1524 Founded the Safavid Dynasty

Shah Tahmasp: 1524-1576 - Son of Shah Ismail I

Shah Ismail II: 1576-1577 - Son of Tahmasp

Shah Mohammad Khodaband: 1578-1587 - Son of Shah Tahmasp, older brother of Shah Ismail II. His younger brother was considered more qualified to follow Shah Tahmasp because Khodaband had poor health and poor eyesight. When Shah Ismail II died early, Shah Khodaband became the 4th Safavid Shah.

Shah Abbas I: 1588 - 1629 – Known as Abbas the Great, son of Shah Khodaband

Shah Safi I: 1629-1642 - Grandson of Abbas the Great

Shah Abbas II: 1642-1666 - Son of Shah Safi I

Shah Suleiman I: 1666-1694 - Son of Shah Abbas II - Historical character - † fictional lover of Zeb-un-Nissa and father of Esther.

Shah Husayn: 1694-1722 - Son of Shah Suleiman I - Historical character - † fictional step brother of Esther.

Safi Mirza: Crown prince of the Safavid Dynasty under his father Shah Abbas the Great. Safi Mirza was executed along with his four brothers and first born son by his father Shah Abbas the Great. Safi Mirza's only living son became Shah Safi I, when Abbas the Great realized he'd executed all the remaining potential heirs.

Safi Mirza's oldest son, the crown prince † **Sultan Abu Hassan Mirza,** (fictional) was born 1610, and secreted away for protection from his grandfather. His son † **Mohammad Ismail Mirza** born 1632, had one son, † **Mirza Akhbar Fikhr** born 1652.

† **Mirza Akhbar Fikhr:** Executed by Emperor Aurangzeb in 1696.

The Mughal Empire

Babur: 1526 –1530 - Founded the Mughal Empire

Humayun: 1530 –1540 - Son of Babur

Akbar the Great: 1556 –1605 - Son of Humayun

Jahangir: 1605 –1627 - Son of Akbar the Great

Shah Jahan: 1628 –1658 - Son of Jahangir. Under Shah Jahan's reign, the Mughal Empire reached the peak of its glory. He was an able military commander, but he is best remembered for his architectural achievement, the best known of which is the Taj Mahal in Agra, in which is entombed his favorite wife, Mumtaz Mahal.

When Shah Jahan fell seriously ill. A war of succession began among his four sons in which his third son, Aurangzeb, emerged victorious. He quickly usurped his father's throne. Shah Jahan recovered from his illness, but Emperor Aurangzeb put his father under house arrest in Agra Fort until his death. He was laid to rest next to his wife in the Taj Mahal.

Mughal Emperor Aurangzeb – 1658 –1707 - Son of Shah Jahan During his reign, the Mughal Empire reached its greatest extent, ruling over nearly all of the Indian subcontinent. During which time India surpassed Qing China to become the world's largest economy and biggest manufacturing power, worth nearly a quarter of global GDP and more than the entirety of Western Europe.

The Maratha Conflict

Prince Muhammad Kam Baksh: Son of Aurangzeb. On one occasion when the Mughal encampments around Jinji fort were surrounded by the Maratha rebels, he actually decided to defect. His plans were foiled.

Asad Kahn: Emperor Aurangzeb's trusted Vizier and father of General Zulfikhar Ali Kahn.

General Zulfikhar Ali Khan: Wrote a letter informing the Mughal Emperor of his son's betrayal at Jinji Fort. When Prince Muhammad Kam Baksh, was brought in chains before Aurangzeb, the Mughal Emperor almost had him beheaded, but Aurangzeb was deterred by the pleas of his own daughter. (not fiction)

Rajaram: Maratha Leader Rajaram Bhosle I was crowned third chatrapati (Type of Emperor) of the Maratha Empire who ruled from 1689 to his death in 1700. He led the Marathas against the Mughals during much of their wars.

Santaji Mahaloji Ghorpade: Santaji was the most celebrated warrior of the Maratha Empire during Rajaram's regime. He led campaigns against Mughal Army continuously from 1689 to 1696. He is considered to be one of the most foremost exponents of ganimi kava (Guerilla warfare).

In and around Liverpool, England 1748:

† **Miss Elizabeth Farrow:** A mid-twentyish young woman on a quest for justice and to reunite with family.

† **Jack:** In his twenties, Jack is doing Captain Remington a favor investigating the knowledge of an old man rumored to know about a 50 year old pirate treasure.

† **Captain Joseph Remington:** In his early 50's, captain of the HMS *Kent*, a powerful navy ship assigned to free the waters of pirates.

† **Mr. Dennison Hillis:** Ol' Denn as he's known, worked for the East India Company and was part of the prison break in Isfahan, Persia when the Afgan's toppled the Safavid King in 1720. Only 60 or so years old his lifestyle leaves him old and weak.

† **Mistress Lonnie Dann:** Daughter of one of Captain Henry Avery's pirates John Dann who was captured and tried for mutiny and piracy. Owner of the Nookery, a quaint tavern/library.

† **Plonker:** Elizabeth's nick name for Emerson Canton who is a regular patron of the Nookery and a dock worker.

† **Lucas Striker:** First mate of Captain Remington on the HMS *Kent*.

† **Captain Brian Bentley:** Captain of the Emerald of the Sea, a converted navy ship sailing from Liverpool to the New World. Dear friend with Captain Remington and thus with Jack.

† **The Tailor: (Francis Deloy)** We never hear his name. A true haberdasher of fine men's clothing and accessories. He helps Elizabeth with her outfits.

† **Belinda Ashford:** A portly woman running the Inn where Elizabeth stays in Liverpool

† **Heinrich Jansport:** A smithy, owner of the livery from which Elizabeth hires a horse and returns the white mare from Porter.

Elsewhere around England 1748:

† **Sheriff Andrew Bills:** Local sheriff of Chester.

† **Victoria Adams:** Victoria is a well educated and well read woman in her mid twenties who fell in love with and married a farmer named John. She and her 4 year old daughter Margaret who they call Mags, and John live on a farm on the southern side of the River Mersey opposite Liverpool in an area known as Chester.

† **John Adams:** Victoria's husband.

† **Isaac Savage:** Victoria's father. A tall strong man.

† **Lord Remington:** of the House of Lords.

† **Charles Miner:** Butler and valet in Lord Remington's home.

† **Abbie:** Abigail Newton, a nurse, cares for Jack in the hospital.

† **Other Nurse:** Abbie's partner. The pale short boring one.

† **Mr. Cletus Underwood:** Record's keeper in London's courthouse, the Old Bailey, in London.

† **Doctor Georg Edmonds:** The attending physician who saves Jack's life following an accidental shooting.

† **Lady Anne Walsingham:** Jack's Fiancé - daughter of the aristocratic Walsingham family from Sommerset.

† **Noah Hoskins:** Young boy given to care for the horses. Lives in a small settlement along the Old Bath Road. Escorts Jack and Elizabeth to Newton Ferrers.

† **Jessica Hoskins:** Helps care for Jack when two highway men stop for fresh horses along the Old Bath Road.

† **Evan Hoskins:** Helps change the highwaymen's horses along the Old Bath road. He and Noah his son escort Jack and Elizabeth to Newton Ferrers.

† **Violet Creagh:** David Creagh's daughter in law, tavern keeper.

† **Elen:** Lars sister from village of Salcombe - outlines the challenge Elizabeth has with Dragons and Monsters.

† **Shanna Lynn Krill:** Young wench in Bristol who propositions Elizabeth when Elizabeth poses as a man.

† **The Calhoons:** An unkind slave owning family, who's son **Simon** violates one of the slave girls, **Cloe. Hariett** is Cloe's mother.

Among the ranks of evil:

✝ **Captain Ali Mutarid Hassan:** In his early 80's, former commander in the Shah's navy sent to recover the Blade of Safavid in 1695. By trade he is a vicious pirate and white female slave trader - harem builder - human flesh dealer. To his men is his referred to as Nakooda - God of the ship. (an actual naval title)

✝ **Krist Thorstein Hassan:** Hassan's son, early 20's. His mother was Icelandic, kidnapped by Captain Hassan.

✝ **Greggson Tandy:** One of Hassan's hired thugs.

✝ **Porter Clark:** An old man who lost his wife to the marauders that also kidnapped his daughter. He's given up on life and serves his daughter who is slave to some of Hassan's thugs.

✝ **Ginger:** Porter's daughter who became a slave to the thugs.

✝ **William Dunleavy:** One of Hassan's thugs posing as an inspector attempting to interrogate Jack.

✝ **Benjamin Potts:** Dunleavy's partner, one of Hassan's thugs posing as an inspector. He along with Dunleavy kidnap Jack from the hospital.

✝ **Drake:** One of Hassan's men.

✝ **Scotty:** Long time pirate serving Captain Hassan.

✝ **Hunter:** Hassan's spy who follows Glen to the island.

✝ **Mr. Gasher:** Killed by Jack when attempting to kidnap ol' Denn.

✝ **Mr. O'Donnel:** Lieutenant among Hassan's thugs. He killed ol' Denn hoping to keep Denn's secrets from Jack. Later in the Nookery he shoots Jack. Jack returns his knife later.

✝ **Mr. Baxter:** Sent by O'Donnel with Granger to bring help. Baxter knew the family was from Sheffield. Baxter threatened Victoria's family and shot at Jack.

✝ **Mr. Granger:** One of two sent to get help. Baxter sent Granger to report back to Hassan and gives ol' Denn's notebook to Krist.

✝ **Begger:** Joe Dip, one of Hassan's spies in Antigua

Other characters:

† **Dr. Alexander Cavinaugh:** Hinch's father, served as the chief of the royal medical staff from 1690 until 1704 when he died of a lung infection. His wife, Mary Hincher, Hinch's mother, died giving birth.

Count da Rio Grande: Commanding officer of the Nossa Senhora da Conceicao, a Portuguese warship of at least 80 guns, captured by Hassan and converted to the Chawbuck.

Thomas Mudge: (1715 –1794) Mudge was an English horologist who invented the *lever escapement,* the greatest single improvement ever applied to pocket watches. Mudge set up his business in 1748 and was considered one of England's outstanding watchmakers. Around this time he invented the detached lever escapement. † **Fictionally,** I credit Rags for inventing this for Mudge. In watches, the lever escapement is considered the greatest single improvement ever applied. It remains a feature in almost every mechanical pocket watch and wrist watch made even today.

John Harrison: (1693-1776) Harrison was a self-educated English carpenter and clock maker who in 1761 invented the *marine chronometer* which solved the problem of calculating longitude while at sea. His work spanned 31 years of persistent experimentation and testing. His invention revolutionized naval and later aerial navigation accelerating the Age of Discovery and Colonialism. † **Fictionally,** Rags' inventive mind helped Harrison solve some of his challenges perfecting the marine chronometer which is actually dated 1761, even though Rags had one of the early versions in 1746 when they sailed to the New World.

Benjamin Huntsman: Crucible steel was developed by Benjamin Huntsman in England in the 18th century. Huntsman used coke rather than coal or charcoal, achieving temperatures high enough to melt steel and dissolve iron. This produced the first steel of modern quality, providing a means of efficiently changing excess wrought iron into useful steel. Huntsman's process greatly increased the European output of quality steel suitable for use in items like knives, tools, and machinery, which helped pave the way for the Industrial revolution. † Fictionally, Walt Huntsman, Benjamin's brother is Rags' and Glen's partner. Glen's knives, swords and machete are all crucible steel.

Islanders:

† **Glen:** Assumptive leader on the island. He saves the families on board the Bringhurst during the hurricane and who looks to their eventual rescue.

† **Martin Skoville:** Lydia's young friend in Sheffield

† **Rosemary:** Glen's wife and mother of 4 children.

† **Lydia:** Young-teen daughter of Rosemary and Glen

† **Jeremy:** Twin son of Rosemary and Glen

† **Jenny:** Twin daughter of Rosemary and Glen

† **Lizzie:** Rosemary and Glen's baby daughter born on the island.

† **Rags:** The only bachelor on the island - inventive and optimistic

† **Louisa:** One of the sages on the island - Walt's wife

† **Walt:** Louisa's husband and business partner of Glen and Rags.

† **Joanna:** Hunter's woman.

† **Marge:** Sal's wife and resident on the island.

† **Sal:** Marge's husband and resident on the island

† **Ben:** Fellow island resident, farmer and Susan's husband.

† **Susan:** Ben's wife and joint farmer with Ben.

† **Clare:** Lars fiance and owner of Clare's tavern in Antigua

† **Amos Arlington:** Spy hired by Captain Remington to be nosey in the new world

† **Darby:** An acquaintance on Antigua.

† **Mereday:** A highly religious man, one of the original slaves on Hassan's island. He and his family lived on the island since before Krist's father conquered it.

The Blade of Safavid began as a business book where writer Kent Merrell sought to teach the principles of influence, persuasion and motivation. Culling from a forty year career in advertising and marketing, Kent was confident his sage understanding of the art of persuasion could be a best-seller. It might have been.

The problem came when his creative story telling intersected with the principles of persuasion. Soon the manuscript included more adventure than instruction. Over time plot took priority, persuasion lost preeminence and The Blade of Safavid stood alone as an epic historical fiction interlaced with characters both real and fictional.

Kent turned his forty year career telling stories to sell products for clients such as Disney, Comcast, Wells Fargo, HBO, VISA, Sam's Club, Discover Card and countless local and regional clients into a passion to create stories proving to be worthy of reading, remembering and sharing.

A preview of author Kent Merrell's new book.

Introduction

Permit me to set the geo-political stage in the early 1500's.

The Iberian Peninsula was known as five independent kingdoms: Portugal, Castile and Leon, Navarre, Granada (Muslim), and the Crown of Aragon. In the year 1492, after the fall of Granada, which was the last of the Moorish strongholds, and with the union of the monarchs, Isabella I of Castile and Ferdinand II of Aragon, the whole peninsula apart from Portugal, converged into a single political entity. With the union of the kingdoms of Castile and Aragon, the term Spain began to refer to the kingdom that emerged from this union.

The final unification of Spain as we know it today still took decades, even centuries. Conquests, revolutions, unifications, and subjugations took years to bring lands, nobles, kings, religions, languages, and races together. For simplicity, in The Conquest of Liberty, we will refer to the Iberian Peninsula as Spain yet we will often be specific with its various kingdoms at the time.

From early Phoenician, Greek and even Roman writings centuries earlier, Hispania with its various spellings became a name used to describe the peninsula. When the Visigoths arrived eight centuries earlier, they referred to the area as Hispania Visigoda.

Thus, during the late 1400s and the early 1500s, the geo-political landscape included diverse peoples identifying with their own cultural heritages, languages, and religions. Throughout Europe, Northern Africa, and the Middle East as we now know it, the same struggle for unification, independence, and liberty has played out for centuries, and continues even today.

Prologue

1499 Cathedral of the Incarnation, Granada, Spain

Isabella's stern countenance softened. A tiny smile crept across her face. Her attendants showed great deference as she entered the cathedral. All bowed but one. As Queen of Castile, only one man was permitted to stand in her presence without her permission. Archbishop Hernando de Talavera stood respectively and returned her smile. A slight nod was all she received. That is all she ex-pected. When they first met, his insistence that he kneel only for the Eternal King demonstrated his loyalty to God. She had not met any other with that conviction or courage. For that reason, he served as her personal confessor those many years and why he was now the first Archbishop of Granada. And today, she came to him rather than summon him to her court.

Her footsteps echoed throughout the church. The Cathedral of the Incarnation was a magnificent edifice. It was built centuries earlier by the Emirate of Granada, and enlarged during the Nasrid dynasty. For two hundred years, it served as the central mosque in Granada. It became one of the largest mosques in the Islamic world during the 1300s. Eight years ago in 1492, after the conquest of Granada by the Catholic monarchs, Ferdinand II and Isabella I, the mosque began its conversion into the cathedral that now served as the principal Catholic Church in Granada.

"My dear Hernando, what is this I hear about you?" Isabella asked.

His smile broadened, he reached out his hand, and ushered the queen to a large red velvet throne-like chair. "Well, what you might hear depends on who you choose to listen to," he said. She nodded.

"I suppose you compare my meager conversions of Arab Moors to the mass six thousand baptisms, of which your Cardinal Cisneros brags," he said. The archbishop wanted so badly to denounce the efficacy of the group baptism where more than six thousand Moors, fearful of losing their homes, knelt at the command of Cardinal Cisneros who then splattered holy water into the air landing randomly on some of the gathered Arabs. Talavera held his tongue.

"Hernando, you are my most faithful servant. It distresses me to receive reports from your detractors that doubt your sincerity."

"Detractors? Sincerity?" he asked. "You know Cisneros and I differ in many ways. Or is it Torquemada? With Torquemada we differ in every way. Conversos unconverted are trouble. You know that. That which is done in fear or by force rather than by one's own will is not lasting. In order to endure, it must be done with love and charity," he said.

"Hernando, Hernando." She put her hand on his arm, "Come with me." Isabella stood. The crowd, so interested in hearing this interchange, came to attention as if they had been oblivious to the gen-tle reprimand given by their queen to her archbishop. She motioned for all to remain back. She led her archbishop from the chapel. They quietly walked to the Courtyard of the Oranges, which fea-tured an elaborate central fountain surrounded by rows of orange trees. The trees were in blossom, which added to the sweetness of the opportunity for Talavera to once again converse privately with his queen. It was not to be. The serenity evaporated when the pounding of boots and the squealing of young boys burst into the courtyard. Cisneros, followed by six of his personal guards, dragged two young boys toward Isabella and Talavera and threw them to the ground.

"This is what your permissive policies create," Cisneros said to Talavera. It wasn't that the cardinal ignored the fact he was in the presence of the queen; it was as if he felt the importance of his demonstration was more serious than respect for Isabella. Cisneros signaled to a guard who pulled a whip and cracked it over the back of one of the boys. The second boy's back was saved when Talavera snatched the whip from the guard and threw it to the ground.

Nothing was said. The archbishop and the cardinal glared at each other for several seconds. Finally, Talavera turned to the boy who received the lash. "Miguel, what is this?" Talavera said.

Miguel stood. For a boy barely ten years old, he stood taller than the other boy and nearly as tall as Talavera. His tousled blond hair and fair complexion testified of his Basque heritage. His innocence, which might have been credible hours earlier, was betrayed by the mud on his tunic and smudges of dirt and blood on his cheek.

Miguel lowered his head in respect to Talavera. When his eyes noticed the hem of the brilliant blue gown, they shot up to the queen, opened wide, and he dropped to his knees.

"Rise," Isabella said. "I am curious. Please answer the archbishop."

Miguel's eyes raised to the queen, but his head remained bowed. "We took bread to the families on San Cristobal Hill." Miguel was talking to the ground as if not daring to face either the queen or Talavera.

"Albayzin neighborhood?" Cisneros spit the words out.

That shook Miguel. He jumped. Miguel nodded.

"Moors? You are feeding the Moors? Is that how you convert the pigs?" Cisneros' coarse insult brought Miguel's humble head sharply around and he glared into Cisneros' eyes.

"Cardinal, you have offended our young friend," Isabella said. She chuckled, then said to Miguel, "Forgive my cardinal, he seems to offer neither of us respect this morning."

Miguel turned back to the queen. The red on his face matched the blood on his cheek.

"Miguel, apologize to the cardinal. You know you must show respect," Talavera said.

Miguel started to answer, "But…" Talavera raised a hand and Miguel held his tongue. Miguel did not apologize.

The other boy stood motionless. He was a local Moorish Morisco converted to Christ. His tunic and thick black hair were no less dirtied by the skirmish than Miguel's. The boy never looked up as he dared to speak. "They called my family pigs and said Miguel was a pig farmer and knocked the bread into the dirt and said we should wallow there if we wanted to eat."

Isabella smiled at the innocent tussle between young boys and how it brought her cardinal to the judgement seat. "You interrupt us for this?" Isabella said to Cisneros.

Cisneros' face glowed red at the queen's rebuke, but not from embarrassment. His demonstration to challenge Talavera's lenient policies failed. Anger pushed all humiliation aside.

Isabella turned to Miguel. "I'm curious to know who got the worst of it?"

The boy and Miguel both smiled. It was enough. Talavera scooted the boys away. "Miguel," he said, "I need you cleaned up by tonight's mass." He reached down, picked up the whip, and handed it back to Cisneros' guard.

Part One

Chapter One

Ten years later

1509 - Cathedral of Incarnation, Granada, Spain

Miguel put his powerful hand on the gilded hilt of his sword ready to pull it free. Soldiers burst open the chapel doors. Archbishop Hernando Talavera, with his deep confidence in God, rested his hand on Miguel's arm, preventing the sword from leaving its sheath.

"If they arrest you, they must take me!" Miguel demanded.

The archbishop looked up into Miguel's defiant eyes, "Isabella is dead. I have no other protector. They will arrest me and if you are here, they will take you. And, you, my faithful friend, they will torture until you confess, and then you will die by fire. You are all I have left. If you care for me, go. Go! May Pope Julius receive you and extend mercy."

Talavera squeezed Miguel's arm, pushing him toward the south transept of the cathedral.

"Go. Appeal to Julius!"

Miguel hesitated only a moment. Looking down into Talavera's beloved deep-set eyes, he obeyed. He turned and rushed from Talavera's side and dashed across the nave and into the south transept chapel.

Outside the cathedral, crowds gathered. Soldiers, fully armed and on horseback, kept the mostly Muslim Granadians back. There had been far too many uprisings for Cardinal Cisneros to risk a riot. Not now. Not while his personal guards were arresting the sole hindrance to his solemn promise made to the queen before her death. He swore to her to convert every soul or expunge them from Granadian soil. He knew the possible danger of an uprising was extreme since Talavera was the sole source of hope for liberty the Muslims clung to.

Escaping through the private exit, Miguel mingled among the crowd and watched as Cardinal Cisneros' officers dragged Talavera outside and paraded him to the center of the large cobblestone plaza. Other officers had already arrested and imprisoned Talavera's friends, family, and fellow clergy—all accused of heresy.

How could Talavera possibly convince him to flee? Miguel anguished.

Miguel thought he knew how Peter felt watching the Christ taken from the garden by the temple guard. So badly he wanted to pull his sword, as did Peter.

Talavera held his head high, unashamed of his dedication to the truths he taught and fought for. Archbishop Talavera intentionally wore the tall white cardinal mirk and his long red cassock with wide sleeves contrasting with his signature white mozzetta, the fur-lined cape, his cappa magna, the velvet fur-lined hooded cape along with his large gold ring. No man looked nor acted more regal and so majestic. There was no question in Miguel's mind why Queen Isabella chose him to be her confessor those many years. Several years ago, Talavera was again her perfect choice when she appointed him Archbishop of Granada, after she finally conquered the city. When Talavera chose Miguel to serve as an emissary for the Moors of Granada, Miguel couldn't have felt more honored.

To Miguel, the stark contrast between the respect and honor the Moors showed his friend and mentor, Archbishop Talavera, and the disdain they showed the archbishop's accuser, Cardinal Francisco Jimenez Cisneros, could not be more pronounced this very minute. Cisneros stood tall in his saddle atop a strong, white Andalusian. To Miguel, the horse seemed to radiate the same arrogance as its rider. Snorting, clawing at the ground with its front hoof, anxious for action.

Cisneros' bright red cassock with black trim fell across the horse's bright white flank. The strong contrast in color and stature broadcast to the crowd; 'do not challenge me.' Miguel watched Cisneros' dark eyes scan the crowd. He was a tall man accented with sunken cheeks and a large narrow nose. Miguel never saw him without a cap, but he imagined his traditional monk tonsure hair style was immaculately trimmed as an example to be followed by other monks.

What is Cisneros looking for? Miguel wondered, victims, threats? Miguel turned back to watch the officers unnecessarily pushing and prodding Talavera toward the center of the plaza. Talavera was not a large man but stood so regally, he appeared to stand heads above all others. Talavera seemed to be focusing on individual faces in the crowd. Miguel's hand on the hilt of the sword itched to free the steel and put it to the work of true justice. When Talavera caught Miguel's eye, he casually raised his hand once again to hold Miguel at bay.

Cisneros, who was closely watching Talavera at that very instant, glanced to see who he so subtly communicated with. He followed Talavera's eyes.

"There! Take him!" Cisneros' command reverberated across the plaza. The soldiers' eyes turned to Cisneros and following the direction of his outstretched arm, quickly recognized the 'him' Cisneros meant.

Miguel stood several inches taller than the native Granadians, most of whom descended from the Muslim Moors of North Africa just across the Strait of Gibraltar. Though his clothing was a blend of colorful Moorish layers, his height and lighter skin added to his difficulty of blending into the crowd.

He dropped to his knees, scooted to a crouch, and tried to shuffle out of sight. Horsemen pushed into the crowd. The sounds of horse on stone and screams as they plowed onlookers out of the way convinced Miguel he could not hide. He stood and ran at full speed. Many from the crowd recognized Miguel as one of the few friends of Talavera and of the Moors. They parted for him and then crowded the horses, giving Miguel an advantage. Miguel left the plaza, but knew within only a few moments the horsemen would be clear of the crowd. He could never outrun them. He decided he needed a higher escape, and went skyward.

A small wall surrounding a fountain pouring crystal clear water into a pool gave Miguel the step to leap to the eaves of the building. He swung himself up. Before clearing the edge, an arrow dove deep into his leg. The shock paralyzed his progress more than the pain. Once over the edge and onto the flat roof, he dropped to his side and tried to remove the arrow. His leg would not support his full weight. He grabbed the arrow free, leaving a trail of blood as he limped across the roof. He had to clear the other side before the soldiers reached and surrounded the building.

Pain slowed his progress. If only he could jump from this flat roof to the next, he thought. His leg grew limp. It would never hold. Stairs along the side of the building provided access to the roof. What was this building? Then he smelled the rancid remains of discarded flesh. A butcher shop! He stopped. Could he hide? He tore a sleeve from his shirt and tied it around his bleeding leg. A faint smell wafted across the rooftop. Pork. This was a Christian business. His heart sank. If it were a Muslim tienda, he might talk the owners into helping him. But not the Christians. They feared being labeled as heretics for aiding a heretic. He reached the edge of the roof and tried to listen for the pounding of horses. Soldiers yelled to one another, giving commands to secure the building. The sound of clanging swords and boots on the stairs reached the rooftop only seconds before four of Cisneros' soldiers surrounded a kneeling Miguel.

In an act of submission, Miguel raised a hand to hold the men at bay as he appeared to remove his sword and climb to his feet. Confident they had Miguel subdued, they relaxed slightly. Taking advantage of their ease, Miguel quickly pulled his sword, then slammed it against the first soldier's sword, which gave Miguel the edge. Miguel drew it so quickly a second guard stood motionless. Empowered, Miguel spun with both hands on his sword and knocked another sword free, sending it flying across the rooftop. It was now two swords against one. That would only last seconds. Stupor ended and the two unarmed soldiers quickly retrieved their swords and, as Miguel parlayed with two soldiers, they surrounded him again, swords well in hand. He could not flee, the pain in his leg would not permit it. With each movement, he depended on that leg. But with each shift of his weight, it screamed for relief. It surprised him how much energy it required to hold the pain at bay as he demanded his leg to support his movements. He was certain he could best two of these men, but not four. A sudden thrust pierced his shoulder, which loosened his grip, and Miguel's sword fell to the ground. A sharp crack on the back of his head and all went black.

The Conquest of Liberty

Order *The Conquest of Liberty* from Amazon,
BarnesandNoble.com or directly from Kent at
jremingtonpress.com.

Kent shares short biographical vignettes about the many
historical characters in his stories. Enjoy these videos as well as
Kent's blog posts and articles when you follow Kent at
https://kentmerrellauthor.com/